The Trouble With Tigers

A Steamy Victorian Romance

Kimberly Keyes

Kimberly Keyes Romance

This is a work of fiction. Names, characters, places, and incidents are either the product of the author's imagination or are used fictitiously, and any resemblance to actual persons living or dead, business establishments, events, or locales, is entirely coincidental.

COPYRIGHT © 2016 by Kimberly Keyes

Revised Edition

COPYRIGHT © 2024 by Kimberly Keyes

All rights reserved. No part of this book may be used or reproduced in any manner whatsoever without written permission of the author except in the case of brief quotations embodied in critical articles or reviews.

Contact Information:

kimberlykeyesromance@gmail.com

Cover Art by Holly Perret

Hidden Hearts Series, Book 1

Produced in the United States

Contents

Before you start reading!

Hi! It's me, Kimberly Keyes, just saying thank you in advance for reading The Trouble with Tigers, book 1 in my steamy Victorian "Hidden Hearts" series, and you should know that if you enjoy it, book 2, If the Slipper Fitsand book 3, Beautiful Viscount, Beastly Bride await you!

Did you know that I have a newsletter? I send way too few emails, (that's what the experts tell me!!) but I do like to keep my readers abreast of my sales, new releases, giveaways (whether one of mine, or a fellow author friend's giveaway), and I always share events where I'll be signing books and talking about the romance genre in general. Visit my website @ www.kimberlyk eyes.net/newsletter-signup.

That's all for now. Wishing you happy reading! I hope you love Kitty and Zeke's love story as much as I loved writing it!

Jesus, she smelled good, and she stood far too close. Something hot and primal filled his veins. Irritated beyond measure—with himself, or her, he couldn't say—he realized he either needed to kiss her or blast her. Very well. He took a mind-clearing breath and went for the latter. "It's crossed my mind to wonder if…"

"Yes?"

"If you might not think it would be easier if the engagement wasn't a sham."

Her unblinking green eyes narrowed. An image of a feral cat came to mind. "Go on."

"I only want to keep things from turning ugly later, Kitty."

"Let me see if I understand you correctly." She aimed a smile at him. "You want to make sure I know you don't want to marry me."

"Ah…" He wouldn't have put it quite *that* bluntly.

"Allow me to ease your mind, my lord. I don't wish to marry you. Indeed, you are the very last sort of man I wish to marry."

He was impressed. She'd managed to communicate her ire without raising her voice above a whisper.

His mouth curved up at the corners. "Really?"

"Really."

His smile broadened, stretching from ear to ear. "You sound serious—as if you've given the matter some thought. You've utterly relieved my mind."

"My life is complete."

Cheeky chit. He laughed aloud. "It's none of my business, I know. But, out of curiosity—what are you looking for in a husband?"

Prologue

L ondon, England, March 1877

"'Ere we are then, miss."

Thunder boomed in the distance, punctuating the hackney driver's words as he rolled to a stop in the fashionable London neighborhood. At least, glancing around at the grand manses looming in the moonlight on the relatively wide, tree-lined street, Kitty supposed it was fashionable. Perhaps a better term would be monied, or of the upper-crust.

She hadn't much to compare it to as she'd only travelled to London once in her adult life. A mere two years before, it may as well have been a lifetime ago. Her previous visit to London entailed seemingly endless, sunny days that passed in a blur of shopping—for gowns, gloves, hats, and slippers, all for a season that never transpired.

If only Grandfather had accompanied her on that occasion. Of a certainly, he would have introduced her to his most trusted friend. Instead, here she sat, alone, penniless, with the meager breakfast she'd ingested at dawn long gone from her belly, and soon to introduce herself to an earl.

Lightning flashed, illuminating thick, low hanging clouds. Another rumble of thunder followed, seeming to rattle her very bones.

"You're certain this is my stop?" She hated the telltale quaver in her voice. She was stalling, and based on the dubious expression on the driver's face as he eyed her over his shoulder, he knew it as well as she.

She couldn't blame him. He'd had his doubts about her from the moment she leapt out of the darkness to hail him as he approached his cab behind the lonely inn. Alarm had squeezed an odorous belch out of him, confirming her suspicion he'd come from the pub. By all appearances, he had not been happy to see her.

But in her defense, she'd been hiding amongst the trees for hours after having spotted the hackney, and could no longer feel her toes thanks to the damp chill. She wasn't about to let him disappear.

To that end, she crawled in his cab, quick as you please, recited the address consigned to memory and huddled into a corner of the worn bench. The driver's hearty cackle threatened to fray her very last nerve. Evidently he found her mud-splattered, rumpled black lace gown and over-all disheveled appearance incongruous with her destination.

He stopped laughing when she fixed him with a glare and thrust her mother's pearl earrings at him as payment for the fare.

Now he pointed to the marquee swinging in the gusting wind above the tall, spiked iron gate announcing for all and sundry this was number 2 Groves Street, Claybourne Manor.

Stiffening her spine, she stepped from the cab.

No sooner had her aching feet touched the cobblestone street than the driver urged his horse forward. He departed without a backward glance.

Kitty shivered—with dread or cold, she really couldn't say. Her bones had long since turned to ice, true, but she also stood in darkness, outside a stranger's home, nothing but her word to recommend her. What if he refused to see her? What if he refused to help?

A frigid raindrop landed on her netted cap with a splat. She almost laughed despite herself. It was the impetus she needed. Lifting her chin, she swung open the gate and marched up the walk.

The skies opened, soaking her as she mounted the steps to the imposing front doors, as if mocking her show of bravery. As if daring her to give up.

Well, she would not. She'd come too far, and besides, she didn't have a lot of options.

She pressed in under the eave, adjusting the dripping netting of her cap, and lifted the heavy brass knocker.

After seconds that felt like an eternity, the thick wooden door opened on silent oiled hinges. A gray haired man, dressed in formal butler attire eyed her from head to toe. He did not look impressed. She read his intent to close the door in her face and forestalled him, using her most authoritative tone.

"Lady Maidstone to see the Earl of Claybourne on an urgent matter, sir, if you please." Her heart hammered in her chest as she stared at the servant through the dotted gauze, willing him to invite her in.

Behind her the rain fell in deafening sheets.

Without a word, the butler closed the door in her face.

She blinked. Turned on the stoop and stared out at rain, so cold it should be snow. *Oh, Grandfather, what am I to do now?*

She waited, but no reply came.

Well, what had she expected? Her grandfather, the eighth Baron of Maidstone, had died a little less than two months ago, and as many times as she'd begged him for advice since, he'd yet to answer. He was gone, as was her brother Collin, and her parents before him. She was well and truly on her own, not to mention frozen, hungry, totally without resources, and now, soaking wet.

The rain lessened to a drizzle, as if coaxing her from beneath the sheltering eave, and her mouth curved in a wry grin. She stepped forward, and, pulling back the mourning netting of her cap, turned her face up to the mist.

She didn't need to ask anyone for guidance. She knew what to do. She straightened, approached the door once again, hands fisted at her sides. She'd come too far, faced heretofore unimaginable dangers, first at home under the so-called guardianship of her cousin, Garrick, then two days on the road to London escaping the monster, to give up now.

By God, she would see the earl or they'd have to call the Yard to cart her away.

She lifted her hand, intent on taking the brass knocker again and banging with all her might.

Before she could grasp it, however, the door swung open wide.

She sucked in a breath, cowed despite herself. The man she faced now was no butler. He was a very tall, broad shouldered man, impeccably dressed, with a shock of white hair, a lean, square jaw, and keen blue eyes. The Earl of Claybourne, she presumed.

Now that she had his attention, she realized, she hadn't worked out quite what to say. How to convince him she was who she claimed, that she needed aid, and more to the point, needed him to provide it. "My lord," she said, and dipped a low curtsy. "I'm Lady—"

Before she could finish introducing herself, the man gripped her upper arm, holding her steady, and flipped up the netting of her cap to study her face.

After the briefest moment, he nodded in evident satisfaction and folded the material back down. "Can't disguise those tiger eyes, m'dear."

Tiger eyes? Oh, dear. Had her grandfather's friend lost his mind? "Excuse—"

He shushed her with a quick grunt, gave the front perimeter of Claybourne Manor a quick scan, then dragged her into the blessed warmth of the foyer. "Let's get you inside before anyone sees. I've been expecting you."

Chapter One

L ondon, England, August 1877

The hackney drew to a halt, rousing Zeke from an uncomfortable slumber. He peeled open gritty eyes and peered through thick evening fog.

There it was, the familiar outline of Claybourne Hall. His birthright. His home. Eventually.

He tossed the driver some coins and dropped to the curb, flicking a glance at the starless sky. God, he hated the London haze.

He chuckled to himself as he opened the iron gate and started up the walk. Already grumbling and he hadn't even been ashore—how many hours now? What time was it, anyway? Well past his grandfather's bedtime, of that he was sure. He'd hoped to arrive earlier.

The massive front door opened as he cleared the top step.

The earl's butler, still in full servant's garb appeared. "Lord Thurgood, welcome home."

"Smethwick, good to see you." Zeke crossed the threshold. "I suppose the earl's abed?"

"Indeed, no, my lord. He's in the den."

"At this hour?"

"Playing a board game with Kit, I believe."

"Kit?" Zeke handed off his gloves and hat.

"The earl's hired a young companion. Shall I announce you?"

"Think I'll surprise him." Though travel weary and sorely in need of a hot soak and soft bed, a broad smile covered his face. He'd missed the old man.

The door to the den stood open and a soft glow of lamplight from the room's interior spilled out over the marble corridor.

"I can't believe it, Kit. You've bested me again." The earl's crusty voice.

A soft laugh reached Zeke's ears. A *young* errand boy, then. The earl had gotten himself a tiger.

He rapped his knuckles sharply on the doorframe. "Hello, anyone here care to welcome home a long missing son?"

He spotted his grandfather looking relaxed and contented in his favorite armchair near the hearth and waited for his reaction.

His grandfather's face lit with joy, followed by an odd expression Zeke couldn't quite discern, before an ear splitting grin took its place.

The earl hoisted himself out of his chair. "Zeke, why didn't you send word you were coming home?"

Chuckling, he crossed the room to meet the earl halfway, where he allowed himself to be thoroughly embraced. "There wasn't time, unless you wanted me to go to my apartments first."

"Of course not. This is your home. Let me look at you." His grandfather grasped his shoulders and leaned back to scrutinize him. "Hair's a bit too long. Face too tanned. But otherwise seemingly none the worse for wear. Brandy?"

"Please."

"Sit, sit, I'll get it," he said, already heading for the credenza.

Zeke made his way to the seating area the earl favored. Only then did he realize the scamp with whom his grandfather had been playing chess had disappeared.

His brows knitted with disapproval. "Where's this tiger I heard you'd employed? Don't tell me he dashed out of here without even bothering to clean up the game."

Zeke studied the board. "Not a bad strategist, eh? Clever check there." He pointed to the boy's well-placed queen.

"I'll say. Squarely beaten again," his grandfather said, his voice muted as he fished a decanter out of the cabinet.

Mission accomplished, he filled two snifters and returned with one in each hand. "Here you are."

They clinked glasses and took their seats. Zeke's was still warm from the absent servant's behind. How had the lad sneaked past him? He must be more tired than he realized.

He shook his head, and swirled the amber liquid beneath his nose. Closing his eyes, he inhaled deeply, enjoying the rich scent before taking a healthy swallow.

"Ah," he said on a sigh and let his head loll back on the plush velvet cushion. "It's good to be home. I say, you're looking well."

His grandfather preened a bit. "Thank you. But I can't take all the credit. Kit's regimen is paying off."

"Kit?"

The earl brandished a sly grin. "My assistant. Companion. Helper." He shrugged.

Zeke snorted. "A tiger who's also an exercise prescriber? That's a new one. You're getting eccentric in your old age."

"Old age? Speak for yourself. And it's not eccentric to enjoy having someone with whom to share the long days of summer."

Zeke shifted in his seat, a stab of conscience pricking him. He met his grandfather's eyes, expecting to see accusation in their faded blue depths, but found none. It didn't banish the sting of guilt, however.

"What of Caden? Tell me he's in London."

The earl arched his brows. "Your brother? Of course not. It's summer. He's currently at a house party in Marlboro."

Zeke frowned. He'd hoped to spend time with his younger brother before he sailed again. Too, he liked to think he kept an eye on their grandfather in Zeke's stead.

"Tell me about this African diamond mine. Was it what you expected?"

Zeke rubbed his palms together. "And then some, my lord. Kimberley is already paying dividends."

"Loaded with diamonds, is it?"

"It is. As usual, my biggest problem is finding a reliable fore-man. There's more than enough willing and able labor to do the digging. Staying to oversee the operations—and thereby ensure our profits didn't walk off the site, was the main reason my stay lasted so long.

"But my time paid off. Matter of fact." Zeke fished in his waistcoat pocket. "I brought back a sample, freshly cut and polished."

He loosed the velvet pouch and shook the contents onto his palm, not bothering to hide his pride in the stone.

The earl leaned forward in his chair. "Magnificent. May I?"

"Please."

The earl took the diamond between his thumb and pointer finger and whistled low. "How many carats?"

"Approximately six."

"Oh, ho, m'boy. Now here's a gem with which to woo a lady. Should I take this to mean you're finally planning on settling down now you're back?"

Zeke snorted. "Hardly. Besides there isn't a woman alive whose finger is big enough to wear that rock."

His grandfather's mouth twisted in a sardonic half grin as he returned the diamond to Zeke.

"Perhaps you should have brought home a more manageable size, then, Ezekiel Thurgood. You are hardly a boy just out of leading strings. It's well past time you got serious about starting a family—"

"Egad. I'm only nine and twenty—"

"No need to act as if I've suggested the guillotine. I got the impression you enjoyed the ladies, and from what I've heard tell, you're quite popular with the fairer sex."

"I adore women. Especially when they're flat on their—"

His grandfather's sudden wheezing fit cut him off.

He sat forward to whack the earl on the back. "How long have you had this cough?"

The earl blinked and wiped moisture from the corner of his eye. "I'm quite well. M' brandy went down the wrong pipe."

He studied the earl with a critical eye. He looked fit, as previously noted. Still broad of shoulder, not all slumped over like some of the old man's peers.

Zeke relaxed back in his chair. "Where were we?"

"We were discussing your family—or lack thereof."

"Ah yes. Brought on by my careless exhibition of the diamond." He dropped the stone back into its pouch and tightened the drawstrings. "But as to your protesting my lack of a family, need I remind you I have one. Namely you and Caden."

The earl scowled. "I won't be here forever."

"I'm well aware of your views, old man, and I plan to marry. But don't forget I'm soon to sail for America to buy into that gold mine I researched. Perhaps you recall I'd planned to go after the completion of the Southern Pacific Railroad."

"Which transpired a bit over a month ago."

"Precisely."

The earl rolled his eyes.

"I suppose I could look for a bride who won't mind being left to rusticate in the country with a brood while I ensure our family's financial future." It was an option.

"You're always planning a trip somewhere. You and your damned mines. And I hate to point out the obvious, lad, but if you never manage to produce an heir, procuring the family's so-called financial future seems a bit moot."

"I'll keep that in mind." Time to change the subject. He drummed his fingers on the arm of his chair. "Have you any idea if Randall's about? Or is he off visiting one of his country estates?"

"Last I heard, your co-conspirator fled the heat in favor of the coast."

"Pity."

"You'll have to make do with me," his grandfather said, blue eyes twinkling, momentary irritation over Zeke's lack of a spouse apparently forgotten. He leaned back in his chair and swirled his brandy. "Now let's hear about your trip. Leave nothing out."

"I have a tale for you, as a matter of fact, concerning the diamond." Zeke gestured toward the pouch on the table between them. "Did you happen to notice the stone's unusual coloring?"

"My eyes aren't what they used to be." The earl picked up the pouch, loosed the stone, and moved toward a wall sconce.

He held it before the flame. "Now I see the coloring you mention. Very unusual, and quite beautiful."

He returned to his seat and set the diamond back on its pouch. "Doesn't color denote inferior quality? As I always understood it, the less color the better."

"Not in this case. This diamond is rare."

The diamond's center was filled with a perfect sphere of pale, bright green, interspersed with flecks of gold that glowed when held to the light.

"According to the journals and experts I consulted, Kimberley has produced only one Tiger's Eye diamond. This one." He grinned. "I named it."

"You"—the earl frowned in confusion—"named it?"

"Evidently when they're as rare as this one, it's what's done." He rubbed a hand over his stubble-rough jaw. "I called it Tiger's Eye. Want to guess why?"

"The diamond's markings resemble the animal's eyes?" the earl offered dryly.

"Brilliant deduction. I had a little help, actually." He broke off.

He didn't need to get into all that nonsense about the dream he had before discovering the diamond, whereby an older man in full military garb came to him with a tiger cub. Without saying a word, he let Zeke know he meant for him to guard the thing. The next day, when Zeke held the diamond, he couldn't help comparing the stone to the tiger's eyes in the dream.

Bah. It hardly signified. Just an odd coincidence, really. Not worth mentioning.

"Never mind, that. The safari I went on, I could talk about for hours, if someone was so inclined to refill a man's drink."

His grandfather gave him peeved look that didn't reach his eyes and headed for the credenza.

Zeke stretched out his legs and laughed. "Remember this moment the next time your young servant disappears on you."

***

How had Kitty wound up hunkered under the desk, stuck for the duration of the earl and his grandson's reunion? Oh, yes, she'd bolted like a scared rabbit the moment the earl's heir had so unexpectedly appeared.

At least their conversation was entertaining. Talk of mines filled with sparkling gems large enough to require names, and plains crawling with all manner of exotic creatures. Kitty enjoyed a good geography lesson. Still.

She inched from under the earl's desk to stretch her neck, confident Lord Ezekiel Thurgood hadn't an inkling of her presence in the room. Did she dare peer around the earl's desk? She ought not. But how else would she see the face accompanying the man's rich baritone and hearty laugh?

She'd barely caught a glimpse before scampering across the carpet in search of cover, much to the earl's horror, though he seemed to recover quickly enough. Tall, blond and tanned, if her eyes hadn't played tricks.

She inched around, moving at a snail's pace until she could just see him. She sucked in a breath.

He was like a golden Greek god from the fables. Wavy, sun-streaked hair, long enough to brush his collar. Wide-set eyes. Sculpted jawline. Sun-kissed skin. And those shoulders. They practically tested the wingback of the chair that swallowed her alive.

He yawned, and she gave a silent prayer he'd take himself off to bed soon. Enjoyable anecdotes aside, crouching beneath the desk had pins and needles pricking her legs, and her already itchy scalp was becoming unbearable. It was past time to remove the dastardly wig.

She had only herself to blame, of course. She shouldn't have panicked when the earl's long absent grandson arrived. She should've stuck to the plan. She was Kit, the earl's personal errand boy, and sometimes-groom should anyone asked. So far no one had. Of course, she hadn't actually had to face anyone other than the household servants.

If they thought it strange she, a servant herself, spent count-less hours with the earl, with no specific duties to speak of, they wisely kept it to themselves. Nor did they comment on the fact she had use of a small bedchamber in the guest wing of the manse.

She wasn't completely naïve. Their lack of gossip in her pres-ence undoubtedly meant they thought Kit was a by-blow of either the earl, or one of his grandsons. Much as the thought rankled, it served her purpose.

But what would Lord Thurgood think? Would he mutely accept the unusual master-servant arrangement?

"I take it you won't remain in London long, Zeke?"

Kitty's ear's pricked at the earl's query, so closely linked with her current vein of thought. It would be far simpler for her if *Zeke* took himself off immediately, even if her eyes reveled in the sight of him.

"Actually I thought I'd stay, a short while at least. I have some business matters to attend."

So much for the easy route.

"I see. Taking a break from your wanderlust? How long?"

"You sound almost as if you want me to leave," Zeke accused with a laugh.

The earl chuckled. "Don't be silly."

"Good. I'd rather hoped you could put me up for a—Now I'm really getting concerned."

"What do you mean?"

"You made a face."

"I did not."

"You most certainly did. What is it? No, don't tell me, let me guess. You have a particular lady friend, and don't want me to cramp your style."

Kitty grinned. Something like that.

"Something like that," the earl said.

Half a snort escaped her. She clapped a hand over her mouth—and held her breath.

"Did you hear that?" Zeke asked.

"Hear what?" The earl sounded far too innocent. She'd been playing chess with the old shark long enough to spot the tell. The question was, would Zeke?

A few heart-stopping beats of silence passed. Finally Zeke went on. "Travel fatigue must be playing tricks on my mind. Where were we?"

"We were discussing your upcoming travel plans."

Zeke hooted with laughter. "So you do have a particular friend. Never fear. I promise to be as unobtrusive as a mouse."

The earl cleared his throat. "Just out of curiosity, what's wrong with your townhouse?"

This time, Zeke's laughter bellowed out of him, warming Kitty from the inside out. "It's not properly staffed. But if my presence is that much of an inconvenience—"

It was the earl's turn to chuckle. "We'll manage. Now, let's off to bed. It's much too late for an old codger like you to be up, you know."

The men abandoned their chairs and strode from the room. Still she remained in place, counting the seconds till she reached five hundred and one.

She unfurled her stiff body from beneath the desk and lay flat on the floor. Now for the hard part. She not only had to tiptoe up the stairs undetected, but she had to pass the chamber she'd learned Lord Thurgood typically used to get to her own.

An easy enough feat, she supposed. After all, the man was clearly bone tired. Tomorrow, however, would be another matter entirely.

***

Kitty jolted awake, heart racing like the hounds of hell were after her. Bad enough, she'd tossed and turned all night. Now this—a dastardly nightmare about the earl's grandson.

She could still see the handsome lord snarling at her and—she rubbed a palm over the crown of her head—could feel the sting as he snatched the wig off her head, pins and all. Only one other nightmare, featuring an entirely different lord, had ever felt so real.

She had no reason to fear Lord Thurgood. He wouldn't actually reach out and de-wig her. He was the earl's heir. He'd be a true gentleman, unlike her cousin, Garrick.

She curled into a ball beneath her covers. The truth was, Lord Thurgood's arrival stirred the winds of change. Although her life as Kit was just temporary, the mad plan had given her more comfort than she'd realized. Still, she couldn't hide out at Claybourne Manor indefinitely. Nor could she huddle in her room all day without raising some eyebrows.

Besides, today was Tuesday.

Throwing back the bedcovers, she forced herself from the warm bed and padded over the cool wooden planks to the window. Parting the heavy drapes, she peered at the dawn sky and smiled. Crystal clear blue skies.

No rain and Tuesday equaled a day trip to the country—assuming the earl wouldn't alter their weekly ritual as a result of his grandson's return.

She practically danced back to her bed. She made it up, neat as a pin, then moved to the chest of drawers to perform her daily dressing ritual.

Off came her nightshirt, which she quickly folded and put away. Naked, she braced and splashed tepid water from the basin over her face and body. She shivered as goose flesh bloomed over her. Oh, for a long soak in a steaming bath. But such a luxury was impossible for months yet to come.

She picked up the remaining sliver of her precious rosemary and lavender soap, and held it to her nose, inhaling long and deep before soaping-up. She could be forgiven this one small extravagance, couldn't she? It wasn't as if anyone would draw near enough to notice the feminine scent on her skin.

Now to don her servant's garments. She didn't mind the rough-hewn mud-brown trousers, jacket, and plain white shirt. The boy's garb represented freedom, and she gave thanks every time she dressed.

The hated wrap was another story. Grimacing, she unfurled it and bound her breasts till her torso resembled a prepubescent lad's.

She eyed the wig. When she and the earl conceived their plan, she'd thought wearing one might be fun. Certainly—if one's idea of fun included denying the mad urge to scratch one's scalp. All. Day. Long.

Still. The disguise, the wrap, the wig were all small prices to pay. She could be married to Garrick, living her own personal hell.

Regarding herself in the mirror, she braided, knotted, and pinned her mass of dark curls.

A vision of her grandfather formed in her mind, when he was still spry, his face lit with a fond grin. "How you remind me of your grandmother, Kitty, love. She had the same mane of raven black hair and frosty green cat's eyes. One look and she had me. Just like you."

A lump formed in her throat, and she pushed the memory from her mind. She must not give in to her grief. Not now. Not till she was free.

Using both hands, she tugged on the wig and studied her reflection. Regardless of the fact the jet black coloring matched her eyebrows, the bowl shaped cut looked ridiculous. A bad do was a bad do.

She beetled her brows and toughened her jaw, wiping away all traces of her gender. Hello there, Kit. She saluted herself, let herself into the corridor, and started for the stairs.

Behind her a chamber door opened with a whisper. The hair on the back of her neck bristled. She picked up her pace.

"You, there." The whip-crack voice of Lord Ezekiel Thur-good.

She halted, inwardly cursing her bad luck. A few more seconds, and she would have been out of eye shot. Measly seconds.

Chapter Two

"Turn around and face me, boy."

Kitty did as commanded, her eyes locked on the brown tips of her boots. She forced herself not to ball her hands into fists at her sides even as her belly fluttered with trepidation.

The still air of the guest wing corridor swirled as he strode toward her.

"You're the earl's helper, are you not? Don't nod dumbly, lad, speak up. What's your name? And look at me when I address you."

She lifted her eyes to his cravat and cleared her throat. "My name is Kit, my lord."

He said nothing.

Curiosity pulled her gaze higher. Her eyes widened in awe before she could catch herself. He was breathtaking, even more so than she realized last night. His aristocratic features did nothing to detract from the rugged, slightly menacing air about him.

Perhaps it was his burnished skin from days spent on the open sea, or his strong, square jaw, now set in unmistakable irritation.

Toward her. She flicked a glance behind her toward the stairs. How far would she get if she ran?

He took a step closer, crossing his arms over his chest. The crisp, male scent of his cologne flowed over her like a summer breeze.

Her urge to run vanished, replaced by the oddest desire to lean forward and inhale deeply to capture more of his intriguing scent.

"Kit," he said as if trying out her name on his tongue. "What are you doing on this floor, Kit?"

Her gaze dropped again to her boots. If he thought it odd to find her roaming the halls, he would definitely take issue with her reason for doing so. There was nothing for it.

"My chamber is at the end of the hall." She gulped, then hastened to add, "My lord."

He rocked back on his heels. "The hell you say? Show me."

Her head snapped up. "My lord?"

"Lead the way."

With no alternative but to do his bidding, Kitty skirted past him, retracing her steps. He stalked at her heels.

The earl's heir was turning out to be a regular curmudgeon. No matter. He could bark at her till the cows came home so long as he never discovered her secret and sent her back to Garrick.

It always came back to that. Should she simply confess to Lord Thurgood and beg for mercy? But then, the earl hadn't opted to go that route. He must have his reasons.

Evidently her hesitation lasted beyond Lord Thurgood's patience because his hand darted past her to twist the brass knob. The paneled mahogany door swung inward.

At least the brute had the decency to wait to enter until she crossed the threshold and turned to face him.

He stepped into the small chamber, hands clasped behind his back, and cast a critical eye over the interior of the room, starting with her neatly made bed.

Kitty gave the familiar surroundings a cursory scan. Nothing out of the ordinary here. Nothing to let on he was she. She smiled inwardly.

Her triumphant feeling faded when the odious man wrinkled his nose as if he smelled something foul. Oh Lord, he was heading for the chest of drawers. Leaning forward, he sniffed the basin like a bloodhound.

She closed her eyes briefly in horror, as he picked up her still damp soap, and held it to his nose.

He shot her a glance, brows arched. "I thought I smelled rosemary."

She glowered at him, and resisted the urge to tell him the soap was infused with both rosemary and lavender.

His deep blue eyes sparkled with amusement, and he placed the soap back on its porcelain dish with exaggerated care.

"It's medicinal," she burst out, hoping he would accept her statement without question since she had no notion what malady the herb might alleviate.

When he didn't immediately scoff, she forged ahead. "May I go now, my lord?"

He gestured with overstated politeness toward the open door.

She stepped into the hall and waited.

A moment later he emerged, shaking his head. "Allow me." He closed the door. "After you?"

"Tha—" She broke off when his sarcasm registered. "After you, my lord, of *course*." Two could play the sarcasm game.

He narrowed his eyes at her.

She blanked her expression and held her breath.

He moved forward at a brisk pace, leaving her to stare after him. Two divergent thoughts sprang to mind. One—he hadn't questioned her disguise. And two—had she really found the arrogant ass handsome?

She waited for his footsteps to recede down the stairs before following. She really did have to hurry now, she thought, irritated. Lord Thurgood's curiosity had eaten into her breakfast time. Instead of heading for the kitchen to grab an apple and some porridge with the rest of the servants, she'd have to go straight to the breakfast hall or risk being late.

Thurgood's booming voice spilled out the open doorway, reaching her before she reached the hall. "...mind telling me why the devil you have a servant staying in guest quarters?"

She held utterly still, awaiting the earl's reply.

"I thought it best. This way, I can call on Kit whenever I need him. He's close at hand, so to speak."

A brief silence elapsed before the younger man's low voiced, "Who is he?"

She closed her eyes, anticipating the earl's confession. Her late grandfather had been one of the earl's closest friends, but Lord Ezekiel Thurgood was his beloved grandson. He'd likely feel compelled to tell him everything, and that would be fine unless—unless Lord Thurgood decided to send her back.

"He's my helper and I'll thank you to mind your own business. And do not go barging into his private chamber again. He's"—the earl paused—"rather timid."

Another pregnant pause ensued, then came some sort of rhythmic tapping. She risked peering around the corner into the breakfast hall. Ah, what a surprise. Lord Thurgood drummed his fingers on the dining room table.

"All right, my lord. For now."

A woman's low humming came from the end of the hall. A chambermaid approaching. Kitty didn't dare get caught eavesdropping.

She hastened forward, bowing stiffly. "Good morning, my lords."

"Good morning to you, Kit," the earl said in a cheerful tone.

Lord Thurgood gave a curt nod and fixed her with a suspicion-laced stare.

He stood before the tall, multi-paned windows lining the breakfast hall. The morning sun spilling in illuminated the magnificent, bottomless blue of his eyes. Not cornflower or powder, but a deep, smoky blue with the richness of crushed velvet.

"Are you quite ready, lad?" The earl's words penetrated her Zeke-induced stupor.

She peeled her gaze off the man. "Yes, my lord, quite ready." She'd even skip breakfast if it meant getting out of this house and away from *him*.

The earl furrowed his fluffy white brows and aimed an accusatory look at his grandson, though he addressed Kitty. "Have you eaten anything this morning, Kit?"

She hesitated, not wanting to delay their departure. "No, my lord."

The earl's expression turned peevish. "I thought not."

Lord Thurgood snorted.

"Run along, Kit, and fetch something from Cook. Then meet me at the stables."

"Yes, my lord. Thank you, my lord."

She swung around prepared to flee the room. She halted at Lord Thurgood's, "Stables?"

A sinking feeling settled in the pit of her stomach.

"That's right, Zeke. Kit and I visit the country every Tuesday."

"Do you, now? Sounds like fun."

***

There was definitely something strange going on here. The earl knew it, Kit knew it, and Zeke knew it. Only, unlike the two conspirators, Zeke didn't know what *it* was. And he didn't like being left in the dark. Not one bit. He sat atop the jostling buggy, sandwiching his grandfather between his hulking form and that of young Kit.

Not long after they'd left London proper, the old man put Kit in the driver's seat. He was giving the lad driving lessons, no less, and from the looks of it had been for some time. That was a job for the head groom. When Zeke said as much, the earl laughed, as if he had made some sort of joke. No explanation was offered.

Was Kit a long lost brother? A by-blow of his late father? A result of one of Caden's liaisons? Zeke quickly did the math. Caden was a mere five and twenty. If he were Kit's father, Kit could only be eight, at the oldest.

Kit was well past nursery age. But precisely how old was he? Zeke tried once more to get a clear look at the boy's face, and once more his grandfather's frame somehow managed to block his view.

No matter, he thought with a glare at his grandfather's too-innocent profile. He closed his eyes and summoned a vision of Kit from this morning, in the dining hall, when the scamp had stared unblinking at him with the brazenness of a peer.

He'd hazard to guess Kit was at least in his late teens. Though he had no facial hair to speak of, the boy's pronounced cheekbones attested any baby fat being long gone.

He supposed the boy could be his grandfather's accident. He contemplated the notion—and promptly came up against a wall. The men in Zeke's family were all fair-haired, especially as youths, with vital complexions. They were also larger than the average Brit owing to their Nordic lineage. In addition, they invariably had blue colored eyes.

Kit's pale skinned complexion looked as if his face had never seen the sun. As opposed to being blond with blue eyes, he had ink-black hair and eyes the color of ice-covered moss. As for his build, Zeke snorted to himself, he was far from Viking material.

Ruling out the possibility of Kit being related to his family by blood left two possibilities, neither of which appealed to Zeke. Either the earl was becoming eccentric as Zeke often joked, or Kit had somehow bamboozled the old man into special treatment.

If the latter was the case, as Zeke suspected, it was a good thing he'd come home when he did. No one took advantage of his family. He'd handle the situation.

Resolved, he settled back, arms crossed over his chest, and allowed himself to enjoy the passing scenery with its increasing degree of foliage and decreasing populace. The air smelled sweeter here than in London. Not to mention he'd spent the past several months cooped up on a ship, unable to walk two feet without running into a fellow passenger or crewman.

"That's it, talk to them a bit, Kit. It puts the horses at ease."

He allowed himself a small smile as the earl's words brought back a similar memory whereby he, and not Kit, had been the recipient of his grandfather's tutelage.

Zeke felt considerably lighter of spirit when, a short time later, Kit guided the team onto a narrow gravel drive.

"This old spot? I'd assumed this place had been sold off. Seems a lifetime ago since you and father brought Caden and I here." The country cottage held good memories, all from before his father's life imploded.

"I'll take it from here, m' boy." The earl pulled the reins from Kit's small, gloved hands.

"Allow me." Zeke took the reins in turn, shaking his head in dismay. Some future groom Kit would make.

"Carry on to the pond," his grandfather directed.

He led the horses past the faded limestone cottage and down the grass covered hill. When the pond came into view, he slowed, reining in the team under a canopy of hawthorn trees.

He hopped down to aid the earl's descent. "As I recall, you and Father gave Caden and I our first pistol shooting lessons here."

From the corner of his eye he saw Kit scramble down the opposite side of the hitch. Good Lord. The boy had his pinkie crooked in the air as if to balance his weight. What an odd bird.

"Exactly what Kit and I have been doing out here these last several weeks."

This was too much. His voice rose an octave. "You and Kit?"

"Never know when one might need protection."

Zeke threw up his hands. "Why would Kit need protection?"

"I was referring to myself," the earl answered. "I prefer my servants trained to defend me.

Plausible. Barely..

The earl's eyes narrowed in sudden contemplation. Never a good sign.

His grandfather glanced from Zeke to Kit and back to Zeke. "The recoil from the blast is a bit much for my shooting arm. Perhaps today you could instruct the boy?"

Kit's head jerked up and his frosty green eyes went saucer-round. Apparently Kit didn't like the idea of taking lessons from him.

Blame it on a perverse sense of humor, but the thought of irritating Kit had a satisfying edge to it.

Kit spoke up for the first time in a long while, his voice at once hoarse and squeaky. "My lord, if your arm troubles you, perhaps we should skip the lesson today altogether. This way you can spend the time visiting. After all your grandson has been so long away."

Zeke could only stare at the boy.

After a moment passed whereby his grandfather didn't rebuke the lad, he found his tongue. "Nonsense, lad. Why should a small thing like a family reunion interfere with your shooting lessons? Not that we don't appreciate your suggestion."

He hoped Kit's intelligence quotient allowed him to detect the sarcasm he'd infused into every blasted syllable.

He glanced at his grandfather, expecting commiseration. Damned if the old man wasn't glaring at *him*. Fine.

"I'm happy to help the boy, my lord." Zeke fixed Kit with a critical eye. "What have you got so far? Can you hit a target?"

Kit glared at him. "Even a moving one."

Oh, dear. She hadn't meant to speak the words aloud. She braced for a through set-down.

Instead Zeke threw his head back and roared with laughter. The earl quickly followed suit.

Her own lips quivered, but she managed to suppress her mirth. Giggling would undermine the accusatory scowl she had aimed at the earl.

What had he been thinking, asking Zeke to instruct her? Sweet, practical, logical Lord Claybourne. His common sense had vaporized the moment his grandson arrived.

"Let's see if you know how to load and unload the revolver," Zeke challenged.

"'Course he knows how. Show him how it's done, lad." The earl set the revolver before her on the overturned hay barrel.

She squinted against the glare of the sun and scrubbed her damp palms on her trousers, mentally reviewing the loading procedure.

She could hardly concentrate, what with Zeke staring and the heat. The afternoon sun beat down on her, baking her monstrous wig onto her head.

Sweat droplets trickled from her forehead down her cheek. One had the audacity to slide to the tip of her nose. She blew it off. How mortifying. But then she was supposed to be a boy, and boys reveled in their perspiration, didn't they?

"I take it I need to load it for you?" Zeke reached for the firearm.

Impatient, arrogant ass.

She waved a dismissive hand at him swiped her brow, and set herself to the task, lining up the powder and ammunition.

The earl had taught her well, and, now that she'd begun, she fell into a routine, unclipping the compaction lever underneath the barrel to fill each of the recesses with powder. Next, she packed a lead ball into each cylinder's receptacle, before placing a cap on the opposite end of each of the chambers.

"There." She crossed her arms over her flattened chest—and winced. The strap did its job all too well.

Lord Thurgood cocked his head and frowned. "Are you un-well?"

Of course the odious man would notice. He watched her like a hawk.

"No, I'm very well. Thank you for asking, my lord."

He shook his head and eyed the heavens as if in a silent plea for patience.

She knew exactly how he felt.

A beat later, he stalked away, his long legs devouring the distance between the grassy knoll and the abutting vegetable garden.

She sent the earl a questioning look. He merely smiled at her. At least one of them appeared to be enjoying himself.

Lord Thurgood fished a smallish pumpkin from the garden, set it at his feet, then strode toward the hoard of firewood piled beside the cottage. After rolling up his shirtsleeves, he crouched to scoop half the logs into his arms. His back muscles rippled under the load, tightening his waistcoat across those broad bands. When he rose, his muscular thighs bulged in his well-fitting tweed trousers.

Kitty heard herself sigh and then coughed to cover it. "Swallowed some dust," she muttered, and ordered herself to stop staring at Zeke. Unfortunately, her eyes refused to obey.

In just two hauls, he moved the entire heap away from the building to make one stack.

He placed the pumpkin on the stack and strode back to where she and the earl waited. "There's your target."

Up close, his bare forearms were thick and bronzed, and dusted with golden hairs. Her gaze moved up his shirtsleeves, suddenly very fitted over very large, very hard looking biceps.

She swallowed with difficulty. Her mouth had gone oddly dry.

"Are you paying attention, Kit? I said—"

"I have eyes. I see the target," she snapped, more irritated at herself than him. She'd been gaping at him as if she'd never seen a man. She was a complete idiot.

"Good. See if you can hit it," he clipped back.

She squared her shoulders and adjusted her stance. Evidently, she didn't move fast enough for his liking.

"Pull the hammer back," Lord Thurgood began in a tone typically reserved for dimwits.

She pinched her lips together and cocked the hammer.

"Now line up your sight, and shoot."

Of all the irritating, obnoxious...she slid him a narrow-eyed glare, and saw his lips twitching with humor. Only out of deference to the earl did she resist throwing the pistol at him.

Gritting her teeth, she leaned forward and braced for the recoil, angling one foot slightly behind her. She laid her shooting arm across the barrel and used her free hand to grasp her forearm. Pinching one eye shut, she aligned the rear sight. Breath held, she squeezed the trigger.

The powder exploded with a deafening bang, and seemingly at the same instant a large chunk of pumpkin disappeared into the atmosphere. A loud ringing clanged in her ears, obliterating all other sound, and a cloud of acrid black smoke stung her nostrils, but she didn't mind.

She put a hand to the small of her back, massaging the area most impacted by the recoil, and smiled in utter delight.

"Good going, lad!" the earl shouted.

She'd have loved to offer Lord Thurgood a satisfied smirk, but how could she?

Claybourne's lion of a grandson had already crossed to the wood stack to reposition what remained of the hapless pumpkin, without having offered one word of praise.

The moment Lord Thurgood rejoined them he broke into a lesson. "When push comes to shove, if you ever need to employ one of these things, there probably won't be a convenient arm rest." He gestured for Kitty to come toward him.

She obeyed, albeit with reluctance.

"Stand away from the barrel. Now aim."

"Very well."

Zeke moved close behind her, and her insides skittered like she'd had too much sugar. It must be the heat. Still, she scooted forward, putting a good foot of ground between them. Taking the pistol in both hands, she held it in front of her.

He closed the distance again. "Don't let your arms droop like a couple of dead fish." He wrapped his arms around her and encircled her wrists with warm, slightly calloused hands, lifting and pulling her arms until they stretched out straight from her shoulders.

The heady male scent of him, intensified by exertion and heat, enveloped her. The jittery sensation in her belly returned with a vengeance, bringing with it the oddest desire to turn her head and nuzzle the salty skin of his neck. Clenching her teeth, she tamped down a nervous giggle.

"Stay just like that," he commanded, squeezing her wrists once for emphasis. He moved away from her, and only then did she realize her knees had gone wobbly. From the heat. Definitely the heat.

Get hold of yourself, Hastings. She closed one eye, setting up her shot, and prepared to fire.

Before she could, Zeke was back, reaching around her and hoisting her arms up again with a quick, impatient tug. He stuck there like a bad rash. "Watch your footing. There'll be a—"

Bang!

The force of the shot lifted her off her feet, jackknifing her into the hard wall of Zeke's chest, bottom first. She bounced off him and, as gracelessly as humanly possible, cartwheeled airborne to land on her feet, arms flung out before her.

She gaped at him through a snaking plume of smoke snaking up from the revolver, which, by some miracle, she hadn't dropped.

"Recoil!" Zeke yelled with a grin.

Bloody, bloody hell.

She glared at him. This was all his fault. He'd flummoxed her so she'd pulled the trigger without preparing for the recoil.

When his grin only widened into a dazzling smile, she turned away to set the pistol atop the barrel. It was that, or aim it at him, the audacious peacock. He had nerve, looking as elegant and poised as ever.

Meanwhile, Kitty could only thank her lucky stars her wig hadn't jettisoned off to land in the middle of the pond.

She sniffed and then grinned despite herself. She had hit the mark again.

"For all the exercise young Kit supposedly mandates for your edification, he seems rather malleable himself. I suggest he join you on some of your prescribed walks," Lord Thurgood shouted to the earl.

Her mouth fell open. Had he just implied she had a large bottom?

"Kit, if you're hot you could try losing the jacket." He lifted a hand to point at her head. "And that felt hat."

Evidently the sweat droplets rolling off her nose and chin had not escaped his notice. Kitty grasped her hat with both hands. She wouldn't put it past the ogre to rip it off her head.

"Let the boy be, Zeke. He needs a break to recoup his arm." The earl waved a dismissive hand. "As for me, I'm starved. Let's to lunch. Zeke, go and fetch the basket."

Zeke shook his head in disbelief, eyeing Kit meaningfully.

Kitty spoke up. "No, my lord, I can—"

"Nonsense, Kit. Zeke, you said yourself the boy's overheated. Kit and I will have a seat in the shade. Lend me your arm, Kit, there's a lad."

Kitty shot the earl a reproving glance as she fell in step beside him.

He winked at her. "Bring the blanket first, Zeke, if you don't mind. We want to sit under the hawthorn without getting dirt on our trousers."

***

As the earl and his grandson supped, Kitty did her best to disappear into the background and Lord Thurgood seemed only too happy to allow her to do so.

He sat with his back to her while devouring his meal and grilling the earl—on his overall health, how he'd been sleeping, whether he continued to work so many hours on the estate or if he'd handed some of his duties over to the manager as Zeke suggested before he last sailed.

His obvious affection for his grandfather quite charmed her, though she maintained a mask of indifference in the event he deigned to glance her way.

Her ears pricked up when Lord Claybourne asked about his upcoming travel plans.

"The American West is next on the docket," Thurgood said. "I believe I mentioned a gold mine I've a mind to purchase."

"Once or twice. Just when do you propose to make this journey, Zeke?" Lord Claybourne demanded, sounding weary.

"Soon," Zeke hedged, ripping off a hunk of bread from the remaining loaf and stuffing it into his mouth.

"What is it with you and mines?" The earl splashed a portion of wine into his goblet.

Kitty wondered the same thing.

Zeke considered the question for a long moment, rubbing his chin with his pointer finger. "I suppose I enjoy mining because"—he paused—"because of what mines produce. We can hold it, measure it, count on it to stand the test of time, and once it's ours, no one can take it away."

As if sensing he'd given some secret part of himself away, Zeke cleared his throat and muttered, "Or something to that effect."

"There are other things in this world even more substantial than gems and metals," the earl said softly.

If Zeke heard him, he made no comment. "All I need now is a bed." He set aside his empty plate, leaned back on his elbows and stretched out his long legs.

Kitty's hand paused halfway to bringing a piece of cheese to her mouth. Her gaze grazed over his well-shaped calves to the contoured muscles of his thighs visible through the fabric.

As if he sensed her eyes on him, Zeke glanced over his shoulder at her.

She shifted her focus away in the nick of time. What in the world was wrong with her? First she'd stared at his arms, now his legs. Arms and legs. Everyone had them.

"My lord, how many times did you bring Caden and I out here to shoot, fish, and hunt? Too many to count, I'd wager."

She heard the smile in his voice and found herself smiling along with him.

"Too many indeed. Do you recall the times your father joined us?"

The tentative note in the earl's voice drew Kitty's gaze back to the two men in time to see Zeke snatch a piece of grass from the ground and fling it back toward the earth.

"I recall the last time. One of the few family outings Father bothered attending after Mother—" Zeke slammed his mouth shut so hard Kitty heard the clash of his teeth.

She averted her gaze, but not before she glimpsed the flash of pain in Lord Claybourne's eyes, and no one could miss Zeke's simmering anger. What had he meant to say before he stopped himself?

She knew little of his parents' history. The earl's son, Zeke's father, had died some time ago, as had his mother. But Kitty had no inkling as to the details. Whatever the case, it appeared neither Zeke nor Lord Claybourne had fully recovered. She could relate all too well.

"Suffice it to say, the cottage holds many pleasant memories, old man," Zeke said in a light tone that almost convinced Kitty she'd imagined the tense moment between grandfather and grandson.

But she'd experienced too much loss herself to be fooled.

Behind her, Zeke bounded to his feet. "Are you finished with your meal? Care to take a stroll? That is, unless you wish to walk the property with Kit while I tidy up, m'lord?"

Kitty had been feeling a degree of kinship with Zeke. Now she had a strong urge to shift around and kick him in the shin.

She turned to glare over her shoulder, and caught Lord Claybourne's twinkling eye.

Guessing he intended to play her against his grandson yet again, Kitty shook her head an emphatic no. "I'll be happy to take care of this, Lord Claybourne."

The older man grinned, then gave her a wink when Zeke's head snapped in her direction.

She nearly groaned. She could practically hear his warranted censure. Kit had no business telling Lord Claybourne what he would or would not like to do.

The problem was, she couldn't seem to recall she was supposed to be Kit, the servant, and not Kitty, the lady.

"Come, Ezekiel, let us walk" Lord Claybourne said, forestalling another dressing down,.

After they moved off, she levered herself to her knees and gathered the used dishes and food containers. She carried the picnic supplies to the buggy and tucked them into the back trap.

The position put the earl and his heir in her sights as they strolled the grounds near the pond.

She drank in the sight of Zeke. She couldn't help it. He was the most compelling man she'd ever met. Beautiful to look at, yes, but more to the point, he had presence. Something in the way he carried himself, like a royal prince, broad shoulders thrown back, head held high, that wavy hair glinting in the sunlight like a golden mantle.

And today he'd shown he had a vulnerable side. A heart that had not escaped this world unscathed. The demigod was human after all.

As she stared, he threw his head back and laughed at something the earl said.

A funny little flutter tickled her belly, and she wished just for a moment, he knew her as a woman, and not an irritating boy. Wished she'd met him as Lady Christine Hastings at a London party, dressed in one of the gowns her grandfather purchased for her come-out. She saw them dancing on a glittering ballroom floor, staring into each other's eyes. The image was so vivid it hurt.

Her eyes stinging, she turned her back on the earl and Lord Thurgood, and her silly, impossible yearnings. She should be grateful for Lord Claybourne's generous willingness to hide her had afforded, not dreaming up impossible fairytales about his grandson that could never come true.

Chapter Three

The ancient grandfather clock in the downstairs hall chimed once, a beautiful, resounding tone that usually delighted Kitty, but tonight had her teeth on edge. Half-past eight.

She huffed aloud and closed the atlas on her lap with a resounding thunk. She'd had such high hopes when she borrowed it from the earl's library, but not even the coastlines, plains, and mountain ranges of Africa could hold her attention. Her mind kept straying. To him.

Setting the heavy tome aside, she uncoiled her body from her cross-legged perch atop her bed and reached for her coat.

The earl had sent word earlier she should join him for a late supper in his den, which meant it would be just the two of them, which, in turn, meant his grandson was going out. Again. Third night this week. She sniffed and re-donned the wig.

She ought to be glad for Lord Ezekiel Thurgood's frequent absences—or Zeke's as she increasingly referred to him in the privacy of her thoughts. But the truth was, with him gone, the house felt cavernously empty.

He'd arrived in London less than a fortnight ago, and somehow had invaded every inch of space in the rambling manse, like air or light, something that couldn't be touched or captured or measured, but when missing left its indelible mark. She'd never experienced anything like the odd mixture of attraction and antipathy she had for Zeke Thurgood.

She ought to feel nothing for him but irritation. He mocked her at every turn. The way she spoke. Too proper for a servant, he had said on more than one occasion. Another time, he'd asked how it was she came to speak with such perfect diction, somehow making what should have been a compliment into an insult. As for her actual voice, he pronounced it too squeaky. When she redoubled her efforts to deepen her tone he accused her of mumbling.

And who could forget yesterday when he cornered her upstairs before breakfast to lecture her on her eating habits. She ought to eat more, he insisted, if she ever wanted to build muscles.

She'd thought to shut him up by escaping down the back stairs en route to the kitchen for her morning meal with the rest of the servants. The brute actually followed her, squeezing that big body down the narrow stairwell with a measure of grace she wouldn't have believed possible had she not witnessed it for herself.

Once in the kitchens, he'd flashed his winning smile and set about charming the hapless chamber and scullery maids. No trouble there, of course. But he'd miscalculated if he expected to get any information from them about her. They hadn't any.

She grinned. She could still see the girls, sitting at the rough hewn wooden table, wide-eyed and dumbstruck, though Kitty wasn't sure if their discomfiture stemmed from Lord Thurgood paying the kitchen a visit or his almost obscene good looks.

Yet for all his peskiness, she—well, she didn't actually miss the man. She more wanted him around. Bother. It made no sense.

Giving herself one last look-see, she exited her room and headed downstairs to join the earl in his den, resolving not to think about Lord Zeke Thurgood for the rest of the evening.

The task proved easier said than done, thanks to the earl's habit of referring to the man in passing conversation. Not that she faulted him for it. In truth she feasted on every scrap of information the earl shared.

After their dinner plates had been removed, Kitty set up the chessboard. "Your turn to go first, my lord."

He reached for a pawn as she settled herself. "Tell me, Kitty, what do you think of my grandson? Be honest."

"Lord Thurgood?"

An image of Zeke formulated in her mind's eye. His wicked, gleaming grin. His hard, broad chest. His rumbling voice uttering some mocking sentiment aimed at her.

"I think he dislikes me intensely, and I think you provoke him to do so, my lord."

The earl let out a hardy laugh. "Indeed, I do."

Her jaw dropped. "So you admit it." She took her turn and waited for the earl's reply.

"The boy's too confident by half. This hoax ought to knock him down a peg or two when all's said and done. He's consumed with curiosity as to who you are, why I've taken such an interest in you. In six months, when keeping your secret is no longer necessary, I'm going to enjoy rubbing his nose in how easily we fooled him. He thinks he's clever, looking to uncover Kit's true identity. He has no idea." Looking extremely self-satisfied, Lord Claybourne bent over the board and contemplated his next move.

Six months. Kitty leaned back in her armchair, crossing her trousered legs at the ankles, and gazed out the window at the night sky. Six months. How she'd longed for the day when she'd fulfill the stipulations of the trust, acquiring the right to her inheritance *sans* husband, and the ability to rule her own life *sans* guardian. She'd be free, no longer subject to the whims of her guardian.

Only now did it dawn on her. She had nowhere to go when the time came.

"Kitty?"

She shifted her gaze to Lord Claybourne, her grandfather's most trusted friend, now the closest thing to family she had. "Yes, my lord?"

His mouth turned down at the corners. "Forgive me. I hadn't considered how humoring myself by teasing Zeke would land you on the hot seat. I'll cease goading him."

She grinned, hoping to set him at ease. "Please don't trouble yourself. Besides, I rather think putting him off my trail will prove nigh impossible, especially as we reside under the same roof."

"One of you is rarely under said roof," the earl muttered, his rook capturing her pawn. "Your move."

"It is quiet with him gone, night after night," she admitted with a frown, her chin in her hand as she took in the earl's devious strategy.

"So you do like him."

Her eyes bugged.

He waved a dismissive hand, though a crafty light gleamed in his eyes. The earl brandished his queen and placed it on the board. "Check." He flashed her a smug grin. "You're losing your touch."

She sent him a mock scowl, and then, with no warning, her face crumpled as love and gratitude flooded her heart. He'd taken her in, treating her like one of his own, no questions asked.

"Kitty?" He prodded, his expression one of alarm.

"You're a dear, you know that?" Horrified by her loss of composure, she hopped up and retrieved the game's wooden storage box, scooping the chess pieces and the board. "I think I'll turn in early tonight if you don't mind?"

Avoiding his eye, she moved to the cabinet and stowed the box.

"Kitty, did you know, during the war, your grandfather saved my life?"

"No." She returned to her vacated chair. "He told me you'd fought side by side. He raved over your bravery. Called you, and I quote, the best and bravest man he ever had the honor to serve beside."

They shared a smile.

"He trusted you implicitly."

"And I him."

"I never said how I consigned your address to memory. He made me recite it. He didn't want it written anywhere. Didn't want Garrick tipped off to my whereabouts should I need to disappear. I thought my grandfather exaggerated the severity of the situation, but then—" She broke off, grimacing as scenes from her last night at Hastings House, what Garrick tried to do to her, flashed through her mind.

How very right her grandfather had been to worry for her. But she got away, she reminded herself, thanks to her grandfather and the honorable man sitting across from her.

The earl with his shock of white hair, aristocratic features, and powerful frame cut quite the intimidating figure. But one glimpse into his kind blue eyes and she'd known he would do everything her grandfather promised and more.

She gazed at the earl through a blurry haze and sent him a tremulous smile. "Thank you," she whispered. "For everything."

The earl's jaw hardened, his look reminiscent of Zeke at his most obstinate. "I vow, I'll see you safe from your blackguard cousin. He won't get his hands on you so long as I draw breath."

Kitty moved to crouch at his feet, taking one of his large hands between hers. "And so long as I draw breath, I vow I'll never forget what you've done for me, my lord." She conjured her sunniest smile. "It seems as if Garrick's called off the hounds, thanks to our efforts. There hasn't been an ad in the *Times* for months."

Admiration gleamed in his eyes. "Yes, sly tiger that you are." He touched the tip of her nose with his pointer finger. "Methinks you threw him off your scent. Now be a dear and pour us nightcap."

She filled a snifter for the earl and escaped to her small chamber, her legs moving as fast as they would carry her. Her will to hold her grief at bay had finally given out.

Ensconced in darkness, her heart burning as if it lie broken in her chest, she dove into bed and sobbed into the pillows. Tears for the grandfather she missed so terribly, for her beloved brother, lost before his time, and even for the parents she knew more from their written adventures than time spent in their company.

Underscoring it all was a pain she couldn't name, a nagging longing consuming her whenever a certain someone was near—and when he wasn't.

Eventually the flood of tears gave way to exhaustion, and exhaustion to fitful sleep. Then came the nightmare she hadn't suffered for months.

She jolted awake, heart racing, skin clammy with fear. Rolling herself into a tight ball, she pinched her eyes closed and tried to shut out the image of Garrick on top of her.

I got away. I'm safe.

Lord Claybourne's genius had devised her clever disguise, making of the whole thing a grand adventure. "One year to play at being a boy," he'd said with a jaunty grin.

Hadn't she spent six full months here without a moment's trouble, hiding in plain sight? In another six months she'd reach the age her grandfather's trust pronounced her free and no longer subject to her guardian's decrees.

But what then?

The image of a golden-haired man with velvet blue eyes, and a gleaming white smile filled her mind. *I knew you liked him,* the earl had teased earlier.

In the darkness, her face flushed with heat anew. She'd die before admitting the truth. She'd developed a silly, hopeless crush on Lord Zeke Thurgood. How could she have done it? Then again, how could she not?

Sharp-witted and beautiful, but critical to a fault—especially of Kit.

Regardless. Zeke captivated her with his robust laugh, stories of foreign lands, and the Heart-melting way he doted on his grandfather, calling him *old man* even as he panicked at every cough or sneeze or flush.

Of course, none of that negated the fact he often acted an arrogant ass.

She pummeled her pillows in frustration then collapsed onto her back. Bother. Despite his many flaws, Zeke could have his pick of women, which meant even if she exposed her secret to him—which she wouldn't—and threw herself at him—which she wouldn't *ever*—she had nothing to hold the man's interest.

Zeke was a man of the world whose tastes wouldn't run toward greenhorn girls who hadn't even had the experience of a London season.

Zeke's perfect mate would be beautiful and exotic and cultured. The exact opposite of her.

She had only passable looks, was as exotic as an apple, and though she knew an awful lot about an awful lot of places, she'd barely ventured outside Maidstone County.

Meanwhile Zeke's wanderlust would soon see him sailing into the sunset in search of new adventure. She ought to think about that the next time his golden good looks or hardy laugh or tender ministrations toward his grandfather turned her brain to mush.

Thanks to her parents and her brother, Kitty knew all about wanderlust and the havoc it wreaked on those left behind. Unlike some people, she knew what really mattered in this world.

Family and togetherness, love and trust, *not* traveling far from home, alone, in a never-ending quest for adventure and fortune.

She rolled to her side, closing her eyes. In several months she would be free to chart her own course in life. Where would she go? What would she do? She lay awake with the questions looping through her mind till the morning sun illuminated the sky.

Zeke still hadn't returned home.

Chapter Four

By two in the afternoon, the heir apparent still had not deigned to put in an appearance.

Kitty tried not to grit her teeth as she placed the small vase containing the fresh flowers she'd arranged on the stand at the end of the hall. She breathed in the fragrant bouquet of lavender and honeysuckle, hoping the scent would soothe her frayed nerves.

It didn't. No surprise there. Someone had worked her into a lather and, maddeningly, that someone was her.

She ought to be ashamed, skulking to her chamber, again, with yet another pathetic excuse. Let's see, first, after breakfasting, she'd come to collect her dirties for delivery to the laundry. An hour or so later, after strolling the private park at the end of the street with the earl, she'd trotted back upstairs to wash. Later, she returned with the laundered clothing.

Now this. Fresh flowers from the conservatory to brighten up the space. Hah. Since when did Kit concern himself with flowers?

The truth was, she'd made the trek to her chamber for one reason, only. She wanted to know if he'd returned.

Bother, bother, bother. It wasn't as if she had any claims on the man, nor did she wish to marry him. Problem was, she didn't have to want to marriage to want...

Oh, that was just it. She didn't know what she wanted. Except that she wanted him here, and not with anyone of the female persuasion—and especially not with a female over night.

She paced the small space and fumed. The earl napped, leaving her free to read or draw, wander the conservatory or entertain herself with any number of pastimes. But she couldn't because all she could think about was him, and where in blazes he was.

This morning's breakfast conversation between several of the maids hadn't helped. While eating her porridge, she overheard Molly, the scullery maid, informing Cook not to bother with Lord Thurgood's meal as he hadn't returned home—again.

Danni, the upstairs maid, added, "Last week he came home with his shirt unbuttoned to here"—she gestured to her sternum—"his cravat hanging loose 'round his neck, and reeking of perfume."

At Kit's shocked gasp, both maids broke into a fit of the giggles, and hadn't reined in their merriment 'til Cook threatened them with a wooden spoon.

"You should follow young Kit's example, girls, and hush up about the family's private affairs. The earl won't take kindly to hearing of gossip spread about his heir."

Kitty instantly regretted her reaction as she'd likely get no further information out of the staff.

Chastising herself as the worst sort of fool, she opened her door a crack and peeked out.

Zeke's chamber door remained closed. Perhaps he'd stayed at his club last night. Gentlemen did from time to time, didn't they?

The tip of her thumb hurt from her incessant nibbling. She yanked her hand from her mouth in disgust, turned from the door—though she left it ajar, and flounced onto her bed with an exaggerated humph.

Footsteps sounded in the hall. Light steps. A chambermaid, she'd wager.

But it could be him.

She flew off the bed to peer toward his chamber. His door was open, and beckoning.

In stocking-covered feet she skulked toward his chamber. *What if he spots you?*

She paused and nibbled her thumb some more, considering. She would say she was on her way to the kitchen. She started forward again. *In your socks?* She shushed her irritating pragmatist.

Hovering outside the threshold, a giddy sense of danger quickened her pulse and made her palms instantly clammy. She wiped them on her trousers and hinged forward from the hips, inch by slow inch, until she could just see into Zeke's antechamber—and came nose to nose with the upstairs chambermaid.

She jerked upright, her heart hammering. "Oh, Danni, you gave me a fright," she said, rapid-fire.

"I could say the same to you. What're you about, Kit? D'ya need somethin'?"

"I...ah...thought Lord Thurgood had returned. I wanted to have a word. Ah, well, cheerio." She began backing away.

"A word about what?" came the haughty demand from the top of the stairs.

She froze in her tracks, her mouth suddenly bone dry. Now? Now he put in an appearance?

Her gaze shifted in his direction as Zeke closed the distance between them. A lion stalking his prey.

A magnificent, debauched lion. The upper buttons of his shirt were undone, no cravat in sight. His waistcoat hung open to his ribs. He'd removed his jacket and had it slung it over his shoulder, hooked over his thumb.

Her skin prickled with awareness as her heated blood rushed through her veins, leaving her shaky and breathless and anticipating something she couldn't name.

His footsteps thumped to a halt directly in front of her.

She noted the golden stubble on his cheeks. Hadn't bothered with a shave, eh? And judging by his unkempt locks, he hadn't employed a comb since rolling out of bed, either. She wouldn't have imagined a head of hair could get that mussed in sleep, unless—her heart seized as the truth struck. A woman had woven her fingers in all that gold silk.

Clenching her teeth against the urge to berate him, her narrowed gaze met his bloodshot, predator's eyes.

"Well?" he demanded.

"Good morning, my lord." Danni slipped away, feather duster tucked under her arm.

Traitor.

"I'm waiting."

She lifted her chin. "I wondered if you had taken ill, my lord, since you missed both breakfast and lunch, and, now that I've gotten a good look at you..." She broke off to sniff. "I see I had reason to worry. You clearly didn't sleep well."

A flicker of amusement danced in his eyes. "Kit, I'm touched."

Her cheeks flooded with heat. "My concern is solely for the earl's sake. He expressed concern."

Zeke inched closer until he loomed over Kit. "Indeed? Where is Claybourne now?"

Alarm spiked through her. Would he actually ask the earl about his supposed concern? She knew her claim to be true, of course. The earl was worried about Zeke, though he hadn't expressed it in so many words.

"He's having his afternoon nap, and I'll thank you not to bother him."

Zeke surprised her with a grin. "Excellent. That leaves you free to help me."

"Help you?" She squeaked.

"This saves me from having to send for my valet." With that, he sauntered into his sitting room, leaving Kitty frozen in place and staring after him.

He disappeared through the adjoining door into his bedchamber. A moment later, his tousled head reappeared. "Kit, I haven't got all day. Move your arse."

She bristled at his tone. Then it hit her. She was about to enter his lair to help strip him of his clothes.

She shouldn't. She couldn't. But how could she refuse?

Zeke's eyes narrowed.

"Very well. Although why a grown man needs help undressing," she muttered under her breath as adrenaline flooded her veins.

"What did you say?"

"Nothing important, my lord."

Kitty entered his private chamber, giddy anticipation bubbling inside her, despite the alarm bells clanging in her head. She must be mad. Ladies didn't venture into gentlemen's chambers, much less help men out of their clothes.

All rational thought ceased at the sight of the large, polished-wood, four-post bed dominating the center of the room. The rich, burgundy velvet coverlet invited her fingers to sink into the fabric.

Without warning, a vivid image of Zeke languishing beneath the sheets sprang to her mind. Her toes curled in her stockinged feet, digging in to the plush carpet.

She pinched her eyes closed and inhaled deeply to clear her mind. Only the room smelled like him. That spicy, clean, masculine scent. A slow burning fire ignited in her belly. *Not good.*

"First my boots." Zeke dropped into the armchair positioned before the empty grate, stretching out his long legs.

She swallowed. She was Kit, she reminded herself, a household servant. Time to get to work.

Problem was, she didn't know exactly how to proceed. Then again, how hard could it be? She squatted before Zeke and tugged. Nothing happened.

"Try unfastening the buckles."

She glanced up at him and her insides...melted. No other word described the sensation.

He gazed back at her with slumberous eyes. His disheveled hair screamed at her to smooth it. His lips were rose-colored, and swollen, as if he'd spent a good portion of last night kissing.

Someone else.

Her chin jutted downward, and she undid the first buckle with short, angry jerks. Then, using both hands, she heaved—and promptly found herself sprawled on her backside before him.

Zeke threw his head back and roared with laughter.

She wanted to maintain her anger, but his laughter proved contagious and her lips curved up instead of down.

"Why, Kit, is that a smile? I'd begun to think you had no sense of humor."

When she would've resumed her crouch at his feet, he waved her off with an easy grin. "I'll get this one. I'll need your help with my garments and I don't want you to hurt yourself before you hang my things. Speaking of which…" He held out his coat.

She took it without comment, her interest in entering his closet outweighing her ire at his high-handed manner. "This way?"

He grunted his assent.

Once hidden from his view, she held the black superfine to her nose and breathed in Zeke's scent.

"What're you doing in there?"

Ever suspicious. She glared through the walls but hung his jacket, shooting the fabric before exiting the closet.

"Kit, how did you come to be in my grandfather's employ?"

He asked the question with practiced nonchalance, but Kitty noted the way the corners of his eyes tightened as if he prepared to catch her in a lie.

No matter. She and the earl had rehearsed the answer. "I met his Lordship at a house party in the country. Acted as his valet, m'lord." The gravelly tone she only partially achieved succeeded in scraping her voice box raw. "He liked my services and asked the host if I could be hired away."

"Evidently your impressive valet skills are rusty," Zeke muttered. "Whose house party?" He set the second boot beside the first and began removing his socks.

She watched, unblinking, as one, hard-muscled calf appeared, followed by a large, but well-shaped foot.

He dropped the dark wool onto the floor beside his boots and frowned at her.

"B-beg pardon, my lord?"

"Whose house party?" he drew out, louder.

"Lord Hastings's." She dragged her gaze from his bare foot. "Baron of Maidstone." Her grandfather. Kitty and the earl figured neither one of them would forget his name and later be fouled up. Plus, she could describe her ancestral home to a tee if pressed.

"Hastings." He rolled the name over his tongue as if trying to place it. He stripped off his second sock, then stood, spreading his arms wide. "Help me with my waistcoat. I daresay you'll be quicker at it than me what with your delicate hands."

She hung back not at all sure she ought to comply.

"You must be the worst servant I've ever—"

"Oh, very well." She darted forward, tackling his fabric-covered buttons as if the devil himself timed her. She bent over her work, and tried without much success to keep her fingers steady. If only he wouldn't notice how her hands shook she could die a happy girl. She leaned closer to block his critic's eye. Almost done now.

An odd scent invaded her nostrils. Her fingers stilled. She sniffed. It almost smelled like...a woman's perfume.

"Ew-w." She grimaced and scrubbed her hands on her trousers and glanced up at him.

His eyes twinkled with confounded amusement. "Did something bite you?" He looked down at his half-unbuttoned waistcoat. "I may as well finish. You're shaking like you overimbibed last night."

"Not I, my lord. *I* don't make a habit of drinking spirits," she said, voicing her indignation, though she knew she shouldn't. But really. A woman's perfume. "Unlike *some* people."

He made fast work of his waistcoat, tossing it on his mahogany valet before moving on to his linen shirt. "I'm sure you don't."

The emerging golden-hair-dusted bronzed-skin chest, all sculpted muscles and flat plains, utterly fascinated her. Her fingers tingled with the urge to touch. His skin would be supple and warm.

"I'm sure you're a paragon of virtue. What I'm not sure of"—he paused, whipping his shirt onto the floor at his feet—"is who the hell you are." He finished on a bellow, his gaze spearing her.

She blinked, startled by his sudden burst of anger. She might've seen it coming if she hadn't been consumed with the man's naked chest. A chest whose hair tapered into a fine line disappearing under the waistband of his trousers.

Her lips parted so she could draw in an even breath. With effort, she dragged her gaze from his flat stomach.

Zeke stared at her, the corners of his mouth curved downward. "You look very strange," he said.

"I do?"

"You do." He cleared his throat. "Whoever you are, I think you'd better leave. I need to get some sleep and I can see you won't be divulging any information other than what you and the old man cooked up."

Right. Time to go. She stood stock still, staring at Zeke's hands, hovering at the waistband of his trousers.

Abruptly he cursed under his breath and stalked to the adjoining door of his suite. With an emphatic sweep of his hands, he said, "Out."

Chapter Five

H e didn't have to be rude. After all, he'd invited her in.

Kitty lifted her chin, and marched through the antechamber door, which Zeke promptly slammed.

The noise catapulted her into motion like a whip crack, and she ran all the way back to her bedchamber, leaped onto her bed, and squeezed herself into a tight little ball. She wanted to cry and giggle and pinch herself all at once.

But what she must do, this very moment, was commit the glorious sight of him to memory. Lord knew she'd never see Zeke Thurgood's bare chest again.

If only she hadn't reacted to that...that woman's cloying perfume, she might've gotten to touch that supple looking skin. Just one little touch. She closed her eyes and imagined doing just that, which morphed into imagining kneading her fingers into his thick hair, and oh, Lord, him touching her.

Truly decadent thoughts. She ought to feel ashamed. But thinking them felt so good. Like the most delicious melt-in-your-mouth chocolate confection.

A while later, an odd sense of frustration eating at her, Kitty headed for the library to join Lord Claybourne.

For the next hour or so, she would munch scones and sip mint-infused tea while the two of them scanned the papers for any posts regarding one Lady Christine Hastings who'd gone missing. It had been a good long while since one had appeared. It was a good sign.

As she approached the open library doors, heated voices reverberated from within, echoing in the corridor. The earl's and, surprisingly, Zeke's. She'd assumed Zeke would be fast asleep by now.

Clearly, that was not the case.

Hovering outside the open doors, Kitty contemplated heading back to her chamber. But the earl's booming voice froze her in place.

"...third night this week you've gone out only to return home well after two in the afternoon. If you're in London only to carouse, perhaps you should take up residence in your bachelor's apartments."

Kitty's heart seized at the thought. She leaned closer to catch Zeke's reply.

"I didn't realize my comings and goings interested you, my lord. Thought you were too caught up with your little pet."

She sucked in a breath. He'd hardly hidden the fact he didn't like her. Nevertheless, hearing Zeke's scathing reference to her, first hand, stung.

"This has nothing to do with Kit," Lord Claybourne said.

"What does it have to do with, then? Speak plainly, my lord."

"Very well. It's crossed my mind to wonder if you've taken to"—he paused—"visiting the gaming hells."

Gaming hells? Thurgood? A gambler? She'd never guess that.

In the lengthening silence, guilt pricked her. She oughtn't listen in on their private conversation. However, by leaving now, her boot steps would practically announce her presence.

On the other hand, if Zeke caught her hanging near the doorway, there would be hell to pay.

"Like my father, you mean?" Thurgood spoke in a low hiss. "I'm nothing like my father. But out of respect for *you*, I'll answer your insult. For your information, other than the odd game at my club, no, I haven't been gambling."

The hurt etched into his words pulled at her insides—not that he would welcome comfort from her...er, him.

"I suppose I don't need to ask what you have been doing, then."

She chewed her bottom lip, half wanting to hear Zeke's reply, half dreading it.

"I was a long time at sea." Amused disdain laced his words.

Naive though she was, she understood his meaning. Her stomach burned as if her morning meal hadn't agreed with her.

"You're always a long time somewhere, aren't you, Zeke? Somewhere far from everyone you know and hold dear. You know what I call it? Running. Even now, when you're home you can't stop running. But where are you running to?"

Zeke made a "pft" sound. "This is ridiculous. A ridiculous nonsensical conversation. I'm right here. Standing right in front of you."

The earl spoke at just above a whisper, and Kitty had to strain to hear. "I worry about you, you know. I fear I've made the same mistakes I made with your father. If only I'd been more watchful, disciplined him more—"

"Is that what this is about? Grandfather, you have to stop blaming yourself. Father was a grown man, solely responsible for the cowardly decisions he made. He gambled away my mother's inheritance and drank himself into oblivion, until it finally landed him six feet under."

"Only after he lost your mother."

"We all lost my mother, and you know his vices didn't start then."

"You're still so bitter, Zeke."

"Can you blame me? In the end what was he to me but an empty place at the table? Oh, don't look so sad, old man," Zeke said in a voice gruff with emotion. "Caden and I didn't suffer overly. We had you."

Tears leaked from Kitty's eyes. How well she understood. She'd had parents who'd disappointed her, and a grandfather who'd loved her through it.

"If you like, I'll move to my apartments for the remainder of my stay."

Everything inside her railed at the statement.

"No. You're where you should be. I'll stay out of your affairs from now on." The earl's defeated tone broke Kitty's heart.

"You seem to forget I rather like spending time with you—when your appointments with young Kit permit it."

The earl's chuckle lacked its usual warmth. "Why don't you like him?"

"Who says I don't?"

"Kit for one."

"Really," Zeke said, sounding amused. "For your information I don't dislike him. I find him"—he paused—"odd."

Odd?

"How so?"

Kitty held her breath.

"He..." Zeke hesitated before blurting, "stares at me. When he thinks I'm not looking, he studies me with those frosty green eyes. It's...it irritates me. It's like he wants something I have, or wants to learn my mannerisms, or maybe eat me for breakfast. In fact, just this morning—what?"

"What do you mean what?" the earl asked, his voice choked.

"You're laughing."

"I have something in my eye."

He thought she stared at him? That wasn't true. Or not often true, anyway. Oh, she could just die. She should leave, now, before she heard any further hurtful remarks. She inched backward, gliding her boots over the marble.

"Is that all?" the earl asked.

"Now that you ask, no."

In an instant, she was back in place outside the library.

"I can't figure out why you're so enamored of him. Other than playing a mean game of chess and being a quick study…"

Warmth flooded her heart.

"…he speaks up far too often, and he has that scratchy voice."

"He takes an interest in my well-being, and he can't help it if his voice hasn't yet changed. You can hardly fault him for that, Zeke. It's not like you to be so unfair."

"Perhaps I'm being, as you say, unfair, because I know you're playing me for the fool. Either that, or he's playing you."

Kitty heard a rhythmic sound and realized Zeke drummed his fingers as she'd seen him do a thousand times, impatient man.

"You could tell me who he is."

"Zeke, my boy, patience. All will be revealed in good time."

"I knew it," he exclaimed. "I knew there was more to Kit. Who is he? Caden's by-blow?"

An odd, scratchy-voiced, ogling by-blow.

"Nothing like that. And I'd appreciate it if you'd leave the matter," Lord Claybourne said.

"It's a little late for that, isn't it? After you've done everything in your power to taunt me, jamming the bugger down my throat at every turn? You've both had a good laugh at my expense, haven't you?"

All too late she heard the telltale whisper of footsteps over carpet. A half second later, boot tips appeared. Then Zeke emerged. He spotted her in an instant, his smokey blue eyes going wide with shock, then smoldering with outrage.

Kitty leapt back and bumped hard into the console, unseating a porcelain vase filled with flowers in the process. She made a grab for it, but Zeke beat her to it, catching the arrangement with one hand.

He settled the vase never taking his narrow-eyes stare off her. She gulped. "Lord Thur—"

"Grandfather!" His bellow reverberated off the walls. He grabbed the scruff of Kitty's coat collar with one hand, lifting her bodily and swinging her around until she dangled over the library threshold. "Look what the cat dragged in."

Kitty couldn't breathe. Black spots danced before her eyes.

"Zeke, put Kit—put the boy down. You're choking him, for pity's sake."

Zeke opened his hand.

She dropped like a stone, crumpling to her knees. An instinctual will to survive bade her drag in air. She wished to be anywhere but here, huddled on all fours. She stared into the red and black pattern of the Aubusson carpet through a blur of tears.

"Don't tell me you're not going to do anything about this? I've a mind to blister the boy's behind."

"Zeke, you'll do nothing of the sort," the earl said, stonily.

For a timeless moment, Kitty heard nothing save the sound of her own choked gasps.

"Well?" Zeke demanded.

When the earl said nothing, Zeke made a sound of disgust and lowered himself until he crouched beside Kitty. He pitched his voice low with menace. "Hope you got an earful, young man. Because it'll be the last time you get one over on me."

His boots made a rapid click over the marble floor as he stalked from the library. A moment later, the front door slammed hard enough to rattle the windows.

She lifted her watery gaze. Utterly miserable, she stared at the earl across the room in his usual window seat overlooking the courtyard.

"My lord," she began in a quavering voice, then broke off. Nothing she said would make up for what she'd done.

"Kitty." The disappointment in his voice twisted her heart.

He deserved an apology at the very least. "I'm so very sorry. After all you've done for me. I don't know what came over me. I was coming to join you, and I heard voices—"

"Kitty, get up off the floor." He patted the empty place on the seat beside him.

She rose and dragged her feet toward him. "I assumed it would be just us for tea. Then I heard the two of you having a row. I thought it would be a brief, meaningless tiff. But instead..." Her words died in her throat. "I eavesdropped. I have no excuse."

"Sit down, Kitty."

She lowered herself onto the bright cushion nestled in the bay window. Outside the sun shone and birds sang. Why couldn't it be raining to match her dismal mood?

"Once I started to listen, I found myself riveted. It struck me how little I know of your lives. Not that I have a right to know. I'm not family, and soon I'll be gone and—" She broke off, unable to speak over the burning lump in her throat.

He patted her hand. "It's only natural you're curious about us. I'm sure you've deduced by now I love my grandsons more than anything or anyone in this world. Perhaps more than I loved their father—my only son."

The earl's faded blue eyes clouded. "Joshua was vibrant, full of life, like Zeke. He also had undeniable charm, just drew people to him like flies to honey. Caden, Zeke's younger brother, inherited that trait."

"Joshua, your son, my lord?"

He smiled. "Yes. We spoiled him terribly, his mother and I. Everyone did. Everyone fell under his spell. There was just something about him. When he misbehaved, when he cheated on exams, when he showed no inclination to grow up—we turned blind eyes. We thought he'd outgrow his reckless ways in time. And then, much to our delight, it seemed he did, when he fell in love with Marjorie—Zeke and Caden's mother." The earl chuckled. "She had a will of steel, that one."

Zeke clearly inherited her trait, she thought, but wisely kept the opinion to herself.

"They married. Started a family. And if he drank a little too much, or gambled a little too freely when Marjorie went to the country or on holiday, we all chalked it up to him being a man's man.

"After she died, and their unborn babe with her—" He shook his head—"Joshua's bad habits came back with a vengeance. He sank into depravity with nary a care for himself, much less the welfare of his two sons who needed him more than ever with the loss of their mother." He paused a long moment, then added in a low voice, "He died in a gaming hell—drank himself to death in a filthy back room."

"I'm so sorry," she whispered. She ached for the earl—and the two little boys who'd deserved so much better.

"Zeke was barely fourteen, and his brother only ten when I tried my hand again. I sometimes wonder if I made the same mistakes."

"That's not possible, my lord."

He gave her a querulous look.

She arched her brows. "Your grandson is a hardly a..."

"Ne'er-do-well?" Claybourne filled in.

"Precisely. Anyone can see he's disciplined. And fit...fitter than most. So that rules out him being a drunken sot, as well."

The earl laughed and covered her hands, clasped tightly on her lap. "Oh, my darling girl, you have such a way with words."

She sent him a tentative grin. "Does this mean you forgive me?" Her grin vanished. "I understand if you can't."

He eyed her, a considering expression on his face. "Maybe I was angry for a moment. But the moment's gone. Besides, how could I remain angry at the granddaughter I never had?"

"Thank you," she whispered, taking his palm and pressing it to her cheek. She glanced toward the door as if she could see Zeke as he stormed out. "I told you he hated me."

Lord Claybourne dropped a finger on the tip of her nose. "He'll get over it."

Kitty sent the earl a fond smile, and kept her doubts to herself.

***

Zeke emptied his tankard and, not bothering to rise from the wingback chair where he'd sulked for the last hour, flagged one of the club's attendants to bring him another.

He pulled at his collar, and inwardly groaned at the close feel of the room. Didn't anyone realize it was summer? What were they all doing in the city, at White's in particular?

He'd come here to get away. To think. But every room teemed with members whose laughter and jovial conversations grated on his every nerve.

He closed his eyes and slunk down into the well-cushioned armchair he'd positioned to face the wall. He drummed his fingers on the armrest, asking himself for the fiftieth time what happened tonight? Why had he blown up at the earl? He never lost control like that, and hadn't spoken to his grandfather with such disrespect since he was a boy.

Recalling his grandfather's worried gaze soured the ale in Zeke's belly. Because he'd done more than bellow at Claybourne. He'd lied to the old man. On one of his recent late nights he had visited a gaming hell.

Why *had* he gone?

Because, at the time, he couldn't think of a sound reason not to, he supposed. Nothing else he tried had quieted the edgy, unsettled tension riding him hard since arriving home. Not over-imbibing, which he'd done on an altogether too frequent basis. Not carousing 'til the wee hours, like a man not quite twenty instead of one closer to thirty.

Perhaps he had inherited his father's traits.

A movement out of the corner of his eye drew his attention. An older gentleman stumbled toward the exit, weaving into one of the large potted plants flanking the door.

In a flash, a vivid memory of his father, months before his death, seared his consciousness.

It had been Winter Break. Zeke and Caden were home from Eton, much to Zeke's displeasure. If he'd had his way, he'd have stayed on campus, or gone home with a school chum. Anything was preferable to subjecting himself to his father—or rather the lack of one. Most times dear old dad spent his days abed, his nights deep in his cups, or absent altogether.

But the earl had assured Zeke Christmas would be a grand affair. He'd called the family to Derby, promising time away from the city would make all the difference.

Zeke remembered the day like it was yesterday. Not a cloud in the sky, but cold enough to freeze his nose hairs—and the air rich with possibility.

He'd set out on his own, much to Caden's displeasure, saddling his favorite horse for a long ride. He recalled the wind in his hair, the sun warming his back. He stayed out of doors, hunting for mischief 'til bone-chilling gusts finally drove him back to Chissington Hall. Red faced and half frozen, he'd raced up the back steps onto the portico, on a mission to find hot cocoa and biscuits.

He practically tripped over his father, retching into one of the potted palms. The sour smell of spirits told Zeke all he needed to know. The usual. He'd over-imbibed. Nothing had changed by coming here.

He'd stood there. Angry. Afraid. To his shame, fighting tears.

His father gazed up at him, bleary eyed, unkept and unshaven. "Never give your heart away, son. It hurts too bloody damn much."

"Is that why you're this way? Because you miss Mother?" Zeke asked, bewildered and disgusted.

"She left me. In the end, she left you, too. No woman's worth this."

"My lord? Your ale."

Zeke's head shot up as the attendant's words dragged him from the past.

The servant took one look at Zeke, placed the tankard on the table, and scurried away.

Zeke scrubbed a hand over his face. Why was he remembering these things? There was nothing to be gained reliving the past, or comparing himself to his weak father.

No? An irritating inner voice asked him. Then explain why you visited the den. Explain your staying out all hours. Explain the emptiness roiling in your gut.

Emptiness?

Ridiculous. He had everything he needed, and then some. He was reading too much into his recent behavior—because of his argument with the earl.

He picked up the ale, considered the foamy brew, then set it down with too much force, sloshing liquid onto the glossy wood.

Hell. Coming here had accomplished nothing. He rose to leave when a familiar voice called to him from the open doorway of the sitting room.

"Thurgood? It is you. I didn't think to see you 'til God knows when, since you disappeared to God knows where, as per usual."

An echo of his grandfather's sentiments. Zeke forced a jovial smile and extended his hand to his life-long friend, Viscount Sterling Randall. "Randall. The earl told me you'd left town."

"I made it back only this morning."

"Fortuitous, then, as I arrived early last week. What's brought you to London this time of year?"

Randall shrugged. "Business at the bank. You?"

"Between trips. Thought I'd check on the earl."

"Looks like you were on your way out. Stay for one more?" Randall gestured toward a small, ornate bar, where one man lingered over a nearly empty cocktail.

"Why not?" Zeke retrieved his abandoned ale.

Randall ordered a stein from the barman then turned his attention on Zeke.

"You look troubled, my friend. Rather unThurgood-like. Let me guess." He narrowed his eyes, his lips twitching with amusement. "Couldn't be woman trouble, unless we're talking about one you can't shake off."

Zeke snorted.

"Let's see. Gaming debts are off the table. Cuckolded husband, as well. A foiled business venture is simply unimaginable. That leaves Caden or the earl. My money's on Caden."

"I haven't seen Caden since my return. The earl, however..." He thought of how he'd left things. Of his own randy behavior of late.

He couldn't discuss such private matters, even with Randall, and certainly not here, where the walls had ears.

But Kit was another matter entirely. "Perhaps you could help me solve a little puzzle."

"I love a good mind bender."

"The earl's got himself a tiger. A young man who's supposed to be his personal assistant, but seems more like a pet monkey."

"And this bothers you precisely why?"

"Because Kit isn't a servant. He's"—he grimaced—"I don't know what he is, but the old man dotes on him like he's another grandson or something. Tell me, have you heard rumors about any"—he broke off, lowered his voice—"mistresses Caden may have left in a delicate condition?"

"Caden?" He scoffed. "What about you?"

"I'd know if something like that happened. Besides, the lad's coloring's all off."

Randall laughed. "Perhaps the old man is simply lonely. Neither you nor Caden sticks close to home of late."

"He isn't lonely," Zeke said, though he didn't meet Randall's eyes.

"Perhaps he likes having a companion at his beck and call?"

"A damned odd companion. The boy's"—He shrugged—"far too proper."

A pale-skinned, wiry man, of average height and with close cropped brown hair leaned across the bar to flag their attention. "Excuse me. What did you say this errand boy was called?"

Zeke didn't answer. Instead he studied the man with narrowed eyes. "I don't believe we've met."

"Forgive me. Name's James. Baron of Maidstone." He extended his hand.

Zeke gave him a firm shake. "Thurgood of Claybourne. My companion, Viscount Sterling Randall."

"Ah, Lord Thurgood, I'm quite familiar with your name. I believe my predecessor, the late Baron of Maidstone knew your grandfather, Lord Claybourne. An interesting coincidence."

Zeke inclined his head, not terribly impressed. James. Didn't ring any bells. Maidstone Struck a familiar chord, however.

"I've been residing in London off and on for some months. On a scouting trip of sorts. I'd begun to think my presence here might prove endlessly fruitless." The baron's mouth twisted in a oily smile. "But enough about me. Tell me more about this servant."

Something about this man grated. The way he'd inserted himself into his and Randall's private conversation, for starters.

Randall slapped Zeke on the back. "Do tell us his name. Maybe it will ring a bell."

"Name's Kit," Zeke said, his eyes fixed on James.

The baron pulled a cheroot from his coat pocket, scraping a match along the underside of the bar. Holding the flame to the cigar, his hand shook slightly. "Kit," he repeated. The tip of his cheroot glowed red as he took a long draw. "An interesting name. Unusual." A long plume of smoke punctuated his words.

Breathing in the sharp scent of sulfur mixed with tobacco, two things became clear. Zeke didn't like Lord James, and he damn sure didn't intend to discuss his grandfather's personal affairs with him. "If you say so."

"Perhaps Lord James will know something of—Ouch," Randall bent to rub his shin where the tip of Zeke's boot had found its mark.

"What's this Kit like? Is he a large boy? Or small? How long has he been on the earl's staff?" the baron pressed.

"Not sure how as I've only just arrived in town myself." He smiled coolly at James and returned his attention to Randall.

Seeing his friend had done him some good. It had given him time to cool his heels—And to hear how ridiculous he sounded.

"I'm off. I promised the old man a game of gin. Now you're in town, perhaps we can coordinate a visit to Jack's."

Randall snorted. "Last time I sparred with you I came away with a shiner that lasted two weeks."

"You're crying off then?"

"Of course not. I could use the exercise, and it's not as if a slew of ladies are hanging about whom I wish to impress with my good looks."

Minutes later, Zeke trotted down the steps of White's. Claybourne was right, he decided. For reasons not entirely known to himself, he'd come down too hard on young Kit, kicking the proverbial dog as it were. Enough was enough.

He smiled, thinking how pleased his grandfather would be to see him arriving home so early. Doubly so when he witnessed Zeke's new and improved attitude toward Kit. He set his lips to whistling, and headed for the mews.

Chapter Six

Kitty and the earl glanced up as the French doors lead-ing to the courtyard opened. The hour for callers had long-since passed. Still, she expected to see Smethwick's shiny head. Instead Zeke emerged, all vital and golden. Her chest ached at the sight of him.

Spotting the earl, he grinned, raised a hand in greeting and started on the path toward them.

She shot a nervous glance at the earl. Her hands gripped the cold wrought iron slat of the bench and squeezed till the metal bit into her palms.

As if reading her disquiet, the earl gave her an encouraging nod.

"Good evening, grandfather. Kit." Zeke said in a friendly tone.

He stood before them, hands splayed on his hips. Lamplight from the courtyard torches spilled over his handsome face. Were her eyes playing tricks, or was Lord Zeke Thurgood smiling?

"Zeke, this is a pleasant surprise," the earl said.

"I hoped you'd feel that way."

His eyes no longer burned with rage. A promising start. She pushed to her feet, conscious of the crunch of gravel beneath her boots. Conscious of her too-shallow breath.

He didn't move a muscle as she stared up into his eyes, twin pools of swirling blue smoke in the lamplight.

Everything inside her clenched. "My lord, I'm very sorry for overhearing—"

"Overhearing?" He arched one tawny brow.

Her shoulders sagged, and her gaze dropped to her boots. He was right. She'd hung on his every word.

She took a bracing breath, and, once again, raised her eyes to meet his. "I purposely eavesdropped on your conversation which was absolutely none of my affair. I beg your forgiveness, but understand if you can't bring yourself to give it to me."

"Kit, thank you for your heartfelt apology. Apology accepted."

She blinked up at him.

And then he smiled. At her. Her heart nearly stopped.

How many times had she fantasized about seeing one of Zeke's smiles aimed at her? She needn't have bothered. Real life was so much better.

A moment later, he sidestepped her. "What do you say to a game of gin, my lord? Kit can even join in if you like."

Kitty whipped around to catch the earl's eyes. As much as a part of her yearned to remain in Zeke's presence, her rational side told her not to push her luck.

The earl winked, and nodded once in the direction of the manse.

She flashed a grateful smile and dashed inside. Half in a daze, she passed through parlor and down the marble hall toward the front stairs. She'd thought nothing could be better than seeing Lord Thurgood half naked this afternoon. She'd been wrong.

That smile. To him, it'd meant nothing more than a kind gesture to an irritating boy. But to her—she could live off it for a week.

With a long sigh she started up the stairs, her hand skimming the cool, silver balustrade. For just a moment, she imagined an alternate reality.

She saw Zeke calling to her from the bottom of the stairs. "Kitty, I've only been acting. I discovered your secret from the start. Your face is too beautiful to belong to a boy. Come back down here and kiss me."

A fierce pounding on the front door tore her from her fantasy, and she nearly tripped on the landing. She peered downstairs.

Smethwick hustled toward the front door, an intimidating scowl on his face. Everyone knew no one of consequence called at this late hour.

The butler opened the massive door. He accepted a calling card. Studied it. His scowl softened. "Come in, my lord. If you'll kindly wait in the foyer? I'll inform the earl of your presence."

The man crossed the threshold. He removed his hat and handed it to Smethwick, revealing close-cropped brown hair, a pale face set with gritty determination and a bit of the street.

A man she knew all too well.

She skittered round the bend, pressing herself into the paneled wall lest her legs give out. She gulped at the air, unable to take an even breath. Garrick? Here? How?

An eternity later, Smethwick returned. "The earl will see you now. Right this way, my lord."

Garrick's receding boot steps announced his determined march down the hall.

After a long moment, she garnered all the strength she could muster. On rubbery legs, she started down the stairs.

***

"Forgive me if my request seems bold or over-reaching, my lords. But my dear cousin has been missing for some time, and our earlier conversation, Lord Thurgood, fostered a hope in me I can't dispel."

Kitty hovered outside the earl's den. Though she'd missed the start of the conversation, she had no doubt James had discovered her presence in the household. Someone had seen her. Someone had talked.

"You refer to my private conversation with Lord Randall this afternoon?" Zeke asked.

Zeke? How could he reveal anything when he knew nothing himself?

Despair swamped her. Why bother with the hows or whys? Soon she would be in her cousin's clutches.

"Lord James, take your accusations and leave Claybourne Manor at once," the earl commanded in a stony voice.

A tiny ray of hope ignited within her.

"Lord Claybourne, I'm afraid I can't do that—unless you don't mind being visited shortly by a member of the Yard."

"You dare threaten the Earl of Claybourne?" Zeke demanded.

"Not at all, Lord Thurgood. Simply asking for a show of courtesy amongst peers. Produce the servant known as Kit, and I will apologize duly if he is, as you say, the earl's tiger."

"Fetch the magistrate or anyone else you damn well please, Lord James," the earl fired back.

Kitty swallowed a sob. She knew something the earl didn't. Garrick would make good on his threat. She couldn't allow scandal to tarnish Lord Claybourne's reputation, not after everything he'd done for her. She took a bracing breath, and crossed the threshold.

"No, Kit," the earl bemoaned from his stance behind his grand desk

Not two feet from her, Garrick stood, legs braced for combat as he faced down the earl. When his gaze lit on her, a feverish gleam shown in his obsidian eyes. "Well, well."

Zeke, to her left, wore a baffled expression as his glance ricocheted from Kitty to Garrick to the earl. "Will someone kindly tell me what the hell is going on here?"

The earl gestured for Kitty to join him.

She bit her bottom lip and took a hesitant step.

"Stay right where you are." Garrick aimed one pointed finger at her.

She halted, uncontrollable tremors wracking her frame.

As if he could hold her captive by will, his finger remained in place, though he aimed his words at the earl. "Tut, tut, my lord. I must say I am very disappointed by your prevarication. Although I can only imagine what lies my cousin fed you." His gaze slid over her. "What sordid tales she used to draw you into her tangled web of deceit."

Zeke frowned at the earl. "Claybourne? *Her* web?"

The earl's ashen complexion worried Kitty. She forced a wobbly smile, trying to project an air of calm she was far from feeling. "It's all right, my lord."

The jig was up, so she'd spoken in her regular, feminine voice, and Zeke's head snapped in her direction.

Without warning he stalked toward her, snatching off her wig in one swipe.

She winced in humiliation more than pain as hairpins scattered on the thick Aubusson carpet. Black coils of hair tumbled around her face and shoulders.

Her face—her entire body—burned. She must look a damned sight. The bulk of her hair, she could only assume, remained ruthlessly attached to the crown of her head.

As if compelled, she met Lord Thurgood's smoky blue stare.

"My God," he whispered, incredulous.

His shoulders shook in what appeared to be a humorless chuckle. Finally he looked away from her, rubbing his stubble-covered jaw as he moved to stand closer to the earl.

"Explains the lavender," she thought she heard him mutter, as if answering his own private riddle.

"I'm ever so relieved you didn't cut off your reigning glory, my dear."

She jumped at the sound of Garrick's voice in her ear. She hadn't realized he'd closed in on her.

His dark eyes gleamed with triumph. He raised his hand as if intending to slide his fingers over her head.

She squeezed her eyes shut, bracing for his touch.

"Just one moment." The earl's voice sliced the air.

She opened her eyes in time to see Garrick's arm fall to his side.

"Aren't you curious as to Lady Hasting's welfare these past months, James?" A crafty smile curved his mouth.

She'd seen that smile before, right before he made a particularly clever chess move.

"Of course." Garrick drew himself to his full height—which still left him a head shorter than Zeke or the earl.

"She has, of course, resided under this roof for months—no chaperone to speak of," Lord Claybourne said.

Garrick frowned. "Are you suggesting some sort of impropriety on your part?"

"Yes, Lord Claybourne, what are you suggesting?" Zeke eyed the earl, arms crossed over his chest.

"I am more than suggesting," the earl said, his eyes locked on Garrick.

Garrick spewed out a hyena's laugh. "You wish me to believe my cousin and you, the late baron's so-called closest friend, engaged in an illicit affair? Next you'll tell me you're engaged to marry the chit."

"No."

Garrick's shoulders seemed to relax, for all his randy bluster.

"She is, however, betrothed." The earl sent Garrick a feral smile. "To my grandson, Lord Thurgood."

Kitty's mouth hung open. She closed it with a snap. Had the earl gone mad? Claiming she and Zeke were betrothed? Garrick would see right through the hastily devised ruse.

As for Zeke—she slid a sidelong glance his way and felt her heart crack a little. His rigid jaw and smoldering eyes confirmed what she already knew. He practically despised her.

His almost certain unwillingness to play the hero in her personal tragedy had nothing to do with the tears stinging the backs of her eyes, or the monstrous lump in her throat. Nothing whatsoever.

"Impossible," Garrick sputtered. "Lord Thurgood's surprise at Kitty's sex couldn't be more evident," he blurted in the crudest of statements. "How do you explain that?"

Rounding his desk, the older man answered. "An act engineered for Lady Hastings' benefit. We surmised, Lord James, you might offer some resistance to the betrothal."

A strange sound, like crunching gravel, came from Garrick. Zeke, conversely, remained mute.

Perspiration trickled down her back and dampened the area between Kitty's clamped breasts. Strange, considering her frozen fingers and toes.

"While we feel certain any such resistance can and will be easily circumvented, we hope to avoid any such unpleasantness, for the lady's sake, as well as the sake of the Claybourne title. Ours is an old, very influential bloodline"—he stressed the word influential—"with ties directly to the royal family. As such, we're reluctant to invite unnecessary scandal." He narrowed his eyes. "But, if necessary, that is exactly what we will do."

Garrick's nostrils flared as he studied the faces of the two Claybourne men. He ignored Kitty. Everyone in the room was ignoring her, she noted, suddenly on the verge of laughter. She bit her lower lip to staunch the inane urge.

"What say you, Lord Thurgood? This afternoon at the club, you expressed no small amount of curiosity concerning the true identity of the earl's tiger known as—" He paused and allowed his gaze to rake Kitty, head to toe. "—Kit."

Anger slammed her like a blast from the furnace. Zeke had done this. Zeke, with his need not to be made the fool, as he'd put it only hours ago.

No wonder he'd arrived home in a jolly mood. He'd met Garrick and somehow put it all together. He waltzed in knowing full well Garrick was coming to take her away.

She wouldn't have thought him capable of such ignoble scheming, or such cruelty.

Her shoulders slumped. What did it matter? What was done was done. Garrick would demand she go with him immediately, of course. To where? A hotel? A boarding house? Or would they head directly to—

"As the Earl of Claybourne testified, Lord James, my purported ignorance was all part of a carefully crafted plot to keep any scandal from attaching to Lady Hastings' name, as she and I have resided under the same roof. Indeed, her bedchamber is just down the hall from mine."

Kitty blinked, unable to believe her ears.

His steely blue gaze shifted to her. Their eyes locked, and he gave her a thin smile. "I can and do attest to the veracity of our betrothal."

Her breath caught. She lowered her eyes, ashamed at the earlier direction of her thoughts. Zeke had taken up the earl's lie. Might the ruse work?

This was Garrick. A little thing like a betrothal wouldn't stop him. As her guardian he could deny the supposed match. Likely would.

Still, this so-called engagement would afford her time. Time she could use to plan another escape.

"I see." Garrick pursed his lips. "You can, of course, produce documents attesting to this betrothal?"

A muscle ticked in Zeke's jaw. He took one step toward Garrick.

The earl stayed him with a touch to his forearm. "Of course. We'll need to contact our solicitor for a copy of the agreement, however."

Garrick made a show of examining his nails. "As a fellow peer, I find it unspeakably gauche you entered into such a liaison without negotiating a settlement with me, her legal guardian."

"With you? No," the earl replied. "We do, however, have a document signed by the late Baron, attesting to his approval of the marriage."

Garrick's eyes flashed with uncertainty. She could almost read his thoughts. Was there any such signed document? If so, could he contest it?

Kitty almost smiled.

"I see," Garrick murmured. "Speaking as her *living* guardian, I must insist on an amendment to the contract, to allow for certain..." He paused, and one corner of his mouth crooked upward.

"You refer to a monetary settlement, I assume, Lord James?" Lord Claybourne asked.

"Indeed."

Zeke glowered at no one in particular.

"That will be no problem—one our solicitors can see to. As for the previously signed documents, we shall provide those at the earliest possible opportunity."

"Tomorrow will work nicely," Garrick bit out.

His hand snaked out to grasp her wrist, and she chirped in alarm.

"What is it, cousin? You're as nervous as a church mouse."

She tried to pull free, but he held tight.

"I can't possibly allow you to remain under the same roof as your betrothed, unchaperoned. You will come with me."

"What's this?" The earl demanded. "You can't take her."

Garrick's grip tightened until her bones screamed at the pressure, yet, when he spoke, his tone was cool. "I can and I will. I'm staying at a reputable boarding house in Albemarle, where I'm certain I'll have no trouble securing another chamber."

He curled his nose at Kitty as if suddenly smelling a rat. "Have you a gown, or must I parade you around town dressed in your boy garb?"

She nodded, unable to speak.

"See you do something with your hair, as well. Quickly. We leave immediately." He finally released her.

She rubbed her aggrieved skin and cast a miserable glance at the earl before starting from the room.

"Oh no you don't, James. You'll produce documents attesting to your guardianship before you to leave the premises with Lady Kitty."

Garrick's eyes bulged in outrage. "I beg your pardon?"

"I can't possibly sanction her leaving with you, with no chaperone to speak of, and no proof to the validity of your claim."

"Kitty can attest..." Garrick's words died in his throat. He realized the unlikelihood of Kitty verifying his sovereignty over her. "My solicitor can provide documents, but it'll take some time. Or we can let a magistrate decide tonight." His tone turned sly.

"Call the—" the earl began in a growl, only to be cut off by Zeke.

"We'll send a chaperone with you for tonight."

"And then what, Zeke? It will take longer than twenty-four hours for James to attain the paperwork needed," the earl growled.

"Likewise, for you to produce your betrothal contract," Garrick snapped.

"It seems we are at a standoff," Zeke said, arms open wide. "Shall we cut the—my fiancé in half?" His lips curved in a grim smile.

"I-I'll go," Kitty said.

"I'll permit it on two conditions. One, the baron agrees to return with you first thing on the morrow," the earl said, his eyes shooting daggers at Garrick.

"Of course," Garrick replied. "And the second?"

"Afterward, we ride for Chissington Hall."

"Chissington Hall?" Garrick asked.

"My seat—Derbyshire."

Chapter Seven

Zeke waited with barely contained impatience for Lady Christine Hastings and her cousin, James, to board his rented carriage and vacate the premises.

No sooner did the earl cross the threshold into the gleaming marble foyer than Zeke pounced. "What the devil do you mean blithely announcing my engagement to that—"

"You'll watch your tongue, Ezekiel Thurgood, if you know what's good for you."

Zeke frowned at his grandfather's menacing tone. It almost sounded as if he was angry—with *him*. "Perhaps we should continue this discussion in the upper parlor."

The earl grunted his assent, and led the way.

The upstairs parlor was masculine, intimate, and as snoop-proof as they were likely to get in a house full of nosy servants. It boasted a well-stocked liquor cabinet, too.

Lord knew Zeke needed a drink now, if he ever had.

Once safely ensconced behind a closed and locked door, the earl set about retrieving the brandy decanter. Zeke turned up the two wall lamps flanking the lone, narrow window, bathing the room in yellow light. The window he left closed. Voices carried.

Not until they sat in two oversized armchairs, full snifters in hand and the brandy decanter in easy reach, did the earl broach his grievance.

"I asked you to leave it alone. I told you I'd give you the answers you sought in good time. Five months and change—that's all we needed. Now, all may be lost."

Zeke's temper flared, but he kept his response measured. "It sounds as if you're blaming me for the fact your *Kit* was discovered hiding out under your roof."

"In a word, yes."

Zeke drummed his fingers on his knee. Narrowed his eyes. "Precisely how is it my fault?"

"Did you, or did you not, go to White's this afternoon, and run your mouth about a certain boy in my employ, named Kit, who seemed oddly out of place?"

Zeke ran a finger under his cravat. The damned thing was a nuisance in the summer months. "I admit to doing so. Will you own the provocation?"

The earl's jaw tightened. He took a large swallow of brandy before replying. "I will, damn my eyes. Kitty asked me repeatedly to stop taunting you, clever, intuitive girl that she is, but I listened too late. If I'd heeded her warning, and kept her hidden, specifically from *your* view, none of this would've happened. I just thought...I hoped... Never mind."

His broad shoulders sagged and he looked like a man utterly defeated.

Zeke could only remember seeing him like this once—after discovering his father died in a gaming hell.

He scrubbed a hand over his stubbled chin. "Grandfather, who is she? Perhaps we should start there, and work our way to tonight's events."

"She's Lady Christine Hastings, affectionately Lady Kitty, daughter of the deceased Lord Charles Hastings, granddaughter of the more recently deceased eighth Baron of Maidstone, Lord Christian Hastings. He and I served together in the Crimean War. I considered him one of my closest friends, a man to whom I owe my life."

"I knew I recognized that name."

"What with one thing and another, I hadn't seen much of him these last years." He shrugged, his familiar blue eyes distant, as if he looked into the past. "Time passes, you lose touch, but you never forget. Not with a history like ours."

He took a long drink, and Zeke followed suit.

"At any rate, some six months ago, Kitty showed up on my doorstep, a royal mess. Penniless, wearing a dirt-crusted mourning gown. Lord only knows how she made it here. What she'd had to endure." The earl chuckled softly. "God bless her, she's got spunk. She made it to London from Maidstone County with nothing but the clothes on her back."

"How did you know she wasn't some con artist, intent on fleecing you?"

"I'd been half expecting her. Several months earlier, Christian had written to tell me he was dying. He expressed concern over his granddaughter's safety upon his demise. He asked me to assist her should the need arise. That and her eyes."

"Her eyes?"

"The last time I saw him he showed me a picture of his late wife. She had beautiful, exotic eyes. Christian called them tiger eyes. Kitty inherited them."

Zeke's turn to grunt. "Did your friend give any indication as to why—" He broke off. He didn't know what to call the chit. "Lady Hastings might need your assistance?"

The earl nodded. "Christian no longer trusted James. Said he recognized James's growing antipathy toward him and Kitty only after he'd filed the documents making him his heir and Kitty's legal guardian. What with Christian's declining health, and the slow wheels of bureaucracy, he had no hope of undoing what had been done. Now I've met the man, I can't help but agree. The ninth Baron of Maidstone's not to be trusted with our Kitty. The bloke actually hopes to marry her."

"You're not making sense. If the baron dislikes her so much, why shackle himself to her for all eternity?"

"Good question. One to which I have no answer. I do know a man can do a lot of damage to a woman once she's legally bound to him."

"And vice versa," Zeke said under his breath.

The earl's eyes went glacial. "This is no time for flippancy. Now listen up, because we haven't much time."

Before Zeke could ask after the time crunch, the earl went on.

"As her guardian, James has the upper hand. He could feasibly force marriage on her, and I do mean force. Legally, we'd have no recourse. The bloodlines are far enough removed, James being a descendent of Christian's half-brother. Which leaves only Kitty's unwillingness to marry him blocking his plans, and for the right amount of blunt, some clergyman can be persuaded to turn a blind eye to a maid's reluctance."

"I don't see the dire aspect here, my lord. Her guardian's not intending to toss her out on her ear. He wishes to marry her. Marriages of convenience happen every day. What makes this one so heinous?"

"If the baron believed James to be a danger to Kitty, then I believe it. Then there's the obvious."

Zeke cocked his head in a silent query.

"She fears the man."

"She told you this?"

The earl scowled. "She didn't need to spell it out for me. She fled in the middle of the night, for God's sake. She's a lady, born and bred, yet she dressed as a servant boy, giving up her freedom, her femininity, her life, for what was to be a year if I hadn't mucked things up. A year, Ezekiel!"

He smashed his fist into his thigh. "I ask you, would a lady go to such extremes if doing so wasn't an absolute necessity?"

"I take your meaning."

"Now the bastard has found her, thanks to me." He set his empty snifter aside and dropped his head in his hands.

Zeke had bristled at his grandfather's accusatory tone. But seeing the old man assume responsibility didn't sit right, either.

"Mark my words. Without our swift intervention, James will force Kitty to marry him, by hook or by crook."

"Enter my betrothal." Zeke downed the remaining brandy in his glass.

The earl straightened, staring over his steepled fingers at Zeke. "I can't make you do it."

Zeke's eyes bugged. "Make me? By God I have no intention of marrying the chit. Until an hour ago I knew her only as an annoying boy—"

"She knew you didn't like her," the earl groused.

Zeke frowned at the earl. "If I have to hear I didn't like him one more time..."

"Her," his grandfather corrected.

"You don't say?"

The abundant swell of breasts visible beneath the high-necked bodice of her black gown when she'd descended the stairs tonight had thrown Zeke. How she'd kept those curves hidden, heaven only knew.

The earl gave him a sly smile. "Rather pretty, isn't she?"

Zeke rolled his eyes. "I didn't notice." *Her face*, he silently added. "I was rather more concerned with the evening's events."

He ticked items off his fingers. "Discovering we've been harboring a runaway. My recent betrothal to said runaway. Your brilliant suggestion all concerned parties adjourn to Chissing-ton Hall for the foreseeable future. Which brings to mind a question. If you dislike the man so much, why on earth the exodus to Derbyshire in the morning like we're one big, happy family, by the by?"

"Simple. It was all I could conjure on short notice to keep watch over Kitty. Her guardian can hardly hope to ravish the girl under the Earl of Claybourne's roof. At any rate, I'm surprised you heard the stipulation."

"Why? I'm not deaf."

The earl raised his brows. "I thought perhaps you'd stopped listening, as you took no part in the discussion after confirming your engagement."

"I do apologize for my apparent lapse in manners."

He sniffed. "I planned to insist he allow Kitty to remain here 'til producing proof positive of his guardianship, when you piped up with that nonsense about providing a chaperone."

Zeke made a silent bid for patience. "I thought he'd make good on his threat to summon the magistrate. By the by, what makes you believe the scamp will make good on his promise to deliver Lady Hastings in the morning?"

"I set up a sort of safeguard."

"In other words, you sent a footman after them to spy."

"Quite right."

Zeke allowed himself a slight smile. He knew the old man well. "If you ask me, it seems like much ado about nothing. All of it: Kitty pretending to be a boy' our so-called engagement;

this idea of holing up together in the country. You don't even have concrete proof she's in danger. Perhaps she's just prone to hysterics."

His grandfather shot Zeke a disgusted look. "I suppose her grandfather was as well?"

Before Zeke could formulate a reply, the earl threw his hands in the air. "I don't know why I bothered discussing this with you. You clearly have no interest in involving yourself in the matter. You may leave. Or stay in London. Or do whatever it is you do. It's my honor in question, not yours, after all."

Zeke felt the noose tightening. "Not so fast, if you please. Perhaps if we put our heads together, we can arrive at a mutually agreeable plan to help her."

The earl picked up his empty snifter to scrutinize the contents or lack thereof. "Such as?"

Zeke refilled both their glasses. "We could secret her away again."

"And have the authorities questioning us? And bring censure down on the Claybourne name? Not bloody likely."

"We could buy him off."

"I think not."

"Why not?"

"He strikes me as one rather set on winning. Also, my intuition tells me this is about more than money. I'm not sure." His grandfather shook his head in frustration.

"Very well." Zeke rolled the snifter in his palms. "What do you suggest? Something other than me marrying the girl, if you please."

"I will have to do it," the earl stated after a pregnant pause.

Zeke froze. "Excuse me?"

"If you won't step in and shoulder the responsibility, and Lord knows I have no right to ask—regardless of the fact you drew the hounds—then I shall do it. It's the least I can do for my dear departed friend." He nodded once, as if his mind was made up. "Now, if you'll excise me? I must prepare for an extended stay in Derbyshire." He heaved himself out of his chair.

"Just. One. Minute," Zeke ground out.

With well-played reluctance, his grandfather dropped back into his seat. "Yes?"

"Perhaps there's another way."

"I really don't see—"

Zeke cut the earl off with a look. "We shall proceed down this crooked path you laid, the caveat being the lady knows from the start the engagement is temporary."

"I see."

"You see," Zeke said flatly. "Does that mean this is agreeable to you, sir?"

"That depends. How shall we accomplish breaking-off the engagement? I don't want Kitty's name dragged through the mud."

Of course. Kitty was the only one involved, after all. "Dear, sweet Kitty will, of course, call things off, after which I will depart for parts unknown to lick my wounds."

He regarded Zeke down the length of his nose. "You must be convincing."

Zeke parted his arms in an *of course* gesture.

"You understand this will require your presence. No haring off on a moment's notice. Not until Kitty meets the legal requirements to thumb her nose at her cousin. In other words, not for at least six months. At least."

Six months?

he must have made a face, because the earl scoffed. "If you're going to be disagreeable—"

"Grandfather?"

"Yes?"

"Don't push your luck. I said I'd do it. Do it I shall. Now I need you to understand something."

"What is that?"

"I'm doing this for you, old man. No one else." He stared at the earl, willing him to understand. "I..." How to phrase this? "Earlier, the things you said. I got the impression you don't know"—no, that wasn't quite right—"that you perhaps question, er...that is, due to my long forays from home these past years—"

"Ezekiel? I love you, too. And your willingness to do this for me means more than you can possibly know."

A feeling of conviction, of doing exactly the right thing for exactly the right reason filled him. At the same time, the incessant clamor inside him pressing him to move, to act, to run, was at once blessedly quiet. It felt good.

Some fifteen years ago, his grandfather had stepped in to care for his brother and him when their father opted out *sans* notice. Now fate, in the form of one Lady Kitty Hastings, had handed Zeke a means to repay his grandfather. Something other than his usual shoring-up of the family's now over-flowing coffers.

How hard could it be, pretending to be betrothed? Child's play. Six months? A wink of an eye. Half a year from now, it would be spring. Who knows, maybe he'd stay in England for the season. Maybe even find a wife. Right now, anything seemed possible.

"We're to Derbyshire in the morning, then?" He pressed up from the chair.

The earl rubbed his chin. "Yes, although I fear the newly named Baron of Maidstone will make this difficult."

Zeke dropped back in his seat. "How so?"

"M' boy, you're asking the wrong question."

"Which is?"

"How are we going to thwart him?"

Chapter Eight

"Wake up." The hissed words travelled up her spine like a spider dancing up its web.

Kitty's eyes flew open to pitch-blackness. "Wh-what?"

A vice-like grip bit into her arm. "I said wake up. We're leaving."

Garrick. In a sickening rush, memory flooded back. Her departure from Claybourne Manor. The earl's encouraging smile. Zeke. Her heart squeezed as she thought of him. But why? Because his loose lips had landed her here? No. Because last night she'd come to the conclusion she'd never see him again.

She silently chastised herself. She had real problems to worry about.

"What time is it?" She demanded of Garrick. Her gritty eyes told her she'd barely slept. "Where are we going?"

He ignored her. A moment later an oil lamp ignited, shedding muted light on the small room.

"My lady?" came a frightened voice from the corner. The poor maid, Mary, whom Zeke had offered up for Kitty's protection.

Garrick cursed under his breath and muttered something about dealing with baggage. He stalked toward the hapless Mary, huddled under her blanket on a makeshift palette.

"Whatever your name is, your services are no longer required. In several hours, Claybourne will send someone to collect you. You will wait here until then. Understood?"

She nodded, wide-eyed, sheets to her chin. She slid Kitty a sheepish look.

Kitty didn't blame her. She'd known from the outset the girl's presence could offer no more than a token shield against Garrick's tyranny. What could a young female servant do to protect Kitty from the likes of him? Less than Kitty herself.

Not to mention the poor girl was terrified. Last night she'd turned to Kitty for comfort after Garrick threatened both of them with bodily harm should either attempt to leave the chamber.

His threats hadn't stopped Kitty from trying the door after he left, much to Mary's distress.

"You shouldn't be doing that, m'lady. What if his lordship hears? He said he'd hurt us." She all but tugged at Kitty's sleeve.

"He's likely to do worse to us if we stay."

She regretted her words immediately as they sent Mary into a frenzy of tears, and all for naught. He'd locked them in.

"You have five minutes." Garrick's menacing voice cut into her thoughts. He let himself out into the corridor, shutting and locking the door behind him.

"Will you be all right, milady?" Mary whispered.

"I'll be fine, Mary, never you mind." She knew nothing of the sort, but why trouble the poor girl with her problems?

Mary rose to help her into her high necked gown.

She hadn't much else in the way of things. Sturdy shoes, yes, but no gloves or hat or pelisse. She eyed herself in the small mirror above the basin.

Dark circles underscored her eyes. A few errant curls hung loose, defying her hasty attempt to secure her hair in a knot at her nape. Her dress was a hopeless, rumpled mess. She looked utterly beaten.

She smiled. Good.

She mentally rehearsed her options, or lack thereof, as she waited for Garrick to return for her. She could fight, or scream for help once in earshot of the inn's other patrons. But no good would come of it. If anyone bothered to intervene on her behalf, Garrick would proclaim himself her legal guardian, with every right to drag, push, or pull her wherever he wanted, whenever he wanted.

She really had only one option.

Minutes later, a gloating Garrick directed her down the narrow flight of stairs. He looked as cocksure as he ever had, certain he led her, a docile lamb, to the slaughter.

Little did he know she was saving her energy, waiting for an opportunity of escape to present itself.

They exited the meagerly lit boarding house, stepping into a a sea of fog that seemed to wrap around her like a vice. No stars shown in the low-domed sky, but dawn's faint light glimmered over the far off rooftops.

"This way." Grasping her wrist as if he feared she might bolt, he dragged her to the street corner where two large trunks stood.

They were really leaving, then. A bone-deep fear almost overcame her carefully crafted decision to play the broken-spirited prisoner, urging her to pick up her skirts and flee for her life. But she had to be smarter than that. He would only run her down, then keep an even closer watch. She sucked in a breath and forced herself to remain calm.

Garrick fixed a sharp eye on her, as if reading her thoughts ."The carriage will be 'round in a moment. Be a good girl and don't give us any trouble, hmm?"

As if on cue, the rhythmic sound of horse hooves and clatter of wheels pierced the morning quiet. Garrick sent her a smile of pure male satisfaction.

She refused to grace his malevolence with a reaction, even as her empty stomach threatened to empty itself right there on the street. What would happen to her once Garrick got her away from London?

She would escape. She had to.

As the carriage neared, the fog seemed to part before it, as if making way for the handsome, matching grays and fine vehicle. He'd evidently spared no expense to ensure his comfort over the next several hours as they made their way to God knew where.

A second carriage trailed close behind the first. Kitty looked around, wondering if more guests were departing the boarding house at this early hour. So far as she could tell, she and her cousin were alone.

The carriage drew to a halt in front of them, a man in livery at the helm.

Was this Garrick's personal coach? Certainly her grandfather had owned one, but not one this fine, and they had not kept a dedicated groom on staff as one had not been needed. The driver hopped to the pavement, placing the footstep.

The door to the carriage opened—from the inside. But that would mean it already carried a passenger.

Kitty shot Garrick a questioning look, and only then did she see his expression of horrified disbelief.

A man emerged from the darkened interior. His broad shoulders took up the entire width of the opening.

"What? No," Garrick gasped.

She shook her head trying to clear her hallucination. She must be seeing what she wanted to see. He couldn't possibly be here.

"Good morning," came Zeke's achingly familiar, completely out of place voice, and her knees threatened to buckle.

He bypassed the step, vaulting onto the curb in one lithe move, then turned to help another passenger, an elegantly dressed, elderly looking lady, from the carriage.

Kitty stared unblinking, afraid if she looked away, the pair would vanish.

In no apparent hurry, Zeke tucked the lady's arm into the crook of his elbow, then turned to Garrick, a wolfish smile on his face. In his dark, fitted traveling attire and flowing black cape, he resembled a figure from a gothic novel. Not so much a hero as a villain. A wickedly handsome villain.

"Good. I thought we might be too early," Zeke announced.

Garrick cleared his throat. "Too early." He held up a gloved hand, gesturing for Zeke to give him a moment.

Zeke waited, a bland smile curving his mouth.

Finally, as if to himself, Garrick nodded. Then he tilted his head back to address Zeke. "It is quite early. I wasn't expecting you quite yet."

The second carriage halted behind Zeke's.

Ah. Garrick's rented carriage, she surmised. No matching grays there.

"No? Surely you didn't expect me to shirk my responsibilities to my lovely fiancé?"

"Your responsibilities?"

"It occurred to the earl and I after you left last night. Now that the cat's out of the bag, Lady Kitty must retrieve her wardrobe. To that end, I shall escort her to Maidstone while you, dear baron, travel ahead to Derbyshire. The earl's already underway. It should take you," he shrugged, "perhaps four days? We shall be behind you but one. Two at the utmost."

After a brief pause whereby Zeke appeared to wait for Garrick to respond—which he did not—he continued. "I, of course, brought along a proper chaperone."

He gestured with his free hand to the elegant woman at his side. "Allow me to introduce my great-aunt, Lady Lillian Thurgood. Aunt Lillian, meet Lord James, the Baron of Maidstone. and his charge, my fiancé, Lady Christine Hastings."

Lady Lillian Thurgood? The earl's sister? She certainly looked the part. Would Zeke actually drag the lady from her bed, and into this mess, only to play-act the part of chaperone?

Lady Lillian, or whoever she was, smiled demurely, and offered her hand to Garrick, who took it after a brief hesitation.

Kitty moved forward and dipped a curtsy. "My lady."

Garrick shifted to stand between Kitty and the two. "Lord Thurgood, you needn't have troubled yourself or your aunt to arise so early this morning. Kitty is my responsibility. As such, I will see to her needs. Indeed I was"—Garrick cleared his throat—"preparing to take her to Hastings House now to collect some of her things for our stay in Derbyshire."

Kitty's eyes widened. She stared hard at Zeke, willing him not to believe Garrick. As far as she could tell, however, Zeke wasn't interested in any input from her. He didn't so much as blink in her direction.

"It's no trouble, Lord Maidstone. Besides, Lady Thurgood is a much more appropriate chaperone. By the by. Where is Mary?"

Garrick looked momentarily nonplussed by the question. "She's...uh...coming any moment."

"Of course she is. Please inform her someone from the household will be 'round shortly to collect her. As for Lady Kitty and I, we will rendezvous with you in Derbyshire in a few days time." Hiss tone brooked no opposition. "I insist."

Garrick's jaw stiffened and he looked ready to argue. "Lord Thurgood—"

Zeke moved forward, crowding in on Garrick. "Yes, Lord James?"

"Your generosity knows no bounds."

He gave Garrick a cool look, and turned to address his coachman.

"A moment with my ward," Garrick said to Lady Lillian.

Taking Kitty's wrist, he pulled her several feet from the small group. He released her wrist only to grasp her bare hand. He crushed the delicate bones in a vicious semblance of a gentlemanly gesture, eliciting a hiss of pain from her as he bent and lifted her hand to his grim lips.

"I was so looking forward to catching up with you today, my charge," he ground out, sending her an icy, warning glare before releasing her.

Zeke appeared at her side. "James," he said by way of parting, then grasped her elbow and steered her toward the coach.

Kitty felt herself handed up into the luxurious Claybourne carriage. In a daze, she settled next to Lady Lillian, Zeke's supposed great-aunt.

Zeke's large frame filled the cab opening, blocking the meager light from the street lamps. He levered himself inside and dropped onto the bench opposite her. The cabin seemed warmer, just from his presence. The smell of him—his spicy, masculine scent—wafted toward her, as inviting and appealing as ever. She wanted to fling herself onto him and shower him with kisses of gratitude.

Instead she massaged her bruised hand and offered a wobbly smile. "Thank you, my lord," she said softly.

He made no reply, merely regarded her in stoic silence as the well-sprung carriage glided forward.

Her smile stalled, and her heart closed in on itself. He might have rescued her, but his opinion of her, if anything, had lowered.

She twisted to face her other travel companion. "Lady Lillian, I presume? Are you Lord Claybourne's sister about whom I've heard so much?"

The lady laughed in delight. "Indeed I am. Enchanted to meet you, my dear."

"I can't begin to express my gratitude for your assistance in this matter, nor can I properly convey my apologies for involving you in"—She gestured vaguely—"all of this, and dragging you out in the middle of the night."

The lady gave Kitty a kind smile that reached her aged eyes. "You are most welcome, Lady Christine. As to my late-night recruitment, no apology necessary. I can't remember the last time I had anything so interesting to occupy my time."

"You're very gracious."

Lady Lillian waved off the compliment and peered at Kitty's face. "Now I see you, I can't believe you played the part of a boy these past months. With your fine bone structure and that porcelain skin, it's a wonder anyone believed the ruse. Bravo."

Kitty's spirits lifted a little. Someone had apprised Lady Lillian of at least some of the facts, and she didn't appear appalled. "Yes, well, Lord Claybourne and I tried to keep a low profile. At least, that had been the plan." She slanted a meaningful glance at Zeke.

He stared out the window at the passing terrain, two fingers holding the curtain aside. He gave no indication he'd heard Kitty's pointed remark.

Just as well, considering he had just rescued her. "Lord Thurgood," she began, "I confess, I'm more than a little surprised *you* came."

When he made no reply, merely shifted his gaze in her direction, she went on. "May I ask where we're heading, or rather, where you're taking me?"

One corner of his mouth kicked up. "Weren't you listening, darling? We're off to Maidstone to fetch some of your things. Such as gowns and dainty little slippers." He waggled his fingers at the last. "Perhaps you've heard of them? Ladies wear them."

She ignored the barb, and instead focused the more important point. "All the way to Maidstone? That's very kind of you. What will you tell Garrick?"

He leaned back, spreading his arms to rest them on top of the seat cushion. He appeared genuinely perplexed. "I don't follow."

"What will you tell my cousin when we—I—never arrive at Chissington Hall?"

"Lady Hastings," Zeke said in a silken voice. "We are heading for Hastings House, where we will retrieve some of your clothes and girly accessories. Afterwards, we will make for Derby, where we will"—he paused to heave a world weary sigh—"act out our brief engagement."

Chapter Nine

Kitty stared at Zeke, recumbent on the coach bench across from her. "You're actually going along with the earl's mad scheme?"

"Leave it to two men," Lady Lillian intoned in disgust. "You didn't bother to fill the poor girl in on any of this?"

"There wasn't time," Zeke replied neutrally. "Grandfather and I worked it all out last night after she'd gone."

"You and the earl worked out precisely what?" Kitty asked.

Zeke glanced at her, his expression inscrutable. "In brief, we shall act out the part of a betrothed couple. Announcements will be posted in the *Times*, documents will be produced, etcetera, etcetera."

"You said...acting?"

"Acting." He enunciated the word with precision. "As a favor to the earl, I've agreed to act the part of your fiancé until you've reached your majority, or your cousin has ceased being a nuisance, whichever comes first."

A nuisance. That was one way to put it. She folded her hands in her lap. "What will happen at that point?"

"You will break off our engagement, and I will get on with my life."

She nodded, thoughtful. It could work. "I don't know what to say. Thank you."

He nodded once. "So long as you don't get the idea our betrothal is legitimate, all will be well."

Kitty felt her cheeks blossom with heat.

Lady Lillian spoke up on her behalf. "Ezekiel Thurgood, that is quite unnecessary. You should apologize immediately."

Kitty sniffed. "That's quite all right, Lady Lillian." She lifted her chin. "To put your mind at ease, my lord, no, I do not expect to find the two of us betrothed in six month's time. In all honesty, I fail to understand why we're bothering with the pretense."

"My sentiments precisely. But the earl was adamant."

So the earl had cowed him into it. It shouldn't hurt. It did. "I could disappear again? It seems a far less convoluted plan."

"For you. But it'd leave the earl wide open to accusation and scandal when your guardian goes screaming to the authorities and anyone else who might choose to listen."

Kitty's shoulders slumped. "I hadn't thought of that."

"That much is obvious."

She gritted her teeth.

Lady Lillian turned to Zeke. "How long did you say 'til Maidstone?"

"With stops, we'll arrive before nightfall," Zeke answered.

"Excellent." She turned a bright smile on Kitty. "My dear girl, I learned of your existence for the very first time last night around midnight, and was given only the briefest of details. I'm exceedingly curious as to how all of this came about."

Zeke eyed Kitty. "As am I."

"You don't know?" Lillian asked him.

"Obviously I'm privy to the basics, as I am the groom in this melodrama. Still, I'd love to hear Kitty's rendition." He sent her a banal smile.

Kitty focused her attention on Lady Lillian. "I'm not sure where to start."

"Start with your relationship with my brother, Claybourne."

Zeke spoke up. "The earl and Kitty's grandfather, the late Baron of Maidstone, fought together in the Crimean War."

Kitty glanced at him in surprise. "That's right. My grandfather trusted Lord Claybourne implicitly. He told me to go to him if ever I felt..." *threatened*. She cleared her throat. "If I needed safe harbor for a time."

"Your grandfather? What of your parents?" Lillian asked.

"Both deceased. They passed some four years ago. Cholera."

Lillian's brows furrowed. "I'm terribly sorry to hear that, Kitty. Do you mind if I call you Kitty?"

"Please."

Lady Lillian flashed a brief smile.

"My parents traveled a great deal due to their chosen professions. Cartographers, both of them. They contracted the disease in America, shortly before they were to sail for home."

"How dreadful. I'm sorry." After a moment's pause, Lillian went on. "Cartographers, you say? They must've travelled extensively."

"Almost constantly, from as early a time as I can remember."

"That must've made for an interesting childhood," Zeke sounded as if he found the notion intriguing..

Kitty slanted him a glance. "They didn't take us, generally. Their destinations were, by design, uncharted territory. Hardly fit for children." Turning back to Lady Lillian she added, "My grandfather filled in during their absences."

Lillian shot her great nephew a fond smile. "Zeke had a similar upbringing."

"Just so." He flashed his Aunt a brief grin, which faded the instant he shifted his attention to Kitty. "You said 'us.' Do you have siblings?"

She regarded her hands in her lap. "I had an older brother." Her valiant, charming Collin. "He died two years ago." If only he had stayed home with her and their grandfather instead of sailing to America, none of this would be happening.

Lillian shook her head and took Kitty's bare hands. "Poor darling. Losing your parents, your brother, and your grandfather, all in the span of four years."

Kitty found she couldn't speak.

"I'm so glad you came to us. So very glad."

"Thank you, Lady Lillian. That's very kind of you to say."

"I still don't understand how James figures in all this—save for the obvious," Zeke said.

"What, pray tell, is the obvious?" Lillian asked.

Exactly what Kitty wanted to know.

"He's obviously the new Baron of Maidstone, obviously Kitty's guardian, and obviously wanted to find her. What I want to know is what he intended to do with her once he did."

An image of Garrick's face caught in a flash of lightning the night she'd fled came to her. *We're going to marry. Tonight I'm going to make certain.* "I believe he wants to marry me."

"Why marry you? After all, he has the title, the properties, the associated wealth. Is it your inheritance?" Zeke asked without preamble.

For some reason, hiss inability to fathom Garrick wanting to marry her for any reason other than mercenary irritated her—never mind his analysis of the situation matched her own. "I don't know his motivation. Only that it isn't love that drives him."

Zeke's brows rose in disdain, as if the mention of love as a basis for marriage was laughable. "What about you? I assume you have good reason not to marry him?"

Kitty felt herself flush under their combined scrutiny.

"Ezekiel, I think it's fair to say Kitty has her reasons. Is that not so, dear?" Lillian asked in a gentle voice.

"Quite," she answered.

"That eases my mind greatly," Zeke drawled.

"Ezekiel Thurgood." Lillian chided, clearly exasperated. She turned to Kitty. "I don't know what's gotten into him. He's normally quite charming."

"Why Aunt Lillian, you wound me," he said with a grin, turning on the aforementioned charm at will.

"Oh, posh," his aunt answered with a fond smile.

Kitty could tell Lady Lillian what had happened to foul her nephew's mood. She had. He'd disliked her from the start.

In fairness to him, the earl had used her as fodder to provoke Zeke's temper, yet here he was, escorting her to Hastings House, then back to Derby to act as her fiancé. She supposed she could extend him a modicum of patience.

"That's all right, Lady Lillian. This situation has put us all on edge, for one reason or another."

When Zeke gave no indication he heard, she went on, "I'm very grateful for what you all are doing for me. I don't know how I'll ever repay your kindness."

"I can't speak for the rest, but for my part, I haven't had this much excitement in years." Lillian's eyes twinkled with warmth.

A lengthy silence ensued, during which Kitty stared out one window and Zeke the other.

After a while, the landscape blurred before her eyes as the rocking and rumble of the carriage lulled Kitty into drowsiness. She fought it, feeling almost as if sleeping would be a show of weakness.

***

Zeke surreptitiously witnessed her struggle. Watched her eyelids drift shut, then widen. Watched her head bob, then straighten. Finally her head lolled back onto the cushion as sleep overtook her.

A soft snore coming from his aunt told him she also dozed.

Good. He could do with some peace to quell his growing irritation, which would be a lot easier if he understood why he was irritated.

He'd left Claybourne Manor this morning feeling damned good about his decision to team up with the earl. It didn't matter if the project involved Lady Kitty Hastings, a pauper from the streets, or the queen herself. The point was, through this endeavor, he had a chance to heal the growing rift between himself and Claybourne.

He'd arrived at the boarding house keen to thwart the baron's attempt to steal Kitty out of town, the lying bastard. Initially he'd scoffed at the earl's suspicions concerning James's intentions. What kind of idiot pulled a fast one on the Earl of Claybourne?

Then the footman the earl had watching the man reported James had hired a carriage from a nearby mews. The telling part hadn't been in the where, but the when. James specified a dawn departure—not midmorning. the time he'd agreed upon with the earl. The fool. Zeke had been only too happy to crush the baron's ill-conceived plot.

When he arrived to find Kitty disheveled and clearly dispirited, he'd had to quell a strong compulsion to squash the newly ennobled baron like a bug.

Then she'd given him one of those looks. Those odd, misty green gazes resembling nothing short of hero worship that at least didn't seem so strange coming from her now he knew her to be a she.

In retrospect, that's when his irritation began.

Which again begged the question—why?

He'd been thoroughly vexed the afternoon he ordered her to help him undress, intent on interrogating the lad, Kit, only to catch him—her—staring at his naked chest like he—she—wanted to lick cream off of him. The dazed look in Kit's eyes now took on an entirely different meaning.

He raked a hand through his hair. What about Kitty vexed him?

His gaze slid to her and a reluctant smile pulled at his mouth. Her cheeks were soft with sleep and looked exactly right on a female.

Now, at least, he understood why she'd always looked so wrong to him. Instead of a square jutting jaw, she had delicate bones, instead of a broad mouth, she had plump, rose-colored cupid-bow lips, instead of bold, thick brows and sprouting facial hair, she had wispy black brows and porcelain skin.

She shifted slightly, murmuring something nonsensical, and brought one furled hand to her chin.

The corners of his mouth curved higher still, remembering the day his grandfather goaded him into giving her shooting instructions. She'd pulled the trigger, reckless in her attempt to get the lesson over-with, and had bounded into his chest. He'd commented on Kit's too heavily padded rear at the time, and she'd glowered at him—just like a woman. Nothing too-lush about that padding, he understood now.

He stifled a chuckle and allowed his eyes to drift over her, taking in the supple curves visible even her staid, high-necked mourning gown. How in hell had she kept those magnificent breasts hidden?

His gaze lingered for several seconds, measured by the steady rise and fall of her chest. Her breasts were perfect. Round and full looking. Exactly the right size for his palms. An image came to him, unbidden, of Kitty *sans* clothing. Her thick black hair unbound, draping over her shoulders, almost, but not quite hiding alabaster white breasts. with small, pink nipples.

An unholy shot of lust tore through him at the conjured image and without warning the fly of his trousers grew uncomfortably tight, protruding with a noticeable bulge. He tore his eyes off her in disgust. She was practically his ward. *Jesus*, his palms were sweating under his gloves. He tore at them, desperate to get them off.

Focus on something useful, Thurgood. Like how to rid them all of Lord James. He pinched the bridge of his nose and gritted his teeth.

"Are we nearly there?"

His gaze shot to Kitty. Her green eyes were open to half-mast. How long had she been awake? Long enough to see him ogling her breasts?

He tossed his gloves over his hips. "Over halfway," he replied in a brusque tone. "Sleep well?"

"Mm," she answered, noncommittal, and stretched, her breasts straining against her bodice as she arched.

"We're due for a stop. The horses could use a break, and I need some fresh air." *And a dip in an ice bath*. He rapped on the trap and instructed the coachman to stop at the next available inn.

Chapter Ten

They would arrive in Maidstone County soon, and what a relief that would be. Kitty had grown tired of the constant jostling of the carriage, of being cooped-up in the small, enclosed space and, aside from Lady Lillian, she especially disliked the company.

Neither of the short breaks they'd taken had done a thing to improve Zeke's sourpuss mood, which meant for most of the day's journey he'd sat across from her looking exactly as he did now. Like a hard-faced curmudgeon.

She set her gaze on the passing landscape and forced herself to focus on something other than him. Even with the sun low in the sky, the grass appeared a bright shade of green. The rolling hills surrounding them sang out in cheerful colors. Red, yellow, pink, and blue wildflowers scattered over the land.

She inhaled deeply, detecting lavender, peony, herbs and flowers of all sorts. The sweet scent on the air told her they'd reached the outskirts of Maidstone County. Home.

She caught the tell-tale scent of coming rain on the wind, as well, and peered up at the sky, Fluffy white clouds crowded out the gray-blue skies of late afternoon, but in the direction ahead, thick black clouds roiled into clustered bands.

"There's a storm coming. It looks like a nasty one. You said we would be making for Chissington Hall on the dawn?"

"Yes."

"I'm not so sure about that," she murmured.

Zeke gave an indeterminate grunt she took for dissent.

This time of year, clouds like those produced rainstorms that lasted for hours, sometimes days. Ensuing floods caused ruts that made the roads less than favorable for travel. She didn't mind. A little rain never killed anyone, and could be very helpful, in fact—especially for someone on the run, hoping to hide her tracks.

When the carriage wheels clattered over the old, familiar wooden bridge at the River Medway, she looked at Zeke, her heart in her throat. "Hastings House isn't far now."

The distant rumble of thunder sounded as they turned up Oak Lane. Kitty could hardly breathe as the red-bricked Georgian manse, her familial home, came into view.

It seemed an eternity before the carriage slowed to a stop and the groomsman opened the door.

Kitty scrambled out, heedless of the two passengers she left behind, or the fat raindrops smattering the cobbled drive. She was home. She half expected to see her grandfather waiting on the front stoop. A sob caught in her throat at the thought of him.

Fisting her skirts in her hands, she tripped up the broad steps to the over-sized double doors. As she reached for the brass knocker, one door opened.

George, her grandfather's faithful butler, blanched at the sight of her.

"George. It's Kitty," she said, her voice choked.

He blinked and a wobbly grin spread over his aged face. "It is you. I thought my eyes were playing tricks." He turned, calling over his shoulder in a loud voice. "Our Kitty's come home!"

A whoop came from the front hall, and scant seconds later, Mrs. Finney's dear face appeared in the open doorway.

Before Kitty could utter the first word, she found herself enveloped in a warm, comforting embrace.

"Oh, milady, we thought we'd never see you again. How we've missed you." After several moments, she loosened her grip and leaned back to study Kitty. "Where've you been these last six months, m'dear? Lord James's looked everywhere for you. When you didn't turn up, some of us worried he'd...that the night of the festival, during that awful storm, he..."

George cleared his throat, and Mrs. Finney broke off, beaming a watery smile at Kitty. "Och, none of that matters now you're home. But who is this you've brought with you?"

Kitty dashed tears from her cheeks with the back of her hand and took a bracing breath. "I have two traveling companions."

Behind her, Zeke's booted heels scraped up the wooden steps.

She glanced over her shoulder and met his velvet blue gaze. She nodded at him, and sent Lady Lillian on his arm a warm smile.

"This is Lady Lillian Thurgood and her great-nephew, Lord Ezekiel Thurgood—my, um, fiancé."

***

Kitty skimmed her fingers over the surface of the now tepid lavender-infused bathwater. Behind her, Mrs. Finney bustled about, packing Kitty's trunks and humming in her familiar, chipper way.

She closed her eyes and tried to banish the nostalgia threatening to swamp her. But it was no use. The gnawing ache inside her refused to subside.

She missed her life, the one that included her grandfather and Collin, and occasionally, her parents. But they were all gone now. All that remained was this mound of bricks known as Hastings House, a handful of aging servants, and her memories.

Memories Garrick James had done his best to erase, the vile creature.

The moment she walked into her grandfather's den the changes he'd wrought slammed into her with the force of a monsoon. The picture her grandfather had commissioned of Collin and her he'd hung above his mantel was gone. Her grandfather's prized globe likewise had disappeared.

Feeling sick, she inspected the sparsely populated mahogany shelves lining the wall to find Garrick had purged them of her parents' works. Their atlases and journals and maps—all gone.

She turned to flee the room only to find Zeke in the doorway. He studied her, eyes narrowed, as if he sensed something amiss.

She refused to break down in front of the man. Somehow, she kept her face impassive as she marched past him, and headed up the stairs to Collin's chamber—where all evidence of her brother's existence had vanished without a trace.

The marble-topped marquetry chest—the one their parents had chosen for him while in France—gone. His ornate snuffbox collection, always proudly displayed on the shelves—gone. The corner by the window where his red-lacquered Oriental cabinet once gleamed now boasted nothing more than empty space. His cologne bottles and ledgers and the Irish paperweight she'd gifted to him were all gone.

From there she dragged her feet to the master's bedchamber. A cursory glance was all she could endure. Garrick had made the chamber his own, eradicating every hint her grandfather had ever existed. Only her chamber had been left untouched.

A perfect illustration if ever there was one. She was completely alone in the world.

The thought brought the sting of tears to her eyes, and she submerged her head under the bathwater. She stayed below the surface until her lungs burned with the need for air. She surfaced, gasping.

"What're you about, girl?" Mrs. Finney asked with a chuckle. "Surely the water's gone tepid by now, Kitty dear. You'd best get dried 'afore you turn yourself into a prune."

Kitty smiled at her wrinkled fingertips. "Too late."

"Well, come on, then, out with you and let's get you dressed."

A small while later, Mrs. Finney finished doing up the tiny buttons lining the back of her green evening gown.

Kitty fingered the fine silk material and smiled inwardly. Six months ago, she would never have anticipated such joy over simply wearing a gown—and not wearing a wig.

"I can hardly believe you're here," the housekeeper murmured. Their eyes met in the dressing mirror and Mrs. Finney gave a wobbly smile. "I only wish you could stay longer."

"As do I."

Lightning flashed, illuminating the sky outside. Seconds later a crack of thunder rattled the windows panes in her bedchamber.

"Why don't you sit while I fix your hair and tell me all about your handsome fiancé. You said you've been staying with the baron's friend in London town. Is that where you met your beau? He has a dashing smile, that one."

Kitty resisted rolling her eyes. Apparently, Zeke had a smile for everyone but her.

What could she tell Mrs. Finney about him? She longed to confide all, to tell her the engagement was nothing but a sham, but she didn't dare. Who knew how the farce would play out? What if Garrick later questioned the older lady and decided she knew about Kitty's deception? He'd sack her with no references, or worse. Kitty couldn't risk it.

"Lord Thurgood is the Earl of Claybourne's grandson and heir."

The housekeeper's eyes widened and her fingers, busily pinning Kitty's curls momentarily paused. "You're to be a countess. The baron would be so proud. But don't stop there."

"As you surmised, I met him while a guest of the earl. Our engagement happened quite recently. In fact, the official announcement will take place at the earl's country estate in Derbyshire, which is why we're heading there straight away. Garrick awaits me there."

Mrs. Finney wrinkled her nose. "I see. Didn't realize he'd be there, too. I don't mind telling you, his lordship was like an angry bee after you left. He'd quiet down for a bit, but whenever one of the runners he hired to find you showed up with no word of your whereabouts..." She blew air out her cheeks. "All hades broke loose. The Lord only knows how the baron's friend—the earl—managed to keep you hidden away so well. But not so well you didn't catch yourself a husband, eh?" She gave Kitty a bawdy wink in the mirror before setting down the silver comb and smiling at her handiwork. "There now. A regular princess."

Kitty stared at her reflection and couldn't resist an exultant smile. Mrs. Finney had piled her long hair high on her crown to allow the curls to spill down over her nape and shoulders. The grubby boy, Kit, was well and truly gone.

"Thank you, Mrs. Finney. It's been a long while since...anyone styled my hair so well."

"No? I'd have thought the efforts of a ladies maid from a fine house like the earl's would far outshine anything I could do."

Kitty sent her an impish grin. "No one has your touch."

Mrs. Finney soon let herself out, leaving Kitty to gather herself before the dinner hour.

She gazed at herself in the long mirror. She may not have had a proper come-out, but at least she had the beautiful gowns her grandfather purchased for her London debut.

How excited she'd been at the prospect of her first London season. Everything had been set. Grandfather rented a house in the fashionable district, enlisted a proper sponsor.

Then Collin sailed for America. When his ship went down at sea, a debut season lost all appeal, despite her grandfather's urgings.

But she didn't want to think of that now. Instead she'd focus on all the dresses she had at her disposal. Maybe they were no longer of the first stare of fashion, yet to her they were magnificent.

As she let herself into the corridor, an unbidden thought emerged. What would Zeke think now?

***

Zeke waited in the parlor of Hastings House for the ladies to join him. He opened his gold pocket watch, checking the time. Ten minutes to eight. He tucked the watch back into his waistcoat and stared out the oriel window. Outside, rain fell in sheets.

Kitty had suggested their early morning departure might be delayed as a result of the storm. The fact she'd been proven correct irked him. Exactly why, he couldn't say. It would amount to no more than a few hours, after all.

But then, if he was being honest, it wasn't the delay so much as the sense he needed to get Kitty away from here. He'd read something in her eyes as she systematically inspected each room in her home. She seemed forlorn. Almost defeated. Seeing the valiant lady who braved the streets to London, then dressed like a lad and posed as a servant, looking like a whipped puppy bothered him.

Approaching footsteps from behind him provided a welcome distraction from his thoughts. He swung around, hands clasped behind his back, and blinked at the apparition standing in the doorway.

Kit had once and for all been put to rest.

Lady Kitty had dressed for dinner in a form-fitting gown, made of a frothy green material that matched her eyes and glinted in the flickering candlelight. Her long hair had been styled high, and soft, fat curls cascaded from the crown of her head, while delicate tendrils artfully framed her face. She looked, in a word, stunning.

He ought to compliment her, as any gentleman would. "Good evening, my lady," he said instead.

She sent him a tentative smiled and moved toward him, her gown making soft, swishing sounds. The unique scent of her reached him before she did—rosemary and lavender. He smiled remembering the tiny bar of soap he'd unearthed in Kit's room.

"Good evening, Lord Thurgood."

His gaze drifted over her, helplessly taking in the creamy expanse of skin revealed by the demure *décolleté* of her gown, and the tiny span of her waist. From there the gown hugged her hips only to flare out again below her knees. She looked damned delectable.

His eyes narrowed on her face as it occurred to him to wonder if she had an ulterior motive.

Her smiled faded, and her pale green eyes widened in concern. "My lord, is something wrong?"

"Not at all. Why do you ask?"

Her feathered brows shot upward as if the answer were obvious. "Because you're scowling."

Damn it all. He cleared his expression. He was smarter than to out-and-out accuse her of trying to seduce him into a real marriage proposal, wasn't he? Besides, whether she was fool enough to try to barter on her looks, pretty girls were a dime a dozen.

"I was thinking how lovely you look in a dress," he said curtly.

Her cheeks bloomed a fine shade of pink. "Er...thank you, my lord?"

"I was also thinking you might need a few things clarified concerning our arrangement."

"Of course," she whispered, and inched closer to him. She peered over her shoulder at the doorway, as if ascertaining they were alone then gazed up at him. "Go on."

His eyes locked with hers, and a shock of awareness coursed through him. Out of nowhere he was gripped with the most idiotic desire to sweep her into his arms and feast on her plump, rosy lips. He blinked. Felt a trickle of sweat course down his back. "Excuse me?"

Her brows furrowed slightly. "You just said you wanted to clarify a few things."

He did want to make things clear. So why did he feel like a cornered hare?

"Later. We'll need privacy. Obviously a walk through the gardens will be impossible thanks to this rain."

"We're alone now," she insisted.

"My aunt will join us any moment."

"Perhaps you can come to my antechamber later, when everyone retires," she whispered "It's the last one on the—"

"I know which is yours. It's out of the question," he snapped.

"Oh? Why?"

"You're a young, unmarried lady. I'm a man. Need I say more?"

She arched a brow. "You're planning on ravishing me, then?"

He drew a hand to his forehead and strove for patience. "I think you know that's not what I meant."

"It isn't as if I haven't been in *your* chamber once before." She had the gall to grin.

"Yes, but you shouldn't have been there."

"You're the one who invited—nay, *demanded* I follow you in."

"That was because I thought you were a lad." He spoke through clenched teeth.

She sniffed. "Very well. Where then?" She crossed her arms under her breasts, drawing his eyes to the hint of cleavage her demure bodice revealed. Her skirt jostled, and he heard a repetitive *tap, tap, tap.* Her evening slipper on the flooring? What cause did she have to be annoyed?

He crossed his arms over his chest, aping her stance.

Tap, tap, tap.

Jesus, she smelled good, and she stood close enough her perfect breasts practically brushed his forearms. Something hot and primal filled his veins. Irritated beyond measure—with himself or her, he could not say—he realized he either needed to kiss her or blast her. Very well.

He drew a mind-clearing breath. "It's crossed my mind to wonder if…"

Blessedly, the tapping stopped.

"…If you might not think it would be easier if the engagement weren't a sham."

Her unblinking green eyes narrowed. An image of a feral cat came to mind. "Go on."

"I only want to keep things from turning ugly later, Kitty."

The tip of her pink tongue darted out to touch on her upper lip. "Let me see if I understand you correctly." She aimed a patently false smile at him. "You want to make sure I know you don't wish to marry me."

"Ah…" He wouldn't have put it quite *that* bluntly.

"Allow me to ease your mind, my lord. I don't wish to marry you. Indeed, you are the very last sort of man I wish to marry."

He was impressed. She'd managed to communicate her ire without raising her voice above a whisper.

His mouth curved up at the corners. "Really?"

"Really."

"You sound serious—as if you've given the matter thought. You've utterly relieved my mind."

"My life is complete."

Cheeky chit. He laughed aloud. "It's none of my business, I know. But, out of curiosity—what are you looking for in a husband?"

Flames leaped in her eyes. She opened her mouth to speak, and he prepared for a thorough set-down.

"Good evening, Ezekiel, Lady Christine," said his aunt from the doorway.

Kitty's mouth snapped shut.

"Good evening, Aunt Lill. Looking elegant as always."

Kitty shot him one last glare before aiming an angelic smile at his aunt.

The parlor clock chimed eight.

"Ladies, may I escort you in to dinner?"

Chapter Eleven

Kitty stood at the window in her grandfather's study, starking out at the fierce storm. Someone had snuffed the candles and the only light in the room came from the moon, its glow eking through the thick clouds in fits and starts.

Lightning shattered the darkness, illuminating the wind ravaged yew trees outside—and the distorted reflection of Garrick's face in the windowpane. Behind her. Almost upon her.

She spun around. Another flash of light, combined with an earsplitting crack of thunder, revealed she'd reacted too late.

She tried to run, but Garrick hooked the tip of his boot behind her ankle. She toppled helplessly to the ground, with Garrick landing atop her.

She wanted to fight, to kick and scratch her way out from beneath him, but she couldn't move. Why couldn't she move?

Even knowing the futility, well aware the two of them were alone in the house, she drew a breath and screamed with all her might.

As if she'd offended the gods, an answering clap of thunder sounded. Again and again.

No, not thunder. Banging. On her bedchamber door.

Her bedchamber? But she was in the study.

"Kitty, be still."

Her eyes flew open at the harsh masculine whisper. A figure moved in the doorway.

She jerked upright in her bed and searched in the darkness for some route of escape. The window.

She flung the sheets aside, but her legs and nightdress were hopelessly entangled in the bedcovers. She wrestled and kicked against the restraining fabric, and succeeded only in cocooning herself further.

"Be still, I say." The figure started toward her.

With no option remaining, she dove from the bed, hurdling toward the floor.

Strong arms caught her, dragging her upwards to place her unceremoniously amidst the heap of sheets on the mattress.

"Good God, woman, wake up before you hurt yourself."

Zeke's voice.

Her mattress dipped with his weight as he sat on the edge of her bed. His hands gripped her upper arms, and warmth from his palms seeped through the sleeves of her night shift.

"Kitty, it's all right. You're safe," Zeke said in a low, soothing voice.

The nightmare's tentacles receded, leaving her weak with relief. She nodded her understanding and drew a shuddering breath.

Zeke's familiar scent—soap, spice, clean male skin—invaded her senses. In her unlit chamber, she could just make out the bold lines of his face. Moonlight glinted off his tousled hair.

Zeke had come and chased her nightmare away, chased Garrick away, just like he had this morning.

"Zeke," she choked, flinging herself into his chest. Her arms locked around his neck and the tip of her nose nestled into the warm curve of his shoulder. She closed her eyes and greedily breathed him in.

His arms went around her, almost tentatively, as if he didn't know where to place his hands.

She snuggled closer, trying to still the random tremors coursing through her.

After a moment, one of his big hands moved, smoothing her hair from the crown of her head to somewhere near her waist. Over and over again he touched her, all the while uttering soothing, nonsensical sounds.

She'd never imagined he could be so gentle.

After a while her breathing steadied, but her stubborn pulse refused to return to normal. Reality leaked in to her consciousness. Zeke was in her bedchamber. She was clinging to him for dear life. And she was fairly certain he wasn't wearing clothes.

With her arms yet around his neck, she allowed her gaze to drift down over the hard plane of his naked chest, then lower. She gulped. He appeared to be wearing trousers.

Reluctantly she unlocked her hands from around his neck and drew back.

He did not restrain her. Neither did he release her, and her skin hummed where his palms grazed her low back. The fact only her thin nightshift separated her flesh from his touch consumed her thoughts.

"I suppose I woke you?" she asked, mostly just to break the silence.

"I heard you screaming, and I thought...I feared James was attempting to abduct you. It's a wonder you didn't raise the entire household." He softened his gruff words reaching up to tuck a lock of hair behind her ear.

She shivered and barely resisted pressing her cheek into his palm.

"I'm sorry I disturbed your sleep. I suppose the storm stirred memories. I..." She swallowed. Clamped her lips together. What was she thinking, revealing so much? "It was only a dream."

Zeke cupped her cheeks between warm, slightly calloused palms. "What memories? Or should I ask of whom? Is Garrick the monster in your nightmares?"

When she didn't reply, his tone grew more urgent. "Did he"—He paused—"hurt you? Is that why you ran? Kitty, so help me, tell me."

"He attacked me," she whispered. "But I got away." She bit her lower lip, unwilling to say one word more.

Zeke cursed softly and pulled her into his chest, trapping her arms between them. She meant to pull them free. Instead her fingers curled into his muscled flesh.

He sucked in a breath, and a shudder coursed through him.

She'd overstepped. Mortified, she drew back, clenching her fists to keep from reaching for him again. She searched his face. His expression was unreadable in the unlit chamber.

"I'm sorry," she choked out. "I didn't mean to..." She had no idea how to finish her sentence.

He didn't speak for a moment, then he whispered, "You didn't mean to...?"

He would make her say it? "To wake you."

He huffed out a breath, that sounded a lot like laughter. "I thought you were apologizing for touching me...here." He grasped both her wrists and placed her palms flat on his chest.

Her breath went choppy and her insides went hot in a way she'd never known. "Zeke?"

He didn't answer in words, but combed his fingers through her hair.

As if of their own accord, her fingers curled into his supple, warm skin. His heartbeat seemed to pound into her fingertips.

He swallowed audibly. "Do you always sleep with your hair loose like this?"

He grasped a handful of her hair and tugged her toward him. Then he relaxed his grip, and let her hair sift through his fingers as his free arm encircled her waist to pull her closer.

When her nipples grazed his chest through the thin lawn gown, they puckered and tightened. She nearly moaned at the inexplicable pleasure of the sensation.

But he'd asked her a question. Something to do with her hair.

"No," she said in a husky voice she barely recognized as her own. "I left it down tonight because I've had it bound for months and I couldn't bear to—" She broke off and closed her eyes.

He was combing his fingers through her hair again.

"Yes?" His voice sounded gruff.

"I...." What had she been saying? Her lashes fluttered open when she felt his warm breath on her cheek.

He'd ducked his head, bringing his face only inches from hers.

She licked her lips as anticipation burned through her. He was going to kiss her. *At last.*

As if he knew he was turning her insides to mush, a lazy smile curved his lips. His white teeth gleamed like a pirate's in the moonlit room. "Perhaps now you see why it's not a good idea for a man to enter a lady's bedchamber in the middle of the night."

Before she could ask what he meant, his mouth covered hers.

The kiss was...everything. Tender. Bone-melting. Intoxicating.

She should protest. Call a halt. Anything other than twining her fingers into his thick mane of hair, and luxuriating in the silken feel of it.

With a low groan, his arms banded around her, flattening her breasts against his chest. His body heat burned through her gown, warming her all the way to her curling toes.

He grabbed fistfuls of her hair like a lusty kitten, finally twisting a mass of it around his wrist. "You taste like honey," he rasped.

She felt herself tumbling back into her pillows. Had she dragged Zeke down with her or had he initiated the fall? She didn't care. She knew she loved the heavy weight of him on her, and absolutely knew she never wanted him to stop kissing her.

Her hands skimmed his shoulders, coursing over the rippling muscles of his back. She couldn't seem to stop her greedy exploration. Couldn't make herself want to. She wanted to touch him everywhere, to commit his beautiful form to memory.

Abruptly his mouth left hers. In one jerky movement, he grasped both her wrists and pulled her arms over her head. A shaft of moonlight stole through the seam of her closed shutters, illuminating Zeke's features. He stared down at her with wild eyes.

She heard his breath, hissing through his gleaming white teeth, frozen in a half smile—or grimace.

Somehow she understood.

She, too, felt something between pleasure and pain, and a delicious hunger only Zeke could assuage. She tugged at his restraining hand, wanting to touch him.

"Christ," he bit out, releasing her wrists as if he hadn't even realized he held her.

She reached for him, but with lightning speed he was up on his feet. "I...this shouldn't have happened. When I came in here I never intended..." He dragged a hand through his hair. "It's past time I go."

"But—"

"We'll talk in the morning." He sounded almost angry.

She vibrated with a need she'd never known, while he turned off his feelings as easily as one would blow out a match.

A moment later he was gone, shutting the door softly behind him.

She lay awake, a long, long time.

***

As Kitty feared, breakfast was an awkward affair—for her, at any rate. She slid a sidelong glance at Lady Lillian who chattered amiably.

If the lady noticed she carried the conversation for the three of them, Kitty couldn't tell.

Zeke's terse responses to his aunt's chipper commentary could indicate nothing more than a disinclination to wake before noon.

Kitty was more inclined to believe him preoccupied with what happened last night in her bed chamber. Certainly it was all she could think about..

Lady Lillian dabbed the corners of her mouth. "Ezekiel, May I assume since the weather's improved we'll be setting out as soon as possible?"

Zeke responded in the affirmative, and Lillian announced her intention to gather her things in preparation.

As the lady made her exit, Kitty quickly scooped the remainder of her soft-boiled egg and salted ham into her mouth, intent on making her own escape.

Zeke cleared his throat and drummed his long fingers on the table.

Kitty chewed faster. If only she'd left the room with Lady Lillian.

"Lady Kitty, if you would be so kind, I'd like you to join me in the gardens for a brief stroll."

She gulped down her bite, eyeing him warily. "Now?"

His velvet blue eyes flickered with amusement.

"As we'll be leaving Hastings House within the hour, now would be preferable."

Kitty led Zeke out to the courtyard garden. The air was soft from the previous night's rain, and filled with the scents of rose and lavender, honeysuckle and peony. It smelled like home.

"Impressive," he said.

"My mother's design," Kitty said with a smile. "She toiled here endlessly on her visits home. When I was a child she let me trail after her, until, by some miracle, I picked up a thing or two. Eventually its oversight fell to me. It looks hopelessly overgrown to me now."

He glanced around. "I just see lush, wild flowers."

They'd taken one of the winding gravel paths and now stood a distance from the manse.

Zeke slowed to a halt. "I think we're safe enough here."

Though the morning temperature was fresh, Kitty felt her cheeks throbbing with heat. Still, she lifted her chin and met his blue stare. "You want to discuss last night."

"I do."

She took a deep breath. "I wanted to thank you for—"

"I wanted to apologize for—"

They both went silent.

Zeke sent her a condescending smile.

She returned the smile. Inwardly she fumed.

While lying awake last night, she'd decided on a course of action should Zeke insist on a conversation. She'd thank him for coming to rescue her and that would be the end of it. They could both pretend nothing untoward had happened and move on.

Meanwhile Zeke, the cur, was apologizing for their kiss, *again*. As if last night's apology, followed by him charging out of her bedchamber like the house was on fire wasn't bad enough. Humiliation swamped her anew.

"May I go on?" He asked.

"Please."

"I've considered the matter, and have come to an inescapable conclusion." He laughed softly, as if he couldn't quite believe what he was about to say. "We must wed."

"Wed?" she squeaked. She had not seen this coming.

His face showed only resolve. "While it's true I didn't enter your chamber with the idea of…" His loss for words and ruddying cheeks gave Kitty a modicum of satisfaction.

She smiled sweetly. "Of ravishing me, my lord?"

A muscle in his jaw ticked. "Perfectly worded, my dear, though, if you wouldn't mind keeping your voice down? I'd be much obliged."

"Certainly, Lord Thurgood," she said in a low tone, that reeked of sarcasm, she hoped.

His eyes danced with merriment. "Ah, Kitty." After a moment, he sobered. "My treatment of you was abhorrent and demands atonement. As such, I am fully prepared to take responsibility for my actions, and as we are already acting under the guise of—"

"No. Absolutely not, my lord."

His brows furrowed in what looked like confusion. "No?"

"I can't allow you to make such a sacrifice."

"Kitty, under the circumstances, you must allow me to decide—"

"Just last night you went out of your way to"—she put a finger to her chin as if searching her mind—"clarify, I believe was the word you used, the nature of our arrangement. If you'll recall, I told you at the time I have no desire to marry you."

He clasped his hands behind his back and gaped at her, clearly perplexed. "You truly don't wish to marry me?"

"Allow me to congratulate you on your excellent hearing, my lord."

His mouth curved in a pirate's smile. "In that case, do you mind explaining your"—he scratched the side of his nose—"participation, for lack of a better word?"

She swallowed hard, beyond mortified now. Participation was a kind way of putting it. She'd practically initiated the whole encounter.

She ducked her head, certain her cheeks glowed red. Her entire face throbbed with heat. "I was curious? That is, I've never...never..." She glanced up, helpless to complete her sentence—and glared at him when she saw his eyes crinkling at the corners with restrained amusement.

"Curiosity, you say?"

"The point isn't what happened between us last night. It's what"—her body bloomed with heat—"didn't. My lord, I wouldn't wish you to sacrifice yourself on the altar of marriage when no one besides us need ever know about our kiss. And, arguably of greater importance, there remains the fact I have certain requirements for a husband you simply do not meet."

His brows shot up.

"You needn't look so incredulous."

"Do I?"

"Indeed."

"Sorry. Still. Morbid curiosity compels me to ask you precisely which requirements I don't fulfill?"

You don't love me. You barely tolerate me. She drew a breath and searched her mind for something she could actually tell him. "You have no desire to settle down. To stay in one place."

When he gazed at her with what looked like genuine bafflement she said, "Don't play dumb, my lord. Are you or are you not planning a trip to the Americas at the conclusion of this pretense?"

"Yes."

"Did you not return less than a month ago from Africa?"

"I did, but..." He spread his large hands wide. "I don't see the problem. It's common practice for married persons to spend great quantities of time in separate locales."

"I don't deny the truth of your statement. Regardless, I find such an arrangement repugnant."

His crossed his arms over his chest, one hand lightly fingering his chin. "I see. You want permission to tag along."

"I want nothing of the sort," she snapped. She took a moment to school her emotions. "You aren't listening. I want a home, and have no desire to shackle myself to someone who has no wish to set down roots."

A slow grin spread over his face. "You're hoping for a love match, or some other nonsensical romantic notion. Is that it?"

His supercilious tone ignited her ire, especially as a love match was precisely what she wanted. She drew herself up regally. "I want a partnership, not a long distance affair. And in your case—" She broke off and raked him head to toe with her haughtiest gaze.

He snorted. "This ought to be good."

"Your habitual carousing leaves much to be desired, as well."

He threw back his head and roared with laughter.

"Shouldn't we see about leaving for Derby?" she gritted out, tapping her toe so hard little mud splatters had attached to her stockings. She didn't care.

He held up a finger as he brought his mirth under control. When he finally sobered enough to speak, he said, "Lady Kitty, you leave me in a predicament. I want to do right by you but can't force you to accept my proposal, short of making a public announcement of our...er...exchange last night."

"You wouldn't dare," she said on a gasp.

He stared at her, unblinking, all trace of humor gone from his face. "You're certain, then?"

Gazing into the smoky blue depths of his eyes, Kitty had the sudden urge to throw all her sound reasoning to the wind and marry him yesterday. She broke eye contact and firmed her resolve. "Quite certain."

"Well, then, Lady Christine Hastings. We'll just have to make certain there are no repeat performances of last night's event."

She nodded. He was right, of course. But hearing him say so filled her with a dull ache she didn't care to analyze.

They walked together into the house.

Zeke delivered her to the base of the staircase and took a step back. "We'll leave as soon as you're ready."

She nodded and started up the stairs, spine straight.

Zeke watched until she reached the landing, then stepped out the front doors to await the carriage.

She'd actually said no.

He'd stayed up half the damned night stewing over how to handle his uncharacteristic lapse in judgment.

He'd thought about the situation frontwards and backwards. How he'd entered her room in the middle of the night. Kissed her as if she were an experienced courtesan rather than a virginal debutante. He was supposed to be protecting her from her guardian, for God's sake, not making advances himself.

Then, too, he'd suffered his grandfather's recriminations, at least what Zeke imagined he'd say if he knew the situation. Replayed his own litany of "I'm nothing like my father."

By dawn he'd reached the unavoidable conclusion he'd have to offer marriage.

He'd actually reached a level of comfort with the idea, too.

By marrying Kitty, he could assuage his conscience, appease his grandfather, rescue the damsel, and satisfy his duty as the heir to the earldom by marrying and, hopefully, siring a son and heir. If their midnight interlude told him anything, bedding the chit would be no hardship.

All that mental cogitation and she'd said no. He didn't know whether he felt annoyed or relieved.

Relieved, he told himself. It had been a near miss. He'd make damn sure he didn't slip up again.

***

The main trouble Zeke had with retiring en masse to Chissington Hall was the fact it was an old castle-turned-residence, and as such one never knew when someone might be waiting in the wings to waylay a person.

As he made his way down the echoing stone stairs and drafty corridors toward his grandfather's study, the overabundant nooks and crannies, short-cuts and alcoves within these old stone walls he noticed had him shaking his head in consternation.

Perhaps the fact he'd hidden in an alcove outside Kitty's door for the last half hour to assure James didn't pounce the first chance he got had made him paranoid.

The manse had been a child's dream-come-true summer home when he and Caden were boys. Now it seemed fraught with dangerous opportunities for James to accost Kitty and finish whatever he started that had frightened her so badly.

Kitty. On the one hand, Zeke wanted to protect her, which meant keeping her close. On the other hand, he wanted to...He jammed a hand through his hair and cursed inwardly. What had the earl gotten him into?

It had been a long four days holed up with the smart-mouthed chit who alternated between looking at him like she wanted to eat him for dinner, or like she'd enjoy using his head for target practice. The latter made him laugh, and the former made him burn. Hell, just being in sniffing distance of her stiffened his cock.

He was damned frustrated. He'd never been so happy to see one of his familial homes as he had today. He'd been desperate to get away from the girl.

Yet off he'd marched to stand sentinel outside her door not ten minutes after they'd arrived.

He reached his grandfather's study and rapped twice on the closed door. When he heard the old man's brusque, "Come," he stepped inside.

"I thought I'd find you here," Zeke said, taking in the old man's aggrieved countenance. "Judging by the scowl on your face, can I assume James made your life a living hell these last few days?"

"How very astute," the earl groused. "You missed the part where I'm irked because it took my grandson an age to get here to report."

"Ever heard the saying patience is a virtue?" He sauntered toward the majestic old desk behind which his grandfather presided.

"Perhaps you should try it, then," he grumbled under his breath.

Zeke dropped into the armchair facing the desk. He stretched out his legs. It felt good after riding in the cramped, if well-sprung carriage for days. "Sorry I kept you waiting. I came as soon as I was able."

"Of course you did," the earl said. "I apologize for snapping. Believe me, you'd be irritable, too, if you'd been the one closeted with the whining blackguard."

Zeke gestured toward the bow window framing his grandfather's desk, and the expanse of rolling green hills and ancient trees spreading out as far as the eye could see. "I'd hardly call Chissington Hall a closet. But I take your meaning. He obviously worked himself into a lather during our absence.

"When we arrived an hour ago, he practically tore the carriage door from its hinges to get at Kitty. But have no fear. Aunt Lillian set Lord James straight."

The earl snorted. "I thought I detected something in the air when I entered the fray."

"You should've seen your sister, all five feet of her, rising to Kitty's defense like a Roman sentinel when the unsuspecting fool thought to corner the chit."

"I'm rather surprised to hear it wasn't you doing the defending."

Zeke plucked at a nonexistent bit of lint on his trousers. Truth be told, he still marveled at his own unexpected and violent burst of anger. Guardian or no, the man had come close to having the stuffing knocked out of him when he rounded on Kitty. Only Aunt Lillian's timely decision to step in front of Zeke saved James.

"It was quite entertaining, actually, watching Aunt Lillian take on the bugger."

James did eventually make it past Aunt Lillian. Then he must've gleaned Zeke's desire to rip him to shreds, because he clamped his mouth shut and scurried back several feet to allow the trio to pass.

"Good ol' Lill," the earl said with a chuckle, and leaned back, his well-used leather chair creaking in protest. "Yesterday, James all but accused me of secreting her out of the country."

"Probably because he came up with the idea first."

The earl lifted a querulous brow.

"Suffice it to say our showing up in Albemarle at the break of dawn proved timely. Five minutes later and they'd have been gone."

"It was that close?"

"Yes. The lying bastard's rented coach arrived directly after ours. James and Kitty were waiting at the curb. Our girl looked downright forlorn before she realized what was happening."

The earl's expression turned wily. "Our girl? Do I detect a degree of softening toward the damsel?"

Zeke snorted. "I'm not an ogre. Of course I don't want to see any harm befall your tiger. Doesn't mean I plan on actually marrying the chit." *Anymore.*

"Speaking of your marriage"—the earl clapped his hands once—"the engagement announcements are due to hit the papers tomorrow."

Chapter Twelve

Zeke's brows shot up. "My. Someone's been busy."

He crossed his arms over his chest and regarded the earl across the massive desk. "I'll admit the wedding announcement ought to give James pause. As a newly titled baron of common origin, he'll think long and hard before pitting himself against us once we've gone public."

The earl nodded and cleared his throat. "Announcements, by the by."

"Beg pardon?"

"Announcements. Plural. As in the *Times*, and the *Chronicle*."

"How thorough of you," Zeke said dryly.

"I thought so, too. Eh, Zeke, I'm curious..." His grandfather paused. Picked up a crystal paperweight sitting atop his desktop and examined it. "Did the two of you have a chance to get better acquainted over the last few days?"

Zeke's mind shot to the moment he'd bounded into her chamber to save her from certain abduction only to find her alone, shrouded in moonlight, hair tumbling down to her waist. Tempting beyond measure.

"Eh, yes. A bit. She's...no lad." He drummed his fingers on his thigh.

The earl hooted with laughter. "I'll say. I still marvel you couldn't see through her disguise."

"Yes." He was getting damned tired of people saying that.

"In any case, I'm counting on your help with a plan I concocted during your absence. A more intimate knowledge of our Kitty will enable you to help me."

Intimate. The word brought all sorts of ideas to mind. "Oh?"

The earl lowered his voice. "The thing is, I rather hoped, since the two of you aren't really going to marry—"

"Definitely not," Zeke interjected, her abject refusal to do so ringing in his mind.

The earl scowled a little at the interruption. "And as she is of an eminently marriageable age..."

"Eminent, eh? How old is she?"

"Two and twenty."

"I'd say she's a bit past prime marriageable age."

The earl stared down the length of his nose at Zeke. "May I finish?"

Zeke waved a hand.

"I thought we might put together a list."

Zeke blinked at the earl. "I don't follow. What sort of list?"

"I want to plan a dinner party, or a garden party or weekend party—something, anything so long as the guest roster includes a few eligible bachelors who might suit Kitty."

"A party. Of eligible bachelors."

"Precisely. So that when Kitty ends your engagement in a few months..."

"Some other bloke can step in to fill my boots," Zeke said, his tone flat.

"Just so."

Annoyance sparked through him. He planted his feet on the carpet and leaned forward. "Supposing I agree to aid your cause, what makes you so sure she'll attract a suitor?"

His grandfather looked at him as if he'd sprouted antlers, then shook his head. "You've evidently got blinders on when it comes to the girl, which is neither here nor there since you're not in the running. Trust me when I say attracting a husband won't be an issue. She's not only beautiful, she's got a certain indefinable charm *most* gentlemen will find irresistible. Add to that a small fortune in dowry, between her inheritance and my offering." He left off with a shrug.

Zeke resisted the urge to scowl. "It sounds like you have it all worked out."

He sent Zeke a crafty smile. "Yes, it does, doesn't it? All I need from you is—"

"A list. I'll see what I can do."

"The sooner the better, please. Oh, and one other thing. Don't breathe a word of this to Kitty."

"Why ever not?"

"Because she'll go all stiff if she thinks she's on display. Not that she'll be on display. In actuality, it's the men who need to impress her. Not that they can know why they've been invited."

Zeke groaned. "This is getting complicated."

"Nonsense. Just think of us as cupid's little helpers." The earl smiled cheerfully. "It'll be great fun.

"Now on to the next bit of business. In two days time, our solicitor will arrive with the proper documentation to make this thing legal. We need to discuss the terms of the arrangement, get all our ducks in a row, so to speak."

***

Kitty gave up. She couldn't concentrate on the local gazette's article, detailing the goings on in and around town. Not with the meeting between the earl, Garrick, Zeke, and the earl's so-licitor taking place, and not with the posted ad in the classified section of the *Times* calling to her like a siren luring sailors to their deaths.

She cast a furtive glance toward the open library doors, and snatched-up the classified section of the *Times* once more. She opened to the engagement announcements.

The Earl of Claybourne and ninth Baron of Maidstone proudly announce the betrothal of Lord Ezekiel Thurgood, Viscount of Claybourne,

*to Lady Christine Hastings, daughter to the late
Lord Charles Hastings.*

If only it were true. The inane thought came without warning. With a self-derisive moan, she covered her eyes with one hand. How ridiculous. If she'd wanted to marry Zeke, she could've accepted his offer days ago. His thoroughly unromantic, obviously grudging, offer of marriage.

She'd had to say no. How could she marry a man who not only didn't love her, but didn't like her?

Witness his grim face on the carriage ride to Maidstone, his air of detached boredom all the way to Derby. His monosyllabic replies to her efforts to draw him into conversation over breakfast, lunch, or dinner.

She refolded the newspaper. Smoothed her fingers over the crisp, cool sheets. Then, very deliberately, set the newspaper aside.

How much longer?

She had a mental image of the four men huddling over the so-called marriage contract.

The earl hadn't provided details, but she had the clear impression he'd promised a small fortune to her guardian for his signing on the dotted line. All for a sham engagement. And Zeke thought she wrought trouble when she was a mere servant. Ha.

No wonder he disliked her.

At least he only had to put up with her for five months more and counting. She'd have the final say so over who she married or did not marry then, as well as access to her inheritance.

She hugged a throw pillow to her chest. lounged back on the chaise, and stared unseeing at the high plastered ceiling.

Five months from now their engagement would end and Zeke would sail away. She'd likely never see him again. That's always how it worked. People made themselves indispensable then left, never to return.

Like her parents, who voyaged the world, exploring and mapping out the far-reaches of the globe for the betterment of mankind.

Like Collin.

She couldn't go through it again.

Hence, her real reason for rejecting Zeke's marriage proposal. Regardless of the spirit in which it had been delivered, the logical move would be for her to leap at the offer, as any other lady would. Not only because of the family's wealth and prestige, but simply because of Zeke. Magnificent, maddening, marvelous Zeke.

But she'd had to say no. She might be halfway to falling in love with the man—what sane woman wouldn't?—but she would never willingly put herself in the position of watching someone she loved sail out of her life again.

She would find someone who wanted a family, and to set down roots. She would, or she'd remain unmarried the rest of her days.

Lady Lillian appeared in the doorway, a cheery smile on her face.

Kitty sprang to her feet, pillow still clutched to her chest.

"Claybourne's office door is open, and I heard him call for his finest brandy from the cellar. That tells me the deed is done."

"Garrick must have signed the contract. I only hope Lord Thurgood doesn't live to regret helping me."

Kitty hadn't realized she'd spoken aloud until she heard Lady Lillian's reply. "I can think of only one reason he would, my dear."

Kitty could think of a thousand, but one in particular rankled beyond measure. "If he meets Miss Right while he's tangled in my web?"

The elderly lady chuckled. "Not at all what I had in mind."

***

Later that night, Kitty nestled in an oversized armchair in the family parlor, legs bent under her, slippers curled under her skirts. She grinned impishly at the earl, sitting across from her.

He studied the chessboard, its black and white surface aglow in the reflected light from the massive grate nearby. "You needn't look so smug, my little pussycat. You haven't beaten me yet," he said.

"Who me?" she asked, all innocence.

The earl snorted.

She felt the air stir around her. Glancing over her shoulder revealed Zeke leaning over her armchair, arms clasped behind him.

He and his catlike grace. He hadn't made a sound crossing the large room. Last time she checked, he'd been reclining on a sofa, reading, legs propped on an ottoman, studiously ignoring the two of them.

"Besting you again, old man?"

The earl's expression turned peevish. "If you think you can do better, you play her."

"I hate to scare her off."

"Ha," she said. "Give me a moment to finish off my first opponent, then you are welcome to try your hand."

"Challenge accepted."

Butterflies erupted in Kitty's belly.

Zeke had never expressed an interest in spending time with her alone. Not that they'd be alone, but she'd have his undivided attention, at least for the length of the chess game.

It was all she could do to keep her mind on the game at hand.

Minutes later, the earl pushed himself out of his chair. "All yours, Zeke. My turn to be the heckling spectator. Just let me stretch my legs a bit."

Zeke took his seat while Kitty reset the board.

He won their first game. "Care to try again?" he asked, flashing his cocksure smile.

She shook her head. "Another time. Perhaps the earl would like..." Her words died in her throat as she glanced around the room.

The earl had slipped out without a word, leaving she and Zeke alone.

She glanced at him, only then noticing how the fire had dimmed to a low burning glow, giving the large room an intimate feel. Her stomach fluttered and she found it hard to draw an even breath. She ought to excuse herself this instant.

Instead, she smiled uncertainly at Zeke, who studied her in turn, an unreadable expression on his face.

He was ever a mystery. With the earl and his aunt, he displayed ample charm, and a proclivity to see the humor in almost everything. Toward her, however, he was distant, bordering on rude.

Over the last few days, however, his chilly veneer showed an occasional crack, and he treated her as someone he almost liked, or at least didn't dislike.

She found herself craving his attention, a smile aimed in her direction. Her name on his lips spoken in his rough velvet voice was like a dollop of thick, melted fudge. Better, even.

"Tell me about your family, Kitty."

"What would you like to know?" She began collecting the chess pieces. She would leave as soon as she put the game away.

He shrugged and leaned over the board, nudging her hand aside with his. "I'll get these."

Her skin, where his fingers had brushed, tingled. "Thank you."

He didn't acknowledge her thanks. "What were your parents like?" He asked, his eyes still on the board. A golden lock of hair fell over his brow.

Kitty folded her hands in her lap rather than give in to the inane urge to smooth it back. "Adventurous. Both of them. And quite learned. My father was a geologist turned cartographer."

"A rather unusual practice for a member of the peerage, isn't it?" He paused in the act of folding the board to study her.

She smiled faintly. "Especially considering father was my grandfather's only son, and by all standards should've begun managing the Maidstone properties when he came of age. He didn't. I never heard it discussed. It was just that way. Father's choice, I presume. He never showed any interest in anything other than my mother and their explorations.

"Not that grandfather complained. He was extremely vital. In fact, I never remember him taking ill, until the last."

She stared into the fire, and willed away the rush of emotion. "Anyway, Grandfather had Collin to take up the helm. I think my father—not that I'm criticizing, mind you—but I think he counted on that."

"I see."

Something in his tone drew Kitty's gaze. His head was cocked to one side, his eyes narrowed and focused—on her.

Her heartbeat skittered, leaving her breathless, as if she'd run up a flight of stairs.

"How did your brother feel about taking on his father's responsibilities?" Zeke asked.

Her lips curved slightly at the memory. "Collin was a natural born lord-of-the-manor. Even as a child he insisted on riding out with Grandfather to tour the properties. By the time he reached adolescence he sat in on grandfather's meetings with his man-of-affairs. He always said things like, 'When I'm baron, I'll do thus and such.'" She altered her voice to sound like a man's.

"There's the voice I remember." Zeke's white teeth gleamed. "No wonder young Kit never sounded right."

"A criticism you never passed an opportunity to make."

"You make a much better female," he said, his voice all silk and smoke.

For the life of her, she couldn't think of one intelligent response.

"How many years separated you and Collin?" He asked, his tone once again neutral.

"Seven. I adored him. If only he hadn't gone on that wild goose chase, none of this would even be happening," she blurted, surprising even herself.

She put a fist to her mouth as if to staunch any further emotional outburst. "I'm sorry. I don't mean to subject you to a fit of female hysterics."

"I asked."

She blinked. The Zeke she knew never missed an opportunity to mock her. Tonight's Zeke unnerved her.

"You can't stop there, Kitty. I'm curious. What sort of goose chase? Where did Collin go?"

She studied her hands in her lap. "He got word a trunk containing our parents' last works had turned up in New York. He set out to retrieve the thing before it went up for auction."

"He couldn't have sent for it?"

"As far as I was concerned, it could rot, and I made my opinion known, but Collin was stubborn as a mule once he set his mind to something."

She curled her toes further under her skirts, and leaned one elbow on her armrest, dropping her chin in her hand. "He even convinced Grandfather to support his fool's errand, though I believe he browbeat him into it. For several weeks—before Collin gave me the news—I'd wake up at night hearing them, well, I don't want to say arguing. That would, be too strong a word."

"And I suppose you happened to overhear these heated conversations?" he asked, a teasing light in his eyes.

She slanted him a peeved looked. "I did not." After a brief pause she added, "I couldn't make out the words."

Zeke threw his head back and laughed aloud.

Kitty grinned, warmed to her toes. "I don't know for certain. Maybe Grandfather wanted the trunk as a memento of his son. I do know I wish Collin had never gone."

"Maybe he had a bit of wanderlust going on?"

"Spoken like someone with first-hand experience," she said softly.

His mouth twisted in a sardonic half-grin. "Have you no desire to see the world, Kitty? It seems to be in your family's blood."

She shook her head.

At one time she had yearned to travel, to go with her parents on their mad adventures. But now she only wanted a home, and a family, and roots.

"I have other priorities." Priorities she had no intention of sharing and inviting censure on herself. "I admit as a child I dreamed of visiting faraway lands."

He looked at her with eyes that seemed to see into her soul. "You wanted to join your parents on their travels, didn't you?"

"What child wouldn't? But of course they couldn't take us into the wilds. Not a very nice existence for small children. To their credit, they didn't begin traveling so constantly until I was past infancy, or so I've been told."

"Very thoughtful of them. Your grandfather raised you for the most part, I take it?"

She smiled fondly. "Yes."

"As did mine."

She studied him through her lashes. "Yes, we have that in common. Except...I think you lost your mother at an early age?"

"I was fourteen, Caden ten. She died giving birth to our sister—who passed with her." He spoke almost without inflection.

"I'm so sorry."

Neither spoke for several minutes. Finally Zeke broke the silence. "I know James is your cousin. I'm shooting in the dark, here, but am I correct guessing your branches of the family weren't close?"

"That's putting it mildly. I first laid eyes on him when his parents brought him to my parents' funeral. My impression was they were a brooding lot." She reflected a moment. "Grandfather explained who they were to Collin. I"—she cleared her throat—"overheard their conversation."

Zeke grinned knowingly.

She raised her chin a notch and fought an answering grin. "All right, I eavesdropped. But sometimes one has to be resourceful if one wants to get at the truth. Especially when the truth embodies dark family secrets."

His smile never faltered. "And just what was this dark truth? If you don't mind my asking."

"You fault my methods, but then wish to savor the fruit of my labors."

His blue eyes glittered with amusement. "Guilty."

Mollified, she went on. "Apparently, Grandfather had an older half brother, conceived on the wrong side of the blanket."

"I see."

"My grandfather knew nothing of his existence until the reading of his father's will, which contained a paltry provision for his illegitimate first-born son. Grandfather, the honorable man he was, tried to right the situation by supplying land and an allowance for his half sibling. From what I...um...overheard, it didn't earn him any favor with his older brother who, apparently, always felt the title rightfully belonged to him."

"An age-old slight. But hardly your grandfather's fault."

"Exactly. How he'd have reveled in the knowledge his descendent, Garrick, would one day hold the Maidstone title."

Zeke steepled his fingers. "Garrick James is the grandson of your grandfather's half-brother?"

She nodded. "Now Baron of Maidstone, and my legal guardian. For five more months."

"Yes." His brows knitted, and he drummed his fingertips on his armrest. "That brings me to another question. How on earth did your nemesis wind up your guardian?"

"Grandfather legitimized him before he knew what a monster Garrick really was."

Her grandfather had thought securing the title in such a way, and making her the man's ward, would keep her safe from ne'er-do-wells who might try to marry her to secure her substantial inheritance and the Maidstone title, in one fell swoop. Too late, he realized he couldn't trust Garrick with the power he'd granted him.

Seconds ticked by with Zeke apparently lost in thought.

Their conversation had reached its end.

But Kitty didn't want to say goodnight. Not yet. Not when being with him felt so—Crimey. She didn't have the words. It was like a hard to reach itch finally being scratched.

"Tell me about you and—Caden, was it?"

Zeke lounged back and grinned. "Yes. Caden and I haven't seen each other much of late. My fault, I admit. I'd hoped to catch up with him during my time in London. Who knows, perhaps since my stay has been unexpectedly extended..." He left off with a negligent shrug.

She bit her lip. "I'm sorry I've caused so much trouble. You've had to alter your plans and—"

"Kitty."

Gooseflesh sprang up over her limbs at the sound of her name, spoken just so, in his rough velvet whisper. "Yes?"

"We've been over this ground. There's no point discussing it further. There is something I'd like to address, however..."

"Yes?" she repeated.

He unfolded himself from his chair and moved to stand directly before her. "I'd like to collect my forfeit."

Her mind went blank. "Excuse me?" He practically towered over her. She untucked her feet, planted them on the ground, and grasped the arms of her chair.

For a moment he stared down at her, his expression unreadable. Then he bent to take both her hands in his, and tugged her to her feet.

"What are you—"

"I won our game," he said, his voice a low rumble.

She frowned in confusion.

"The chess game. Now I'm claiming my prize." He cradled her cheeks in his warm palms.

Her insides melted like wax over a flame. "What do you—"

His mouth covered hers in a searing kiss.

Chapter Thirteen

He hadn't meant to kiss her, but sometime between the start of their chess game and the mid-way point of their conversation, the need to taste her lips became an all-consuming craving, until he burned with it.

Her lips were sweet, and damned delectable, and his insides clamored for *more*. But he held back, waiting for a sign.

Seconds passed during which she held herself statue-still. He half-feared, half-hoped she would push him away.

Then those plump lips softened beneath his and her body, wraithlike, swayed toward him. Something hot and primal flared to life inside him.

He cupped the crown of her head with one hand, anchoring her in place, while his other hand skimmed her lower back, drawing her closer.

Her body, pliant and lithe, contoured to fit every hard angle of his. He grasped a handful of the long hair hanging down her back and the scent of her floated up at him like lavender vapor.

He wanted her. Wanted to explore every inch of her creamy skin, inhale the sweet feminine elixir of her that had him so drugged he couldn't think.

A soft moan escaped her, and the proof of her desire for him was like fuel on an already blazing inferno.

"Kitty, touch me," he said against her mouth, his arms tightening around her, as an instinct he could not fight took control of his will.

Her hands fluttered in the air before landing, feather light, on the pockets of his waistcoat. Too much damned material. He wanted her flesh on his.

He held his breath as her fingers crept upwards to clutch his shoulders. Then she was cradling his nape, her cool fingers toying with the hair at his collar.

Lust unfurled low in his belly. *More* his body screamed. He slanted his lips over hers as hunger tore at his insides. His tongue flicked at the corners of her mouth, seducing her lips apart little by little until, finally, he slipped inside. *Sweet Jesus*, she tasted like heaven. Better even than his memory of her, plaguing him day and night.

She mewed and pulled closer. The teasing weight of her hips through the layers of fabric barraged his self-control, urging him to carry her to the hearth, lay her down, and pull up her skirts. It would be so easy. So sweet.

He must be out of his ever-loving mind.

Calling on a will he no longer knew if he possessed, he forced his mouth from hers. He pressed his forehead against hers to stare down at her.

Her eyes were closed, her lips parted. Her breaths, coming in short little pants, whispered against his jaw.

Her lashes fluttered open, and their gazes locked. For a moment he lost himself in those pale green eyes, shining with desire and wonder.

Like a girl who'd never been kissed.

Guilt smote him, hot and swift.

His hands dropped, and he took a faltering step back.

A scuffing noise sounded in the open doorway, and he glanced up in time to see James skulking past the threshold. Perfect.

Kitty didn't appear to have noticed him. "Zeke? Why did you"—she swallowed—"do that?"

Because I'm an idiot who couldn't leave well enough alone. He attempted a smile that felt more like a grimace. God, he hated himself in that moment.

"Why did I kiss you? Have you never surrendered a harmless kiss as penalty for losing a parlor game?" In self-defense, or maybe self-recrimination, he wielded his supercilious tone like a knife, knowing it would put her off him for good.

Hurt flashed in her eyes.

"Plus, we had an audience to impress."

Her eyes widened in horror before her gaze shot to the doorway. She took a step back, wobbling a bit when her legs collided with her chair. "Who?" she choked.

"Who else? Who better?"

She covered her lips with shaking fingers.

"Dear cousin James. His seeing us in a passionate embrace can only aid your cause."

Icy green fire lit her eyes. "I suppose I should thank you, then?"

"That's not necessary."

"You are intolerable," she hissed.

He chuckled, even as his gut clenched with an aching need to pull Kitty into his arms and kiss away her ire.

Without another word, she fisted up her skirts and flounced from the room.

He stared for a moment at the empty doorway, then a humorless smile pulled at the corners of his mouth.

Good for her. Come to think of it, good for him. Now maybe she'd keep her guard up around him. Maybe she'd resist looking at him with those guileless eyes, stop plaguing him with that honeyed voice. Maybe she'd lose all her softness and sweetness and ability to wriggle her way under his skin like he hadn't allowed any woman to do, ever.

Hell. He wasn't being fair and he knew it.

He strode toward the wall cabinet and unearthed the earl's brandy decanter. He poured himself a healthy portion— then added another splash for good measure

She hadn't broached the subject of her family, hadn't intended for her words to reach inside him and wreak havoc on his emotions. What was it about her? Why did she test his self-control?

He downed a large swallow of the expensive brandy like it was swill. He was a player in this charade as a favor to the earl, damn it. Seducing Kitty was not part of the deal. He would not touch her again, whatever the cost.

***

Kitty entered the breakfast room and scanned the faces of those present. Lady Lillian, the earl, Garrick. No sign of Zeke. Again.

For the past two days he'd made himself scarce with the sole exception of appearing for the evening meal, and that was for Garrick's benefit no doubt. They mustn't appear disinterested in each other. Oh, no, not that.

His frequent absences were for the best. She lost her mind around him, went all weak-kneed, and according to the man himself, stared.

"Good morning, everyone."

A round of good mornings followed as she marched to the sideboard to fill her plate. Even Garrick issued a polite greeting.

Surprising. Contrary to the plan, the marriage contract between she and Zeke hadn't improved Garrick's attitude at all. If anything, he seemed more hostile. More dangerous. Not that he'd said or done anything specific.

It was there in his eyes. A silent threat directed at her when no one else was watching. The cold, stillness in his dark gaze reminded her of a snake, lying in wait in the grass. He wanted her to know he hadn't given up. Was, in fact, only biding his time.

So long as she never allowed him to catch her alone, she'd weather this storm. Five months to go now. Less. She could outlast him. She chose a seat near the earl, who had his nose deep in a copy of the *Times*.

"Anything interesting, my lord?"

"Just the usual dismal news from town."

Lillian spoke up from across the table. "Speaking of town, do you know Lady Torrington has eschewed her London home in favor of the country? She's asked me to tea this afternoon." Lillian's eyes glowed with undisguised pleasure. "I expect she's anxious to hear all the juicy details."

"Details?" Kitty asked.

"About the wedding. She's well aware Claybourne and I have waited a long time to see Zeke married."

"Indeed we have," the earl said, not looking up from his paper.

Kitty's cheeks radiated with instant heat. Lillian and the earl made a habit of speaking as if this betrothal were legitimate. She supposed they wanted to put on a good show for Garrick, but it made her more than a little uncomfortable.

Lillian dabbed her lips with her serviette. "If you'll excuse me, I have some correspondence to see to before leaving."

Garrick spoke up after Lillian left. "Kitty, I'm thinking of going to the Derby market this morning. When I went in to town last week to post my correspondence, I noticed the vendors had an assortment of eye-catching baubles, perfumes, hair ribbons, and such."

"Nice little village, isn't it?" the earl asked, off hand. "Been meaning to mention you have no need to venture into town to post your items, James. You can leave all correspondence with Giles in the front hall. He'll see everything gets taken care of."

Garrick smiled cooly. "As your butler informed me. However, documents related to important affairs in Maidstone I prefer to see to personally."

The earl's brows rose a fraction. "Good to know you take your responsibilities to your estate so seriously."

"Indeed I do, my lord." Garrick switched his attention back to Kitty. "As I was saying. Kitty, we've hardly had a chance to catch up since arriving to Chissington Hall. Go into town with me for lunch, and I'll purchase you whatever little trinket you desire." A wry smile curved his lips. "Call it a wedding gift. Lord knows I can afford it."

Did he really think she'd go anywhere with him, willingly? Still, she found his improved attitude encouraging. "Thank you, cousin, but I already have plans for this morning." After a moment's pause, she added, "And this afternoon."

Garrick's eyes tightened at the corners. "Another time, perhaps." He shoved back from the table and vacated the breakfast hall. "I'm off. Enjoy your day, Lord Claybourne, Kitty."

The earl re-folded his newspaper and turned an affectionate smile on Kitty. "May I inquire as to your pressing plans? Anything to do with Zeke?"

"No, my lord. I plan to scour the library for a map of this weaving estate walk you mentioned."

"Robert Adam's famous rabbit trail? I wish I could join you. It's been a long while since I ventured that path. Alas, I fear my knees are acting up. I could ask Zeke—"

She held up a hand, palm out. "Thank you, my lord, but no. If you haven't noticed, Zeke has no desire to be in my company." Heat snaked up her neck. She didn't want the earl to think she minded Zeke's paucity of attention.

"My dear girl, Ezekiel is still adjusting to"—He paused as if searching for the right words—"to being back in England. Soon enough he'll settle in. You'll see. Everything will work out."

***

Kitty lifted her face to spy the shafts of sunlight stealing through the canopy of trees. What a glorious day. She grinned, silently thanking her cousin for making her solo jaunt possible. Had he not taken himself off to the village, she'd have been forced to drag a servant along. No one else was available.

An image of Zeke flashed in her mind, and she shook her head. No. She wouldn't waste a moment of time thinking about him.

She resumed her walk. Thus far, the graveled path had woven through a myriad of flower gardens, to a pond with a burbling fountain in its center.

She crossed the pond on a wooden footbridge and stopped. The river lie ahead, in sight, with its man-made waterfall, and marked the halfway point.

Which meant, if she read the map correctly, she would find a footpath stemming off the main thoroughfare just ahead.

She spotted it, congratulating herself on her fine map reading skills. She followed the worn ground through a patch of forest, and emerged into a grassy clearing.

She found herself facing what looked to be a solid wall spanning the perimeter of the property.

She approached the fence and felt along the vine covered stone wall until she located the hidden gate. Holding her breath, she pushed. The gate opened.

Laughing with delight, she ducked inside. A real secret garden, equipped with stone bench, birdbath, fountain and all.

She settled on the slatted bench centered in the garden. Above, an open lattice-dome roof topped the enclosed space. No direct sunlight shone through the vines, leaving the secluded grounds shaded in green-tinged mystery.

Flowers—Jasmine, peony, roses, clematis—abounded. Their blossoms and the plethora of herbs she spotted, rosemary, thyme, lavender, and mint, and other flora she couldn't name, sweetened the air.

Singing birds and the faint tinkling of water filled her with a sense of peace and wonder. No doubt about it, the place had been designed for dreamers—and lovers.

Zeke's father probably brought Zeke's mother here for stolen kisses, once upon a time. And Zeke? Had he ever brought a girl here?

A fierce longing squeezed her already bruised heart. She'd banned him from her thoughts ever since the kiss in the parlor, and his subsequent total rejection of her.

But now, just for a moment, she indulged her fantasies, closing her eyes and allowing herself to picture Zeke passing through the open entrance.

He would approach her unhurriedly, a lazy smile curving his lips. His eyes heavy-lidded would fix on her mouth. He would—

The sound of leaves crunching underfoot brought her fantasy to a crashing halt. Someone walked the footpath. She stared at the opening, a sick foreboding causing the hair on her nape to prickle.

"Ah. Here you are, dear cousin." Garrick ducked into view.

Chapter Fourteen

K itty's blood hammered through her veins. She blinked, trying to clear her vision of Garrick, in this very private, very enclosed, very remote space, blocking the only exit.

But her vision wouldn't clear. He was here.

Don't panic.

She gripped the edge of the bench and forced her gaze to meet his. "Garrick, I'm surprised to see you here. I thought you'd gone into the village."

He gave her a canny smile and sauntered toward her. "Change of plans."

He lifted one booted foot to set it on the bench entirely too close to her hip. "I thought I'd surprise you on your walk. Surprise."

A chill skittered down her spine. He'd followed her, and she hadn't had a clue.

"Kitty, you must know by now if I want something, I'm bound to get it." His eyes gleamed with a sort of mania. It frightened her more than the loathing she'd come to expect.

"What is it you're after, Garrick?"

"What do I want," he said, as if savoring the words. "A private word, for one. It's been so long since we've had a moment alone."

She slid to one side of the bench. "Why don't you sit down. We can talk here." And if he sat, instead of looming over her, he'd clear a path to the exit.

He glanced deliberately over his shoulder before lowering himself to sit beside her, much too close for comfort or propriety. His thigh pressed into hers, deliberately goading her, she'd wager.

She kept her expression carefully blank. "What did you wish to discuss?"

Garrick stared at her, his dark eyes stark against his too-pale complexion. "I saw you the other night, you know."

"S-saw me?"

"Whoring with Thurgood."

A hot flush burned her cheeks. That anyone should see her in such an intimate circumstance, much less Garrick, mortified her beyond words.

"Nice effect with the missish blush." He crooked a hard finger under her chin, forcing her eyes to meet his. "Seeing the two of you did make me reconsider Claybourne's claim you'd been compromised. Not that it changes things." He paused a beat, and dropped his hand. "He'll never marry you, you know. Not after you've let him sample your wares."

"I've heard quite enough," she said, vibrating with a righteous anger she welcomed over the fear he inspired.

She half-rose, but Garrick grasped her forearm, his fingers like bands of steel. "We're not finished here," he said through gritted teeth.

She could not hope to best Garrick in an out-and-out struggle. Frustrated impotence burned in her stomach, but she resumed her seat.

He loosened his grip to run his thumb over the tender skin at her wrist. "Kitty, you must see I'm trying to help you."

His new tack didn't fool her for a second. But to buy time, she nodded once.

He opened his fingers.

She snatched her arm back and massaged her aggrieved skin.

"Cousin, what do you think will happen to you when it comes out you've been living with Thurgood for the last several months? After he casts you aside, your reputation will be ruined beyond repair. You'll be a social pariah."

"What do you care what happens to me? You've claimed your reward. You've got the Maidstone title, a substantial inheritance, and now a tidy sum in exchange for marrying me off. I would think you'd be satisfied."

A cold smile spread over his face. "The funds will soon be in my account, and they're mine to keep whether or not Thurgood goes through with the ceremony."

"Which he will." She hoped she sounded convincing. "Garrick, you must know if you do anything to obstruct my engagement, the earl will exact retribution."

His lips tightened. "I have no need to act. I have only to wait. But for your sake, I'm asking you to come away with me now. We can forget all the ugliness of the past."

She stared at him. "Come with you and do what?"

"Marry me, of course."

She laughed. "Are you mad?"

His jaw clenched. "I'm trying to save you from disaster, cousin, as any good guardian would. Do you remember the first time we met?"

His question caught her off guard. "It was at my parent's funeral."

"I watched you prissing about in your finery, you and your spoiled brother. My father told me how your side of the family held itself superior. And that day, I saw it myself, first-hand. Do you think I didn't know you whispered behind our backs?"

She frowned. She hadn't even known who he was until he left and she overheard her grandfather discussing Garrick and his kin with Collin.

"I still see it. You think you're above me. Just like the old man thought 'til the day he died." Garrick's upper lip curled into a sneer.

"You're wrong, Garrick. Grandfather took you in, accepted you as family, made you his heir."

"Ah yes. His heir. Because there was no one else to name after your dear, sainted brother disappeared. But he treated me like so much dirt under his nails."

His slander was too much. "He welcomed you into our home. And you repaid his generosity by—"

"Generosity." Garrick erupted. "Everything you took for granted all your life—position, wealth, prestige—all of it should have been mine by birth."

"And now you've got what you wanted, haven't you? What have I to do with any of your delusions of grandeur?"

"Delusions?" he roared, spittle flying as temper exploded out of him. Grasping her face between his gloved hands, he forced her to meet his wild eyes. "It's you who has delusions. When I get through with you, there will be no doubt who is superior, *countess*."

"Let. Go. Of. Me." She clawed at his leather gloves, more terrified than she'd been in her life.

Breath hissing through his clenched teeth, he pressed forward, forcing her bodily from the bench onto the thick ground cover, pinning her with his weight.

His dark eyes sparked with manic rage. He spread his legs, straddling her, trapping her skirts with his knees and immobilizing her from the waist down.

But her arms were free. She shoved at him 'til she felt her bones might snap from the strain, but he barely budged except to slide a hand between them to grasp a handful of her skirts.

"G-garrick, p-please. You really d-don't want to do this."

"No, Garrick, you really don't." Zeke's deadly calm voice shocked Garrick into stillness.

A moment later, Kitty's body was freed of his suffocating weight.

She scampered back into a sitting position and stared at the unlikely sight of Garrick dangling in midair.

Zeke looked like a Viking warrior with his golden hair wildly unkempt, his white teeth bared, his chest muscles rippling as he held his quarry aloft with one clenched fist.

"Release...me...at...once," Garrick wheezed.

"Very well." With a flick of his wrist, he flung Garrick across the courtyard.

He landed facedown.

Zeke's gaze shifted to Kitty. "Are you all right?" His voice was surprisingly gentle.

"Y-yes." She gripped the bench, pulling herself up with the intention of going to him, but her legs wouldn't support her. She dropped onto the seat.

Garrick, now on all fours, gasped for air. "You knocked...the...breath...from me."

"Get up and face me like a man." Zeke ground out.

Kitty cried out in alarm.

Garrick dragged himself to his feet, glowering at Zeke. "If you attack me, I swear I'll take her from here so fast your head will spin, contract be damned."

"She's not going anywhere."

"I agreed to the marriage, Thurgood, but the contract stipulates nothing about her living arrangements for the length of your betrothal."

"Nor does it say I can't issue you a formal challenge," Zeke replied, not missing a beat.

Kitty's heart seized. She would die if anything happened to Zeke because of her stupidity. "No, Zeke. Please." She may as well not have spoken.

Garrick seemed to realize the direness of his situation. "I didn't hurt her," he said, his voice rising an octave. "She said so herself. You can't challenge me over such a minor offense."

"A minor offense? Is that what you call—" Zeke gestured toward Kitty, his mouth clamped shut almost as if he couldn't bare to say the words aloud. "I could kill you with my bare hands."

Garrick lurched backwards, and his eyes darted toward the exit. "It looked bad, that's all. We were simply having a disagreement. She spoke out of turn and I had to teach her a lesson. Ask her yourself."

Zeke rolled his shoulders. He turned to Kitty, nostrils flaring, twin blue flames burning in his eyes. What would he do if she told him Garrick had attacked her with the intent of forcing himself on her—again?

He would defend her. She knew it like she knew her name. What if he ended up hurt? Or facing criminal charges for harming Garrick, however well-deserved?

"H-he's right. It was a mere disagreement," she lied.

Seizing his chance, Garrick pressed on. "Look, Thurgood, if you agree not to blow this whole thing out of proportion, I'll agree not to remove her from Chissington Hall this very afternoon."

A muscle ticked in Zeke's jaw. "You'll agree not to remove her from the premises for the duration of our engagement."

Garrick's mouth flattened into a grim line, but he nodded.

"Hear me well, James." Zeke's upper lip curled. "Lay a finger on my fiancé again, and it'll be the last thing you ever do. Now get out of here before I change my mind and give you the thrashing you deserve."

Garrick ran for the exit.

"Don't let me see your face for the remainder of the day." Zeke did not spare Garrick's retreating form another glance. But he fixed Kitty with a hard stare.

She could not look away if she tried. "It appears you've come to my aid yet again, my lord." Her voice sounded small. Powerless. She bit down hard on her lower lip.

"Something I wouldn't have had to do if you'd used some common sense."

She sniffed, fighting tears. Because, of course he was right.

"Why would you venture out alone to this secluded location knowing the sort of threat your cousin poses?"

She lowered her gaze to her hands, twisting in her lap. "He said he was heading to town. I had no notion he followed me until a few moments ago."

"Yes, but you know how crafty the man is. Why would you come here alone?"

"I made a mistake." She rose from the bench, moving on unsteady legs to a patch of wildflowers. Anything to hide her face, to keep herself from cracking into a million pieces in front of Zeke. She couldn't bear it. Not that, too.

"A mistake? Has it occurred to you what might've resulted here if I hadn't arrived when I did? Or did you simply expect me to come to your rescue again?"

He may as well have slapped her. She rounded on him. "I didn't expect anything from you. I didn't ask for your help. I didn't ask for any of this."

He arched a brow at her. "I seem to recall hearing you showed up on my grandfather's stoop."

"I did. Of course I did. What do you want me to say? I'm well aware I'm a burden on you and your family." She balled her hands into fists at her sides. "I tried to right the matter. That's why I revealed myself to Garrick at Claybourne Manor. Because I didn't want your family dragged through the gossip mill.

"I swear to you, I had no intention of involving the earl further. I didn't ask for this phony engagement—with you of all people. It's not as if I don't know you resent me for dragging you into this. If I could, I'd call a halt to this farce right now. And as to this"—she made a sweeping gesture with her hand—"I'm sorry to have troubled you. It may not have looked like it, but I was managing the situation just f-fine..."

She broke off, unable to speak over the lump in her throat. To her horror, her mouth contorted and her eyes welled with helpless tears. She turned her back on him, and pressed a hand to her quivering chin.

Zeke cursed under his breath and closed the distance between them. He grasped her shoulders. "Kitty," he said softly, his mouth close to her ear. "Enough." Using a gentle pressure, he turned her to face him.

"No," she wailed in protest as he wrapped his arms around her, enveloping her in his warmth and strength. She held herself rigid, resisting her body's disloyal inclination to melt into him and accept the comfort he offered.

He ran one hand down her spine. "I'm sorry I came down on you so hard." She felt his hard swallow. "Did he hurt you?" He asked in an achingly tender voice.

"No," she nestled into his chest, going pliant against him in spite of her good intentions. He felt so good. Smelled so good. Like soap, and cologne, and sunshine and Zeke.

He heaved a sigh. "You're wrong, you know."

Dear God, what now? She tilted her head back to gaze up at him and found herself caught by his velvet blue stare.

"I don't resent helping you."

"Yes, you do," she insisted. "Why wouldn't you? I've been nothing but trouble, and you couldn't make it more obvious you dislike me."

He gave her the lazy smile that never failed to turn her knees to jelly. "That's ridiculous."

"Is it? Not five minutes ago you lambasted me for embroiling you in yet another of my conundrums."

"I was wrong to do that. I reacted like an ogre because—" He broke off, but did not look away. "Because I didn't like seeing you hurt."

"Oh."

"And I do like you."

"You do?"

"I do. Which is why I want you to promise you won't go off on your own again so long as Garrick resides here."

"But—"

"Promise me, Kitty. Unless you want to see me face the gallows?"

She bit her lower lip. "Very well. I promise."

He tucked a loose lock of hair behind her ear, his long fingers grazing her cheek.

She shivered. Felt something warm and liquid swirl low in her belly. Time to get herself in hand. She took a small step backwards, and his arms fell to his sides.

She lowered her lashes, lest he see the sharp disappointment swamping her. "I should get back to the manse."

"I'll walk with you."

She nodded. He gestured for her to precede him out of the garden, and her gaze skimmed over him, pausing at his bare throat. No cravat? For that matter, no coat jacket. She hadn't noticed his odd state of dress until this moment, preoccupied as she'd been with more pressing matters.

He wore his shirtsleeves with the arms rolled up to his elbows and his waistcoat partially unbuttoned. Strange he should be wandering the estate in such a state of *dishabille*. It looked as if he'd dashed from a burning building.

"Zeke, how did you happen to be out here, a good mile from the house, at precisely the same moment as Garrick and I?"

Chapter Fifteen

Zeke wasn't precisely sure how to answer Kitty's question. How he'd ended up at the hidden garden at precisely the moment she needed him was simple, but also complicated.

He couldn't tell her how, for two days, he'd set out to avoid her. Ever since he'd made the grievous mistake of kissing her again, in fact.

Today, he'd been at his desk in an upstairs study reviewing a property prospectus. Repeatedly. He hadn't been able to focus. Truth be told, his mind kept straying—to Kitty. He couldn't tell her that, either.

Then, something outside caught his eye. A splash of robin's egg blue on the lawn. Without even looking, something inside him told him it was Kitty.

He damn sure couldn't tell her that.

He'd set aside the ledger, looked out the large bay window, and spotted Kitty traipsing along the famous Chissington Hall walking path in a frothy, powder blue gown—an unlikely walking dress if he ever saw one.

He followed her progress longer than he should, something he'd never dare admit, imagining what she thought when she spied the gardens, brooks, bridges, and fountains he'd seen a million times, and wishing he were there with her to experience her first time, first-hand. When she disappeared from sight, he started to turn back to his work.

Then he saw James, heading in the same direction.

He didn't exactly remember what happened after that. One minute he was at his desk, the next he bounded down the stairs, through the manse, and across the portico, practically deafened by the sound of blood rushing in his ears.

He'd known exactly where he'd find them. No way would Kitty be able to resist visiting the secret garden, and her bastard guardian would take full advantage.

The muted sounds of a scuffle coming from within the private courtyard infused him with bloodlust unlike anything he'd ever known. He still suffered the aftershocks.

He had no recollection of passing through the concealed entrance.

Unfortunately the image of Kitty, trapped beneath the animal she called cousin, would likely haunt him forever.

"Zeke?"

"Mmm?" he murmured, buying time to calm his tempestuous emotions.

"I asked how you happened to be on the same path as Garrick and I?"

Yes, she had, and he wasn't about to tell her the truth. "I often stroll the path."

"I...see." She didn't press, which was decidedly unlike her.

Zeke slanted her a curious glance.

She gazed straight ahead, her arms clasped behind her back. Her usually porcelain complexion glowed a becoming shade of pink either from exertion, or her recent altercation, or both.

Her ebony hair, caught in a ribbon at her nape, gleamed blue-black in the shafts of sunlight stealing through the thick foliage surrounding them. The length of it reached nearly to her waist, and swung side to side with every step she took.

He liked the look of her lustrous, dark mane. Liked that she usually wore it down. Liked the feel of it sifting through his fingers. An image the glossy mass fanned over pristine white sheets appeared in his mind.

The simmering lust he'd done his best to tamp down this past week exploded into a full boil—and he couldn't do a damned thing to assuage the hunger. He swallowed a groan and cursed himself, but fool that he was, didn't look away. She thought he didn't like her? He liked her too much. It was damned inconvenient.

Beside him, her pace slowed to a crawl. She started examining her clothing. "You're staring. Am I covered with dirt?"

He felt like a kid caught with his hand in the cookie jar. "Just wondering what's going through your head." It was a true statement, as far as it went.

"Oh." She blew air out of her cheeks. "If you must know, I was thinking about what Garrick said, before he..." She shook her head. "He insists he and I should marry, supposedly for my benefit."

"By God, he's got nerve." *Damn* the man.

She flashed him a grin. "I don't buy the supposed magnanimity, especially as he hasn't made any secret he holds me in contempt. I asked him why he'd wish to marry me."

"Did he give you a straight answer?"

"If I understood him correctly, and I'm not at all certain I did, he sees marriage to me as his due."

"Come again?"

"Apparently he bears a bone-deep grudge against my grandfather whom he believes usurped his grandfather's title. It's all so absurd. After everything grandfather did for Garrick, too."

She beetled her brows. "Grandfather welcomed Garrick into our lives. He thought having him around would be good for me after...Collin."

"You'd lost your parents and your brother in a relatively short span of time. He probably hoped providing you with another family member might ease your pain."

She smiled sadly. "I could have told him—should have told him how I felt around Garrick, before he contacted the solicitors."

"Garrick made you uneasy from the start?"

She wrinkled her nose. "It was nothing I could name. Just a feeling something was off."

"In that case, why didn't you tell your grandfather?"

She raised her eyes to his. They were like green mist in the muted afternoon light, and he couldn't look away if he tried.

"I didn't want to worry him and I hoped Garrick might bring him some comfort." She sighed. "I'd lost my parents, but he'd lost his only son. No parent should outlive his child."

Zeke nodded, thinking of his own grandfather's loss in a new, less selfish light.

"Grandfather was getting older and I hoped having Garrick at hand might allow him to begin the process of handing over the reins—again.

"By the time grandfather realized Garrick wasn't the man he thought, he'd relinquished much of his control over the estate. Then his health took an unexpectedly sharp decline. Otherwise, he'd at least have tried rescinding what he had done with the help of a solicitor. In the end, there simply wasn't time."

That filled in a few blanks for Zeke—like why the baron hadn't tossed James out on his ear.

"It must've galled the baron to no end."

She nodded. "The worse things got, the more he pressed me to leave Hastings House." She smiled fondly. "Silly man. As if I would ever leave him to fend for himself, especially while ill."

No. Zeke couldn't see her doing that, even though it would've made things far simpler for her. "So you came to my grandfather for help after your grandfather's passing."

"Yes," she said softly.

"We..." He broke off, suddenly needing to clear his throat. "The earl has told me how glad he is you came to him."

"Lord Claybourne has been so kind," she said, in that same soft tone.

For pity's sake, why didn't he just say it?

"I'm also glad you came to us." He meant what he said. He wanted to help her, and not simply to please his grandfather.

"Thank you for saying so, Zeke." She linked her arms behind her and lowered her head. "I wish I didn't have to trouble either of you."

Zeke had to wrestle an almost irresistible urge to haul her into his arms again. His grandfather was right. She did have a way of getting under a person's skin.

***

They cleared the arbor on the backside of the sprawling stone mansion, and Zeke uttered a muffled curse. "Damn if I didn't order James to make himself scarce."

Kitty followed his gaze to the upper terrace, where she saw not one, but two men. Both were of a height similar with Zeke's, with one having short cropped golden hair, and the other sporting a thick head of chestnut locks.

"I'm not sure either of those men is Garrick. Neither their height nor coloring seems right."

"I see what you mean. We can rule out the earl, as well."

"Are you expecting guests?" She worried her lower lip between her teeth. She hadn't anticipated having to act out this farce in front of perfect strangers.

Without a word, he took her hand, and tucked it in the crook of his elbow.

The simple gesture warmed her to her toes.

He continued to scrutinize the men as they moved closer. Suddenly he hooted with laughter. "The devil I say, but who's his partner in crime, I wonder?"

"Do you know one of them?"

A broad smile lit his face. "Indeed. It would appear my brother has come to meet my fiancé."

"Your brother? Here at Chissington Hall?" This was terrible. An absolute disaster.

Zeke eyed her wide-eyed terror with amusement. "You appear somewhat vexed. I assure you, Caden is an amiable sort."

"Hmm." If he was anything like Zeke, she'd have her work cut out for her.

The dark haired man shouted down at them as they neared the manse. "About time you showed up, Thurgood."

Zeke lifted his free arm in a brief wave. "Mystery solved as to the identity of my brother's second," he muttered before calling, "Shall we come up, or are you coming down?"

"Let's meet in the private parlor, second floor," said the golden haired man Kitty assumed must be Caden.

A moment later, both men disappeared from view.

Kitty lowered her chin to inspect her gown. The tussle with Garrick had left her favorite blue walking dress much worse for wear. Lord only knew how her hair looked. She couldn't meet Zeke's brother in this wretched state.

She slipped her hand from his arm as they reached the portico. "Thank you for accompanying me. I'll just leave you to—"

A grinning Zeke, as lighthearted as she'd ever seen him, cut her off mid-sentence. "Oh no, you don't. Caden will run me through if you escape to your room without an introduction."

She gave him a dubious look.

"Come now. What if he concludes you've something to hide?"

"I do," she exclaimed.

His white teeth flashed in a glamorous smile. "Just say hello."

"Zeke, I look like I've been rolling in the gardens rather than touring them. What will your brother and his friend think?"

"Caden and Randall?" Zeke's smile faded and his brows knitted in a considering manner. "Perhaps you're right."

"I am?"

"Wait here." He disappeared into the shadows of the portico, leaving her to brood.

She'd wanted to escape, but his agreement rankled. Especially since he looked so bloody marvelous. How was it possible? He wasn't even dressed properly, yet he still exuded masculine elegance. He'd nearly gotten into fisticuffs with Garrick, yet he still smelled of…that lovely Zeke smell.

He returned with a footman. "He'll escort you to your chambers."

The footman looked at her expectantly.

A dismissal if ever their was one. She stuck her nose in the air and started for the doors.

"Kitty?"

She tossed Zeke a withering look.

"Try not to get into any trouble between here and your bedchamber, hmm?"

She decided not to dignify his question with an answer.

Zeke watched her flounce away, head held high, hips swaying in an entirely too appealing fashion. He shook his head and started for the private parlor.

***

He hadn't intended to insult her. Had, in fact, wanted Caden to meet her. But then he'd considered the possible ramifications of Randall's presence.

He reached the parlor, and poked his head through the doorway. "Gentlemen."

Caden, standing with one hip propped on the back of the sofa, jumped up, an expectant look on his face. He craned his head to peer past Zeke. "Where is she?"

"She?"

Caden crossed his arms over his chest and frowned. "Very poorly done, mate."

His brother looked good. He'd filled out during Zeke's absence, and his complexion had a healthy cast—the product of a sport-filled summer, no doubt.

A flash of movement drew Zeke's attention to the window.

Viscount Sterling Randall uncoiled his body from the window seat to fix Zeke with a mocking accusatory stare. "Come now, Thurgood, don't play dumb. Where is this fiancée the papers claim you've acquired? Surely she's the lovely creature in whose company we just caught you." He shook his head, making a tsk-tsk sound even as his eyes gleamed with amusement.

Zeke sauntered into the room, hands tucked into his trouser pockets. "The lady sends her apologies. She's looking forward to meeting both of you at pre-dinner cocktails."

"Riddle me this: Where the devil did she come from? By God, you've only just returned from halfway 'round the world." Caden spread his arms.

"It's good to see you, too, brother."

With a huff of laughter, Caden wrapped his arms around Zeke's shoulders to thump him on the back. "Welcome home."

He returned to his perch on the sofa and crossed his arms over his chest. "Randall tells me you've been in town several weeks. Nice of you to send word."

"I would've gotten 'round to it once I discovered your whereabouts. Been a bit busy. But now you've saved me the trouble by showing up." He flashed Caden a smile, then slanted Randall a glance. "Randall. Rather surprised to see you here. Last we spoke, you had pressing business in town."

"As did you," Randall replied, not missing a beat.

"Curiosity compels me to ask how the two of you joined forces." Zeke's gaze flicked from one man to the other.

Caden spoke up. "One minute I'm breakfasting with Prinney, the next I'm reading about my brother's engagement. Naturally I made haste to London, only to find you and the earl had quit the city for Derby. At the club I ran into Randall, who informed me he'd seen you only last week. We both found it extremely interesting you'd made no mention of an imminent engagement at the time."

Randall grinned. "I do recall you being in a bit of a snit over the identity of your grandfather's servant." He paused briefly to study his nails. "Kit, wasn't it?"

Zeke nodded slowly. So Randall had reasoned out his fiancé and Kit were one and the same. Too smart for his own good.

"Kit's short for Christian, isn't it?" Caden asked in a too-innocent tone.

Zeke concentrated on unfurling his shirtsleeves as two sets of unblinking eyes honed in on him.

"As I recall, we met Lord James, Baron of Maidstone at White's the afternoon our paths crossed. Maidstone. Say, isn't he the guardian of your betrothed? Or did I misread your announcement? Oh, excuse me. Announcements,"

Zeke met Randall's eyes. "Quite right."

Randall gave a satisfied smile.

Caden glanced from Zeke to Randall, and back again. "Right, then. Zeke, do you want to tell us what the devil is going on here?"

Zeke very deliberately shut the parlor door and leaned against it. Propping one booted foot behind him, he crossed his arms over his chest and asked, "Where shall I begin?"

"At the beginning, naturally." Caden dropped over the back of the sofa, long legs extended over the cushions.

"A perfect starting place," Randall quipped, fitting his back against the frame of the window seat.

"I may as well make myself comfortable, too." Zeke went to a row of wooden chairs lining the wall, grabbed one and set it equidistant between Caden and Randall. Flipping it around, he straddled the seat.

He spent the next half hour giving them the breakdown. Detailing how Kitty had come to the earl for assistance. Her subsequent role as the earl's tiger. James's discovery of her—thanks to him.

"Once she'd been found out, Grandfather and I worked out a plan whereby she and I would get engaged. And that, gentlemen, is that."

Silence descended as Caden and Randall digested his truncated summation.

"I see." Caden finally said, steepling his fingers. "I just have one question."

Zeke raised his brows inquiringly.

"How long is this so-called engagement to last?"

Zeke began a study of his upturned boot tips. "I'd have thought you'd know by now how it works. But, for your edification, the engagement typically concludes at the wedding ceremony."

"You seriously expect us to believe the engagement's not a sham?" Caden pressed.

Zeke inclined his head at his brother. "Why would you think otherwise?"

"Because we're talking about you, dear fellow," Randall said, entering the fray.

"Oh, ye of little faith," Zeke rejoined.

"Never say you plan on marrying the chit?" Caden pressed.

Zeke arched a brow. "I have to marry sometime, don't I?"

"That's not an answer," Caden accused, aiming his pointer finger at Zeke.

"I'll wager it's the only answer we're going to get," Randall put in.

Zeke rose, replaced the chair against the wall. "If only I'd known it would take nothing more grand than my engagement announcement to shake you loose from the woodwork, Caden. I half feared I wouldn't see you before my next trip abroad."

"Actually, it took two," Caden muttered.

"Two?" Zeke asked.

"Wedding announcements," Caden clarified.

Randall threw his head back and roared with laughter.

Both brothers looked at him as if he'd grown two heads.

"You Thurgoods slay me. Quibbling over the minutiae while totally missing the big picture."

Zeke glanced at Caden, a silent query in his eyes.

Caden shrugged.

Randall sighed. "Clearly, it's no love match. Zeke, you haven't yet married your bride and already you're planning your next foray from England." He laughed anew and wiped at the corners of his eyes. "I really can't wait."

"For what?" Zeke and Caden asked in unison.

"Why, to meet the future Countess of Claybourne, of course."

Chapter Sixteen

Kitty paid special attention to her evening toilette in anticipation of meeting Zeke's brother and his traveling companion. After Zeke's implied insult concerning her appearance this afternoon, she needed to prove to herself she could make an entrance. She needed to prove it to Zeke, too, the swine.

She selected one of her favorite gowns for the occasion—the one fashioned of watered green silk the dressmaker said brought out her eyes. She asked her maid to wash and dress her hair with special care, as well. The end result was an elegant coiffure, pinned to the side to fall over one shoulder in the grecian style.

Heading down to dinner, her heart in her throat, she chided herself for her vanity. It mattered naught what Zeke's brother and his friend thought of her. It wasn't as if she and Zeke were truly engaged, and by now, no doubt, they had been versed on the private details of her life to boot.

How utterly mortifying.

The moment she stepped into the drawing room, she decided she'd made the right choice in primping to the extent she had. Because the three of them together, Zeke, Caden, and the unnamed third gentleman, fairly took her breath away. All appeared freshly shaven, expertly groomed, and had dressed for dinner in tailored dark suits. Their cravats were crisp white, starched, and tied in the simplest of knots.

Funny, she'd always liked the flamboyant bows her brother favored, but now comparing the two styles, she vastly preferred the sophisticated elegance.

What really made them stand out had less to do with their stylish looks than their demeanor. A certain shoulders-back, self-assured, confidence. Corinthians. She was in the presence of a team of aristocratic Corinthians.

Gathering all her nerve she entered the room.

"This, I assume, is the infamous Lady Kitty Hastings," spoke the man she assumed to be Zeke's brother. He and his dark-haired friend crossed toward her, offering warm smiles of welcome that set her instantly at ease.

Zeke held back, evidently intent on scrutinizing her appearance. His eyes flowed over her from head to toe, then reversed course to settle at her décolletage. His brows furrowed.

Irritation sparked through her. What complaint could the blasted man possibly have now?

At last, he sauntered forward to stand beside her. "Gentlemen, may I introduce my fiancé, Lady Christine Hastings, affectionately Lady Kitty. My lady, meet Viscount Sterling Randall, an old and dear friend of the family, and, of course, my brother Mr Caden Thurgood."

She dipped a proper curtsy, and murmured a greeting.

"My lady, welcome to the family. I must say, you're even lovelier than my brief glimpse of you from the terrace revealed." Zeke's brother bowed over her hand.

"Mr. Thurgood, how very kind of you to say."

"Nothing kind about it. Just a simple truth. And you must call me Caden."

She nodded her assent. She rather liked Zeke's brother.

Viscount Randall spoke up next. "Lady Kitty—may I call you Lady Kitty?"

"Please."

"Lady Kitty, may I offer congratulations on your recent betrothal?"

"Thank you, Lord Randall." As she spoke she slid an uncertain glance toward Zeke. Surely he'd told them the truth?

The viscount gave her a crooked smile. "I confess, after reading the announcement in the *Times*, I jumped at the chance to accompany Caden to Derbyshire to meet the lady who'd finally hooked the wily Claybourne heir. But now I see you"—he shot Zeke an accusatory look—"I begin to think it's he who hooked you before anyone else had the chance to throw his hat in the ring. That is, I assume you never visited London during the season? I'm positive our paths never crossed. I would have remembered."

"I...no," she answered.

"My loss, entirely." The viscount held his hand over his heart in a dramatic gesture.

"You'll stop groveling if you know what's good for you, Randall. Zeke's staring daggers at you," Caden said, chuckling.

"Is he indeed?" Lord Randall asked, his bland smile proclaiming his indifference to the supposed threat.

A quick glance at Zeke told her Caden had merely been teasing the viscount; something outside the parlor's large window had Zeke's full attention. She scanned the lawn and shrugged inwardly. She saw nothing but grass and, a short distance off, trees.

Soon, the gong sounded for dinner, and everyone made their way into the dining hall.

Kitty was greatly relieved to note Garrick had taken Zeke's admonishment to heart, and had opted not to put in an appearance. Between his absence and her good fortune in being seated between Caden and Lord Randall, she was having a grand time.

Which was more than she could say for Zeke. His affable mood from earlier had vanished. Oddly, witnessing his surly countenance had a satisfying edge to it for once.

Still. A moodier man she'd never known. One would think he'd be in fine spirits, what with the arrival of his brother. Yet he had hardly spoken two words since making the introductions.

He sat across from her, beside Lady Lillian, with the earl taking up the head of the table. The earl, she was heart-warmed to see, looked pleased as punch, probably owing to the fact both his grandsons were present.

"So, Lady Kitty," Caden began. "I'm trying to accept what Randall reasoned out prior to our arrival, and what Zeke confirmed only this afternoon, but I'm having a dastardly time of it."

She angled her face toward him. "Your question concerns me?"

His blue eyes, similar to, but slightly lighter in color than Zeke's, gleamed with amusement. "You could say that. I'm trying to understand how a lady as utterly feminine as you ever fooled my brother into believing you to be a lad."

The table went silent. Forks and knives froze mid-air. All eyes fixed on her.

Her stomach dropped as realization struck. Everyone knew everything. How she'd pretended to be a boy, and been caught red-handed. The subsequent false engagement she and Zeke had entered into to protect her from her guardian. Everything. She couldn't look at Zeke, the blackguard. He hadn't even warned her.

From the corner of her eye, she saw him throw up his hands. "So I'm an idiot who needs his eyes checked. Can we please move on from this?"

She ignored the outburst, and turned to Lord Randall. "You reasoned out who I was before you arrived at Chissington Hall, my lord?"

He inclined his head. "I surmised."

"How, may I ask, when we'd never met?" She had to give herself credit. She sounded very calm, even to her own ears.

"Zeke's odd manner when last I saw him. I've almost never seen him in such a snit. Definitely never over someone as, you'll pardon me for saying so, inconsequential as a tiger." Lord Randall leaned back in his chair and eyed Zeke.

Oh, how she loved seeing Zeke on the sticky wicket. "You mean he isn't always irascible and hypercritical of the hired help? I swear he'd have scarred me for life had I truly been a young man. My voice was too squeaky. My hands too dainty. My muscles poorly developed."

"Poor darling," Lillian said, with a scowl for her elder grand nephew.

Zeke winked at his aunt before tossing out, "Not to mention a horrible eavesdropper. But I wasn't all bad."

At the head of the table, the earl snorted.

Zeke sent the older man an affronted look. "Didn't I give her one of her shooting lessons?"

The earl nodded. "Quite right. Quite right, m' boy."

"You shoot pistols, Lady Kitty?" Caden asked, sounding intrigued.

She inclined her head slightly. "I know enough to be a danger to myself."

"I'll say," Zeke muttered, before taking a sip of wine.

Lucky for him, she didn't have a pistol handy now.

"Come now, Lady Kitty, you're much too humble. We practiced for weeks." The earl addressed his next words to Caden and Randall. "Girl's a crack shot." He turned to Zeke. "Zeke, tell them."

Zeke gave her a long, considering look as his fingers drummed a lazy staccato on the table. "She's a fair shot. It's readying her stance for the recoil she needs to work on."

A crisp memory of her lesson, when she'd fired and the recoil hurled her into Zeke's chest, bottom first, flooded her mind, as well as his observation concerning her soft derriere. She glared at him.

He merely smiled, his blue eyes gleaming with amusement at her expense.

She dragged her gaze down to her plate and forced herself to fork up another bite of roast beef.

"I'd love a demonstration of Lady Kitty's skills," Caden enthused. Directing his next words at Kitty he added, "What say we make a match of it? Tomorrow, if the weather holds. You and I can make up one team, with Randall and Zeke making up the other."

Randall piped up. "I think you brothers should make up a team—as per usual, the Thurgood brothers banding together against the world—and Lady Kitty can partner with me." He flashed her a winning smile.

She beamed at him.

"I don't think so," Zeke said in a brusque tone, not bothering to look up from cutting his meat.

Kitty swallowed her disappointment. Zeke made it clear he didn't fancy spending his days with her, but she thought he'd make an exception this once. And hadn't they made some headway this afternoon toward something resembling a friendship? She grabbed her wine and took a healthy swallow.

"Lady Kitty will be my partner. As her fiancé, I claim the right."

She nearly choked on her wine.

"I don't see why—" Caden began, only to be interrupted by the earl.

"Zeke is quite right. Lady Kitty and he are betrothed. It's only right he be allowed to claim the honor."

Kitty toyed with remaining food on her plate. She'd been convinced Zeke had revealed all to his brother and Lord Randall. Now she wasn't so sure. Had he kept the phony engagement secret, and if so, why?

"Very well, spoil sports. Shall we say noon? Who's in?" Caden asked.

Lord Randall, Zeke, and finally Kitty all assented to join the match.

"Excellent. Grouse or pigeons? Or deer?" Caden asked.

Kitty felt her eyes bug. She quickly schooled her features, but not before Zeke, evidently, noted her distress.

"I think the lady prefers a still mark, preferably one that was never alive. How about paper targets? If you like, we can have them cut in the shape of a bird." Zeke grinned at his brother.

"Don't let me spoil the fun. You all go on without me." She sent Caden an apologetic smile.

"Nonsense. Only your absence could spoil our fun. Paper targets it is. No animal shapes necessary," he added dryly. "We'll use concentric rings, like in archery. Does that meet with your approval, Lady Kitty?"

"Eminently. You are too kind." She folded her serviette and laid it across her plate.

"It was my idea," Zeke muttered.

She flashed Zeke an encouraging smile. "So it was. And quite a surprise, too."

Zeke flashed her an answering smile which faded in an instant. "Why a surprise?"

Kitty went blank. Had she said the last bit aloud?

Lucky for her, Lord Caden picked that moment to exclaim, "Hastings. I knew the name sounded familiar. It's plagued me all night."

Kitty turned to Lord Caden, completely ignoring Zeke's expectant expression. "Why is that? Did you know my grandfather?"

"No, I can't say as I ever had the pleasure. But I'm wondering if you have a brother...although now I think of it..." He shook his head and reached for his wine.

"Indeed I did. He passed several years ago. Lord Collin Hastings. Were you thinking of him?"

Caden gazed at the painted ceiling tiles as if trying to recall. "You know, I think I did meet your brother. In London."

"Oh?" A little thrill shot through her at the thought of Caden and Collin being city friends. Unable to contain her excitement, she sent Zeke a brilliant smile. "My lord, your brother knew Collin."

He paid her no notice. His assessing gaze was fixed on Caden.

She returned her attention to Caden. "Where did you meet in London? In one of the infamous gentlemen's clubs? Or perhaps you met at a ball during the season?"

Caden blew out a breath. "I can't say for certain. Sorry, love. But I do remember he was a...well-liked chap, wasn't he? I have a vague recollection of him going about with a rather large following."

Kitty smiled fondly. "Collin always could make friends easily. I used to hate it when he went to town, mostly because he never took me. Now I understand, of course. I was far too young to accompany him."

"Very wise of your brother, dear. And your grandfather, the baron, God rest his soul," the earl said.

A short while later, the footmen removed the last of the dinner plates.

"Shall we leave the men to their brandy, dear? Let's away to the library. I need to find a book," Lady Lillian said.

Kitty rose and accompanied Lillian from the room.

Zeke watched her leave. He waited for the ladies' footsteps to recede then turned to Caden. "Interesting you knew her brother. What aren't you saying?"

Chapter Seventeen

Zeke smoothed the white table cloth before him, striving for patience with Caden's obvious reluctance to talk. "You know something unsavory about Collin Hastings, do you not?"

Caden scratched the side of his nose. "I'm not even sure I'm thinking of the correct man."

"This ought to be good," Randall murmured before scratching a match on the heel of his boot. The faint scent of sulfur tinged the air as he cupped the flame and held it to the tip of a cheroot. "Care for a smoke, anyone?"

"Not for me. Makes me snore," the earl said.

"Love one." Caden extended his open hand.

If Zeke hadn't been convinced Caden was hiding something before, he was now. His brother detested the taste of tobacco.

He drummed his fingers on the table. Waited 'til Caden had his cigar lit and was puffing away. "Out with it," he barked.

Caden coughed.

The earl glanced from one brother to the other. "Out with what?"

Caden's eyes widened. "I haven't the vaguest notion."

Zeke motioned to the footman distributing the last of the brandy-filled snifters 'round the table. "Leave us and close the door behind you."

He brought his snifter to his nose and inhaled deeply of the strong liquor. He took a large swallow. Felt the liquid burn its way down. Then fixed Caden with a steely-eyed stare. "Tell me about Hastings."

"Something told me not to miss this family reunion," Randall drawled.

Zeke sent Randall a quelling look.

The earl spoke up, his quiet voice, but carrying the weight of unmistakable authority. "Caden, do you know something about Kitty's brother's death?"

Caden drew back, appalled. "Good God, no, my lord. Nothing like that."

"But you do know something." Zeke was trying very hard not to lose his temper.

"For pity's sake. I spoke without thinking. If you must know I kept mum for Lady Kitty's sake, and because I know it's"—Caden drew a finger under his cravat— "kind of a sore subject for you."

"Go on," Zeke said.

"I met Hastings in London." Caden glanced briefly at the earl. "At an establishment near St. James Street."

"An establishment," Zeke repeated. "A new gentlemen's club?"

Caden licked his lips and rolled the stem of his snifter between two fingers. "Not a club, per se."

Zeke's mouth hardened. "A den."

The earl turned to Zeke. "Of course not, Zeke." He switched his gaze to Caden. "Tell your brother..." His words died as he read the apology in Caden's eyes.

"How long have you been frequenting the hells?" Zeke demanded.

Guilt assailed him. If Caden was in trouble again, the blame would fall squarely on his shoulders. He'd been gone far too often over recent years. He hadn't been here to guide him or keep him out of trouble.

"Good grief, I see the guilt written all over your face, which is precisely why I didn't want to say anything." He pointed a finger at Zeke. "You're not my keeper, and I'm no child."

They glowered at each other.

"You Thurgoods do know how to keep a party entertaining," Randall said, laconically. "I really should take notes."

The earl waved Randall's comments aside. "Please, m'boy. You're practically one of them."

The genuine look of shock Randall sent the earl would normally have had Zeke laughing aloud. Not today. "After what happened last time, Cade? I really can't believe it. I expected better of you."

Caden sighed. "It's not that I frequent them. I visit them on occasion, for fun. What happened at university was a one-off. A terrible mistake. And you know I regretted it, because I had to come to you to bail me out."

Zeke glowered. "How deep are your losses?"

His jaw hardened. "You aren't listening. I have no losses to speak of. I'm not a regular at the hells. I haven't gambled with monies I don't have to lose since...that time at university. You can believe me or not. Now can we please move on?"

Zeke regarded his brother stonily. "Swear it? You're not in any trouble? You could..." He heaved a sigh. "You can always come to me. No matter what."

Caden rolled his eyes. "If you're in the country, you mean?"

Zeke winced.

Caden scrubbed a hand over his jaw, his expression contrite. "That was a low blow. I apologize."

"Good lad," the earl said.

Caden sent his grandfather a wink and a nod before continuing. "I thank you for your kind offer, Zeke. However, I'm telling you the truth. I am not in any trouble with the dens, have not been in any trouble, and will not be in any trouble. I can't say it more plainly than that.

"I didn't want to talk about what I know of Hastings because, suffice it to say, it occurred to me Lady Kitty would not be pleased. Aside from that, I know how you feel about dens and how you associate them with our father. I didn't want you looking at me like you are now, like I'm nothing but a bloody disappointment."

"Be glad I'm only looking. A moment ago I was prepared to beat some sense into you."

Caden bristled visibly. "You could try, old man."

"Boys, is this really necessary?" the earl asked wearily. "Zeke, Caden has already told you there's no need for concern."

Randall cocked a brow. "My lord, are we certain this is your eldest grandson sitting here? Because the Zeke I know was never so serious. He laughed constantly, oft times, out of turn. He goaded and bossed his younger brother with impunity, but never resembled an out and out curmudgeon. Come to think of it, the Zeke I know would get engaged to be married kicking and screaming, not with such cool aplomb."

Well, hell. Randall's description hit a little too close to the mark. He'd overreacted just now with Caden, in large part due to his own guilt.

As to going into his engagement with alacrity—well, there, Randall also had him pegged. Witness his initial reaction to the idea of marrying Kitty. He'd pitched a bloody fit.

To his surprise, Caden spoke up in his defense. "It's not entirely Zeke's fault. He has reason to despise the hells. We all know the fate that befell our father."

The earl smiled like a proud father. "Quite right, Caden. And more to the point, Randall..." He slid the viscount a look.

"Perhaps Zeke's just growing up. Marriage is the natural consequence of such an occurrence. Perhaps you're next."

Zeke and Caden laughed both at Randall's appalled expression.

"You, too, can become surly and staid in your old age." Zeke lifted his snifter in a silent toast to his friend.

Randall arched a brow and returned the gesture.

"Now, then." Caden leaned back in his chair. "The truth about Hastings. He was a known regular at some of the seedier establishments, as I recall. I might not have remembered him at all, but there was one incident in particular that etched itself forever in my brain.

"Hastings had been on a winning streak for several nights running, and more than a few of us followed his triumphs on tenterhooks, rather like watching a speeding carriage that everyone but the driver knows is about to lose a wheel. As expected, Hastings' luck ran out. He went all-in on a horrific hand—and lost."

Zeke narrowed his eyes. "How much?"

"If memory serves, something to the tune of three thousand pounds, give or take a shilling."

"Did he make good on his debt?" Randall took the words from Zeke's mouth.

"I couldn't say. He left town the next day, as far as anyone knew. I never saw him again. That was some two years ago."

"Right about the time he sailed for America."

Zeke scrubbed a hand over his jaw. "You were right to say nothing of Hastings' foolishness to Kitty. As far as I can tell, she idolized her brother. I see no reason to tarnish his memory for her now he's dead and gone."

"Here, here," the earl said.

"Now that's out of the way," Randall began after a moment, his brown eyes gleaming with speculation, "we can move on to the far more interesting subject of your betrothal."

The earl grinned. "An excellent notion."

"I'll admit, I had my doubts as to the veracity of your plans to wed, at first. But no longer," Randall said.

Zeke arched a brow at his long-time friend. "Indeed. What changed your opinion?"

Randall inclined his head toward Caden. "Hard not to see the merit is all, after meeting her, wouldn't you say, Cade?"

Caden nodded.

"Well said." The earl grinned proudly. "She's extraordinary. A real gem."

Randall switched his attention to the earl. "Yes. She's different than the usual London set. Not afraid to speak her mind." He slanted a look at Zeke. "Or take a certain person to task."

Caden shrugged. "Randall, I don't know why you're dancing around the obvious. She's remarkable to look at. Those pale green eyes of hers almost make a man forget what he's saying." He lifted his hands and began tracing a shape in the air. "And then there's her figure."

"I'll thank you not to discuss my fiancé's figure," Zeke snapped.

Caden chuckled with glee, and Zeke realized he'd been played.

Randall directed his next comment to the earl, gesturing toward Zeke with one hand. "There's the clincher. Zeke's attitude toward the damsel. Like she exists for his pleasure alone, and God save any man who challenges him. Do you know he refused to let us meet her this afternoon? Sent her right up to her room, rather than introduce us."

"Is that so?" The earl's gaze lit on Zeke.

Zeke rolled his eyes.

"I half feared she'd be banished from the dining hall this evening, locked in her room with a tray of food slid under the door," Randall went on.

"That's utter nonsense, and you know it," Zeke said, but he felt the stirrings of a grin.

Caden yawned. "Much as I enjoy any discussion that puts Zeke on the defensive, the day has caught up with me." He rose, and gave Zeke a fond smile. "It's good to have you home, brother."

"It's good to be home," Zeke replied, realizing only as he spoke the words they were true.

Randall expressed his intent to retire for the night, as well. A few minutes later, only Zeke and his grandfather remained in the room.

"I'm surprised you didn't retire with the other two, my lord," Zeke said.

The earl glanced toward the now open doorway. He lowered his voice. "I had to congratulate you on your clever ploy."

"Ploy?"

"You really took our discussion to heart. Way to show initiative."

Zeke frowned, confused. He'd expected his grandfather to grill him for answers, as in, why hadn't Zeke told Caden the entire truth. "Come again?"

"When I asked you to come up with a list of suitors, you did so in spades. A short one, I'll grant you, but I approve of your choices."

Zeke's frown deepened.

"Your brother or Viscount Randall would both make fine husbands for our Kitty," the earl continued. "Bravo on your tactical strategy. Since neither has any idea your engagement is a pretense, they'll both act quite their normal, charming selves around the girl. By the end of the week, Kitty and the boys will be fast friends."

Zeke heard a crunching sound. Realized, belatedly he was grinding his teeth to stumps. Randall was right. He'd lost his legendary sense of humor. He forced a smile. "May the lucky horse win."

The earl slapped his thigh and winked at Zeke. "That's rich, Ezekiel." He pushed back from the table. "Goodnight, m' boy." He was still chuckling as he left the room.

Zeke's pretense at amusement vanished. He supposed he should be glad his grandfather hadn't gotten any more ideas concerning he and Kitty in his head. But how he could think Zeke would assign himself matchmaker to Kitty was beyond him.

He finished his drink in one swallow, then pushed up from the table. He exited the dining hall, and stood for a long moment in the corridor. Turning right would take him to the front of the house, and the grand staircase leading to his bedchamber.

He ought to go up directly. Ought to turn in. Get a good night's sleep.

That was the thing. He wouldn't sleep. He'd lay there, like he had every night for the past week, staring at the ceiling. And imagine her. Kissing her. Touching her. Whispering things to her—things he'd never said, never wanted to say, to any woman.

He put his face in his hands. When had any of this become about Kitty? He'd entered into this nonsense for one purpose—to honor his grandfather.

Blast it all. No woman was worth this. This prowling energy. This worry over her damned wellbeing. This burning, nameless need that couldn't lead to anything good.

Tunneling his hands through his hair, he cursed, turned left and stalked down the hall.

Chapter Eighteen

Kitty loved the earl's library—the scent of leather permeating the air, the rich red and green striped silk-covered walls, the floor-to-ceiling shelves filled with books on every subject imaginable.

Seating areas comprised of comfortable wing-back chairs and sofas invited a person to settle in, while the thick Persian carpets blanketing dark pine floors tempted one to step out of her slippers and tiptoe around the room in just her stockings.

A log in the hearth popped, reminding her the fire would soon be nothing but glowing embers. She ought to go to bed and get some rest before facing the impressive bunch of Corinthians that had descended on her. She smiled. They were an entertaining lot, save Zeke.

He was something else entirely.

She needed to quit thinking about him. Which was why she opted to stay behind when Lady Lillian suggested they turn in for the night. A book to occupy her mind seemed like just the thing.

She approached the book shelves, stopping in front of the section on architectural design where she'd picked up the tome on Chissington Hall's construction. Fascinating reading, but it had landed her in a hill of trouble. She moved on.

Books on scientific study, psychology, politics. None struck her fancy. She could go for a good novel, but so far hadn't spotted any fictional works.

Which left...she closed her eyes. Smiled. *Of course.*

She adored books on travel and geography. Atlases contained more than simply maps. Their first-hand descriptions of far-away lands and cultures satisfied her thirst for knowledge and adventure, while keeping her safely at home.

Someone like Zeke would never understand.

But she wasn't supposed to be thinking about him. She craned her head, eyeing the top shelf. Should she climb the gliding ladder tonight, or wait for another day?

She wasn't exactly dressed for it. She fingered the delicate green silk of her evening gown, disheartened that no one complimented her on her finery. True, the earl had, as had Lord Randall and Caden. Come to think of it, Lady Lillian had remarked on her gown. Oh, bother. *He* hadn't noticed.

Zeke, Zeke, Zeke. She had to get him off her mind. She grasped the rails of the ladder and started up. Her slippers skidded on the rails, so she kicked them off and continued climbing.

Halfway up, she peered down to where her shoes lay. They seemed very small from this distance. Probably best to set her sights on the top shelf and press on.

Reaching the top, she saw right away her perseverance had been worth the effort. Grasping the ladder rung with one hand, she used her free hand to finger the spines, reading the titles as she went. Milner's *Descriptive Atlas, S.D.U.K. Family Atlas,* Bromme's *Illustrated Hand Atlas.* They all looked promising.

There looked to be more atlases further down the shelf. Which meant climbing down, sliding the ladder over and climbing back up. Or she could glide sideways on the ladder. How hard could it be? Grasping the curved mahogany edge of the bookshelf, she gave a little push.

The ladder took off at breakneck speed toward the other side of the room. Using one hand, she grasped the passing shelf. The ladder came to a jerking halt. Her body did not.

Chirping in alarm, she clung to the ladder's rails as the lower half of her body levitated. Heart racing, and feeling rather like a monkey, she wriggled toes of her right foot back onto a rung, then swung her left foot to join the first. She closed her eyes and leaned her forehead on cool railing—and giggled. Monkey indeed. A bloody lucky one.

"Is there a bird nesting up there, or was that you I heard just now? And what the devil are you doing up there, with no one about to hear if you fall?"

Zeke. Of course. She giggled harder and prayed he hadn't actually witnessed her graceless flight.

"Are you quite all right?"

She opened her eyes and peered down at him. "Quite. Why do you ask?" Another giggle escaped her. She bit her lip.

He stood, hands on his hips, directly beneath her, staring up. "Oh, I dunno. Your death grip on the side rails, perhaps?" His gaze roamed over her, searching for further ways to insult her no doubt. "Your..."

She waited, but he didn't go on, merely continued to stare up at her. No, not at her. Under her. She scooted her stocking-clad feet closer together. "What are you doing in here?"

"Looking for you. What're you doing up there?"

"Looking for a book."

"You couldn't find one down here?" He moved his hand in wide sweep.

"Are you saying you'd like me to come down?" she asked.

He appeared to give her question some thought.

Mostly just to annoy him, she perused the titles she'd risked her life to reach. "Oh, my. Hullo there." She traced the spine of the book with one fingertip.

"Yes, I'd like you to come down," he finally said. "Are you having a conversation with yourself up there?"

She couldn't wipe the grin off her face. "Did you know you have one of my parents' works? *Atlas to the Historical Geography of Europe.*"

"Wonderful. Feel free to bring it down with you. Now."

"Yes, my lord," she said with a tiny salute. She pulled the tome from the shelf and hugged it to her chest with one arm. Hmm.

Getting down would be tricky with only one hand holding the rail.

She stretched one foot downward till her toes contacted solid wood, then shifted her weight. Sliding her gripping hand lower, she lifted her upper foot and navigated it to meet the lower, then began the process again.

"At this rate, you'll be up there till morning."

She gritted her teeth. "I'm going as fast as I *caaaan...*" A blur of leather book spines passed before her eyes as she plummeted toward her death.

She landed in a pair of strong, masculine arms.

Breathless, speechless, Kitty gazed up into Zeke's face. His smoky blue eyes shimmered with suppressed emotion. Anger? Amusement? She couldn't tell.

"Thank you?" she said.

He shook his head and strode from the bookshelves. "I can't leave you to your own devices for five minutes."

At least he sounded more exasperated than annoyed.

He dropped heavily onto a well-cushioned sofa located in the most dimly lit, private corner of the room.

Displaced air swirled softly around them, mingling the scents of leather, smoke, brandy, and Zeke. Her belly trembled with giddy delight at being in his arms, the feel of his warm, hard chest against her ribs, his face so close she could kiss his lips if she dared—which she wouldn't, any more than she would twine her arms around his neck and burrow her face into his warm skin.

But she wanted to. Like nothing she'd ever wanted before. It was maddening.

Meanwhile he probably didn't even realize he still held her.

He shot her a sullen look. "It's a wonder you survived this long."

She searched her brain for a smart reply—but no words came. She couldn't focus on anything beyond the intoxicating scent of him. She shifted and he loosed his hold enough so her her bottom settled onto his hard thighs. Heat swirled through her low belly. It felt oddly...good.

"At least you have the good sense not to argue." One corner of his mouth hitched upward in grudging amusement. "By the by, you're welcome."

Helpless to resist the urge, her gaze locked on his lips, on that captivating hint of a smile. "You do appear at the most opportune moments."

He pulled his arm from beneath her knees, freeing his hand to toy with one of the loose tendrils of hair framing her face. His fingers were warm and gentle against her cheek. "You could've been seriously hurt."

Their eyes met and held.

"You look very beautiful tonight," he said, his voice gruff.

Had she knocked her head during the fall after all? Because it sounded like Zeke had just complimented her. "Thank you."

He shrugged.

She lowered her lashes and, seeing what she still clutched in her arms, remembered the treasure she'd nearly broken her neck to retrieve. "Do you want to see my parents' book?" She held the tome out for his inspection.

"Yes." He plucked the atlas from her hands and set it on the side table. "In a moment. First, I want to talk."

"All right." She tried to sound self-assured, as if she wasn't sitting across Zeke's lap. Was he waiting for her to extricate herself, she wondered? "What about?"

He reclined his body into a more comfortable position, pulling her along with him, and stretched out his long legs. "For starters, promise you won't go up that ladder again without someone standing by to catch you." His tawny brows knitted together. "Scratch that. Either send one of the footmen up to do your foraging, or wait until I'm available."

Here was familiar territory, Zeke and his proclivity for issuing orders.

"You and your 'promise this' and 'promise that.' Soon enough you'll have me promising not to leave my bed."

"An interesting choice of words," he drawled. His gaze lowered to her lips.

"I..." How could she think with him staring at her mouth like that?

Abruptly he dropped her onto the sofa beside him. "That's a fine bit of gratitude."

She struggled to maintain her dignity after being unceremoniously dumped off his lap, righting her skirts and curling her slipper-less feet under the hem. "I only meant I'm not totally helpless."

He ignored her, choosing instead to pick up the atlas. He set it on his lap and read, "Atlas to the Historical History of Europe, by Lord and Lady Charles Hastings. Very impressive." He flipped open the book and began leafing through its pages.

"I don't find you helpless. More like reckless, or at the very least unlucky. I want your promise, Kitty. This looks to be a fine bit of scholarship," he added, as if he'd been discussing the atlas all along.

"Very well. I promise."

He nodded and continued perusing the atlas.

Decorum forgotten, Kitty hoisted herself onto her knees to peer over his shoulder. "I'm familiar with this volume. Grandfather had a copy of every one of my parents' published works, as well as their personal travel journals in his library. I read them all a thousand times. It made my parents seem not so far away."

She leaned forward to get a better look at the page he studied, just as he lifted his head to glance at her. Her heart started a wild staccato in her chest. Any closer and their noses would collide. Or their lips. From here, even in the dim light, she could practically count his thick, tangled lashes. Could almost taste his soft, warm breath fanning over her cheek.

Zeke's brows hitched. "Had? Past tense?"

She licked her lips and told herself to ignore his, mere inches from hers. "One of the many ways Garrick has taken revenge against my family for the slight he feels he received."

"James sold off the collection?"

"Sold. Burned. Tossed. Your guess is as good as mine. I only know when we arrived in Maidstone last week, my grandfather's library had been decimated."

"I see. I hadn't realized." Zeke's eyes held a wealth of empathy—as if he truly understood how much those inanimate things meant to her.

"I did manage to salvage one totem. Something I'd tucked beneath my mattress, before I knew I'd be ru—before I knew I'd be leaving Hastings House indefinitely."

He arched a brow. "What's that?"

She pulled a long ribbon from her bodice. On the end, dangled a shiny gold band. "My grandfather's pinkie ring. See here, it has the Maidstone insignia." She held the band out to him.

He fingered the ring, studying it briefly, then lifted his gaze to hers. "The metal's warm."

Kitty inched back, tucking the ribbon into her bodice.

He huffed out a breath. "I should go," he muttered. "It's getting late. Our discussion can wait until morning."

"If you don't mind, I'd rather press on tonight. There's something I wish to discuss, as well. Something I'd rather no-one else overhear."

He slung one arm over the back of the couch, angling his torso toward her. "Very well. Go on."

"You go first."

"No, I insist." He gestured magnanimously toward her while bending one long leg to prop his foot on a small ottoman.

Good God, they could be at this all night.

She drew a deep breath and took the plunge. "I was wondering...that is, unless I misunderstood at dinner, you haven't filled your brother and Lord Randall in on all the pertinent facts concerning our engagement?"

He gazed at her with slumberous eyes. "Correct."

"Explain yourself, my lord."

"Are you so anxious to have our betrothal denounced?"

"No. I merely assumed, Caden being your brother, you would tell him the whole of it."

He studied his bent knee, plucking at the fabric. "The best way to assure your safety is to maintain the utmost discretion. There'll be plenty of time to explain everything to Caden and Randall after your cousin is no longer a threat."

She gazed at him, wonder unfurling in her chest. "You kept quiet for my sake?"

He shifted in his seat. "In my experience, secrets work best when shared with the fewest people possible."

"You don't trust them?"

"I trust them." He slanted her a look. "Do you have a particular wish for Randall or Caden to know the whole of it?"

She huffed. The truth was complicated. She didn't like to lie, but telling them now would be beyond embarrassing. "No."

He leaned forward, slapped his hands on his thighs, and rose. "It's settled, then. We'll leave things as they are." He strode toward the bookshelf, pausing near the ladder when something on the floor drew his attention.

Kitty followed his gaze. Her cast off slippers. Her toes curled reflexively into the carpet.

He scooped up the slippers and sauntered toward her. "Caden and Randall will probably stay at Chissington Hall for several weeks. You do realize we'll need to do a better job of acting the part of a soon-to-be-wed couple."

"I do? I mean, we will?"

"Don't you agree?" He stopped directly in front of her.

"I...er...yes." She reached for her slippers.

He pulled his arm back, putting the pair just out of her reach.

She wouldn't fight him for them. She laced her fingers together on her lap. "How do you propose we go about—how did you phrase it?—acting the part?"

Chapter Nineteen

Kitty perched on the sofa and waited expectantly for Zeke to clarify exactly how they could make a a more convincing couple for his brother and the viscount.

"We'll spend more time together. Doing...things." Zeke's voice had gone low and smoky.

Still holding her slippers, he crouched before her.

"Such as?" She swallowed, her eyes tracking his every move.

Without warning, he slipped his hands beneath her skirts to grasp one of her feet.

She gasped, partly from shock, and partly from the unexpected thrill of feeling his warm hands cupping her arch.

His palm skimmed upward, encircling her ankle. He squeezed gently, then slid his other hand below her foot to cup her heel. He drew the pad of his thumb over the length of her arch in a delicious sweep.

"Oh," she uttered helplessly as the tickling sensation rippled through her. "Zeke," she breathed, trying to pull free of his grasp. "I hardly think—"

"Hush," he whispered. "I'm making sure you didn't twist anything when you slipped." His words made perfect sense, but the heat she glimpsed in his eyes told a different story.

She didn't trust herself to speak, so she merely nodded.

He bent his head to his task, and his golden hair fell over his brow. He began his exploration anew, as if her interruption had caused him to lose his place.

She almost groaned from the sheer pleasure of his strong hands massaging her feet. She'd never been touched in such an intimate way, and regardless of Zeke's stated reason for doing so, she knew she shouldn't permit it now. Odd, delicious things were happening to her insides.

"Where was I?" he asked. Evidently finished with the one foot, he set it gently on the carpet, and reached for the other.

"Pardon?" She fought the urge to close her eyes and sink back onto the cushions.

"Ah, yes. You asked me what things we should do."

Through her lashes she saw his lips curve in a lazy smile as his hands stroked and squeezed.

"Yes." Her limbs felt as solid as warm jelly.

"We should undoubtedly make a habit of riding together. Perhaps each morning after breakfast. During certain entertainments, we'll team up. And...hmm."

Kitty's breath froze as one of his hands reached her calf, the path of his palm leaving a trail of fire. She bit her lip, unable to speak.

His brows knitted in apparent concentration. His palm moved higher, almost to her knee.

Dizzying heat spiraled through her. She should do something. Stop him. "Zeke?"

"Yes?" he whispered, his eyes at half-mast.

"I don't think this is at all proper."

Removing his hands from beneath her skirts, he dropped onto his knees before her. He cradled her head between his hot palms and leaned forward, his hard, muscled thighs pressing into her shins. "We are engaged to be married, are we not? We're permitted a small amount of latitude." His gaze fixed on her mouth, his eyes glittering with a hunger that stole her breath.

"But we're not," she argued without any heat. "Not really."

His gaze had not strayed.

Her lips parted of their own accord, a silent demand for his kiss.

"Finally, we're getting somewhere." His fingertips skimmed over the curve of one ear, then danced feather light across her cheek. "How are we to convince anyone if you don't believe yourself?"

She closed her eyes and nibbled at her lower lip.

She heard his soft laugh, then felt his hair tickle her nose as he dipped his head, bringing his mouth to hover over hers.

"For the next several months," he said, brushing his lips over hers, "you must believe yourself engaged to me. Can you do that, Kitty?"

The best she could do was nod as a desperate hunger tore at her insides. "Please," she heard herself whisper, a moment before his lips sealed over hers in a hot, drugging kiss. Kitty grasped his hard, broad shoulders and held on for dear life. Combustible heat flooded her veins, burning her from the inside out.

She tugged, urging him closer. Maddeningly, he refused to budge. She wanted his body touching hers, everywhere, and she never wanted him to stop kissing her.

When the tip of his tongue played at the corners of her mouth, her lips parted in a gasp of pleasure.

"That's it. Let me taste you, sweetheart," Zeke murmured. When his mouth covered hers again, his tongue slid past her lips.

Tentatively, she touched the tip of her tongue to his.

Delight surged through her as, instantly, his arms banded around her.

Braver now, she traced her tongue over the soft inside of his full lower lip.

His hands coursed over her back, her waist, her nape, the sides of her face, as if he were as desperate to touch and feel all of her as she was desperate for him to do so. Tiny tremors vibrated through him.

She wanted to purr in awe as she recognized her own womanly power over this confusing, seductive, enigmatic lion of a man.

Her arms twined around his neck, her greedy fingers slipping into his thick mane of hair. She kneaded like a kitten, loving the feel of the silken gold.

"Kitty," Zeke gasped against her lips, and pressed her back into the sofa cushions.

The weight of him felt so good. Still, he wasn't close enough. She whimpered with a nameless need and arched into him.

He hissed in a breath, and loosed an agonized groan. A moment later his lips left hers, leaving her dazed and oddly desolate.

His face pressed into the curve of her neck like a hot stone, his body heaving with ragged, labored breaths.

"Zeke?" she whispered.

He didn't respond immediately, and Kitty wondered if he'd heard. Then she felt the scrape of his stubble against the underside of her jaw as he smiled. Though his heart pounded into her chest like a base drum, he pressed a light kiss against the abraded skin and asked in an amused tone, "Yes?"

"Was Garrick watching from the hallway again?"

His shoulders began to tremble, then his entire body shook. A moment later, he pushed himself off of her to balance on his knees. He threw his head back and bellowed with laughter. "Oh, Kitty," he breathed when his mirth finally subsided. "Was that a serious question?"

She glared up at him from her reclined position on the sofa. "The last time you kissed me, you told me you'd done so to impress Garrick and—"

He shushed her holding one finger to her lips. "No. To my knowledge, we had no audience."

He unfolded from his kneeling position to sit beside her on the sofa. He reached out to smooth the damp tendrils at her temples, an indulgent smile curving his lips.

"Then why?"

His smile grew cocksure. "Why did I kiss you?"

She nodded in growing impatience and dragged herself to a proper sitting position.

He shrugged. "It suited me to do so."

His words cut her to the core. But what had she expected? A declaration of love?

Her cheeks burned and the backs of her eyes stung. Oh, no. She would not humiliate herself by crying in front of him. She hinged forward and searched at her feet for her slippers.

"You horrible man," she bit out as she jammed her feet into the slips of satin and sprang from the sofa. She launched herself toward the library door, still choking on outrage. "You perfectly odious—"

"Kitty," Zeke said, his voice the only warning she had that he'd closed in on her before his large hand grasped her elbow, halting her mid-stride.

"Let go of me," she said through her teeth.

"Kitty. Look at me."

She glared at him over her shoulder.

"That came out badly. You misunderstood what I meant. I only—"

"I understood perfectly. Now understand this. I never want you to do that"—she waggled her fingers toward the vacated sofa—"ever, again. Do you hear me?"

A boyish grin spread over his damnably handsome face. "I hear you, but I'm afraid I can't promise to comply. I liked it way too much. As did you."

She swiveled to faced him. She drew her hand back, prepared to slap the smile off his lips.

Zeke caught her wrist before her palm got anywhere near his face. Adding insult to injury, he laughed. "I can see you're upset, Kitty. Let's table this discussion 'til tomorrow."

She huffed and jerked her arm free. "This discussion is over now."

She marched past the threshold, then spun to glower at him. "I'll tell the earl. I'll..." She frowned realizing the flaw in her plan. The earl wouldn't want Zeke to stay away from her. He'd force him to marry her.

Zeke rubbed his chin between his thumb and forefinger. "You know, I think you should tell him."

She shook her head in frustrated disbelief. Zeke knew very well the earl would demand they wed, probably by special license. He'd entrap himself to outwit her? Just like a man. Evidently none of them had any sense till they reached the age of her late grandfather or the earl.

"This is lunacy," she said, throwing her arms up.

His eyes narrowed on her face. At least he no longer appeared quite so delighted with himself. "Go to bed, Kitty," he said softly. "We *will* talk in the morning."

***

Zeke stood in the doorway, listening to the receding pitter-pat of Kitty's footsteps. Amazing how she could scream *vexed* with nothing more than the sound of her feet on the stone floor.

He wished he could read his own emotions so easily. Wished he could understand what in hell had come over him, not only tonight, but since he met Kitty.

From the beginning, the infusion of Kitty into his life had heralded inexplicable results. Like tonight, when she glided into the parlor looking like a princess, or sea nymph, or whatever you called someone so damned beautiful she stole your breath.

The minute he laid eyes on her he'd wanted to scoop her into his arms, carry her to the first available bedchamber and devour her. That reaction he could almost understand.

But what of the almost palpable anger that followed? He hadn't known where to direct it. At Kitty, who'd waltzed in showing more skin than Randall or Caden or any man ought to see, or at his brother and friend for fawning over her? Wasn't that grand? He'd never been jealous in his life.

He covered the lower half of his face with both hands and prowled the dimly lit room. Anything to alleviate this restless, simmering energy. This feeling of losing himself, who he was. All because of one tenacious, audacious, irresistible wench.

He stopped in front of the oriel window. Leaned his over-heated forehead against the cool glass. No woman should have so much influence over a man. Should make him crave her. Her laughter. Her spirit. Her attention. Her body, for Christ's sake.

Witness his father. His ever-smiling, quicksilver father, who had lost his will to live, his ability to care for anyone or anything, when Zeke's mother had the bad grace to die.

He didn't want to want Kitty like he did, and he refused to confuse want with need. He did not need her. It was that simple.

He pushed away from the glass. The heavy atlas on the side table caught his eye.

She'd held onto the thing and had barely made a sound, brave little idiot, as she'd tumbled to the earth. He smiled, thinking how easily he'd caught her. He hadn't wanted to let her go.

He approached the seating area where he'd taken her. The darkest, most private corner of the large room.

He dropped onto the sofa, his head lolling over the backrest.

Maybe he was looking at this all wrong. He liked Kitty. What was so wrong with that? He wasn't spouting poetry. Wasn't promising undying love. Far from it. He'd barely even told her he found her attractive. Clearly he didn't worship her like his father had done his mother.

So he thought about her when she wasn't around. Who wouldn't, given the circumstances? The threat James posed, this phony engagement, not to mention the shared living arrangements.

If he was being honest, he had to admit he liked her, as well. More than once he found himself glued to her every word. Found himself enthralled with the woman who, unlike him, had overcome the handicap of seemingly uncaring parents. A woman who'd risked everything to stand by her grandfather, and who never doubted her own ability to rise above whatever circumstance life threw at her.

But none of this—not the danger, not the pretense, nor even liking her—explained his physical hunger for her. He wanted her. Wanted to grab her and drag her down and pour himself into her. His fingers dug into the velvet sofa cushions as need ate a hole through his insides.

It only made it worse she hungered for him equally. She might not like it, beyond a shadow of doubt didn't understand it, but the truth was there in her response to him. In the way she clung to him, opened for him, inviting him to touch and taste and...God, he was rock hard again.

Groaning, he tunneled his fingers through his hair. He ought to feel bad about his behavior tonight. He'd behaved without scruple. Again. He'd taken advantage of her innocence, of her desire for him.

But the truth was, he felt good. Better than he had in days, aside from the hunger gnawing at his loins.

What now? What was he to do about Kitty? He flung himself lengthwise onto the cushions, his legs hanging over the front of the sofa. For a long minute he lay there, staring at the plastered ceiling. Then the answer came to him and he couldn't stop the grin spreading over his face. Because the answer was as obvious as it was simple.

By God, the answer had fallen right into his hands—literally. He stood up, scooped the heavy tome off the table, and marched from the room, whistling.

Chapter Twenty

Kitty awoke to the rumble of thunder. Snuggling deeper into her bedclothes, she recalled the most delicious dream. Zeke, in the library, kissing her into oblivion. Except...

She scanned the room and spotted the crumpled green silk gown draped over the post at the foot of the bed. Groaning, she rolled onto her belly and crushed her face into the down pillow.

As if the heavens seconded the magnitude of her idiocy, an ominous crack of thunder reverberated through the windowpanes, followed by a rising din of rain, pounding the roof tiles and grounds below. She lifted her head and smiled. Good. The nasty weather meant no shooting match. She could mill about the bedchamber all day if she so chose.

She grinned as Zeke's edict from the night before came to her. *We'll need to spend more time together. Doing...things.*

"Doing things, my big toe," she muttered—and dragged the covers over her head.

****

Zeke had spent about as much time dawdling over his kidney beans, eggs, and toast as he could stomach, and still Kitty hadn't come down for her morning meal.

Was she ill? According to the housekeeper, Kitty hadn't missed breakfast once since arriving at Chissington Hall.

Perhaps he'd arrived too early in his zeal not to miss her. No matter. He'd wait her out. He allowed the hovering footman to remove his plate. Drummed his fingers on the white tablecloth. Frowned into his coffee cup.

Boot steps sounded in the corridor seconds before Caden and Randall entered the breakfast room.

Zeke sighed inwardly. If she presented herself now, there'd be no chance for a private conversation. He dropped his cheek in his palm and regarded his brother and Randall.

"Sadly, our shooting exercise will have to wait," Caden said as he heaped food onto his plate from the sideboard. "The sky's positively black, not to mention the grounds are soaked." He started for the table and glanced pointedly at the empty chair beside Zeke. "Where's your lovely fiancé this morning?"

Zeke ignored the question. He flicked a bored glance over Randall, currently eschewing food in favor of tea. "What's wrong with your appetite, Randall?"

"Tea first, food later." He scraped back a chair. His eyes drifted over the empty plate before Zeke. "I see you got an early start."

Zeke shrugged.

Caden grinned. "Let me guess. You hoped to catch your fiancé alone before the rest of us descended on you." He waggled his brows. "Better luck next time. Pass me the *Times*, will you?"

Zeke snorted and slid the paper toward Caden, hoping neither he nor Randall noticed his cheeks going ruddy. His brother's jest hit too close to the mark.

Aunt Lillian swept into the dining room. "Good morning."

The earl appeared a few moments later, followed by James who pointedly avoided glancing in Zeke's direction.

Probably a good thing. So far he'd managed to hang on to his pleasant comportment. But the day was young.

"Ah—the infamous Lord James, I presume?" Caden asked equably.

The earl made the formal introductions.

More plates of food filled. More pots of tea and coffee drained. Still no Kitty. Zeke seriously pondered the notion she'd come down with something—though she hadn't seemed the least bit ill last night. His mouth curved in a self-satisfied grin.

He suddenly became aware of a heavy silence in the room. Glancing around the table, he noted every set of eyes, save James's, centered on him. "Did I miss something?"

"Only the last five minutes of conversation," Caden said.

"Ah, but Caden, the crafty grin on your brother's face tells a tale all its own. One can only hazard to guess what's brought that devil's gleam to his eyes."

Zeke ignored Randall. "Forgive me, Caden. Kindly repeat whatever it is you said."

Caden shrugged. "I asked how your trip to South Africa went. Grandfather says you purchased a diamond mine and brought back some sort of rare stone."

"Yes, I purchased majority shares for the family, and the mine promises to be a fruitful. I'm glad to hear you're interested."

"What of the diamond?" Randall asked.

Zeke leaned back in his chair. "For starters it's huge—and rare, thanks to its unique coloring. It's got a bright green orb, with little flecks of crystalline gold in its center."

"So rare it has its own name," the earl added. "Your brother came up with it."

Zeke answered the unspoken question. "Tiger's eye."

"Prescient, your having brought this tiger's eye back with you, eh?" Caden asked.

Zeke knew what his brother referred to. He assumed Zeke would make the diamond into a ring for his bride to be. He started to deny any such thing, but his mind filled with an image of Kitty, gazing up at him in that way she had of looking at him, some combination of hero worship and gratitude and womanly desire all swirling in those frosty green eyes of hers.

Footsteps sounded in the corridor. He glanced at the open doorway.

Not Kitty but Giles appeared. "My lord? Mr. Hallis has arrived from London. He's awaits you in your den."

The earl's man-of-affairs.

The earl shot Zeke a look. "Good. Zeke? Care to join us? We're going over the books for the last quarter."

In fact, Zeke did want to talk to Hallis. He had questions for which the solicitor might be able to provide answers. He just hadn't wanted to talk to him today. Today, he had another conversation in mind entirely. On the other hand, Kitty clearly wasn't going to make that conversation easy.

He pushed back from the table. "Lead the way."

***

Kitty rose from the pretty, rose-colored wingback chair in her sitting room, and moved to her open window. The breeze had picked up, carrying with it the thick scent of wet earth. She peered through the mist-cloaked air at the rain soaked lawn. It was indeed a fine day to laze about. Too bad the excitement she'd felt at the prospect of evading Zeke had faded with the passing rain.

She had to get out of her self-imposed prison, even if it felt as if she'd be losing a battle of wills, against herself, if not Zeke.

Had Zeke noticed her absence? Doubtful. But say he had, and she had the unfortunate luck to cross paths with him, he'd take one look at her and know she'd done little more today than relive the memory of last night. The thrill of his hands on her skin, the magic of his lips sliding over hers. The intoxicating awareness of his sharp desire for her.

Turning from the window, she glanced at the treatise on Chissington Hall she'd been leafing through, again, and thought longingly of the atlas she'd gone to such lengths to unearth last night, then promptly abandoned in the library, thanks to Zeke.

Bother. Snatching up the Chissington Hall treatise, she made for the door.

She raced through the meandering corridors, a woman on a mission, eyes peeled for any sign of *him*. She passed only a chambermaid scurrying from one room to another, duster in hand. Much ado about nothing.

Except...as she approached the open doorway of the library, she overheard masculine voices coming from within.

Her pulse kicked up a notch as a golden haired scoundrel with a dashing white smile and hot, wet lips sprang to her mind. She wiped her suddenly damp palms on her skirts and crossed the threshold.

Caden and Lord Randall sat across from one another, bent over a board game of some sort. Zeke was nowhere in sight.

Her traitorous heart sank.

She fixed a bright smile on her face. "Good afternoon, Caden, Lord Randall." She strode toward them. "I've come to exchange my book." She held it out in front of her like she needed to show proof.

"Good afternoon, Lady Kitty. This is a welcome surprise. I've had enough of this bloke's company to last me the week." Caden rose. He clipped a slight bow.

Lord Randall followed suit. "I had begun to lament we might not see you this afternoon at all. Spending time with a beautiful lady on a rainy afternoon is one of my favorite pastimes."

A smile tugged at her lips. "If only I'd known." She hugged her book to her chest and rocked back on her slippers as she eyed the half-played game. "You've been playing chess?"

"Playing? More like losing. A tedious endeavor, really," Caden said.

"Meanwhile, I've quite enjoyed myself," Randall quipped.

Caden scowled. "Perhaps we should come up with another game, for three this time. Unless you're set on resting further, Lady Kitty?"

"In truth, I'd love to. I was beginning to feel like a caged rabbit, staring at the same four walls all morning."

"Silly, goose, why'd you lock yourself away all day, then?" Caden asked.

She blinked. She could hardly tell them she'd been thoroughly kissed last night, had liked it way too much, and as a result, had hidden all morning. "I...er, had the headache. But it's better now."

"Excellent," Caden said. "I daresay it's a good thing the rain delayed our shooting match. Explosive firearms would not have helped matters."

She smiled and approached the shelves to return the book. The less said the better. After re-shelving the treatise, she glanced at the seating area where she and Zeke had...where she'd left her parents' atlas. It was nowhere in sight.

"Have either of you seen the atlas that was on the table just over there?" She pointed to the side table, her face burning as if they could see into her mind and know what had transpired on the sofa beside that table.

The men shook their heads, looking at each other as if to confirm neither had moved it.

"Sorry, Lady Kitty. It wasn't there when we came in," Lord Randall answered for both of them.

So it had been re-shelved. Now she'd have to go searching for it again. "Have either of you seen..." *Zeke* "...the earl today?" she asked, re-joining them.

"At breakfast," Caden replied. "After which his man-of-affairs arrived. I believe he and Zeke are still meeting with the fellow. Lady Lillian's made herself scarce, as well. Said something about retiring to her chambers to see to some correspondence."

"As for your guardian, he claimed he received some reading material from his solicitor. If you were interested." Randall offered, with a shrug.

Her smile brightened at that news. "What should we play?"

"Too few for whist," Randall said.

"Too many for chess," Caden said, before muttering, "Thank God."

Kitty giggled, delighted to be free from her room, safe from the threat of running into Garrick, and in the company of two good natured, non-surly, gentlemen. "Most parlor games involve a greater number of people than three." She glanced around the room. Her eyes lit on a familiar object. "I have an idea. Follow me, if you please."

She marched toward the sitting area she'd dubbed the man corner, due its sturdy burgundy leather sofa and matching armchairs. It also boasted a good-sized globe, situated between the two chairs.

The globe's glossy surface and brass axis gleamed, reflecting the muted daylight eking in through the window. She touched the surface lightly and set it to spinning. "Do either of you gentlemen know anything about geography or anthropology?"

The men slanted competitive glances at each other.

"I can't speak for Randall, but I certainly do." Caden looked supremely self-assured.

"I was top of my class in world studies," Randall rejoined.

They faced off a moment longer before switching their attention to her.

"What have you in mind, my lady?" Caden asked.

She gestured for them to sit before lowering herself onto one of the armchairs. "I propose a game whereby we take turns spinning the globe. I will close my eyes, and when the player whose turn it is calls time, I will place my finger on the globe, like so." She broke off and spun the globe again. Next she closed her eyes, and after a brief hesitation, dropped her finger onto the rotating world map, thereby stopping the rotation. Then she opened her eyes, peeling her finger slowly back to read the name of the target location. "Antarctica," she said.

"In this instance, whoever spun the globe would recite a little known fact about Antarctica. Such as the median temperature, the first known settlers, the indigenous population, or anything factual, just so long as it's not too well-known. The other two players must decide whether the information is true or false. If they choose correctly, they win a point."

"How would any of us know whether or not the person citing these little known facts is being truthful?" Caden asked.

Kitty gave him a tut-tut look.

"In other words, this is to be a game of honor," Randall stated.

"I have no intention of lying." She glanced from one man to the other.

They both gave grave assurances they had not, either.

"What shall be the forfeit for the winner?" Caden asked.

"Ah...." She remembered the kiss Zeke claimed in forfeit the night he'd beaten her at chess. Praying her face hadn't gone pink, she said, "Winner's choice."

***

Zeke let himself out of his grandfather's study, leaving the earl and his long-time man of affairs, Carson Hallis, to share a well-earned glass of cognac. Irritable after spending what amounted to the entire day poring over estate reports rather than settling things with Kitty as intended, he declined to join them.

He descended the stairs two at a time, anxious to get to the ground floor and finally get down to the business at hand.

At the base of the stairs, he plotted his hunt. Surely Kitty had emerged from her bedchamber by now. She was a social creature by nature and wouldn't abide staying hidden away all day unless she was ill. Something told him that was not the case.

He'd go room by room, hitting all the shared living spaces 'til he found her. He smiled and set off at a comfortable pace.

At least the morning hadn't been a total bust. He'd discussed the investigative work he wanted Hallis to assume. Primarily, he sought information on dear cousin Garrick. His history, his friends. Anything that might explain what made the man tick.

Of equal importance, Zeke wanted Hallis to check into his claim on the Maidstone title. Now that Zeke understood Garrick James' relation to Kitty, he had questions regarding his ascension to the Maidstone barony. Not that inheritance laws came up in Zeke's world often. Hell, never. But he seemed to recall learning in one of those stuffy classes on codified law a man had to be legitimately linked to the titleholder to inherit.

Laws could change. Probably had. But Zeke believed in being thorough, especially when it came to Kitty. She was his future wife, after all.

***

Kitty preened, having just answered another question correctly. She was having a marvelous time, and hadn't noticed Zeke's continued absence at all, or so she kept telling herself.

"We're all tied. Someone will have to work a bit harder at her trickery." She waggled her brows and spun the globe.

Peeling back her finger, she read. "New Zealand." She sat back. "New Zealand's native people, the Maoris, descendants of the Australian Aborigine—"

"Again with the Aborigine." Caden threw up his hands. "Let me guess. Another story of British brutality against the natives. I'm beginning to think you proposed this game merely as a way to illustrate Britain's global villainy. Much more of this and I'm likely to defect."

Kitty stared at him, a stern expression on her face.

"Yes, my lady?" Caden looked suitably cowed.

"May I go on?"

Caden, ducked his head, grinning. "Please."

"The Maoris were brutally—"

"You see?" Caden exclaimed, turning to Randall for commiseration.

Kitty didn't miss a beat. "...expunged from their lands by invading foreigners, until the year 1840 when they signed a treaty with Great Britain, promising them protection."

"Speaking as a fellow defector," Randall winked at Kitty, then muttered to Caden, "Where is she getting these facts? Does she have a notepad with history lessons tucked under her skirts?"

Kitty giggled. "True or false?"

"It's too depressing not to be true," Randall said.

Caden's eyes gleamed with triumph. "False."

Her mouth fell open. "How did you know?"

"The Maoris aren't descendants of Aborigines. They're from Polynesia."

She laughed and clapped her hands together in approval. "Bravo."

"Blast!" Randall flopped back on the sofa in defeat.

"I believe that point makes me the winner," Caden said, with a grin.

Chapter Twenty-One

Zeke heard Kitty's laughter before he came within a stone's throw of the library. An answering smile spread over his face at the unbridled joy of it. He paused just outside the open doorway, curious as to what or who had aroused her humor, and reluctant to cut it short.

When her laughter died-down and conversation resumed—he recognized Caden and Randall's voices in the mix—he stepped into the room. The trio sat on the far side of the room, making use of the sturdy leather furniture he usually favored.

The two men were clearly hanging on Kitty's every word, so much so his arrival appeared to go unnoticed even though nothing but a few potted plants and one seating area stood between him and them.

From his vantage point, he had a clear view of her profile, limned by the muted afternoon sun spilling in from the bay window.

As usual, tendrils of gleaming, inky black hair fell in delightful disarray from her loosened chignon. She twisted a fat curl around one of her fingers, and he felt something twist inside of him.

She did something to him. He couldn't put his finger on how, or why. Not that it mattered anymore. His brilliant solution made it a moot point.

Something Caden said caused Kitty to laugh and clap her hands with delight.

An answering smile curved his lips.

She nodded at Randall, and Zeke saw the flash of her crystalline green eyes as they reflected the waning sunlight. Tilting her head thoughtfully, she began speaking.

He moved a little further into the room, grateful the thick carpet muted his steps.

"My parents' first-hand descriptions painted a more thorough picture than I would find in a book."

A stab of annoyance pricked him. Why was Kitty discussing her parents with Caden and Randall?

"Your parents taught you about the Australian Aborigines and the New Zealand Maoris you lectured us about earlier?" Caden asked.

"Lectured? I did no such thing."

Zeke grinned.

Kitty went on. "According to the rules of the game, each player had to cite little known facts about the locale upon which he or she landed." She sniffed and plucked at her skirts. "I just happened to land on Australia and New Zealand. Just as I happen to have an interest in the natives of those lands."

"The"—Caden cleared his throat—"misused, downtrodden, *miserables*, I believe were some of the adjectives you used."

Kitty flashed her imp's grin.

She would take up the cause of the underdog.

A warm sensation filled his chest—along with an odd possessiveness he didn't care for at all. Damn it, he didn't know if he was coming or going these days.

He did know he was ready to have that talk with her. He took a step forward.

Caden cleared his throat. "Now, then. We need to settle the small matter of the forfeit owed me."

"Very well. What's your demand?" Kitty asked.

Zeke froze, sensing the scoundrel's reply before he uttered another word.

"A kiss from the lady, of course."

Like hell. Zeke stalked toward the group.

His eyes skimmed accusingly over Randall, the accomplice as far as he was concerned, before landing squarely on Caden.

Randall looked sufficiently cowed, but Caden, by God, had the gall to lounge back, link his hands behind his neck and grin.

"Hello, brother, finished with your meeting so soon?"

Zeke flexed his fists and imagined wiping that banal smile off his brother's pretty face. "Caden, Randall." He slanted Kitty a glance. "Lady Kitty."

She inclined her head, but kept her gaze averted. "My lord."

"We missed you at breakfast. I thought perhaps you'd taken ill," he said.

"Not at all," she replied. Then her eyes went wide as saucers. "I mean, I had a headache. Earlier. This morning."

Zeke opened his mouth to inquire further, but Caden forestalled him. "I was about to claim my forfeit from your fiancé."

"What game were you playing? Perhaps I can atone for her loss. Unless the lady objects?" He looked at her, all innocence. He hoped.

She flushed, hesitated slightly, then said, "By all means, if Caden agrees."

He bit back a smug grin. Kitty's natural inclination would be to deny his offer of assistance, but doing so would give the appearance she was vying for Caden's kiss. She would hardly wish to convey that sentiment.

"See here, what's in this for me? I was quite happy with the outcome of our game," Caden groused.

Zeke pasted a bland smile on his face, though he wanted nothing so much as to beat his chest and snarl at his brother. Kiss Kitty indeed.

"Let's say, if you win, I'll grant you"—He broke off, searching his mind for an enticing prize. He reclined his hip on the arm of Kitty's chair in a deliberately possessive posture—"The tiger's eye diamond I acquired from our mine in Africa."

Caden's face went slack.

Zeke flicked a glance at Randall, then Kitty in turn.

Everyone looked stunned.

Well, what did he expect? His words shocked him, and he'd said them. The tiger's eye diamond? What inspired him to lay such a valuable object on the table?

He'd had to come up with something fast. That was all. Besides, he had no intention of losing. "Well?"

"I'll allow the challenge," Caden relented.

Kitty briefly, and none too warmly, explained the rules of the game to Zeke.

Caden spun the globe.

"Manitoba, Canada," Kitty read.

Caden thought a moment. "So named in 1870, after the Canadian confederation purchased the land from the Hudson's Bay Company—a company in which we had shares, for a time, if you recall, Zeke."

"True," Zeke said.

Caden conceded the point.

Zeke winked at Kitty, which she pretended not to notice, but the flush stealing up her neck gave her away.

He flicked the globe and set it spinning. "Time."

Kitty stopped the globe, then peeled back her finger. "The River Nile."

Zeke considered what he knew about the river.

"Today, if you please," Caden said.

"The longest river in the world," Zeke blurted. Instantly, he regretted his choice of facts. Everyone knew that much.

"It's supposed to be—" Kitty began.

"False," Caden said, his expression smug.

"—little known," she finished lamely, before fixing Caden with a bemused gaze.

"False?" Randall aped, looking at Caden as if he'd grown another head.

Zeke couldn't believe his luck. "It's true," he said, before Caden could try to change his answer.

"Damn," Caden said with a scowl. "I was sure the Rhine River was longer. I suppose you win. What prize do you claim?"

Zeke concentrated on ignoring Randall and Kitty, who both continued to gawk at Caden in a most irritating manner. "I claim your prize. A kiss from my lovely fiancé."

Out of his peripheral vision, he saw Kitty's head snap in his direction. "But...I didn't lose to you."

"You lost to Caden, however, and I believe he'd already named the forfeit."

She frowned. "Is that legal?" she asked, glancing from Caden to Randall.

Not really, but he'd challenge anyone who said so.

Randall shrugged, his eyes bright with humor, the cad.

"I'm afraid so, darling." Caden aimed a you-owe-me look at Zeke.

Zeke ignored him. "I reserve the right to claim it later, how-ever."

"Do you, now?" She asked dryly.

He smiled down at her, just an adoring groom-to-be, gazing at his intended.

Abruptly Kitty rose, forcing Zeke to straighten quickly or risk toppling the armchair with his weight.

Only then did she grace him with a smile, the vixen. He almost laughed aloud.

A kitchen maid appeared in the doorway with a rolling cart, laden with pastries and finger sandwiches and steaming pots of tea. Come to think of it, he'd skipped lunch.

"Tea time," Randall enthused. "Thank God. I'm famished."

"If you'll excuse me gentlemen, I'll be taking tea in my cham-ber. I thank you for a thoroughly enjoyable afternoon, Lord Caden, Lord Randall." She hesitated, "My lord."

A moment later she was gone. Apparently she was still angry over last night. Zeke stared at the empty doorway, resisting the urge to trail after her like a lost puppy.

"I could do with some nourishment," his brother intoned cheerily. "Losing a kiss and an invaluable diamond in one swoop tends to work up one's appetite. What say you, Zeke?"

"I've eaten," He lied. "I'll catch up with the two of you later. I have something I forgot I needed to do." He left the room before either of them could ask what.

Neither man spoke until the sound of Zeke's boots, eating up the cold stone floors, receded.

"Since when don't you know the Nile's the longest river in the world?" Randall finally asked.

One corner of Caden's mouth kicked up. "Since my brother bet a priceless diamond rather than risk letting me kiss his lady."

"You should've seen his face when you claimed your forfeit," Randall said with a laugh.

Caden's mouth curved in a crooked grin. "Who says I didn't?"

***

Kitty didn't know why she ran. Yet here she was, pacing her sitting room like a caged animal. Again.

It was all Zeke's fault. Zeke and his pesky habit of sneaking up on her.

She could still see the handsome rogue, forcing his way into their game, looking so bloody sure of himself as he claimed her kiss like it was his right to do so. As if they truly were engaged.

But they weren't engaged, and he had no business kissing her, only...She closed her eyes, and touched her fingers to her lips, silently admitting the truth.

She'd run from herself. From the unrelenting ache within her for more of Zeke's bone-melting, heart-stopping kisses.

She wandered to the open window and looked out on the rain-soaked earth. In the beginning, she'd wanted just one kiss from him.

But one kiss made her crave more—more kisses, more touching, more...she didn't know, precisely, only that whatever it was, she wanted it from Zeke in spades.

She wished she had someone to turn to for advice, but, as always, she had no one.

She must rely on herself and hope she got it right.

What *was* the sensible thing to do? She might want Zeke to kiss her, and hold her, and stir feelings within her she never knew existed. But what good could come of giving in to such desires?

A sinking surety filled her. None could.

Five months from now he'd leave England. She couldn't let him take her heart with him. She knew all about the hardship being left wrought.

Time to employ your long absent willpower, Christine Hastings, she silently commanded herself. She could withstand both Zeke's seductive charm, and her own weakness for the man, by God, and she'd start now, this instant, by not hiding in her room.

She marched to the door, yanked it open, and found herself face to face with Zeke, fist poised to knock.

He grinned boyishly, looking almost, *almost*, unsure of himself.

Just like that, her insides melted. She was off to a banging start.

"May I come in?" He didn't wait for an answer, but pushed past her into the antechamber.

Still holding the door lever, she spun around, prepared to blast him for his audacity. Instead, the sight of his large, masculine frame in her terribly feminine chamber, with its delicate flower-papered walls, pastel furnishings, and rosewood escritoire, struck her as nothing short of hilarious.

She brought her fingers to her lips to cover her smile.

"I brought you this." He held the missing atlas toward her, his expression one of hopeful expectation, as if bringing her pleasure meant something to him.

She blinked, fighting the wave of tenderness his thoughtful act elicited.

"Now you say, *thank you, Zeke.*"

His mocking tone broke her momentary trance. Twisting around, she craned her neck past the door jamb to glance up and down the corridor. Lucky for both of them, no one was about.

She turned back to Zeke. "Thank you for delivering it. Now you may leave."

Zeke's brows furrowed. He tossed the leather bound book onto her settee. "Why?"

"You know very well you can't be in here."

He looked down at himself, then spread his arms wide. "I can't?"

"You know what I mean. You shouldn't be. Someone might see you."

He reached past her, closed the door, then flattened his palm against it. Mere inches separated them. Heat emanated from his body, transmitting itself to hers like an intimate caress.

His eyes, the color of blue smoke, locked with hers. "Better?"

"You deliberately miss the point." she said, but couldn't muster any heat.

His unblinking gaze dropped to her mouth. He licked his lips and parted them slightly.

Kitty went hot all over and her knees threatened to buckle. He was too close. His intriguing masculine scent too tempting. She pressed her palms behind her into the cool wood of the paneled door and tried to steady herself.

He brought his free hand to her face, tracing her cheek with one knuckle.

That one tiny caress started a tremor in her belly that spread through her like wildfire 'til it seemed her entire body vibrated.

She must remember her vow not to cave at every turn. Pinching her eyelids shut, she ducked under his arm and put some much needed distance between them.

He swiveled to face her, and leaned negligently on the door, his arms crossed over his chest.

She'd had to call on all her reserves to keep from wrapping her arms around his neck and clinging to him like a vine, and he had the nerve to stand there looking cool as a cucumber. How very irritating. "Why are you here?" she asked. "Really."

"I thought you'd appreciate having the atlas you risked life and limb for last night. And"—He inclined his head—"I wanted to talk to you. I would've preferred a more appropriate venue, but you've given me no choice, sequestering yourself in your chambers—and don't bother denying it."

So he had noticed her absence. Ruthlessly, she quashed the little thrill the revelation wrought.

"You could've employed a bit of patience. Perhaps you've heard of the notion?"

"Not my strong suit." One corner of his mouth kicked up as he shoved himself away from the door and began a slow exploration of her sitting room.

She moved as he moved, keeping the distance between them constant. "Then how about decorum? You know very well you shouldn't be in my bedchamber. You told me as much yourself. Why, if anyone found us—" She broke off as she recognized the corner she was backing herself into—again.

Zeke flashed her a brilliant smile. "The earl would insist we become engaged?"

Clever, arrogant ass.

"For the last time, what do you want?"

Zeke's playful smile vanished. He straightened and closed the distance between them in two strides. Liquid blue heat smoldered in the depths of his eyes as he grasped her shoulders. "I should think that's obvious."

She gazed at him in dumb fascination.

"If you wish to hear the words, I want you."

And she wanted him. But it was no good. A haze of pain clouded her vision. She batted at his hands suddenly desperate to get away from him.

He put a stop to her flailing by grasping her wrists, one in each of his hands. His thumbs coursed over the tender underside of her wrists.

"Kitty," he said in a low tone. "Marry me."

His words caused her heart to crack into a million little pieces, as yearning and reality clashed within her. "I've already explained why I can't do that."

His jaw hardened. "Yes, and your stubbornness borders on the ludicrous. It's high time you faced reality, lady."

She laughed with derision and tugged her wrists free of his scorching ing hold. "Of all the—"

"Point one. You have to marry—at least you do if you want to have a family. I assume that's a priority for you, but if I'm wrong..." He left off with a shrug.

"Well, of course I want a family, but I—"

"Why not marry someone you're wildly attracted to? It would certainly make the process pleasurable."

She opened her mouth to refute his arrogant, albeit true, assumption, but he held his hand, palm out. "Please don't try to deny the obvious, and thereby insult both our intelligences."

She closed her mouth with a snap.

"Imagine the alternative. If you don't marry me, you'll likely end up with some elderly, decrepit, boring sot."

She threw up her hands in exasperation. "I hardly think a boring old sot is my only option."

He appeared to give her words serious consideration. "I suppose you're right."

"Of course I am," she said in triumph, even as disappointment filled her at his too-easy capitulation.

His eyes fixed on her mouth and his tone turned gruff. "But will your numerous suitors' kisses make you want to forget you're a lady the way mine do?"

Her breath caught, and without thinking she drew her fingertips to her lips.

He gave a huff of laughter and crowded in on her, pressing forward till her backside came up against the wall. He planted his forearms on either side of her.

"Point two. Forget your so-called majority. You won't be free of James until you're well and truly wed. You know that, don't you?"

He didn't give her a chance to answer, but instead continued to make his case.

"Point three. The earl enjoys your company, and you enjoy his." He angled his face over hers, and his eyelids went to half-mast. "Do you know how badly I want to kiss you, Kitty?"

Her legs turned to jelly. She struggled to focus.

His lips brushed hers in a feather light kiss. "So sweet," he whispered.

She bit back a moan as her eyes drifted shut. "W-what does the earl have to do with our hypothetical marriage?" she asked, breathless. His lips almost, *almost* covered hers. Everything in her wanted to grab his lapels and pull him closer.

"You'll keep each other company while"—*Finally*, he pressed a tender kiss on her lips—"I'm away."

He may as well have tossed a bucket of ice-cold water on her. Her eyelids flew open, then narrowed to slits.

He wanted to marry her so he could wash his hands of both his grandfather and her in one fell swoop? She placed her palms on his waistcoat lapels and pushed.

He sighed and allowed her to put an inch or so between them before putting on the brakes. "What have I said to cause you to bare your claws, Kitten?"

"You want someone to stay with the earl so you don't have to feel guilty for leaving him alone? You selfish blackguard."

He drew back as if she'd slapped him. "How does keeping you both safe make me selfish?"

She considered trying to explain, and finally threw up her hands. "What does it matter? I already told you, I don't want a marriage like the one you're offering."

His blue eyes went steely. "You little fool. You want to fall in love, no doubt with a paragon of a man, one who'll glue himself to your side and read sonnets to you day and night. Sweetheart, such a man doesn't exist, and if he did he'd bore you to tears."

The backs of her eyes stung. "I don't need a paragon, just a man who wants a family as I do. And yes, I do want to fall in love, and to be loved in return. What's so wrong with that?"

His hard expression turned almost pitying. "Kitty, you're not a child. You should put away these childish notions and face reality."

She set her jaw, and glowered at him with stubborn resolve.

He cursed silently. "You want to fall in love, do you? Fine. Where are you planning on finding this perfect specimen of a mate? And when? You're nearly three and twenty."

His words stung, badly, but she dug in her heels, jutting out her chin. "I don't know."

He spun away, dragging his hands through his hair. "Have you considered this might be the best offer you're going to get? At least you want me, and don't try to deny it," he rasped out, turning to point an accusing finger at her.

"You want a family? You'll have one. You'll have my grandfather, whom you claim to love, and Aunt Lillian, and God willing, my children. For the love of the saints, woman, I'm rich as Croesus. You'll want for nothing." He broke off, and gazed skyward. "I can't believe I'm having this argument."

She lowered her eyes, misery settling over her like a shroud. How could she explain what he offered was tantamount to dangling a carrot in front of a starving rabbit—and holding it over a bottomless crevasse? The thought of being pregnant with his child, and alone—never mind that he didn't love her, filled her with an unbearable ache. Like never ending loneliness.

"If you're so rich, why do you continue to leave in search of more wealth? Why not stay put in England, your home?" she asked, grasping at straws.

Her question seemed to take him aback. "I have to. Otherwise the profits from the mines tend to walk off the site. The laborers aren't the only ones who need supervision. The foremen do, too."

"That's not what I meant. I meant why more mines. Not to mention, have you ever considered the cost of mining to the laborers and their families?"

He scrubbed a hand over his face. "Kitty, do we have to make this a socio-political discussion, *now*?"

She shook her head. "Just answer the first question."

His nostrils flared, as if her question angered him. "I seek out mines because of what they produce. Gold, silver, things I can hold in my hand." His hand curled into a fist. "Real things I can grasp to keep my family secure for generations to come. You don't know what it's like to have your father fall apart like so much dust before you, all because he held onto things that weren't real. Things he staked his life on, then lost."

Her expression softened. She lay her hand on his still-clenched fist. "Things, like your mother?"

A muscle ticked in his jaw, but he refrained from answering, which told her all she needed to know.

She cupped his jaw and a shudder went through him. "Zeke, have you considered love is the only thing in this world that is real?"

He barked out a harsh laugh. "No."

Her heart seemed to fold in on itself. For him. For her. She couldn't differentiate between the two. "I see. Well, then. Do you mind telling me what would be in this marriage for you—besides seeing to your grandfather's wellbeing?"

He crooked a warm finger under her chin and tilted her face up 'til their eyes met, his shimmering like the sea before a storm.

"Don't you know?" he asked in a voice both gruff and tender. "I want you. So badly I can taste it. You're the last thing I think about at night when I fall asleep, and the first thing on my mind when I wake. If I could, I'd take you right here. Right now."

Liquid heat poured through her veins.

"Kitty, marrying you won't be any hardship for me. I simply won't promise something I can't give. I'm not like you. I don't believe in fairytales. Don't believe another person can make you complete. Relying on someone like that—it's, well, I'm sorry but it's weak. I'll never subject myself to such a damning illusion. And you shouldn't either. It only leads to ruin."

She frowned. Was he trying to convince her, or himself?

"Promise me you'll think about my proposal, Kitty."

"I will," she whispered.

A moment later, he was gone.

Chapter Twenty-Two

At a quarter 'til eight Kitty entered the formal parlor. She fixed what she hoped passed for a genuine smile on her face and scanned the room. She counted five persons. Everyone was present—save Zeke. She didn't know whether she felt relief or dismay. She started toward the earl.

Her smile faltered as Garrick sidled into her path.

"Kitty, my dear." His black as night gaze drifted down her body. "Lovely," he murmured.

She inclined her head and made to move around him.

He placed a staying hand on her forearm. "Now you're here, I can share my news. I received the most extraordinary letter this morning. Can you guess what it was?"

"No."

"An official Writ of Summons to the House of Lords, for the spring session. My first, as Baron of Maidstone. I've already shared the news with the earl and your fiancé." His eyes glittered with exhilaration bordering on madness.

Certainly he had no concern for the losses she'd endured in order for him to procure his precious title.

"Congratulations, my lord. Your heart's desire fulfilled, no doubt."

"Not quite." He lowered his mouth to her ear. He smiled, giving the outward appearance of sharing a private joke with her. "That will happen, my sweet, in due time, I assure you." His eyes slid to hers, sending a silent but unmistakable threat.

"Hope I haven't missed anything." Zeke's robust voice sounded from the open double doorway.

Kitty turned to see him striding toward her, and released the breath she hadn't realized she'd been holding.

As always he was a sight to behold, dressed in his black su-perfine evening clothes, golden hair gleaming.

When he proffered his elbow, she placed her gloved hand in the crook of his arm, without hesitation. A veritable cloak of warmth and security engulfed her.

He'd deny it if she called him a hero outright, yet the truth was there, as plain as the nose on her face. Zeke had somehow appointed himself her knight in shining armor.

"When I didn't see you, I wondered if you had made other plans for the evening."

He smiled. "Would you have missed me, my darling?"

She tried to smile at the teasing tone, but Garrick's odd warning still rang in her ears.

Zeke sobered. "I had pressing estate business, but I'm here now. I think we have time for a wander to the portico before dinner. Walk with me?"

***

Zeke led Kitty through a maze of shadowed corridors to a door opening to the section of the portico running along the western perimeter of the manse. He urged her through the door with a hand pressed to her low back.

A small shiver went through her at his touch. Satisfaction roared through him. She was already his. He knew it. Her body knew it. It was only a matter of time before her mind grasped the truth, as well.

He pulled the door closed, cutting off the diffuse spill of lamplight from the corridor. The sun had long set and only moonlight, and low burning wall lanterns illuminated the open-air space. A soft, steady breeze rustled the leaves of the strategically placed potted plants adorning the rails and columns of the portico. Somewhere out of sight, a wind-chime sang its soulful tune. It was damned romantic.

He led her toward the railing, the sound of their shoes indecipherable above the night din.

"I've never been out here after sunset," Kitty said in a soft voice.

Zeke said nothing. He didn't want to have a meaningless conversation. He wanted to know what was going on inside her head. Wanted to know what James had said to drain her cheeks of color—though he could guess it had something to do with that writ, proclaiming him Baron of Maidstone and calling him to the House of Lords.

As they neared a hanging lantern, he broke stride. "Kitty, wait."

She turned to him, without hesitation.

He cupped her face in his hands, searching her eyes in the flickering light.

She returned his stare, brave creature that she was. Though she tried to mask it with that defiant tilt to her chin, he could see the shadows lurking in her ice-green eyes.

"You looked as if you'd seen a ghost in there. What's James said to upset you now?"

She drew a shaky breath. "His writ of summons arrived. It's nothing I hadn't expected."

He nodded. "I guessed that had something to do with it. But there's more you're not telling me." He smoothed his thumbs over her cheeks.

She covered his hands with hers, before pulling them from her face. She moved to the railing and looked out over the night-dark grounds. "It wasn't so much what he said, as how he said it. I probably imagined things."

She didn't believe her words any more than he did.

Cursing softly, he shoved a hand through his hair, and followed her to the railing. Grasping both of her shoulders, he turned her to face him and surprised even himself with his gruff words. "Kitty, I can't stand that madman looking at you, much less speaking to you. If I had my way, he wouldn't come in spitting distance of you, ever again. I could make that happen—and yet you refuse to see reason."

Rather than argue, a small smile played at her lips, throwing him further off kilter than he already was. "If I didn't know better, Ezekiel Thurgood, I'd mistake you for a—" She lowered her eyes.

"A what, damn it?"

"A man who cares," she finished on a whisper. She lifted a hand to trace his cheek with her fingertips. Her scent, lavender, rosemary, something uniquely Kitty teased his senses. Every thought in his head vanished, save one.

"You make me crazy." He pulled her into his arms. "I'm beginning to think you do it on purpose."

"Maybe just a little," she said, sounding breathless. She grasped his collar, lifted herself onto her tiptoes until her nose brushed his cravat. "You smell divine."

"You see?" he asked, his voice hoarse. "There you go again, driving me out of my mind."

She tilted her head back to gaze at him, and his meager resistance crumbled. He took her mouth in a desperate kiss.

When she wrapped her arms around his neck and pressed herself into him, his meager restraint vanished. His hands, as if they had a mind of their own, roamed over her, imprinting her shape on his brain.

"Kitty," he breathed against her lips. His mouth traveled over her cheek, seeking the sensitive area below her jaw.

She tilted her head back, giving him greater access as she clung to him.

A low groan sounded in his throat. Every fiber of his being burned for her. He needed her naked beneath him, her legs tight around him as he sank himself into her.

She made a soft mewing sound, drawing his lips to hers again like a magnet drew steel.

He slanted his mouth over hers, seeking entrance. The tip of his tongue played at the corners of her mouth, teasing, prodding, 'til her lips parted on a sigh.

Sweet Jesus. His tongue slid home. She tasted like heaven.

She touched the tip of her tongue to his, and a helpless shudder went through him.

He pulled her closer, holding her to him as one of his hands cupped her buttocks, lifting her slightly off her feet to bring their hips in line. His pulsing erection strained against the restraints of his trousers and layers of her skirts, and he silently cursed the fabric separating her sweetness from him.

She whimpered with need, rocking against him.

He hadn't thought he could get any harder, any more desperate. He was wrong. He scooped her into his arms, ready to carry her off to—where?

She whispered his name, her lips grazing his neck. He bit back a roar. Now. He wanted her now. The conservatory? It was just west of the manse.

Somewhere in the house, the gong sounded for dinner.

Reality crashed in, tearing a groan of pure frustration from him. Calling on all his will, he set her on her feet though he didn't release her. He couldn't take his hands off her. Not yet. He rested his forehead against hers and gulped the cool night air.

Kitty gazed at him, looking delightfully dazed and thoroughly kissed. She took a shuddering breath. "Did you...did you bring me out here for that?"

"No," he replied. "Maybe," he admitted a moment later, as much to himself as her. "I don't know. I just wanted to get you alone."

She only smiled.

He straightened and traced a tendril of her hair. "Come on, then." He took her arm, leading her toward the door.

"Ask yourself this, Kitty." Hand on the door lever, he lowered his mouth to her ear. "Will your paragon of a boring husband make you want to be touched in places you never knew existed?"

He yanked open the door and ushered her ahead of him.

She stumbled inside and stared at him, wide-eyed, looking, to his mind, more than a little intrigued.

He gave her a lazy grin. "I'm giving you 'til tomorrow to accept my offer. I expect you'll come to your senses by then."

"And if I don't?" she said in a belatedly peevish tone.

He winked, and refrained from laughing at her delayed show of resistance. "I'll cross that bridge if I come to it."

At the moment, he was more concerned with getting the bulge in his pants to subside before they reached the dining hall. That was going to be a real feat.

***

The following morning Kitty sat beside the earl at the breakfast table, quietly brooding. She'd reached one decision in the wee hours of the morning. She would marry Zeke. He was right. It was the logical thing to do. Garrick would pose a threat so long as she remained unmarried, and, if she was being honest, imagining life without Zeke left her feeling desolate.

Maybe he was right, and that did make her weak.

"I see you've picked up one of Zeke's habits," the earl said.

She looked a question at him.

He had his nose in this morning's copy of the *Times*. Without looking her way, he inclined his head toward her fingers, poised over the white tablecloth beside her barely touched plate.

She'd been drumming her fingers. Very carefully, she laced her hands in her lap.

The earl folded his newspaper. He turned to Kitty, eyeing her with concern. "Kitty, I know you're a private person, but I must ask. Is something troubling you anew?"

"I have a few things on my mind, but nothing overly troubling."

She wrestled with when she ought to tell Zeke she'd decided to accept his offer of marriage. But that was nothing she could share with the earl. She had every intention of seeking the earl's blessing on her and Zeke's plan to wed. She just felt Zeke ought to know first.

"If you need someone to listen, I'm always here to lend an ear."

She beamed at him. "I appreciate that, my lord."

"Good morning." Caden burst into the room on a cloud of energy and vigor, dashing in his sportsman tweeds. He headed straight for the sideboard. "I've come from overseeing the placement of the shooting targets. All is set. It's going to be great fun."

"I, for one, am looking forward to getting out-of-doors. This constant rain business gets old," Randall said, strolling into the dining hall.

Zeke emerged from the corridor on Randall's heels. He stole her breath in his crisp white shirtsleeves, his dark brown, fitted sports breeches and glossy boots.

The other two men were handsome and well dressed. But somehow they didn't compare to Zeke. One glimpse and her heart set to racing.

He smiled at everyone in turn, saving Kitty for last. "You're looking lovely this morning, my dear," he said. He winked and sauntered for the sideboard.

His cocksure attitude made her decision for her. She would definitely tell him after the shooting match.

Lady Lillian entered the room, followed by Garrick.

"Gang's all here," Caden said, cheerfully. He lifted his coffee cup in a mock toast.

Rapid footsteps sounded in the hall.

Giles, looking oddly flustered, appeared in the open doorway. "Excuse me, my lords, my ladies."

"Yes, what is it, Giles?" the earl asked.

"My lord, there's someone here claiming—rather, a man who wishes to...If I could speak with you in private, Lord Claybourne?"

Claybourne's brows furrowed. He pushed back from the table and rose to make his way, unhurried, toward the waiting Giles.

Zeke turned from the sideboard, a half-filled plate in his hand. "What is this, Giles? Should I join—"

His words died as a dark-haired man burst into the room. His eyes scanned the faces of everyone present, finally landing on Kitty. A broad grin lit his face. "What's all this talk of my baby sister getting married?"

Chapter Twenty-Three

The room erupted in excited chatter. She could make out bits and pieces. She heard Garrick's whispered, "Impossible." Felt Zeke's warm hands on her shoulders. She thought he asked her if she knew the man.

She couldn't answer. Couldn't speak. For what felt like an eternity, she could only stare. Then she erupted from her chair and raced around the table.

"Collin!" She threw herself into her brother's open arms, nearly toppling them both.

"Hello, love." He held her, patting her back gently.

She couldn't stop her tears of joy. Not letting him go, she leaned back, drinking in the sight of her beloved brother. "Collin...where...how... Oh, Collin." Overcome, she buried her face in his chest, soaking his tailored jacket.

"Lord Collin Hastings, I presume?" The earl asked.

"Kitty, love, a moment?" Her brother peeled her fists from his lapels.

Sniffling, she took a small step back. She sent the earl a misty smile. "S-sorry." She held a finger up, and tried to get her emotions under control long enough to introduce them.

Collin tucked her hand into his elbow. He faced the earl, clipping a bow. "Lord Collin Hastings, brother to this beautiful watering pot at my side, at your service."

The earl took Collin's free hand and shook it between two of his. "Very pleased to meet you young man, very pleased."

Kitty finally had herself under some semblance of control. "Collin, please meet the Earl of Claybourne."

"I'm honored, My lord. I believe you were a close friend of my grandfather's."

"Indeed. The closest of friends."

She eyed the rest of the room's inhabitants, each and every one of them standing, each staring at she and her brother.

Zeke had eyes only for her, and they held a wealth of concern. She sent him a bemused smile. This was Collin. Her brother.

"Welcome home, cousin." Garrick's flat sliced the air.

Kitty glanced between him and her brother.

Collin studied Garrick as if he couldn't quite place him. "Ah. Mister James, isn't it?"

"Lord James, now."

"I see," Collin said. A muscle in his jaw ticked as if the situation was becoming clear.

After a brief, tense silence, Lady Lillian cleared her throat. "I'm sure we'd all like to meet your brother, dear, but perhaps the two of you might like a moment alone first?"

The room emptied of everyone, save Zeke. "Kitty, perhaps you'd be so good?"

"Of...course," she stammered. "My lord, may I present Lord Collin Hastings, my brother. Collin, dear, this is—" She broke off, suddenly unsure.

Zeke extended his hand. "Lord Ezekiel Thurgood of Claybourne. Kitty's fiancé."

Collin grinned and pumped Zeke's hand. "Very good to meet you, Lord Thurgood. May I congratulate you on your excellent choice of brides."

Zeke gave Collin a polite smile, bowing his head slightly. "On that we agree." He turned his gaze on Kitty. "I'll leave the two of you. If you need me..." He left off, departing and closing the breakfast hall's seldom-used double doors behind him.

Kitty barely knew where to begin. "Where have you been? How did you find me? Collin, they said you died."

Her darling brother. A bit fuller 'round the middle. Deeper lines etched across his forehead now. But Collin. Here. Alive.

"Obviously they were wrong, to my ever-loving relief. Sweetheart, do you mind if we sit? I've ridden straight from Maidstone County, and I'm rather exhausted, not to mention famished."

"Yes, yes, of course." Kitty pulled out the chair beside hers and flapped her hands for him to sit. "I'll fix you a plate while you fill me in on everything. Starting with where in the world you've been these last two years, how long you've been home, and how in the world you found me, and—"

He chuckled. "Not so fast, poppet."

"S-sorry. I'm just so happy," she choked out.

Collin withdrew a white linen handkerchief from his coat pocket, and held it out to her in exchange for the breakfast plate she delivered. "Thanks, love." He scooped up several large forkfuls of eggs.

Kitty sat and stared at him, her chin in her palm, content for the moment to simply watch him eat.

When he'd consumed most of the food on his plate, he sighed and set his fork aside. "It's not a pleasant tale, I'm afraid, so I won't belabor the details. The ship upon which I sailed came upon another vessel, in trouble, or so we thought. Our good captain offered assistance. Once he dropped anchor, he summarily lost his ship to the hailing crew."

She gasped. "Never say so. Grandfather and I were informed your ship went down."

"A ship did indeed go down—burned into smithereens by its crew. It just didn't happen to be the one I was aboard." His eyes took on a faraway look. "I'll never forget the smell of burning bodies." He shuddered. "The ship that overtook us was a slave runner. Do you understand what that means?"

"A sea vessel used for the despicable practice of human trafficking," she said.

"Yes—manned by a bloodthirsty lot of pirates. They pressed me into service."

"Forced you to work on a slaver's ship? For two years? How did you survive? Oh, if only you'd sent word." She wrung her hands, imagining the horror.

Collin gave her an aggrieved look. "Don't you think I would've if I could? Kitty, you have no idea what I've lived through, or to what lengths I had to go to make my way home."

She was instantly contrite. "Collin, forgive me. I didn't mean to diminish what you must've endured. It's just that I've missed you so terribly."

He took her hands in his. "And I you. Only imagine my disappointment when I arrived to Hastings House to find you gone."

She swallowed past a lump in her throat. "Then you know about Grandfather."

He nodded, face grave.

"I wish you could've been there to say goodbye." She paused. "What will happen now? Collin, Garrick's inherited the title."

He gave her his signature crooked grin. "He merely borrowed it, love. By rights, it's mine."

She gazed at him in pure adoration. Of course he'd set things right. "Baron Collin Hastings of Maidstone."

"Precisely. Speaking of titles. My only sister's getting married, to a future earl, no less?"

She shook her head. "We're not really..." She'd been ready to refute her engagement to Zeke, out of habit. Because up until last night, her engagement had been only pretense. But that was no longer precisely the case.

"Not really?" He prodded.

"We're not really going to get into all that now, are we? I want to hear more about you, and introduce you to the rest of the family."

***

"Is he the man you remember from the hells?" Zeke asked Caden the minute the four men reconvened in his grandfather's den. He paced to the far corner of the room, unable to quell the restless energy coursing through him.

"One and the same." Caden sprawled on the armchair before their grandfather's desk, behind which the earl presided. "Did you see the look on James's face? Hasting's arrival heralds a major upset in his life, more so than anyone's, save Kitty's."

"How long did you say he'd been presumed dead?" Randall asked, hip propped on the edge of the desk.

"Over two years," the earl replied.

"Where's he been all this time? That's what I'd like to know." Zeke started back toward them.

"You and the rest of us," Randall quipped. "I wouldn't miss this for all the tea in China. You people really know how to entertain. Tomorrow I leave for London to see to some estate matters I've neglected far too long, and I really hate to go. One never knows what surprises a day in Chissington Hall might offer."

"Ha ha," Zeke replied without humor. "Caden, I think London is calling you as well."

Caden frowned. "I have no pressing business."

"Oh, but you do." Zeke clapped a hand on Caden's shoulder.

Caden's brows shot up. "I take it I'm to be your errand boy?"

"Something like that."

"What will you be doing, that you can't manage your own tasks?" Caden asked.

"Guarding my bride," Zeke answered without preamble.

His brother gave him an assessing look.

"What?" Zeke asked.

"Who are you?"

Zeke opened his mouth to ask what the devil Caden meant, when Randall spoke. "I thought we'd already established the fact your brother's beyond smitten."

Zeke snorted. "Don't be absurd. I'm merely being pragmatic. Someone's got to keep an eye on things here."

Caden smirked. "He doesn't know."

"Hasn't a clue," Randall concurred.

"Will you two cease discussing me as if I'm not in the room?" Zeke turned to his grandfather for support, who was trying to disguise his own amusement by holding a fist to his mouth.

Zeke threw his hands in the air, exasperated. "You, too? Can we please dispense with this nonsense and move on to relevant matters?"

The earl sobered, though his faded blue eyes retained a trace of mischief. "Forgive us, Ezekiel. Pray tell what errand have you in mind for Caden."

"As Hallis is already engaged in learning all there is to know about James. I need someone to dig into Hastings' background."

"Zeke, he's to be your brother-in-law," Caden said, his tone disapproving.

"Exactly. That's why I want to know what I'll be dealing with. I want to know about his gambling, his past relationships, about the bloody ship he was on that went down. I want to know where he's been these last two years in lieu of protecting his sister. In short, I want to know anything about him that has the potential to hurt Kitty."

Caden scratched his chin. "When you put it like that. I'm not sure where to begin, though. I'm not schooled in the art of spying."

"Hire a private investigator. Hire runners. Whatever it takes. Just make sure whomever you hire is discreet. Hallis can assist you there. You might let him know my question regarding inheritance law is a moot point." Zeke paused. "On second thought, ask him how the Crown will handle the prodigal son's return."

A soft knock sounded on the door.

"Come," the earl said.

Lillian entered, followed by Kitty and Lord Hastings, linked arm in arm. "Look who I found heading this way," Lillian said, her eyes bright with emotion.

"I thought to finish making introductions. May we join you?" Kitty asked in a shy tone Zeke wasn't accustomed to hearing from her.

"Please." The earl rose and moved toward the center of the room.

Caden, Randall, and Zeke followed.

Kitty beamed up at her brother. "You've met the earl, and," she hesitated, "my fiancé. "Now may I introduce Mr. Caden Thurgood, grandson to the earl and Lord Thurgood's brother, and the redoubtable Viscount Sterling Randall, a close friend of the family's. My lord, Caden, my brother."

She gazed up at Hastings, as if he hung the moon and stars.

After exchanging greetings, Caden said good-naturedly, "We planned a shooting match for this morning, but clearly that's out now."

Unable to resist the compulsion, Zeke moved to flank Kitty on her other side. "We'll do it another time. You'll want to spend the day catching up."

"I see." Hastings gave a considering frown. "There's no need to cancel the match. Not on my account, anyway."

Kitty blinked. "But Collin, you've only just arrived. We have so many things to discuss."

Amused indulgence reflected in Hastings' eyes. He patted her hand. "Darling, I've already given you the facts concerning my recent history."

She opened her mouth to protest.

He stayed her with one palm, held out. "The truth is, I'm exhausted. It would do my heart good knowing you were occupied, and not pacing the halls outside my door, holding your breath 'til I emerge."

"Oh," she said, visibly deflated. "Of course. Of course you must rest."

The earl spoke up, ever the gracious host. "Lord Hastings, I took the liberty of setting Giles on preparing a room for you. It's ready whenever you are, and of course you must stay as long as you like."

"I greatly appreciate your kindness, my lord." Hastings released Kitty's arm to execute a crisp bow.

Before his eyes, Kitty's disappointment faded, replaced by an expression of utter sisterly adoration.

It made Zeke feel...he couldn't quite name the feeling. Didn't exactly recognize it.

She laughed gaily at something her brother said. Lost in his thoughts, Zeke had missed the particular repartee, but the inexplicable sensation grew more insistent.

At least now he could name it. Insignificant.

Damn it, he'd been the one looking after her, protecting her from the circumstances caused in large part by her brother's absence, while darling Collin had been God knew where doing

God knew what. And yet she gazed on him like he held the answers to all life's mysteries.

Never mind Zeke had actually saved her from her cousin. Well, Zeke and the earl. But Zeke had been more than willing to take that final step to ensure her long-term safety that only a husband could offer.

Except...now her brother was here, did she even need saving?

"Zeke? I asked if you'd show Lord Hastings to his room in the bachelor's wing," the earl said, evidently repeating himself, based on the expectant looks of everyone present.

"I'd be happy to." Zeke forced a polite smile. Truth be told, he felt slightly nauseated. Probably because he'd missed breakfast.

"Allow me a moment alone with Collin, my lord? We'll meet you in the foyer directly." And off she went, brother in tow.

Chapter Twenty-Four

Several minutes later, Kitty and Hastings arrived in the foyer, as promised.

Caden and Randall swooped in to escort Kitty to the shoot site. "We promise not to start without you," his brother said with a grin before the three disappeared down the hall.

Zeke turned to Hastings. "If you'll follow me?"

They walked a short distance in silence during which Zeke considered mentioning anything from the weather to what he'd almost eaten for breakfast. For some reason, he didn't feel comfortable with the lapse in conversation. Maybe because he and Hastings were strangers with a lot at stake between them, all housed in the form of one pretty package named Kitty.

He drew a deep breath and pushed past his instinct to hide behind small talk. "Lord Hastings, you can't know what your return means to my fiancé. She has spoken of you so often, I feel I almost know you."

"Lord Thurgood, I have missed my sister every bit as much as she's missed me, I assure you."

And there it was, Zeke realized grimly. He had claimed Kitty as his fiancée, and Hastings had responded in kind, referring to her as his sister.

He was probably making something out of nothing. What had that woman done to him?

Hastings shook his head and continued, absently twisting a pinkie ring. "These last two years, there were times I longed for home so much I almost wished for death, rather than face another day in the hands of my captors."

Zeke's brows shot up. "It was like that, was it?"

They had nearly reached the bachelor's wing, and Hastings' guest bedchamber.

"Touching foot on English soil never felt so good. Of course, the first thing on my agenda was to make my way back home to my sister."

"Of course." Zeke fought the urge to claim her again. "I hope you'll share a bit of your recent history with the earl and I. If there's anything we can do to help smooth your return, please let us know."

He drew to a halt in front Hastings chamber. "Here we are." He opened the guest door and stood aside.

"Certainly I'll bore you all with tales of my trials and tribulations. We'll have time enough for that, now we're to be family." Hastings punctuated his words with a warm smile, giving Zeke a glimpse of the famous charm Kitty was always boasting about.

Hastings hesitated, one foot across the threshold. "Lord Thurgood, tell me, is my cousin staying in a room in this wing, as well? Perhaps one near mine?"

"Yes. Is it going to be a problem, being near him?"

Hastings patted his waistcoat absently, and Zeke noted the flash of gold on his hand. The pinkie ring he'd been twisting. It looked similar, if not an exact replica of the ring Kitty wore around her neck, the one having belonged to the recently deceased baron.

"Oh, gracious, no. I simply need to have a talk with him, sooner than later, preferably."

"I imagine you have many things to discuss with the man," Zeke said.

"Yes." Hastings once again twisted his ring.

"I couldn't help noticing your pinkie ring. It reminds me of one Kitty once showed me," Zeke said, curiosity getting the better of him.

He held out his hand, regarding the band. "One and the same. It belonged to my grandfather. Kitty just gave it to me. It feels like a good omen, wearing the old man's ring."

So she had given her brother the ring, the sentimental fool. The backs of Zeke's eyes stung suddenly.

"Your things should already be unpacked, the bed turned down. There's a toilet with running water just there." He pointed to a door down the hall.

"And, uh, you'll let me know which is James' chamber?" Collin asked.

He was in a hurry, then, wasn't he? Zeke supposed he couldn't blame the man, considering he'd come home to find his grandfather dead, his sister gone, and his inheritance relinquished to another.

"The one at the end of the hall on the left."

Hastings reached out to squeeze his shoulder. He fixed Zeke with a steady gaze. "Thank you, Lord Thurgood. For everything. For taking care of my Kitty, seeing to her wellbeing when fate took me away from her. Hopefully it hasn't been too much of a burden on your family."

"Kitty is..." He paused and blew out a breath. "She's worth any amount of trouble," he said finally, finishing with a soft laugh when he realized he meant every word.

***

"I thought we'd take the long way. We have some time to kill since Zeke's meeting us, and if I haven't missed my guess, you've never taken this particular route." Caden guided her to a narrow footpath opening off the eastern edge of the property, with Randall taking up the rear.

"Thank you, my lord. You guessed correctly." Holding her hat with one gloved hand, she tilted her head up to regard a cloudless, blue sky. It would be hot later, but at not quite ten o'clock, the air still held a pleasant chill. She inhaled and caught the sweet scent of yesterday's rains hanging in the air.

"My dear, let me say again I fully understand if you want to cry off. It's not every day one's long lost brother returns to the fold." Caden fixed her with an assessing eye.

She linked her hands behind her back, and regarded the tips of her boots as they peeked out from the folds of her yellow walking skirt. "Collin has the right of it. If I stay indoors, I'll be climbing the walls, waiting for him to emerge from his chambers. A day spent out-of-doors while he rests is just the thing."

"In that case," Caden said with a jaunty grin, "the markers are in place, the targets spaced properly and staked into the ground, pistols are oiled, bullets laid out—"

"—I've brought refreshments." Randall cut in, patting a canvas bag he wore slung over his shoulder.

"Oh?" she asked.

"Whiskey," Caden and Randall said in unison.

Kitty laughed. "I see."

"We have much to toast," Randall said with a wink at Kitty. "Seriously. With the return of Lord Hastings, not only do you get your brother back from the dead, but your whole world changes for the better." He paused. "Your brother will take over as your guardian, will he not?"

"Randall, no need to get into the nuts and bolts of the thing just now. It's enough to celebrate he's alive at the moment," Caden said before Kitty could answer.

"Quite right," Randall agreed. "Please know we are very, very happy for you, my lady."

"Thank you," she said softly.

The group fell into an easy silence, punctuated by the sound of boots scraping along the stone path.

But Kitty's mind was far from quiet. Her thoughts spun so fast she felt dizzy.

Lord Randall was right. Everything was different now Collin was back. Garrick's guardianship would be no more. His say over her life, null and void. Which meant...

She was free. No more looming threat of a lifetime of marriage to Garrick.

She didn't have to marry Zeke.

She stumbled a little, and Randall caught her by the elbow. "My lady, are you all right?"

She nodded numbly and murmured an apology.

Collin was back, she scolded herself fiercely. She ought to be thrilled, and she was. So why did she feel like she might be sick any moment? Like she'd had too much candy. Like she'd just lost someone dear to her forever.

She concentrated on breathing. On placing one foot in front of the other. On not stumbling again or doing anything equally as foolish— like crying.

Silly little fool. She had her brother back, alive and well. Everything else was secondary.

Besides, now Zeke could keep running toward whatever it was he sought out there in the great unknown, and she wouldn't have to suffer a lifelong commitment to a man who openly avowed never to love her.

To think, just an hour ago, she'd wrestled with how best to accept his marriage proposal. Thank goodness she hadn't actually spoken the words. How much worse it would have been to have him rescind his offer.

What was she thinking? Zeke was honorable to his toes. He wouldn't break things off. Instead, he'd feel honor bound to marry her.

"Hello, brother." Caden's voice crashed through her private storm of emotions.

Heading in their direction, Zeke's long legs closed the distance with ground eating strides. "I hurried down and found the match site very much deserted. I'd begun to think Kitty had changed her mind about the outing." He maneuvered himself into position beside her.

"Our Kitty's a trooper," Caden said.

"Why the devil did you come this way, anyway?" Zeke asked.

"Because I wanted to give you time to take care of Hastings, and because I figured our girl hadn't taken this route." Caden craned his head to see past Zeke to Kitty. "I'll be happy to point out some interesting sights we'll be passing shortly."

"Thank you," she said. "I would appreciate it ever so much."

Zeke picked up his pace, all but dragging her with him so they moved ahead of Caden and Randall. "That's all well and good, but we haven't the time," he said crisply. "I'll be happy to take you on a tour of the property another afternoon, my lady."

"Very well," she said, slightly taken aback.

"Are we in a hurry?" Caden asked Zeke. "If it's Lord Hastings you're worried about, I gave specific instructions for a footman to send word if he should awaken before we return, as you very well know."

Kitty glanced behind her at Caden in delighted surprise. "Did you? How very considerate of you."

"I live to serve," he said with a grin.

"I only meant the weather may turn foul again," Zeke muttered.

Randall darted a few paces ahead of them and pivoted in a broad circle, his hand to his brow, his face upturned to the blue skies. "Because the clouds on the horizon look so fierce?"

Kitty laughed.

"Everyone made fun of Noah, as well," Zeke groused, though a smile played at the corners of his mouth.

As if it were the most natural thing in the world, he tucked her hand into the crook of his arm, then covered her hand with his. She delighted in the small gesture. For now, she belonged here, with Zeke.

"If I'm not mistaken, after we round the bend here, we'll reach a small, stone bridge. Is that right?" she asked, hoping no one noticed the breathless quality of her voice.

Zeke had begun lightly caressing her knuckles. Though they both wore gloves, the stroke of his fingers created a charged awareness in her. She felt flushed and feverish even in the fresh morning air.

"That's correct," he and Caden answered simultaneously.

Soon they crossed over the bridge.

Caden leaned forward to loudly whisper, "Observe the bridge we shall not discuss at this time."

Kitty laughed aloud, enjoying the ribbing at Zeke's expense.

.

"Ouch," Caden said a moment later.

"These family outings are so much fun," Randall announced to no one in particular.

"I'm not sure Lady Kitty would agree, Randall. Unless she considers one sibling kicking the other for no apparent reason, fun," Caden replied.

"She'll get used to us," Zeke quipped.

Which was the absolute worst thing he could have said. Because she knew, even if he hadn't worked it out yet, she wouldn't. She would never have the chance.

***

Kitty yanked off her earmuffs and squinted to see the target through the gun smoke.

"I say, you're a crack shot, Lady Kitty." Caden half-shouted since all their ears were ringing, even with the use of protection. "I'm duly impressed."

"So you keep mentioning," Zeke tried to mutter, though the intended effect was lost in as he had to speak loudly enough to assure he'd be heard.

She sent Caden a brilliant smile. "My shooting lessons seem to have paid off."

She wondered if any besides her had noticed Zeke's increasingly dour mood, or what lay at the root of it. Wounded male pride.

All morning he'd attempted to charm her, engage her in conversation, stand close enough to touch her. The small of her back, her elbow.

Once, while the other two men argued over a shot, he twisted a lock of her hair around his finger. "Kitty. Why does it seem like you're avoiding me?"

Because I am? But she couldn't say that. Nor could she explain that being this near to him made the pain of knowing their relationship had reached its end ten times worse. That his sweet attentions made her ache almost intolerable. Instead, she shook her head in feigned ignorance, and promptly inserted herself into Caden and Randall's conversation.

After that, he'd taken the hint, while letting her know he hadn't liked the message.

Well, too bad. With one little word, he could fix the whole bloody problem. Love. But no. He only wanted her.

"I knew I should've had you on my team," Randall complained, distracting her from her morose thoughts. He planted his hands on his hips and eyed the four targets. "Although I feel I must point out, once again, I haven't had much practice of late as I've—"

"—been city bound," Zeke finished for him.

"You're not doing so badly." Giving Randall's shoulder a pat, Kitty added, "Your score almost equals Caden's, and his score is only a tad below mine." She refrained from mentioning Zeke's score, as he'd left them all in the dust.

"Yes, not so bad at all. Just because you're being squarely beaten by a female. You're at least hitting the target. Most of the time," Zeke said.

Caden hooted with laughter and clapped the viscount on the back.

Randall shot the brothers affronted looks.

"Caden, do you realize you and I will have to pay both Zeke and Kitty a forfeit? Did we ever discuss prizes?"

He paused to reflect, then aimed a sly smile at Zeke. "I have a capital idea. How about you claim sole right to the forfeits again, and demand kisses from Kitty? By the by, did you ever collect on that debt?"

Zeke slanted Kitty a heated glance, and to her mortification, appeared to be considering answering Randall, the rogue.

Kitty deliberately turned her back on the three of them and approached the staging tables. "I'm positively parched."

She bypassed the first table, laden with boxes of unused bullets and pistols they'd fired, and went straight for the dripping pitcher of ice-cold lemonade sitting like a beacon on the refreshment table. She waved off the approaching footman with a smile, and filled one of the four crystal glasses. "Lemonade anyone?"

Whistling a carefree tune as if he hadn't just stirred the proverbial pot, Randall rummaged in his sack. "I do need a beverage, but I don't care for lemonade." He pulled out a large, holstered pistol and set it on the table before brandishing a shiny silver bottle.

"I'm for that." Caden rubbed his palms together.

"I could definitely do with a drink," Zeke said sourly.

"Ladies first." Randall offered Kitty what she now saw was an ornate silver flask. "If she's game."

Holding her lemonade in one hand, she accepted the flask with the other. "Thank you." She took a dainty sip. The horrid liquid burned its way down. "Delicious," she choked, and forced down another sip. The second heralded an uncontrollable coughing fit.

"That's the spirit," Caden said. "Allow me." He moved toward her, arm raised to administer a helpful pat on the back.

Zeke beat him to it, moving with catlike speed.

After several thumps, she sidled out of his reach. "I'm fine, thank you," she said with a glare.

Caden took a healthy swallow of the spirits. "Zeke?" He held the flask out to Zeke who took the container with a grunt of thanks.

The early afternoon sun shone on his golden mane as he threw back his head for a long draught. He was so beautiful it almost hurt to look at him.

She tore her gaze away.

"I think it's time we go in," Zeke said.

She felt his stare on her. As if she had no choice in the matter, her gaze met his. Heat, and promise, and something volatile swirled in the blue depths of his eyes.

One thing was certain. Her time was up. They would talk once they arrived back at the house, and then it would be over between them. Over before it even began.

Deliberately, she shifted her attention to the viscount—and stalled. "Lord Randall, I see you've brought another firearm. Rather larger than the ones I've handled. Quite impressive really. Might I have a closer look?"

Chapter Twenty-Five

Viscount Randall picked up the weapon and displayed it against his flat palm.

"What you see here is a Colt, model 1873. Affectionately, the peacemaker. I imported it from the States. It's a .45 caliber, and packs quite a bit more punch than the .22s we've been firing today. Would you like to try it out before we pack it in?"

"I'd be delighted to," Kitty said with feeling. Although she was keen to try the firearm, she was more pleased about the short delay she'd bought herself. Telling Zeke goodbye was going to kill her.

She and Lord Randall approached the starting mark.

"Its sight is here." The viscount gestured to the rear of the barrel, as opposed to the hammer.

"Oh, that is different, isn't it?"

"You'll hold it like..." He stretched out his arm, adjusted his stance, glanced at her. "You angle your body and stack your—"

He broke off. "Perhaps it would be best if I showed you." He stepped toward her tentatively, as if he meant to position her arms himself and felt awkward over the notion.

Zeke practically shoved Randall out of the way. "I'll show her."

Kitty thought she heard muffled laughter coming from both Caden and Randall.

Her cheeks burned as he crowded in on her. How mortifying. She wriggled and elbowed him in the ribs.

He chuckled low in her ear and refused to give an inch. Widening his stance to place his booted feet on either side of hers, his arms came around her, encircling her, before his warm, large hands covered hers.

"I comprehend the basic operation, my lord," she said through gritted teeth. "I don't require your assistance."

"Nevertheless," he said in a velvety soft voice, his lips close to her ear, "I insist."

Kitty closed her eyes as liquid heat rippled through her. She took a fortifying breath, and struggled to maintain her righteous indignation. But how could her will prevail against sandalwood and spice and Zeke's hard muscled body cocooning hers?

Best to take the shot and get this over with. She pinched one eye closed, and used the other to sight the target.

"Make sure your footing is secure," he purred. "Do take your time."

"How can I adjust my stance with your feet in my way?" she hissed.

No question about it; the two observers' laughter rang through the air.

And then, the brazen peacock propped his chin on her shoulder. "Am I?"

"Seriously, Zeke, you must tell her to—" Randall began.

She squeezed the trigger.

A deafening explosion sounded in her ears, while seemingly in the same instant the most powerful recoil she'd ever experienced pulled her off her feet, pounding her into Zeke's chest, while her firing arm shot back, pistol in a death grip in her hands. Or Zeke's hands. She couldn't tell. Instinct bade her pinch her eyes closed and crane her neck sideways to avoid the gunstock's impact. The wood collided with something solid.

And then time slowed.

In the eerie silence and through the acrid smoke, she flew up and up—then back. Trees, then treetops, and finally blue sky, passed before her eyes.

She landed with a thud that stole her breath.

Before she could begin to right herself, rough hands patted her arms, grasped her shoulders, her head, then lifted her to her feet.

"Are you all right?" Caden asked, his throat muscles cording so she knew he shouted, though she could barely hear him over the ringing in her ears.

She nodded and craned her neck searching for Zeke, then stared in horror at the ground behind her where Zeke lay, motionless.

Randall crouched beside him. Garnet red blood matted Zeke's beautiful golden hair.

She had no coherent thought of twisting out of Caden's arms, nor of lunging forward and dropping to her knees beside Zeke. She cradled his face in her hands.

"Zeke," she cried over and over till her throat felt raw.

He gave no response.

Dear God, she'd killed him. She'd killed him and she never told him she loved him. "You'll make yourself ill, Kitty. You must calm yourself," Lady Lillian urged.

"My lady, I appreciate your concern." Kitty executed a sharp pivot. She was well aware she was making a spectacle of herself, crying, pacing outside Zeke's closed chamber door, wringing her hands till her fingers ached. She didn't care.

"Perhaps a cup of tea, then?" Lillian asked.

"Tea would be lovely," Kitty lied.

Lillian seemed grateful for the task. "I'll see to it myself."

"Lovely," Kitty repeated. Dear God, didn't anyone understand she just needed to know Zeke was all right? That she hadn't permanently maimed him—or worse.

Certainly the men in the room with Zeke all thought her ridiculous. Oh, they hadn't said so directly. No, the words they'd used had been perfectly reasonable and rationale. Perfectly polite. What was it Caden had said? Oh, yes.

"Kitty, love, he came to in the buggy on the way up to the manse. It's the laudanum we gave him that's kept him knocked him out. He'll be fine, trust me. No small tap could crack that hard head."

Small tap indeed. She'd brained him.

She hadn't argued the point however. Neither had she mentioned she could do without the condescending pats, indulgent smiles, and not-so-subtle speaking glances passing between Caden, Viscount Randall, and even the earl inferring she suffered a fit of the vapors.

She couldn't blame them entirely. They were looking at things with their man eyes. Whereas her more reliable women's intuition kept screaming at her something awful was about to happen. The proverbial other shoe was about to drop.

She paused to scrub the heels of her hands over her burning eyes. She wanted to ignore the innate knowing. Really she did. Wanted to dismiss her fears as simply owing to her idiotic love for the man. Unfortunately, in her experience, whenever her inner messenger of doom spoke up, it proved unerring. Like the time Collin left for America. She'd known tragedy would follow.

Collin has come safely home, a tiny voice inside her argued. The thought brought a tremulous smile to her lips. Collin.

Where was he anyway? She'd sent a footman for him a good half hour ago, well before the doctor arrived.

The good doctor. She snorted and resumed her pacing. Summoned from the nearby village, they awaited his arrival the better part of an hour. An eternity as far as Kitty was concerned. And then the stuffy old goat ejected her from Zeke's chambers.

Said he couldn't do a thorough examination with a female was present.

"What's all this, puss?" Collin said, sauntering toward her.

She launched herself into his arms. "Collin, oh, Collin, it's Zeke. I bashed him in the head with a revolver, and now he's unconscious."

"You what?" Collin held her slightly away from him to study her, a horrified expression on his face.

She almost laughed. "Not on purpose, silly."

"That's a relief. I say, this has been quite a day for you, hasn't it, poor darling? And I'm afraid there's more to come."

"That's what I'm afraid of. I knew you'd understand, Collin."

His brows knit.

"The doctor's with him now. They kicked me out for decorum sake." She stamped her booted foot.

Collin's frown deepened. "Of course you can't be in the room. Unless...you haven't already seen the man...eh...that is..."

She cut him off with an impatient tsk. "Of course not, Collin. What kind of person do you take me for?"

He gave a self-deprecating laugh. "I do apologize, darling. It's something James said."

"James? Did you speak with him this afternoon?"

Collin gave his fancy cravat a small tug, as if he'd tied it too tightly. "Indeed we had a lengthy, rather productive conversation. In point of fact, I have some important things to discuss with you, and the sooner the better." He glanced meaningfully at Zeke's closed door. "Are all the Thurgoods in with your—in with the patient?"

The hair on the back of Kitty's neck lifted a fraction. She smoothed a hand over her nape.

"Everyone save Lady Lillian." She eyed him. "Why?"

"Because I need a private word with you."

Kitty blinked. "Now?"

"No time like the present."

"But, Collin. I can't leave now. I have to know the extent of Zeke's—Lord Thurgood's—injury. I'm responsible," she said, her voice rising an octave.

He gave her a look of impatience. "Is the injury likely to lead to his death?"

"No, but—"

"The doctor's in with him now?" Collin gestured toward the closed door.

"Yes, but—"

He threw up his hands. "For God's sake, Kitty. I'm your brother. Your family. One would think you'd have a little more partiality for my well-being."

She winced at the direct hit. "Collin, nothing means more to me than having you here, alive and well. It's just—" She eyed Zeke's chamber door, then, resigned, relented. "You're right, of course. We can talk now. Only...can we do it somewhere close by? So that I may be here in the event the doctor deems Lord Thurgood's injury more serious than I've been led to believe?"

Collin sighed with impatience, but conceded the point. "Very well, someplace close. But private."

"There's a small, family parlor at the end of this corridor." She was already hurrying toward it.

The room was cozy, with burnished gold papered walls, two comfortable seating areas, with soft throws and pillows strewn hither and yon. Several oil lamps burned, illuminating the small space. A baize covered billiard table stood to one side, set and ready for a game.

"Will this do?" Kitty asked.

Collin nodded, his expression once more affable. "Quite. After you. Let's sit, shall we?" He reached behind him to close the door.

Her fingers flew to her lips. "Oh could we…that is, I'm certain we won't be interrupted here. It's just I want to hear if—"

He rolled his eyes and half smiled, as he finished her thought. "If someone comes or goes from Thurgood's chamber. You know, I'd almost forgotten your tenacity. Almost. Very well, love. Now do sit and listen to what I have to tell you."

She perched on the edge of an armchair, folded her hands in her lap, and waited expectantly.

Collin sat across from her. In spite of having pressured her into this tête-à-tête, he didn't immediately broach the subject. Instead he glanced around the room, taking in the hanging portraits and ornately tiled ceiling. "I'm not sure where to start."

"Something to do with Garrick?" Kitty offered. Anything to get this over with so she could return to Zeke's chamber.

"Actually, yes. As I mentioned, I had a long discussion with James this afternoon, initiated by him, to his credit."

"Oh?" In her experience, conversations launched by dear cousin Garrick were never to his credit. One of her feet began to tap with nervous energy.

"Yes. He said he expected I was anxious to discover the status of the Maidstone title." Collin's face flushed with feeling. "My title. As you noted this morning, the Crown's awarded the Barony to him."

"But surely they'll rescind their decision now you're back? They'll have to transfer the entailment to you, the rightful heir, won't they?"

Collin's mouth curved in a humorless smile. "It's what's right. It's what should happen. But it's a legal matter now, and as such, subject to all sorts of delays and missteps. For instance, what if I contest James' claim, and the courts simply refuse to undo their decision?"

Kitty's mouth dropped. "But they can't."

"Can't they?"

"Surely we could find a way…"

"We could fight. Appeal to the courts. But a drawn-out legal battle eat up every shilling." Collin's voice went low, and intense. "On the other hand, if James and I jointly petitioned the crown to overturn the decision, why, I'd be assured of success."

Kitty's brows furrowed at her brother's obvious naiveté. "Collin, I hope you're under no illusion James will cooperate with such a scheme."

Collin shifted off his seat to kneel in front of Kitty. His green eyes held hers in an intense stare. "That's just it, Kitty. He is willing, more than willing, to return the title."

The dread whispering through her as she paced the corridor outside Zeke's chambers turned into a deafening drumbeat.

"Why would he do that?" she whispered.

"In exchange for a good faith effort on our part," Collin said.

She swallowed hard. Tried to clear the buzzing in her ears. "On our part?"

"My darling. He asks only for the honor of your hand."

Chapter Twenty-Six

Zeke ran through a forest so thick with foliage and bracken the light of the moon barely eked through. Pain lanced his head with every foot strike. His lungs burned. Brambles and thorns tore through his clothes, pricking his skin.

But he couldn't stop. He had to find her.

He came to a place where the treetops merged, blotting out even the meager moonlight. North and south, east and west, vanished in the darkness. He could as easily be running away from her as toward her.

He strained his ears, desperate for any clue of which way should he go. Only the competing chorus of croaking frogs and night crickets answered his silent plea.

Guilt and fear ripped at his insides. He'd let this happen. If he didn't find her soon, it would be too late.

From nowhere and everywhere, came a swirling, luminescent fog. It closed in on him, congealing before him to form the distinct figure of a man, austere in his officer's garb—the man he'd dreamed of in Africa. Kitty's grandfather. He knew it as surely as he knew his own name.

Like before, the old man said nothing, just stared, eyes grave. He lifted his hand, pointing at Zeke as if in accusation.

Zeke blinked and found himself flat on his back. The man had vanished. A woman, bathed in moonlight, hovered over him.

Kitty. Touching him with those delicate fingers, cooling his burning skin, soothing his tortured soul. He needed her like air.

"Kitty."

"I'm here."

The dream receded. Zeke lay still, eyes closed. His head throbbed, miring his very thoughts in quicksand—as if someone had put a bullet in his skull, then poured an entire bottle of whiskey down his throat.

He inhaled slowly, filling his lungs. For his efforts he caught the subtle but distinct notes of lavender and rosemary. Relief cascaded through him. Kitty *was* here.

He opened his eyes a crack. Recognized immediately he lie in bed in his private chamber. Night had fallen, and someone had lit the wall sconces. Kitty hovered over him, her cool fingers resting atop his forehead, her creamy complexion bathed in the stuttering golden light.

God she was beautiful.

He liked looking at her, and relished her soothing touch. But why in hell was she here? Something had happened. It was there on the edge of his memory.

She lifted her hand from his forehead and traced her fingers down his cheek, her gaze trailing over his face until she noticed him studying her. Her eyes went wide. Swollen, red-rimmed eyes. She'd been crying. Why?

"You're awake," she said softly.

"Apparently," he rasped out. His mouth tasted like dirt.

She started to pull her hand from his face, and he reached up to press her palm in place. "May I have some water?" came his hoarse plea.

"Of course." With gentle force, she withdrew her hand from beneath his. She disappeared from his line of vision, returning seconds later. She slid an arm beneath his pillow and levered him up.

She held a glass to his lips and he took a long drink of lemon-tinged water. Some of the cobwebs from his sleep mud-dled mind cleared. He nodded when he'd had enough and she adroitly lowered.

Feeling more himself, He flattened his palms on the bed and hoisted himself up, much to Kitty's distress. Though he ignored her pleas to desist, she clearly had a point. His head pounded, and for a moment the room spun, but he refused to concede defeat.

When he finally sat upright, his shoulders pressed against the cushioned headboard, he closed his eyes and sucked in a fortifying breath.

That or wretch.

"You shouldn't have done that. You're hurt."

He opened his eyes and slanted her a glance. "I rather noticed that on my own. Now, kindly tell me what the hell is going on. Why does my head feel as if it's cracked open, and why are you in my bedchamber in the middle of the night? And more to the point, why've you been crying?"

She dropped into the chair someone had pulled to his bedside, a morose expression clouding her crystalline green eyes. She opened her mouth to speak, closed it, and out came her quivering lower lip.

The moment that plump lip caught his eye, his loins stirred to life. He would laugh if he didn't think doing so would make the pounding in his head worse. He shuffled his legs to rumple his bedcovers over his groin, and dropped a hasty glance down at himself.

He was bare-chested, leading him to wonder if other body parts were equally bare. He peeled back the covers and peered beneath. Drawers, and nothing else.

He threw Kitty a suspicious look, and was gratified to see a rosy flush stain her cheeks. "I'd also like to know who undressed me."

Mainly he wanted to provoke her out of her gloom. She was still in the yellow gown she'd worn to the shooting match earlier, so he couldn't be half naked for any good reason.

Shooting. They'd had their match.

She sucked in a breath, then her words poured out. "I nearly killed you with Viscount Randall's pistol. I don't know who undressed you since the doctor demanded I leave during his examination, after which Collin insisted I wait 'til morning to see you, but I refused."

She lowered her voice to a confessional tone. "Actually, I acceded to his request, then snuck back here after everyone was asleep."

He lifted his hand to stop her diatribe in case there was more. He closed his eyes, taking a moment to digest her rapid-fire speech. He'd forgotten about Collin showing up this morning. He needed to revisit that fact, but one thing at a time.

"You fired Randall's firearm." He drew out the words as the memory congealed. He'd crowded her, purposely provoking her. He could almost hear his grandfather saying, I told you so.

"And almost killed you," she said in a plaintive tone.

The corners of his mouth curved upward. "Kitty, no."

"Yes."

"It was an accident."

She shook her head emphatically. "No. You made me angry, standing so very close behind me and..." She swallowed, fanning her face as if to calm her quaking nerves.

The scent of lavender wafted over him. He grinned and crossed his arms over his chest. Now that he'd righted himself and taken several steadying breaths, he felt much better. In fact, he felt good enough he had to wonder if he'd had some help of the medicinal nature.

"I shouldn't have reacted to your sour-puss disposition, by firing so hastily.."

His grin wavered. He did vaguely recall her avoiding his gaze while also brushing off his every attempt to draw her into conversation. Why had she done that? But he had no time to reflect further as she barreled on.

"I remembered how, once before, I'd knocked into you from a gun's recoil. Do you recall? At the cottage? This morning I thought I'd teach you a lesson by not bracing myself properly again and...*bam*,"--She clapped her hands together, the sound reverberating painfully in his head--"I brained you." A fat tear rolled down her cheek.

He lifted a hand to wipe it away, but she sprang to her feet like a skittish cat.

"Oh, Zeke. Does it hurt much?" She leaned toward him, placing her cool fingertips gently on his forehead. Her sweet, utterly Kitty scent surrounded him.

He sighed in contentment. "It does a little," he said, mostly so she'd keep touching him. "You're watching over me even against Collin's express directive not to? I feel special."

She bit her lip and averted her gaze, but not before he saw her chin quiver, and tell-tale moisture dampening her lashes as if she might cry anew.

Dear God, anything but that. "May I have a cold towel for my brow?"

"Of course." She dashed toward his bureau, returning with a damp towel. She took her time, dabbing his forehead and cheeks. Then she reached around him to drape the cloth over the back of his neck. Doing so brought her bodice eye level.

"Mmm."

Her mouth curved in a tremulous smile as she straightened. "Randall and Caden said the accident caused us to lose points, and declared the match a draw."

"Like hell," he said. The cold towel really was easing his headache. "Not that there's any prize I want from them. You, however…"

His gaze drifted over her disheveled appearance. Her coiffure had lost most of its pins, and only a sagging coil at her nape remained. Several silky tendrils, gleaming blue-black in the candlelight, framed her face.

"Poor darling. You never even got to clean up."

She lowered her lashes and put a hand to her brow. "I look a mess."

She looked like heaven. "Turn around," he commanded in a rough voice.

She shocked him by obeying without question for once. She probably assumed he intended to adjust his sheets or his drawers.

He didn't. Using both hands, he grabbed at the remaining pins in her hair and tossed them onto the floor. The thick coil unwound.

She spun around, her hand to her nape. "Why did you do that?"

"Because I like your hair down." He took advantage of her distraction, wrapping one hand around her waist to pull her toward him. "Sit."

She rested her slender hip on the edge of the mattress, glancing over her shoulder at the open doorway linking his bedchamber and the night dark, adjoining antechamber. "This isn't proper. I'm not even supposed to be here. What if someone comes?" She licked her lips.

His eyes fixed on those rosy lips. He didn't give a damn if anyone came. He just wanted to taste her. To feel her glossy hair brush over his naked chest. To hold her in his arms. "What time is it?"

She scrubbed her hands over her skirts. "Nearly two a.m., I think."

"No one's coming," he announced. "But if it will make you feel better, go lock the adjoining door."

"Why should I do that?"

"Because I'd like to claim my forfeit now." He held his breath, aware what he suggested was wrong, and not caring one iota. He wanted his mouth on hers.

He watched her wrestle with her conscience.

In desperation, he played his ace. "You did almost kill me."

Without a word, she pushed to her feet and hastened for the door.

His cock seemed to thicken with every step she took. He mounded up the bedcovers around his waist so she wouldn't notice the telltale bulge and run. Not before he kissed her.

She returned to her perch on the edge of his bed, eyes roaming his naked chest in a charming combination of alarm and something resembling hunger. "Oh, dear. Your bedclothes."

"What about them?"

She swallowed visibly. "They've fallen." She reached for them with both hands, evidently intending to yank them up.

Better she see his chest than what his sheets concealed.

He caught her wrists. "Too hot. I likely have a fever, due to my injury." He had a fever, all right. It just had nothing to do with his head injury. "Feel for yourself," he said, his voice husky.

Taking one of her hands, he unfurled her fingers and placed her palm flat on his chest.

"You are quite warm," she said, breathless. Her fingers pressed into his skin in tiny pulses, almost kneading, and he had to fight the urge to drag her into his arms and plunder her sweet mouth.

"Come closer."

She inched further onto the bed.

She looked so sweet, so intent on pleasing him, he almost felt guilty. He silenced his conscience, telling himself he didn't intend to ravish her. He simply wanted—needed—to kiss her. Thoroughly.

"Closer."

"I'm right beside you." She loosed a nervous laugh and moistened her lips with the tip of her tongue, drawing his gaze to her mouth like a moth to a flame.

"I can't kiss you from here."

"Oh." She leaned forward, not stopping till her face was inches from his. Her warm breath fanned his lips. "Better?"

In answer, he cradled her head, spearing his fingers into her hair, and brought his mouth slowly, inexorably, to hers.

At the touch of their lips, molten heat poured through his veins. Somehow he kept the contact light, brushing her mouth with feather-soft kisses again and again until her lips grew damp and pliant, her breaths shallow and choppy.

His slow seduction cost him. His body shook with the effort it took to reign in his own pent-up desire for her.

God, but her lips were sweet. He nipped and sucked and teased the corners of her mouth until, finally, a small mew escaped her and she parted her lips, inviting him in. With a low groan, his tongue eased into her damp warmth. She tasted like mint tea and sugar and Kitty.

Another little whimper of pleasure sounded in her throat, hammering a crack into the wall of his restraint. He moaned, tangling one hand in her hair and splaying his other hand on the small of her back to urge her closer.

In a rustle of skirts and sheets, she half leaned, half fell toward him. Her hand, still pressed against his chest, kneaded his flesh in the rhythm of a purring cat. Her fingernails scored his skin, each tiny stab shooting lightning bolts of pleasure straight to his groin. His hips rocked as nature and lust collided. *Sweet Jesus.* Cold sweat beaded on his brow, but he stilled his riotous flesh.

"Touch me," he commanded in a hoarse whisper.

Her other hand crept up to explore the hollow of his neck, then moved higher, tracing his Adam's apple, and toying with the hairs at the back of his neck.

A helpless shudder racked his body. "Kitty," he rasped against her lips. Unable to stop himself, he wrapped one arm around her slender waist, and pulled her fully against him.

She responded with a sweet, innocent ardor, twining her arms around his neck, and clinging to him.

Though she still wore her chemise, she'd removed her wired corset at some point during the day, and the weight of her plump breasts taunted him through the thin material of her gown. Her small, hard nipples grazing his flesh acted like fodder to the inferno of need raging inside him.

He grabbed a fistful of her hair, twisting it around his wrist. Using gentle force, he tugged her head backward and deepened the kiss. His tongue plunged into her mouth, again and again, mimicking the intimate joining he longed for. He wanted her. So. Badly. His swollen cock literally ached to be inside her.

He must be mad to torture himself like this, indulging in the taste and feel of her, here in his bed, in the middle of the night, his body half naked, and fully, desperately aroused.

Calling on all his will, he broke off the kiss. He had to, now, while he still could.

Kitty stared up at him with heavy-lidded eyes. "No, Zeke. Don't pull away again. Not tonight," she whispered, and threaded her fingers into his hair, tugging his mouth back to hers.

Just like that, he lost the battle with himself. His lips sealed over hers, and he twisted with her in his arms. He fell on her, crushing her into pillows and mattress. He pulled his mouth from hers long enough to gaze down at her face, framed with her lustrous waves of inky black hair. "So beautiful," he whispered.

She gazed back at him with passion-glazed eyes, shifting beneath him 'til the base of his cock settled snugly between her legs.

He gasped lung-fulls of air and his hips pressed helplessly into hers. "You make me...crazy. Make me...want things...I shouldn't."

He drew one shaking hand to trace her cheek, lowering his forehead to hers. "Kitty, do you know what torture this is? You, here, at my bedside, with me wanting you more than the air I breath?"

"Should I go?" she asked softly.

God, no. Shaking his head, he drew a ragged breath and traced circles around her lips, coaxing them apart.

Her slender arms snaked around his waist, her silky fingers tracing the muscles of his back, cruising lower, to the band of his drawers.

"Mary, mother of God," he muttered as his body shuddered with need. Without making a conscious volition to do so, his knee wedged her thighs apart beneath all the layers of fabric and sheets. He swiveled his hips, aligning them with hers, not stopping till the tip of his cock pressed into her hot center. He closed his eyes and ground his teeth.

It would be so easy. Just move the sheets. Pull up her skirts. Spread her thighs. They would be creamy white and silky smooth and would feel so good locked around his waist.

No. He pushed the image from his mind. He couldn't take her like this, no matter how badly he desired her. Unless...

He grasped the desperate thread of hope like a lifeline.

"Tell me why you're here, Kitty," he demanded in a harsh whisper.

Chapter Twenty-Seven

Zeke waited, tense and desperately aroused, his body pressing hers into the mattress. If Kitty told him what he wanted to hear, everything would change. If not...He swallowed hard.

Kitty gazed up at him. "I snuck here to your chamber after everyone was abed because of your injury—"

"That doesn't explain your presence in my bedchamber. Not really."

Her hands stilled on him. She lowered her lashes, shielding her eyes from his view. "I don't want to talk. Kiss me, Zeke, please."

He didn't want to talk either, but he forced out the words. "Kitty, last we spoke, I made you a proposition. You promised to think on it. Did you?"

She nodded.

His heart hammered into his ribs hard enough to crack bone. Longing and fear threatened to choke him. Fear she might not give him the answer he so desperately needed to hear. "And?"

She lifted her lashes and gazed up at him with inscrutable eyes. "You must know the answer, Zeke."

Blood roared through his ears. He could hardly breathe as lust and satisfaction converged within him, flooding his senses.

She was his. His to do with as he pleased, from this moment forward. He lowered his head and pressed his mouth over hers, his lips moving slowly and deliberately, claiming her. *His.*

She clutched his shoulders, her nails digging into his skin, while her body arched against his. He had never wanted a woman so badly.

"Kitty, tell me you want me," he said against her lips, her cheek.

"I want you," she whispered.

"Again," he murmured into the column of her throat. His hand came up and cupped her breast through her bodice, then retreated enough to skim one tight nipple with his palm.

"I want you," she said, panting as he rolled her nipple gently between his thumb and fingers. She let out a low mew, then said in a voice barely audible, "I love you, Zeke. I'll always be yours."

✳✳✳

She closed her eyes and pressed her burning face into Zeke's hard shoulder. She hadn't meant to profess her love for him.

The words had simply fallen from her lips, pulled from the depths of her being as surely as his hands were coaxing the most delicious sensations from her body.

She pressed up into his palm, shamelessly encouraging his caress. This was all that mattered. Her, Zeke, their bodies entwined.

While his fingers played over her breasts, his lips traveled to the base of her throat where his tongue delved. She sucked in a breath.

He nibbled his way to her ear. "You love me, do you?" he breathed, before taking her earlobe between his teeth in a gentle nip.

In answer, she angled her chin upward to give him greater access.

He gave a throaty chuckle and hefted his weight off her to rest on his forearms, bracketing her upper body. His rumpled hair fell forward, tickling her nose as his face hovered inches above hers. His choppy breaths fanned her fevered skin as he gazed down at her.

She drank in the sight of him. The flickering, golden candlelight, played over the hard line of his jaw, the contours of his full lips. But it was his eyes that caught at her heart. They burned with desire and a tenderness she'd never hoped to see from him.

He brushed his knuckles over her cheek. "I know I should tell you to go. You deserve roses and champagne and a wedding night for your first time. But—" He shook his head. Using the lightest of touches, he cupped one of her breasts through her gown, then smoothed his palm down her ribcage to her hip. He squeezed. "I have one small problem. I want to touch you everywhere. Taste you. Everywhere."

"I want to touch you, too." She cupped his cheek.

A look akin to pain crossed his face. "Kitty, I'm not sure you understand." He gave a shaky laugh. "Hell, I don't even understand this madness."

Sobering, he traced her collarbone with his fingertips. "What I'm trying to say is... What I mean is..." He emitted a low curse. "If you don't extricate yourself from my bed this instant, I'll use everything in my arsenal to coax your legs apart, and sink myself into you."

His words both shocked and enthralled her. "I'm not going anywhere." She barely recognized the husky voice as her own.

Heat flared in his eyes. "In that case..."

His hand drifted to the bodice of her bodice. He toyed with the ribbon-trimmed edge, slipping his fingertips beneath the fabric. "I think one of us has on too many clothes."

"I'll need a bit of help with the buttons," she said. Inwardly, she marveled at her calm tone. Her insides were quaking.

In one easy move, he rolled off her, taking his body heat with him.

She sat up, twisting so her back was to him, and slanted a glance over her shoulder.

Propping himself up on one elbow, he wordlessly set to his task. His burnished gold hair and bare chest gleamed in the candlelight. An artfully draped sheet concealed his hips and one leg, while the other tanned leg rested, knee bent, foot flat on the twisted fabric. He resembled nothing short of a debauched demigod.

She held her breath as he pushed the fabric of her gown apart. The cool night air whispered over her shoulders, causing gooseflesh to rise all over her body.

"Are you cold?" Zeke ran one fingertip down the length of her spine, stoking the hot and needy ache pulsing low in her abdomen. She shook her head.

He inched closer, and the heat from his body swathed her. He reached around her to push her bodice low, sliding her arms out of the puffed sleeves. The fabric pooled around her hips.

His large hands encircled her waist. "Better," he murmured in her ear as his fingers drifted up her ribcage.

He bent his head to kiss her neck, and slowly, so slowly, his fingertips grazed the undersides of her breasts.

Body humming with sensation, she fell into the wall of his chest, and gasped when she felt a hard ridge against her buttocks.

His body shuddered at the contact, and he half-growled. His hands slid roughly upward, to cup and squeeze her breasts through the sheer silk of her chemise. He rolled her nipples between his thumbs and forefingers, each tug sending intoxicating darts of pleasure deep in her core.

She closed her eyes, glorying in the heady sensations, and every ragged draw of his breath in her ears. Nameless, dizzying need clawed through her.

He turned her to face him, his gaze traveling down her torso. His mouth curved in a wicked grin as he shoved her gently into the pillows.

"Still too many damned clothes." He shimmied her gown and petticoat down her legs and flung them to the floor.

The sheets ensconcing him had disappeared. Candlelight limned the tapering V of his torso, illuminating the band of his white drawers—and the very definite, very large bulge.

The first flicker of doubt assailed her. But she couldn't leave. Not now. She would have to live on this night for years to come.

Zeke hinged forward, planting his forearms on either side of her. As always, the scent of him—sandalwood, spice, and pure Zeke, numbed her mind to all but an insatiable craving to be closer to him. Her doubts receded. She loved him, and for tonight, nothing and no one else mattered.

He pressed feather kisses across her collarbone, his soft hair tickling her nose. Then his warm, wet lips encircled one nipple through her chemise.

A kaleidoscope of pleasure spiraled through her. "Zeke," she half-whimpered.

He gave a low groan, as his tongue danced over her nipple, flicking softly, before his lips closed over her again to suck and pull at the heated flesh.

His hand skimmed down, over her waist, her hip. He bunched a handful of the skirt of her chemise. The sheer lawn inched upward. He grasped another fistful of material, exposing the lacy ruffle of her knickers.

A moment later, her underskirt reached her hips. Cool air whispered over the bare flesh where the fabric of her crotchless knickers parted. She'd never felt so vulnerable, or so alive.

His hand settled on her knee. Stilled. He brought his mouth back to hers and kissed her so tenderly she thought her heart might burst from her chest. "All right, kitten?"

Unable to speak, she nodded.

Staring into her eyes, he smoothed his lightly calloused palm up her thigh, pushing her knickers higher until his fingers slipped into the loose folds of fabric to cup her bare bottom. Goose flesh rose over her entire body.

She bit her low lip and pressed her face into his damp, hot neck.

"Shh," he whispered. His fingertips traced slow circles on her tender skin, 'til her insides bubbled like hot wax and the area between her legs thrummed with need.

His fingers slid higher, grazing her curls. On instinct her legs squeezed together despite her desire to give him everything she had.

"Open for me, darling. Trust me to know what you need," he purred.

Her heart pounding in her throat, she inched her shaking legs apart.

He feathered kisses on her lips. "More." He drew up her knee, planting her foot flat on the mattress. His fingers traced down the underside of her thigh, sliding inexorably toward her core.

This time, when he eased his fingers into the petals of her sex, she sucked in a breath but left herself open to him.

"Sweet Jesus," he breathed, his eyes narrowing as if he were in pain. "So wet. So ready."

He brushed his fingertips over the slick flesh near to her opening, and she quivered helplessly at his tantalizing touch. Then, he slid one finger inside her while his thumb slowly massaged her sex.

Pleasure unlike any she'd ever known unfurled within her. "Zeke," she cried in desperation. "Please."

She heard his husky laugh before he murmured in her ear. "Shhh, darling. Just let me..."

She made a choked noise and fisted her hands in the sheets. Her hips undulated as his thumb moved over her in a deliberate, circular motion, relentlessly twisting her insides tighter and tighter, like a coil ready to spring.

Her hips swayed and shuddered, and she was past caring. Past embarrassment. Zeke was taking her body to a place she never dreamed existed. A place where love and desire, tenderness and sensation, excitement and need entwined.

"*Zeke, Zeke.*" She clutched at him, dragging herself into his chest as if, by being close to him she could reach that unknown pinnacle, just out of reach.

She sensed that illusive peak growing nearer as his whispers of encouragement gave way rasping breaths. His body, half covered hers, and his own gyrating hips told her his need matched her own.

"Now, Kitty. *Now*," he choked.

No sooner had his words left his lips then glorious release swept through her. Wondrous pleasure bloomed inside her, like a thousand shards of sparkling light spreading as far as the eye could see.

Time stood still as Zeke wrenched every last drop of the heady sensations out of her until her stuttering breaths slowed and her body went limp in his arms.

When she turned to gaze at him with wonder, he pressed his forehead into hers. He stared at her with hot, possessive eyes the color of a stormy dusk sky.

"Kitty, I—" He hissed in a breath, and in one rough move, ripped off his drawers. Then he eased himself on top of her, pressing her pliant body into the mattress.

Zeke reached between them with a shaking hand.

Pressing her chemise up and out of the way, he brought his hips into alignment with hers, nestling the tip of his throbbing cock into the entrance of her swollen sex. Her sweet, hot liquid welcomed him, daring him to thrust into her. His entire body shook with the effort it took to resist his own carnal need.

Her release had nearly undone him—something that had never happened to him, even as a greenhorn lad. But, then, he'd never wanted a woman the way he wanted her.

She was his. He would be the only man she would ever know.

She lay beneath him, a siren gazing at him with passion-drugged eyes. Black hair tumbling around her shoulders in sensuous waves. Creamy skin aglow from the climax he'd coaxed from her body.

She smiled shyly. Love and trust shone in her green cat's eyes. Love. She loved him.

His insides twisted with gut wrenching need. "Kitty," he rasped, her name sounding like a prayer to his own ears. "I don't want to hurt you, but I'm afraid it's unavoidable." At least he thought so. He'd never had a virgin. Never wanted to bear the responsibility before now.

"It's all right, Zeke. I trust you."

Blood roaring in his ears, he closed his eyes and pressed into her heat. Her sweet flesh pulsed around him. It was like nothing he'd ever known. He opened his eyes and looked down at her.

Kitty's brows were furrowed. "I think...this may not work."

Sweet Jesus. He'd laugh if he weren't so desperate for her. Sweat trickled down the center of his back. He pressed forward another inch, then another.

She shifted, probably trying to accommodate herself to his size, but it was too much.

"Kitty," he said in a strangled voice as his hips jerked and he thrust past the fragile membrane, sinking himself to the hilt. The sound of his ragged breath filled the air.

She felt so good. Too good. He held himself perfectly still, for his sake as much as hers.

A teardrop escaped the corner of her eye and rolled down her cheek.

He kissed the salty track. "I'm sorry, sweetheart." He wanted to tell her the pain would recede, that making love would improve with practice. But he was past the ability to speak.

"I'm all right. Are we…is it done?"

This time he did give a shuddering laugh, before pressing a kiss to her temple. "Not quite."

He eased himself nearly out of her, then pressed back in, kissing her all the while.

Again and again he buried himself in her. Long, slow, delicious, tortuous thrusts. Time stopped. Only Kitty existed. Her sweet body, her mouth, her sighs, her heat. Her love.

She wrapped her arms around his neck and pulled him to her. Then her hips arched up to meet his, matching his rhythm. Oh God. Torture. He fought the urge to thrust harder, faster, deeper. Fought it with everything in him.

A low keening sounded in her throat. It built, growing louder. Then her thighs tightened around him as her second release gripped her.

She choked out his name, and he was gone. His climax tore through him. He poured himself into her, gritting his teeth against the overwhelming ecstasy.

Afterwards he collapsed on top of her, utterly spent, and inwardly shaken by the power of the release she'd wrenched from him.

He didn't know how much time passed before he moved again. Five minutes? Ten? "Kitty?"

At her muffled response, he cracked one heavy eyelid and saw his blankets practically engulfing her. With a world-weary sigh, he rolled to his side, taking her with him so she nestled in the curve of his body. He draped an arm over her and closed his eyes. They'd earned the right to rest. Just for a few moments.

It occurred to him his head no longer hurt. A satisfied smile spread over his face. The old wive's tale was true. Sex really was a remedy for the headache.

***

Zeke came awake with a start. A bright beam of daylight seeping through a crack in his drapes told him it was morning. He was cold. He was lying on his stomach, atop seriously rumpled sheets instead of under them, and he was naked.

Last night's events came back in a rush. He jerked upright and scanned his bedchamber for Kitty. She was gone.

He erupted from the bed and combed the floor for telltale signs. Hairpins. A petticoat.

He found nothing except his drawers. The lady had covered her tracks. Except...

He turned back to the bed and searched the bed covers. Dried blood marred the sheets. A brief memory of he and Kitty, tangled in the linens, of Kitty's soft flesh, yielding to his insistent hardness, flashed before his eyes.

It shouldn't have happened like that.

Despite the prick of guilt, the lower part of his anatomy came to full attention. He grinned. He wanted to see her. Now.

First the sheets. The injury he'd suffered could explain the blood, not that any of the servants would question him. But why court trouble?

He finished stripping the bed, and had them balled in his arms when two knocks sounded on the outer chamber door. He shoved the sheets in the bottom of his wardrobe, and pulled up the bed covers before throwing on his dressing gown and striding through the antechamber.

He found his brother in the corridor, leaning against the wall, arms crossed.

"Caden. Since when have you ever waited for me to open my door?"

Caden craned his head to look past Zeke. "Since you acquired an adorable fiancé who had to be forcibly ejected from your bedchamber." He crossed the threshold.

Zeke gave his brother an innocent look. "Kitty was here?"

"Yes. We let the doctor bear most of the blame for ousting her, out of fear for our lives. Cowardly, I know, but we were fairly sure she'd spare him for your sake. Even after he pronounced you the most hard-headed man alive, and her brother dragged her to her bedchamber, I half feared she'd sneak back." Caden gave Zeke a shrewd look.

Zeke moved to the open door leading to his bedchamber, propped his hip against the doorjamb, and met Caden's eyes with—he hoped—a guileless stare.

Caden let the subject drop. "How are you feeling, by the way?"

Zeke smiled broadly. This he could answer truthfully. "Aside from a nagging headache, I'm on top of the world. And starving. Have you eaten?"

"I'm about to, but thought I'd check on you first."

"Very thoughtful."

"As I mentioned, I half feared I'd find you in bed. With company."

"Kitty's hardly some trollop likely to throw her reputation away for a quick tryst."

"Wasn't her character I was worried about," Caden muttered. "Do you remember anything?"

Zeke was beginning to get irritated. "I just told you, I had no idea she was even in my bedchamber."

Caden arched a brow. "I meant, do you remember the accident?"

"Oh. That. Not much. I assume I got assaulted by the butt of Randall's gun?"

"Exactly." Caden pushed past Zeke to wander his bedchamber. He glanced around the room as if he'd never been inside it. Nosy bastard.

"Don't get any notions about blaming Kitty, either. You brought it on yourself, standing too close to her. Poor thing was quite beside herself."

"I'll do my best not to hold anything against her." Zeke turned his back on Caden to hide his grin and disappeared into his closet. "I'll see you downstairs, eh?"

***

"Speak of the devil," the earl said. "Zeke, we were just discussing you."

"Good morning to you, too, Grandfather, Aunt, Randall. Caden I've already had the pleasure of greeting." Zeke sauntered into the breakfast hall. "What, no Lady Kitty yet?"

"Perhaps all that nurse duty tired her out," the earl suggested.

Caden drained his coffee and rose from the table to approach the sideboard alongside Zeke. "I just informed Zeke of Kitty's vigil. Apparently he had no idea he had an angel watching over him."

Zeke grinned down at his plate and piled on the eggs.

"It is a bit odd neither Lord Hastings nor Kitty have put in an appearance this morning," Lillian said. An odd tenor in her voice had Zeke glancing her way.

Her hand fluttered at her throat in an agitated manner. "Lord James hasn't breakfasted yet, either."

Zeke waited for her to say something more, but after a moment she dropped her gaze and resumed eating.

"No, indeed," the earl said, not seeming the least concerned as he read this morning's copy of the Times.

Zeke took his filled plate and sat across from the earl. He picked up his cutlery and set to work on his salted ham.

"My, but someone's in a good mood today," Randall marveled.

Zeke glanced at his friend, his brows arched in query. "Are you referring to me?"

"I am."

Zeke chuckled for no apparent reason. "True. Not sure why you'd say so, however."

"Because you were whistling."

He thought a moment. "So I was."

"Odd to be so jubilant after getting a nasty knock in the head, don't you think, Randall? Perhaps we should have tried that on him earlier in the week."

Zeke refrained from rising to the bait. By George, he was in a grand mood.

"Ah. That ought to suffice for the journey back to London," Caden said a few minutes later, when he'd consumed a copious amount of eggs, ham, beans, and toast.

"Alas, it is that time, is it not?" Randall asked.

"We'll miss you," Zeke said with a grin.

"Don't pay any attention to him. The house won't be the same without the two of you here to wreak havoc on us all," the earl said. "Isn't that so, Lill?"

Aunt Lillian appeared lost in thought. With everyone's eyes on her, she gave a start. "You were saying?" she asked of no one in particular.

Caden threw his head back to laugh. "On that note, I'm off to my chambers to gather my things."

"I'll do the same," Randall said.

Both men rose. "What, you're leaving today?" Lillian asked them.

Her look of indignation had no effect on the hoots of laughter her question heralded, though Zeke's affectionate wink seemed to mollify her.

Chapter Twenty-Eight

After his brother and Randall left the room, Zeke checked his pocket watch. Late. Soon, breakfast would be cleared from the sideboard. Damn it, why hadn't she come down yet? Was she so mortified by last night's events?

Didn't she know he'd only pushed the bounds of their relationship because she'd agreed to marry him?

As to that, the sooner the better. To date Kitty hadn't proven herself the most practical girl when it came to marriage, but he assumed she'd be on board with the idea of a hasty wedding.

After all, she loved him.

He'd be happy to ask her opinion on the matter. If she ever came downstairs.

"What's got you all bothered?" his grandfather demanded. "When you first walked in here, you seemed grand."

Zeke cocked his head, considered his grandfather's words, then said, "Matter of fact, there is something on my mind.

Something I wish to share with both of you, as it happens, since you're both privy to certain pertinent facts."

"You actually plan to marry our girl, am I right?" the earl surmised, calm as you please.

Zeke frowned. "Yes. How did you guess?"

The earl waved a dismissive hand. "It was only a matter of time."

"Oh, dear," Aunt Lillian said.

Both men turned to look at her.

"I wasn't sure I should say anything, but now…" She trailed off, her expression pained.

"Say anything about what?" Zeke demanded.

"Late yesterday afternoon, after Dr. Caswell arrived, and Kitty and I adjourned to the corridor outside Ezekiel's chamber, she was beside herself. She kept muttering something about it all having been her fault, and a few choice words concerning the good doctor I'd rather not repeat."

A smile tugged at the corners of Zeke's mouth. "She was upset. Seems a normal reaction for a concerned fiancé."

"You didn't see her. You don't know," Lillian insisted. "I suggested she retire to her chamber, or the family parlor at the end of the hall, at the very least. She wouldn't hear of it. Not knowing what else to do for her, I finally went to fetch her a cup of tea.

"When I returned, Kitty was nowhere in sight. I first thought she'd retired. Then I noticed the parlor door stood ajar. I tiptoed toward the room, not wanting to intrude if she was resting. I heard voices."

Zeke stiffened. He and his grandfather exchanged a meaningful look.

Had James waylaid her? Zeke remembered now she'd been crying. If her cousin had harmed her, if he'd so much as frightened her, Zeke would tear him apart. Slowly. "James's voice among them, no doubt?"

To his surprise, Lillian shook her head. "I listened a moment. Not to eavesdrop, you understand, but because I know the danger her guardian—er, previous guardian—poses." Her eyes narrowed. "Finally I heard Kitty call the man by name. Collin."

Impatience stirred within Zeke. So Kitty and her brother had a private conversation. So what. "Go on."

"It was obvious their conversation was upsetting Kitty."

The earl cocked a brow. "Why do you say that, Lill?"

"Because she was crying."

Zeke stifled a sigh. "Didn't you say she'd been crying over my injury?"

"Yes. I thought the same, until I heard her ask Lord Hastings if there wasn't some other way."

Lillian broke off a moment to reflect. "Yes, those were her exact words. Collin, isn't there some other way? To which he replied, quite testily, no, there wasn't, and how could she think of objecting after all he'd been through."

She took a moment to lock eyes with both men, alternately. "He also told her she mustn't to breathe a word of their plans to any member of the Claybourne household. He made her promise."

The earl's white brows furrowed with concern. "What could he have asked her to do he would demand her to keep secret?"

Lillian frowned. "I don't know. I stopped listening when she started crying in earnest. It broke my heart."

Zeke slapped his palms on his thighs and rose. "One way to find out."

Lillian's eyes went round. "You won't tell her I—"

Zeke gave her a reassuring smile. "Don't worry your pretty head, aunt. I'll be discreet. I only plan to..."

Hell. He had no plan. Just a feeling of dread urging him to move. "...to talk to her," he finished lamely.

"But you can't simply descend on a lady's private chambers. It's not proper," Lillian insisted.

Zeke didn't stick around to argue the point.

A few minutes later—minutes that felt like bloody hours—he stood outside Kitty's door. Now that he was here, he found himself somewhat chagrined. She clearly had no desire to speak with him.

On the other hand, he wasn't leaving without answers.

He rapped twice. Waited. And waited. Rapped again, harder.

Still no response.

Something was very wrong. He grasped the doorknob, swallowing hard. "Kitty, I'm coming in," he said loud enough for her to hear from her inner chamber. He turned the lever, and after a beat, pushed open the door.

Her sitting room was all wrong. His gaze raked the area, trying to pinpoint exactly what seemed off. Then it struck him. It was perfectly tidy, not a single item of hers in sight. He stalked forward, yanked open the adjoining door, and felt the blood drain from his face.

Kitty was gone.

Operating on instinct, he bolted from her suite, and raced down the corridor toward the bachelors' wing. He came to James's chamber first. He flung open the heavy walnut door, slamming it into the papered wall. Empty.

He crossed the hall to Hastings' chamber, already knowing what he'd find.

He was gone.

Heart racing, he jammed both hands into his hair and stalked the hallway. Why? Why would they leave and take Kitty? Surely they didn't plan to harm her. Not Hastings at any rate.

He could not lose her. Especially after last night.

"Think, damn it," he growled to himself, and started for the stairwell.

Lillian said she'd heard Hastings demanding Kitty do something for him. Something she mustn't tell a soul. And now he, Kitty, and James were gone.

Pounding footsteps sounded in the corridor. He looked to see Caden and Randall charging in his direction

"Zeke, what is it?" his brother demanded.

"Kitty's gone. They've taken her."

"What do you mean, Kitty's gone?" Caden asked.

"And who's they?" Randall added.

Zeke shoved past them.

"Where are you going?" Caden demanded.

"To the stables. I want to know when they left, and where in hell they're going."

"We're coming with you," Randall said.

"Suit yourself."

Zeke cut a swatch through the servants' wing and kitchens, the most expeditious means of reaching the stables.

One of the stable lads greeted him. "My lord? May I saddle a horse for you? Oh, there's several of you here."

"Where's George?" Zeke asked, not bothering with the niceties.

The young groomsman's eyes went wide with alarm. "I'll fetch him."

But George was already coming their way, wiping his hands on a towel. "My lords, what might I do for you? I understood only the viscount and Mr Thurgood would be leaving this afternoon."

"My fiancé," Zeke snarled.

George's salt and pepper hair riffled in the wind as his gaze flicked between Zeke, Caden and Randall. "Are you asking about the party what went out this morning?"

Zeke rolled his shoulders, interlaced his fingers, cracked his knuckles.

Caden stepped forward, positioning himself between Zeke and the head groom. "Precisely, George."

Anxiety tightened George's features. "Is there something wrong? I only did what was asked of me."

"Just tell us of their departure," Caden said.

George nodded. "I got word last night to prepare Lord Hastings' barouche for an early morning departure, and have it waiting at the carriage house, by the front gate."

"How early?" Zeke ground out. He was incapable of pushing full sentences past his lips. His insides felt like he'd swallowed broken glass.

George cleared his throat. "They were here at the break of dawn. Roughly five hours ago, I'd say."

Caden Frowned at Zeke. "Up at the gate house, eh? Explains why no one heard anything."

"They said as they wanted to keep the horses quiet 'til they got a ways down the lane. Didn't want to disturb anyone's sleep at the main house. I didn't think anything of it at the time. Did I do wrong?" George asked for the second time.

Caden opened his mouth to speak, but Zeke beat him to it. "You did fine, George. Just fine. Now kindly saddle my mount. I'm leaving in ten."

"We're leaving in ten," Caden corrected.

"Not a good idea," Zeke tossed over his shoulder, already striding for the manse.

"Why is that?" Caden demanded, dogging his heels.

Zeke took the servant's entrance, judging it the quickest route to his private chamber. Bloody inconvenient to bother with a change of clothes, but he could hardly drive his mount like the devil in his current state of dress. More importantly, he needed his pistol.

"Damn it, Zeke, I asked you a question." Caden grabbed his shoulder.

Zeke shrugged him off, waiting 'til they'd cleared the kitchens to reply. "Because I wouldn't want you dragged into a murder investigation."

Rather than having the intended effect of shaking the two men loose, they stuck to Zeke like glue as he navigated the twists and turns of corridors leading to his suite.

He rounded the corridor leading to his chambers and found his grandfather standing sentinel outside his chamber door. Evidently he had to suffer through a damned family reunion before he could depart Chissington Hall. Bloody damned hell, couldn't anyone see he was in a hurry?

"I take it you've heard the news?" Zeke reached past the old man to shove open the door. He sidled through the narrow space between his grandfather and the doorjamb. He'd made it half way through his antechamber, when Claybourne's words froze him in his tracks.

"Zeke, I think you should read this."

He turned. Took in the folded sheet of parchment clutched in the earl's fist. "Did she leave me a note?"

The earl extended the letter toward Zeke.

He took the paper, and unfolded it. He scanned to the bottom and saw Kitty's signature. He slid his grandfather a look. "I don't understand why it was delivered to you, and not me." He sounded petulant to his own ears.

His grandfather cleared his throat. "I am sorry, son. I found it on my desk."

Zeke heard the words, but they didn't sink in fully. Not 'til he read Kitty's neatly penned note in its entirety. He fought the base urge to crumple the letter in his fist and grind his teeth 'til they cracked. Instead, he refolded the sheet with care, and handed it back to his grandfather.

The letter trembled in his hand, damn his eyes.

Caden's voice sliced the tension-filled air. "What does it say?"

The earl answered. "It's from Kitty. An apology and a good-bye. She says she and her brother thought it best to leave quietly, without upsetting the household."

Zeke barked out a humorless laugh.

The earl went on. "Apparently, as Kitty's legal guardian, her brother deemed the marriage contract agreed upon and signed by James, Ezekiel, and I, null and void."

Zeke wanted to toss the lot of them from the room. He wanted to throw something. Break something. He wanted a drink.

Randall came toward Zeke and laid his hand on his shoulder.

The pity in his friend's eyes whipped at the impotent rage boiling inside him. For a moment, he couldn't speak.

Finally, he drew in a long breath and forced out the words, "Never fear, Randall, I got an honorable mention in Lady Kitty's letter to Claybourne." He cocked his head and recited from memory, "Please thank Lord Thurgood for all he's done for me, and tell him I wish him Godspeed on his forthcoming venture abroad. Collin and I will, of course, handle the engagement retraction with the utmost discretion, in the most expedient manner possible. Blah, blah, blah." A joker's smile split his face.

"A damned honorable mention," Caden hissed, shaking his head.

The earl frowned. "Don't leap to conclusions. We don't know the circumstances she may have faced while writing her-her—"

"Her crying off letter?" Zeke still wore a broad, gruesome smile. He couldn't seem to wipe it from his face.

The earl waved the damned letter in the air. "You're all missing the point. I, for one, am not willing to assume she left on her own recognizance, not after everything she went through to be rid of James."

Caden glanced from the earl to Zeke, his expression considering. "What, exactly, does James have to do with this? I thought it was her brother, Hastings, who nullified the marriage contract."

"Maybe you noticed the three left the premises, en masse," Randall said in a low voice, his eyes on his boot tips.

"And?" Caden asked.

Zeke spoke in a gravelly voice he barely recognized. "James has something Hastings wants. Hastings, as Kitty's guardian, has something James wants."

Caden frowned. "You're saying...but that would mean her brother, her own flesh and blood..." His words died in his throat.

"Means to trade her for the return of his title," Zeke finished.

Caden's eyes went cold. He fixed his stare on Zeke. "You don't plan to let him get away with it?"

At Caden's question, something loosened inside of him. He had a choice here, he realized. He wasn't a powerless youth, forced to sit on the sidelines and watch as some outside force wreaked havoc on his world. He could fix this. Take control of the situation.

"She did ask that none of us interfere in her decision," he said.

"So you plan to leave her to the wolves." Caden threw up his hands in disgust.

Zeke's smile was grim. "No, as a matter of fact, I don't."

***

He rode from Chissington Hall alone, after garnering Caden's promise to leave for London, as planned. Now, more than ever, Zeke needed answers. Anything he could use as leverage should he be forced to strong-arm Kitty's dear brother.

With the wind burning his cheeks, he raced his mount toward Maidstone. His gut told him Hastings would take her there, to their ancestral home. He prayed to God he was right, and that her fool brother wouldn't marry her off first.

Hastings was an experienced gambler. He ought to know to hold onto his ace—in this case his sister—'til he saw the prize—his title—on the table.

On the other hand, Hastings had a habit of losing when the stakes were high.

Chapter Twenty-Nine

Kitty sat on the edge of the bed of the small room Collin had generously procured for her at the inn where they'd stopped for the night. She stared at nothing.

She should have left Zeke a letter. Something private, a proper goodbye. She'd tried, but every time she'd picked up her pen, all she could think to write was that she loved him, and didn't want to marry Garrick, or anyone else in the world except him. She wanted to build a future with *him*, to forge a real marriage with *him*—none of which he'd offered.

He planned to marry her, impregnate her, then leave the country. In the end, she'd given up altogether.

She could only guess at his reaction to finding her gone. Maybe he was relieved. Maybe he hated her.

A small sob escaped her, and fat, hot tears coursed down her cheeks. She let them fall. She'd held them back all day.

Meanwhile Collin and Garrick talked, even joked, as if everything were fine. As if they hadn't sneaked away from Chissington Hall like thieves in the night after everything the earl and Zeke had done for her.

As if Kitty's future wasn't forfeit.

Last night had been so…so…everything. She could still feel Zeke's warm, aroused body pressed to hers. Could close her eyes and imagine he was here, holding her in his arms, whispering sweet nothings in her ear—which only made knowing she would soon belong to Garrick that much more repugnant.

Her stomach emitted a low growl. Little wonder since she hadn't eaten all day. But the thought of food made her want to vomit. Had she ever been this hopeless in her entire life?

"Collin, Collin, why are you doing this to me?" she choked, dropping her head in her hands.

But she wasn't being fair. Collin didn't wish to ruin her life. He was simply doing what he must to recoup his title.

He'd been through so much. Enslaved. Likely beaten and starved. Kitty had to remember that. He needed her to do this to get back the life fate had so cruelly stolen from him.

A soft rap sounded at her door. Collin come to fetch her for dinner, no doubt. With a weary sigh, she scrubbed at the salty tracks on her face and dragged her feet toward the door.

Her brother stood in the hallway.

She attempted a smile.

He did not reciprocate. Instead, he hustled into the room and closed the door. "For heaven's sake, Kitty, you look…" He broke off, eyeing her head to toe with evident disgust. "Haggard is the word that comes to mind."

Kitty sniffled. "What a lovely thing to say," she retorted, but with no heat. She knew she looked a fright. She'd never been an attractive crier.

"You know very well seeing you miserable makes me feel just awful. If that was your intent, you've succeeded."

"I'm sorry, Collin. Of course I don't wish you to suffer on my account."

Collin took Kitty's cold hands in his. "Sweetheart, listen to me. It's just marriage. A formality really. After you're wed, you will live in Hastings House, with me, like before."

Like before. Except grandfather wouldn't be there. "Where will *he* live?"

Collin laughed. "He as in Garrick? He'll live there, as well, love. He will be your husband, after all."

She repressed a shudder of revulsion. "Of course."

"Stop looking so glum. Splash some water on your face, pinch your cheeks, and for heaven's sake, put on a fresh gown. I'm going downstairs to see about our supper. I'll have a quick pint, then return to fetch you. How does that sound?"

She nodded obediently.

"Give us a smile." He chucked her under her chin.

She forced the corners of her mouth upward.

After he left, she stripped off the simple muslin traveling gown she wore and opened her trunk. She pulled out the first dress she touched. What did she care what she wore?

Except shaking out the green day dress, she saw she'd need assistance getting into it, what with all the tiny buttons running up the back. She replaced the gown, and pulled out another. The yellow linen? Hmm. It laced up the back, as well.

She dug deeper—and found a dark blue gown of watered silk. Fancier than the moment dictated, especially considering her mood, but as the velvet ribbon tightening the bodice laced up the front, it would do.

She washed at the basin, for once taking no solace from her lavender and rosemary soap.

She was pulling on her gown when Collin knocked. He hadn't given her nearly enough time to freshen up after he'd expressly asked her to do so. How like her brother.

"It's open, Collin. I'm just finishing." She did her best to sound cheerful as her fingers tugged at the velvet ribbon tie.

The door swung open with unnecessary force, hitting the wall with a bang.

She glanced up—and froze. It couldn't be. Zeke? Here? It wasn't possible.

She must've spoken the thought aloud, because the man in her doorway bearing a striking resemblance to Zeke growled a response.

"The devil I can't." He swept into the room, golden hair wind-tossed, nostrils flaring, cheeks flushed, and coat tails flying. He looked glorious—and mad as hell.

Kitty couldn't speak. Couldn't form a rational thought. Not with the myriad emotions whirling within her. Joy and pain, hope and sorrow, and unbearable longing.

Zeke shook his head, as if bewildered by the sight of her. "I've ridden like the devil all day to find you. To save you from your abductors. And I find you like this." He gestured toward her. "Dressing for dinner."

Her mouth fell open. He sounded as if she'd hurt him. Zeke—who refused to care about anyone. "I...it's just a dress."

He took one halting step toward her, hand outstretched. "Has he touched you?" he asked in a hoarse voice, studying her with tortured eyes.

Her heart melted in her chest. "No. I'm quite safe, Zeke. It isn't like that."

"No?" he bit out, peeling off his overcoat and throwing it to the ground as if it were aflame. Next he stripped off his riding gloves with impatient yanks, and slapped them onto the discard pile. Shoving his fingers through his hair, he stalked toward her.

She stumbled backward until her legs hit the mattress.

"Kitty, tell me what the hell is going on here," he said through his teeth. "One minute we're getting married. The next you've disappeared without so much as a goodbye."

She gazed up at him, hands fisted at his sides. Heat emanated from his body, and he smelled of wind, and leather, and Zeke.

"Kitty? Say something."

"I-I left a note."

His nostrils flared, and his jaw went rigid. "For. The. Earl."

She had hurt him. She blinked back a fresh onslaught of tears and slumped onto the edge of the mattress.

Zeke sighed heavily and lowered to crouch before her, dropping his head onto her lap. His arms fell on either side of her thighs. "Please don't cry, Kitty."

Her heart ached. Literally burned. "All right," she choked past the lump in her throat. Helpless to resist, her fingers sifted through Zeke's silky golden hair.

A shudder went through him at her touch, and his hands coiled into fists on the bed. "I thought...I feared—" He broke off.

Why he'd come was all too clear. He'd come to save her. Again.

Meanwhile she'd skulked away at dawn, without even leaving him a note. She'd thought only of herself. Of the fact he didn't love her. She'd conveniently overlooked how he'd repeatedly come to her rescue. How he'd been there for her when her own brother had not. She didn't deserve this man. But he did deserve an explanation.

She took a bracing breath, and forced out the hated words that would finally free him of all obligation to her. "Zeke, I had to leave because it wouldn't have been right to continue accepting your hospitality when...I'm marrying Garrick."

***

Zeke's head shot up. Had he heard correctly? Because it sounded as if she'd just blithely announced she was marrying her cousin.

She cupped his wind-burned cheeks with hands as cold as ice. "You're free. You needn't worry over me any longer."

Blood hammered in his ears. He wanted to punch something. Make that some*one*. "This is your brother's doing."

She lowered her lashes, averting her gaze. "He asked me to marry Garrick, yes, but"—she bit her lip—"Garrick's going to return the Maidstone title to him in exchange."

At the vicious curse Zeke hadn't realized he uttered, Kitty flinched and started to pull away. He covered one of her hands with his, holding it to his jaw, then angled his head to press a kiss into her palm.

A tremor ran through her. Good. He was beginning to think her completely inured to him.

"You're not a piece of meat to be bartered at market. Hastings has no right to ask this of you. And you—how can you agree to such madness? After everything that's happened?"

Her pale green eyes turned zealous. "That's exactly why I must. Collin—he's been through so much. How can I not do this for him? As for Garrick, I know he's behaved in a deplorable, despicable manner, but—"

"I was talking about what happened between us," Zeke said through clenched teeth.

His chest burned, like someone held a red-hot branding iron to the underside of his ribs.

"You gave yourself to me. You belong to me now." As he spoke the words, his eyes roamed over her, hungry, desperate. "We made love, kitten. I put my seed in you. Even now, you may carry my babe."

A sob caught in her throat. She shook her head.

He rose to his feet, grasping Kitty by the shoulders to bring her toe to toe with him. His gaze settled on her rosy, quivering lips. "You're mine," he said in a voice he barely recognized as his own.

Those soft sweet lips parted, and the tip of her tongue peeked out to dampen them in unconscious invitation.

It was too much. With a low groan he bent, claiming her mouth with his, half devouring her as he sought to vanquish the anger, fear and need roiling within him.

After a moment, a whimper sounded low in her throat, and her arms twined around his neck.

Satisfaction like he'd never known slammed through him as she clung to him, pulling him closer, even as he strained to press every inch of his body into hers.

With a moan, He cupped her bottom, lifting her off her feet, then dropped with her onto the poorly sprung bed. "Mine," he breathed against her lips.

"Zeke, oh, Zeke, always," she said on a sigh. Her fingers trailed up and down his back in gentle, long strokes, slowly soothing the wild beast inside him.

His mouth covered hers, savoring her tender surrender as his hands roamed her body, alternately squeezing and caressing her through her damned evening gown.

Unerringly, his hips found hers, his erection nestling within the apex of her thighs, and he ground into her rhythmically, unable or unwilling to stop himself.

"Christ, I want you. I always want you." How did she do this to him?

Her body went pliant beneath his, legs parting. She wriggled, arching slightly until his hips settle snugly against hers. Pleasure and torture collided. She wanted him. But wanting him wasn't enough.

"You love me," he purred into her ear. "Say it."

"I do love you, Zeke. I love you so much," she avowed, banishing the darkness engulfing him since discovering her gone.

He hefted himself onto his forearms to stare down at her. "And you're going to marry me. Not that bloody fool cousin of yours. Not anyone else. *Me.*"

God, she was beautiful with her luminous green eyes, her creamy white skin, and blue-black hair.

"Why?" she demanded, her eyes intent on his.

Her question caught him off guard. He brought his fingers to trace her hairline. "Because..." He grunted. "What do you mean why?"

"I mean why do you want to marry me, Zeke? Do you..." She bit her lip. "Do you love me, too?"

Alarm bells clanged in his head. There was no right answer to this question. None she would understand, at any rate. He didn't believe in love. But he knew what he felt for her was different than anything he'd ever experienced with a woman. He wanted her. Wanted to protect and keep her. "Kitty—"

"You don't," she whispered.

He blew air out of his cheeks. "I told you, I don't believe in love. Not the way you do."

He was losing her. He could feel distance creeping between them though neither had moved an inch.

"Kitty, I want you. You know I do. And you want me."

Tears welled in her eyes. "But wanting's no reason to marry. I think you'd better leave. Now." She tried to hoist him off of her.

"I'm not going anywhere. Not without you." He knew in his gut he'd missed the mark. She had no intention of leaving with him. The darkness inside him returned with a vengeance.

"Why should I marry you instead of Garrick? What's the difference if love means nothing?" she demanded.

This again. He rolled off her and sat up. "The difference is your brother is marrying you off to save his own sorry hide," he ground out.

"And your reason is so much more noble?" Kitty propped herself on her knees behind Zeke. "My brother seeks to regain his title. You want to marry me so you can leave your grandfather alone in good conscience."

"It isn't like that," he hissed.

"It's exactly like that."

A knock sounded at her door.

"Collin," she mouthed, eyes going wide.

Zeke bared his teeth. "Excellent."

In a flash of movement, Kitty dove forward, clutching at his shoulders. When he would have brushed her off, she skittered onto his lap, locking her arms around his neck. "No, Zeke, please," she begged, pressing her face into his neck.

With a frustrated sigh, he relented, unable to resist her pleas. When he felt a quiver course through her body, his arms came up around her, gentling her. "Shh. It's all right. I'll stay right here."

She nodded, snuggling deeper into his arms.

A hot rush of tenderness swamped him. There was no way he would let this fiercely loyal, brave, utterly foolish vixen marry James.

"Kitty?" Collin called from the hall sounding irritated. The doorknob rattled.

In his arms, Kitty went tense as a bow string.

Zeke tilted her face up with the crook of his finger. "Calm yourself," he murmured. "I locked it."

She closed her eyes in evident relief.

When the doorknob rattled again, she raised her voice. "Collin, I'm not quite finished with my toilette. Be a dear and go ahead. I-I'll meet you in the dining room in a few minutes."

"Very well," her brother replied. "But do hurry."

After a moment, Kitty traced the side of his face with her fingertips.

Jesus. Helpless to stop himself, he lowered his head, dropping tiny kisses across her cheek, making his way to her earlobe, then down the column of her neck.

"I don't think you should...we should...be..." she stammered, tilting her head back to give him greater access, despite her protests.

He chuckled and bent to nuzzle the swell of her breasts above the half tied décolletage of her gown. "You see?" he asked, laying her back on the bed. "See how good I make you feel, sweetheart?"

"I know," she breathed. She agreed readily enough, but she still hadn't conceded the bigger point.

He closed his eyes briefly and played his ace. "Have you forgotten you might be carrying my baby? There's no way in hell I'll let another man raise my son."

She spoke in a soft rush. "I'm not pregnant. So you can stop worrying about the possibility of a baby. Because there isn't one."

He ignored the punch to his gut her words caused. "You can't know that. Not yet."

Except there was one way she could know. He stared into her eyes and waited for her to offer that unerring proof.

When she lowered her lashes, a tiny flicker of hope ignited in his chest. "Kitty, don't play games with me. Not about this."

She nibbled at her lower lip. "It was only the one time."

He stifled his laughter. "Yes," he said, going for a serious tone, "very often, that's all it takes."

Her sooty lashes fluttered upward. She looked dazed, as if she truly hadn't considered the possibility. "I promise if it turns out I'm carrying your baby I'll send for you."

"The hell you will."

She blinked several times. "Zeke, what are you saying?"

"I'm saying I'm not leaving your side until I know for certain, one way or another. If it turns out you aren't with child, I'll do the gentlemanly thing. I'll bow out and let you ruin your life to save your miscreant brother. Until then, you're stuck with me."

***

"Define stuck with me," Kitty said to the two hundred plus stone of gorgeous male currently pressing her into the mattress.

He glanced at the ceiling as if giving her question serious thought. "Stuck with me. As in not leaving this hotel until you leave." He paused to toy with a lock of her hair. "As in traveling to wherever you travel when you do leave."

He grinned at her. "Basically, I'll be shadowing your every move until we get this resolved." He slid a hand between them and caressed her belly.

"That's ridiculous," she sputtered, and shimmied out from beneath him before his magic hands could distract her from her point.

He rolled lazily onto his side, propping his head in his hand to study her.

She tried to ignore him as she tugged at the ribbons of her bodice and re-tied the ends into a less than picturesque bow. "Be serious, Zeke. You can't possibly join us."

Zeke sat up, all trace of humor vanishing from his face. "I'm deadly serious."

Her hands fell to her sides. "Do you doubt me? Zeke, I would send word if—"

He cut her off with a slash of his hand. "Kitty, you're one of the most loyal, steadfast people I know. It isn't you I distrust. It's that brother and cousin of yours.

"You might very well be dragged to the altar in the time it took me to learn of a baby. No, I'm not taking any chances with my babe's, or your safety." His voice softened and a corner of his mouth crooked upward. "As the mother of my child, you'll be under my protection for the rest of your days and nights. Included in the service is protection against any unintended marriages."

Her traitorous heart swelled in her chest. She spun around, making a show of neatening the items on her vanity—her brush, her comb, her hair sash—lest he see how profoundly his words affected her.

No one besides her grandfather had ever cared for her enough to stand by her and see no harm came to her. Not her parents. Not her brother. Definitely not her cousin.

For Zeke, caring for her seemed to come natural. A natural born hero. If she were pregnant with his baby, what a father he'd make. A horrible, aching hope took up residence in her chest. She dropped onto the stool before her vanity.

She needed to get a hold of herself. Of course she wasn't with child. She couldn't be. She should tell Zeke how she'd long suspected her inability to conceive.

"Kitty, quit fussing with your accoutrements and tell me what you're thinking."

She raised her gaze to the mirror and met his eyes.

She opened her mouth to tell him the truth, and heard herself saying something else entirely. "You can't join our traveling party. Collin would never permit it, and Garrick—he'd probably insist on marrying me yesterday."

"I'll stay out of sight."

She meant to argue, but her curiosity got the better of her. "While we're traveling, you could trail a bit behind us. But inns tend to be smallish, like this one. How would you keep from being seen? Like tonight for instance?"

"Tonight?" He shrugged. "I'll stay with you."

She sprang to her feet, rounding on him. "You can't."

He crossed his arms in front of his chest. "You have a better idea?"

She glanced around the small space. "Where will you sleep?"

His lips twisted in a sardonic grin. "I suppose, as we're trying to rule out the possibility of a baby so you can marry your brother out of his current jamb, your bed is out of the question?"

She glared at him.

"I'll take the chair."

They both eyed the spindly legged armchair in the corner.

"On second thought, I'll take the floor." He sighed. "I've fared worse."

***

"I'll be back as soon as I'm able," she said, repeating the sentiment for the third time since accepting the fact he wasn't going anywhere, any time soon. She gazed up at him, hand on the door lever, that luscious lower lip caught between her teeth.

He forced his eyes from her mouth. "As we're evidently repeating ourselves, I'll remind you, again, not to act out of the ordinary. Stay as late as you normally would. Later, even. Keep your ears open. I want to know if I have to thwart an attempted wedding ceremony." *Before I talk you out of this nonsense*, he silently added.

She nodded. "Right. Well, then…"

He pulled the door open and pushed her into the corridor. "Bon appétit.' He shut the door in her face.

He thought he heard her indignant hmph, and smiled. He listened at the door for her footsteps to recede, then started a slow count to three hundred, pulling on his coat and gloves.

At three hundred one, he let himself out into the deserted corridor. He strode for the servants' stairs at a brisk pace. He needed to get his business done and return to Kitty's chamber before she came back to discover him gone, and that he'd lied to her.

But of course he had lied.

He had no need to hide out in Kitty's chamber to avoid detection by the duo made up of her idiot relations. He knew how to stay out of sight. Yet he'd insinuated himself into her chamber for the night before he'd even made the conscious decision to do so.

Why? Momentary insanity? A streak of masochism? *Needing to be near her?*

Bah. He didn't have time for these mental cogitations. Kitty needed guarding and he was the only man he trusted for the job and that was that.

He must focus. He had much to accomplish, and very little time to do so.

First on the agenda, track down Hastings' groomsman to discover their ultimate destination. He didn't want to risk losing them on the road.

Second, he must send telegrams to both Caden and the earl, advising them of his whereabouts and immediate plans. He had to be careful there, informing them he meant to shadow Kitty while leaving out the part about staying in her very chamber.

Outside the inn, he pulled out his pocket watch. Mentally allotting himself thirty minutes, he tucked the watch away, pulled up the collar of his great coat to shield his too-distinctive hair from casual view, and crossed the courtyard toward the inn's stables.

He'd have a five minute conversation with James' groom, and then he'd away to the post to send the telegrams.

He didn't foresee any problems. His real challenge lay ahead. How in hell was he going to spend the night with Kitty without going stark raving mad from the need to have her again?

The answer was simple. He wasn't.

Chapter Thirty

Hands trembling, Kitty turned the key in the lock, and stepped into the chamber. Zeke had left only one wall sconce burning on low. Pressing the door shut, she leaned into it and allowed her eyes to adjust.

She scanned the small bedchamber for Zeke, and found him stretched out atop the bed, arms crossed beneath his head. She couldn't tell if his eyes were open or closed. She did know seeing him lying on her bed, with the lighting just so, did funny things to her pulse.

Devil take it, she should have insisted he leave, or, barring that, told her brother he was here, and let him deal with the situation.

Instead, she guarded the secret because...she wanted this time with him, desperately, brief as it would be.

"Welcome back. How was dinner?" Zeke drawled.

She allowed herself a little smile. He was awake.

He sat up, swinging his long legs over the side of the bed. "I hope you don't mind. I rode hard all day to find you and thought to take advantage of the mattress considering I'll have use of the floor for the rest of the evening."

He stood. Stretched.

"I don't mind." She sounded as breathless as she felt. Gad. She cleared her throat. "I brought you some rolls. It was the only thing I could take that wouldn't rouse suspicion."

She moved toward him, extending the bundled serviette.

In the deeply shadowed chamber, she thought he looked amused.

"Thank you." Rather than accepting her offering, he captured her hands. He pulled her closer, bending to brush his lips over hers in the sweetest, softest kiss.

She raised up on tiptoes and leaned forward, deciding then and there if he initiated the two falling onto the mattress she'd allow it—just for a moment.

Instead of deepening the kiss, he snagged the bread from her hands. He unfolded the serviette, examining one of the rolls with interest, and moved away.

"I found an extra blanket in the wardrobe. Between that and the seat cushion, I should sleep well enough." He set about arranging his makeshift bed for the night.

Kitty began her nightly ablutions. She cleaned her teeth, splashed water over her face, removed her hairpins.

She heard him remove his boots. Then his belt hit the floor.

Unable to resist, she glanced at him in the mirror as she brushed her hair.

He sat propped on his elbows near the unlit hearth, legs stretched out before him. Light from the wall lamp gleamed off his shiny, mussed hair, and cast shadows over his sun-burnished skin.

He stared back at her, unblinking, and her blood began to simmer.

"Did you learn anything interesting while dining with your brother and...fiancé?" Zeke asked dryly.

She set down her brush and swiveled to face him. "I don't know what you mean by interesting."

"Do you know where you're headed, for one thing?"

"Oh. Yes. We're going home to Hastings House."

"Any pertinent topics of discussion over the dinner table?"

"Pertinent to whom? I don't see what this has to do with—"

"Kitty? Humor me. I have, after all, stood by you during your entire nightmare, at least since being made abreast of it."

She dropped her chin. "I'm aware. I just don't want to argue during the little time we have left."

"Who says answering my questions will lead to an argument? For that matter, why assume our time together is limited?" His mouth curved upward giving her a glimpse of gleaming white teeth.

She shook her head, grinning despite herself. "Fine. Have all the boring details. Evidently Garrick sent a message to his solicitor requesting a meeting to discuss how best to proceed with the title exchange."

"I see." He glowered at no one in particular. "And everyone ends up happy, with each a tidy little sum and his just desserts. Tell me, how do you like being served up like a steaming apple turnover?"

"Zeke," she warned.

"Once you're wed, there goes your inheritance, as well. All your hard-earned independence, gone, in one fell swoop, 'til death do you part."

She turned back to the mirror, and resumed brushing her hair with sharp, angry strokes.

"Or you could leave with me, now."

"I'd be so much better off then, wouldn't I?" she snapped. "An independent wife of an absent lord. A brood mare, set out to pasture."

"Suit yourself," he bit back.

She heard a plunk on the floorboards and hazarded a glance at Zeke in the mirror.

He lay flat on his back, staring at the ceiling.

She longed to go to him. To wrap her arms around him and confess her undying love. Couldn't he see this was the last thing she wanted? Her only bright spot in this lamentable ordeal was having her brother returned from the dead.

"Are you sleeping in your gown?"

She blinked at Zeke's unexpected question. "I thought I ought to."

"I'm not going to ravish you."

She knew that. He hadn't even kissed her goodnight.

"You'll be more comfortable sleeping in your night dress. Do you need help undressing?"

"No. The ties are in the front."

He was right, of course. She would be more comfortable in her nightrail. "Don't look."

Zeke pulled his blanket over his head. "Can't see a thing."

She stripped out of her gown, stockings and slippers with her back to him, pressed in close to the side of the wardrobe, though it didn't actually shield her from Zeke's view if he looked, which he wasn't.

"There was one thing I didn't mention. More of a coincidence, really," she said.

"Oh?"

She folded her gown, then rolled up her stockings and piled them neatly on a shelf in the wardrobe.

"An old acquaintance of Collin's happens to be staying here. He stopped by our table to say hello. Collin acted strangely, practically running the man off without introducing Garrick or me. He explained himself later, of course."

Zeke's blanket rustled as he ripped it off his head. "Do you recall the man's name? Did you recognize him?"

She squinted her eyes, studying him. His lids still appeared sealed shut.

"Let me think. When the man approached the table, he said something to the effect of, 'Hastings? Is that you? Haven't seen you in an age. It's me. Peters.' Or Parish. Something with a P."

She shook out her nightshift, debating her chemise. Scowling to herself, she decided to leave it on and shimmied the white lawn over her head.

"The thing is, after Collin walked me to my door, I noticed he didn't go on to his chamber, but turned for the stairs. When I called after him, he told me he was going to have a word with Mr. Peters." She smiled. "Yes, Peters it is. I'm sure of it."

"The same man he didn't want you to meet?"

She paused in the act of buttoning the neckline of her gown. "I asked him that very question. He had a sound reason for not doing so, Mr Fault finder. He told me he hadn't introduced us because he didn't want to get into the whole title issue in front of Garrick."

"I see." Zeke yawned loudly.

Kitty hadn't liked the look of Mr. Peters. He had a coarseness about him that made her uneasy—but she didn't want to say anything else that might further sour Zeke on Collin.

She tiptoed across the cold wooden floor and slid beneath the bedcovers, pulling her sheets to her nose. "You can open your eyes now."

Zeke did not respond.

"Zeke?" She strained her ears—and heard the slow steady breath of one fast asleep.

The blasted man had nodded off. She couldn't say exactly why his ability to do so annoyed her.

With a hmph, she reached up to extinguish the lamp, then rolled to her side and pinched her eyes closed. And proceeded to lie awake. She tossed, turned, and beat her pillow.

It was no use. How in the world could she relax with Zeke mere feet away? So very close, yet they may as well be oceans apart.

She still couldn't quite believe he'd come for her, and then refused to leave until he knew for certain she wasn't with child, no matter she'd told him she wasn't.

What if, by some miracle she was pregnant?

Zeke would insist on marriage. And what sweet torture that would be, married to a man she loved desperately, whose kisses left her breathless and whose touch brought her body to the height of ecstasy, but who flat-out told her he would never love her.

And she mustn't forget he said nothing about staying in England, baby or no. In fact, he made it clear he would be off at the first opportunity to dig a fresh hole in the earth, half a world away.

Through it all, there was Collin to consider. Why hadn't she thought of him before bedding the man?

Because she loved Zeke, and thought she'd never see him again.

Because she hadn't been thinking at all.

"I can practically see smoke coming out your ears, you're thinking so hard," Zeke said in that rich, velvety voice of his.

She nearly jumped out of her skin. "I thought you were asleep." She aimed a glare at him in the darkness.

He propped himself on his elbows. She couldn't make out his features of his face, but the moonlight seeping in through the window told her he gazed in her direction.

"I thought it was the best way," he said, his voice gruff.

"The best way for what?"

"To keep my hands off you."

Her heart beat so hard she thought she might crack a rib. "Maybe I don't want you to," she said, her face burning at her own audacity.

"Kitty, don't play games with me. My restraint is already at its limit. Now close your eyes and go to sleep." He dropped onto the floor with a thud and, if she wasn't mistaken, rolled onto his side to face away from her.

She stared at his dark shape, wrestling with her conscience. He was right, of course. She should let sleeping dogs lie. But...

"I just want you to kiss me goodnight, Zeke. Because you're here..."

Zeke threw off his blanket.

"...and I can't think of anything but you lying there and..."

He reached her bedside before she finished her thought.

"That makes two of us," he growled, cupping her face. His hands were warm against her cheeks, and if she wasn't mistaken, shaking.

His mouth came down on hers, hot and demanding.

She made an urgent little sound, low in her throat, and wrapped her arms around his neck. "Oh, Zeke," she breathed against his lips. "I thought you didn't want to kiss me anymore."

He gave a humorless laugh. His flesh was burning hot and slightly damp. "You little fool. Haven't you heard a damned thing I've said?"

"Will you lie with me? Just for a little while?"

He groaned. "You may be the death of me, kitten. You know that?"

***

Lying atop the bedcovers, he reached for her. He pressed his face into the thicket of her lush hair, and breathed in the scent of her. Lavender. Rosemary. Kitty.

"You feel so good, sweetheart. So damned good."

She felt so right in his arms, and the thought of someone else holding her, someone else kissing her tore him up inside. He had to make her see.

"Kitty," he began, but lost the ability to speak when she twisted her body under the sheets to mold herself to him.

She rained tender kisses down his neck. When her lips reached his collar, she pushed it out of the way and nuzzled into the hollow at his throat.

He closed his eyes and reveled in her sweet ardor, in the weight of her breasts through the sheets and fabric of their clothing, firm and ripe against his chest.

She slid one sinewy leg up over both his. Knee bent, her thigh grazed the rigid length of his cock and he groaned.

His eyes flew open when he felt her fingers traveling down the front of his shirt, undoing buttons.

Whether or not she'd done it by accident, she had pushed the bedcovers to just below her waist. Thanks to the quick work of her wandering hands, nothing separated their upper torsos but the thin lawn of her gown, and chemise.

He swallowed. Her hips squirming against his, her leg sliding over his and, occasionally, over his erection, and now the absence of anything of substance separating them all conspired to push him past the point of desperation. *Christ.*

"I want to touch you," she whispered, fueling the inferno of his need. Her breath feathered over his naked chest, sending a spray of gooseflesh over his entire body.

He reached for her hands, trapping them in one of his. "I don't think..."

She freed one hand, bringing it to his lips to press two fingers there. "I only want to touch you." She pressed a kiss to his chest. "And kiss you."

Blood rushed like liquid fire through his veins, aiming south. "This was not a good idea."

He gritted his teeth. If he had any chance of stopping this runaway carriage, he had better remove himself from her bed this instant.

He stayed put, damn his own eyes.

Her fingers trailed down his center, not pausing 'til she'd reached the waistline of his trousers.

His erection jerked against the restraining fabric, and he nearly came. Damn it, he was like an untried youth. Wasn't she supposed to be the innocent here? Time to take control.

He grasped her shoulders and rolled her onto her back, then threw a leg over her to straddle her. He rose up to his knees and ripped his unbuttoned shirt off, flinging it across the room.

His eyes had adjusted to the darkness, and he saw feverish anticipation burning in hers, saw her chest rising and falling with each inhalation as she panted for air.

"You want to play?" he asked on a hoarse whisper.

She slid her silky palms up his chest. When her fingertips grazed his nipples, she traced their edges with painstaking care, her lower lip caught between her teeth.

Jesus. He groaned and dropped his hands to the neckline of her prim gown. He fumbled with the row of tiny, seemingly endless buttons. Emitting a low growl, he gave up, tearing the thin material apart, surprising himself, and, going by Kitty's gasp, her as well.

"I'll buy you a new one."

She reached for him, urging him down to her. "I don't care. I want...please..." She lifted her face for his kiss.

"Not so fast." Gently now, he rent her shift to her waistline. He sighed. "You're still wearing your chemise. Well, then. Let's see it."

He rolled onto his hip and with one swipe yanked the remaining bedcovers from between them. He palmed her ribcage and eased his hand up to cup the underside of one breast.

She made an urgent little sound at his touch, sending his pulse soaring. "You're making me crazy. You know that, don't you?"

She didn't answer, just shifted and shimmied on the bed, her body calling to his. He grasped the two sides of her ruined nightgown and helped free her of the garment, leaving her clothed in only her sheer chemise.

In the moonlight he could clearly make out her shape, and the hint of dark at her apex. Mouth watering, he lowered his head, his mouth seeking and finding one hard nipple.

He drew on it with greedy pulls while his hands roamed. One found her other breast. Squeezed. The other grasped the hem of her chemise and tugged upward. One of his knees speared between her legs, parting them. She opened them with no resistance.

His loins screamed with the need to melt into hers. But he held back. First he had to touch her. To make her as hot and desperate for him as he was for her. He traced his fingertips up the inside of her silky thighs, not pausing until he found her curls. He parted her, discovering slick, swollen flesh.

It was too much. He laid his cheek against her chest and sucked in air, while his palm cupped her sex.

The first time, when he thought she'd agreed to marry him, it had been easy to convince himself bedding her wasn't wrong. He'd assumed it would be only a matter of days or weeks between that night of sheer pleasure and their wedding ceremony. But now he didn't know if or when she'd become his wife.

He wanted her—and not only in the physical sense. He wanted to marry her with an intensity that scared the living hell out of him. But he didn't want her coming to him because she had to. Because she was pregnant.

He would laugh at the irony if he weren't in such delicious agony. Because wasn't that the pretense under which he was here? To see if she was pregnant and claim her as his wife?

He should stop this madness, but he ached to bury himself inside her and show her she was his, to claim her so she would never, could never, accept another's touch.

"Zeke?" She spoke his name tentatively. Her fingertips trailed over his low abdomen to his waistband. She rand one finger along the length of the band and he shuddered.

"Kitty—"

"I want you to make love to me, Zeke."

"You'll let me have you, but you won't marry me, is that it?" He muttered a curse. "I don't understand you."

She reached down, covering the hand that still cupped her at her apex. She pressed one of his fingers between her petals. "But you understand this?" she asked in a soft whisper.

He nearly whimpered. Nodded. Helpless to stop himself, he slid one finger into her slick, tight channel.

She shivered with need, and he felt himself come just a little. His groan was half desire, half frustration.

"Please, Zeke. Please. Make me feel like...before."

He choked on disbelieving laughter. "So I've created a monster, eh?"

She pressed her face into his shoulder and nodded.

His fingers went to work. Circling her, slowly. Caressing. Teasing.

"You want this?" His mouth found one nipple. Suckled. Then moved to the other. "And this?" He found her swollen nubbin, bringing her to the brink of orgasm, then easing back.

Her hips trembled and bucked. Her arms twined around his neck. Her fingers tunneled into his hair, and raked down his back. It was by far the most erotic experience of his life.

He touched her, faster, faster, bringing her ever closer to sweet release at the expense of his own sanity.

Abruptly, she rolled away.

"What the hell?" he demanded, out of his mind with need.

"Not like that," came her words, muffled by the pillow.

He dropped onto his back, one hand ripping at his hair. She was literally driving him insane.

She rolled again, climbing on top of him, and the leap to insanity was complete.

His hands gripped her hips, staying her attempts to wriggle up to the tip of his cock. "Please. Stop. Moving."

She leaned over him, her ebony locks falling around him like a curtain of black silk. "I want you inside me," she whispered.

"We're playing with fire."

"I thought you wanted to marry me." She sounded petulant now, like a child denied her favorite toy.

He shook his head and tugged her down, 'til her face was less than an inch from his. "I do want to marry you. I don't want to force you. Can't you understand that?"

Her eyes filled with dawning comprehension. She smiled an angel's smile and smoothed a cool hand over his brow, sweeping his hair back. "Then do it so we can't make a baby."

A hoarse bark of laughter erupted from deep within him. "Woman, how do you know such a method even exists?"

She slid him a glance. "I can read."

"It isn't foolproof."

She dropped a kiss to the corner of his mouth. Then the other. Then feathered kisses over his face.

A hot, aching, tenderness—distinct from the screaming lust tearing apart his insides—filled his chest 'til he thought he might explode from the pain of it.

"Make love to me, Zeke. This might be the last time."

God, no. The words reverberated in his head like heavy church bells clanging. Kitty was his, and by God, he would show her.

He rolled with her on the bed, pinning her beneath him. With his eyes locked with hers, he removed his trousers and undergarment, adding them to the growing heap on the floor. As for her chemise...he simply couldn't wait any longer.

He slid one hand between them, pushed up the paper-thin material, and brought the tip of his erection to the entrance of her channel.

She started to close her eyes.

"No," he said, hoarse now. "Look at me. I want to see your eyes as I enter you."

She raised her chin a notch and stared up at him unblinking.

He pressed into her. One deliciously slow thrust that cost him at least a year of his life.

Her muscles tightened and flexed around him, making room for the length and breadth of him.

When he'd sunk himself to the hilt, he started a slow retreat.

Kitty's lips parted on a silent gasp of pleasure.

Jesus she was beautiful. So damned beautiful. The most perfect creature he'd ever seen. He wanted to tell her. Tell her...what he was feeling. How she moved him. But he couldn't. Couldn't speak.

His eyelids closed. Couldn't stay open any longer as he pressed slowly into her, as he fought to maintain that teasing, slow tempo. Once. Twice. Three times.

But his warring need to claim her overpowered his self-control, and his hips pumped harder, faster, pushed deeper as instinct and desire merged.

Kitty met his driving passion with her own. She arched up inviting his thrusts, her insides pulsing around him, 'til he was dizzy with desire and hanging on to his control by a thread.

"Zeke." She cried his name as her release crashed through her.

He took her mouth, swallowing her moans, feasting on her gasps. She wrapped her arms and legs around him, half climbing his body as hers quaked beneath his.

God, oh God, she felt so good as she came, and came, and came, the walls of her womanhood gripping his cock, milking him 'til, with a hoarse roar, he pulled out of her and exploded like he never had in his life.

He toppled across her, boneless.

Beneath him she sighed, long and deep, as if utterly sated. She pressed the sweetest kiss to his shoulder, and, if he wasn't mistaken, her lips curved into a smile.

He felt an answering smile of his own. "Was that what you had in mind, vixen?"

She giggled.

His heart seemed to crack open. To fill with light. She'd done something to him. Changed him somehow. God help him, he liked it.

He rolled onto his side, reached down with one arm, and hauled the covers up off the floor. Covering them both, he pulled her into the curve of his body. "Good. Maybe now we can get some sleep."

She snuggled her hips into his, and, unbelievably, he felt his desire stirring to life.

On second thought, sleep was vastly overrated.

Chapter Thirty-One

Kitty was having a hard time grasping this latest twist in her situation. Granted she was tired, owing to a lack of sleep the night before and a long day of traveling, but she suspected she'd be confused even if she'd slept the night through. Confused and, all right, slightly suspicious.

She stood aside and allowed the innkeeper's wife to open the door to her guest chamber at the *Inn at Aylesford*, which was located in the quaint village of Aylesford, which was decidedly not en route to Maidstone.

"Thank you," she murmured on cue as the portly woman opened the wardrobe, parted the curtains, and performed all the usual tasks associated with showing a guest to her chamber.

"You've missed tea, but supper'll be served starting at half past six. Until then, there's much to be seen out on Main Street. Food vendors, craft markets, trinket hawkers and such."

Because there was a festival going on, which Collin explained when they arrived.

"The Carmelite friars come back every summer for the End o' Summer Festival. They put on a nice show, singing their hymns and such up at the church on top of the hill. The fair draws a fine crowd."

Kitty smiled and nodded mechanically. Finally, the woman let herself out.

Normally a summer fair would be right up her alley, and it wasn't as if she minded the delay in reaching Maidstone and what awaited her there.

The problem was, of course, Zeke.

She stripped off her gloves and tried to remember exactly what he'd said this morning, pre dawn, before leaving her. Something about seeing her later. But he left under the assumption they were heading for Maidstone. How would he find them now?

It'd serve you right if he didn't, her inner critic sneered.

She slumped onto the edge of her bed, tossing her gloves and travel bonnet on the nightstand.

She'd gotten herself into a fine kettle of fish. She'd promised Collin she'd wed Garrick knowing his future depended on it. Meanwhile Zeke wasn't going anywhere 'til he knew she wasn't pregnant. Meanwhile she'd lain with him again, and instead of feeling guilty as she ought, all she could think about since arriving to this out-of-the-way village was whether Zeke would find her and make love to her again tonight.

She rose and moved to the window. The sun hadn't yet set. Warm bands of fading daylight shone into the room from the west, silhouetting the church dome from its perch on the hill, and casting long shadows on the quaint, bustling town below. Street vendors, open air markets, and people abounded on the cobbled streets.

It was certainly a festive scene. But Kitty couldn't help wondering what on earth they were doing here.

She'd asked Collin once out of Garrick's earshot. According to him, he'd made this detour for her. To give her a buffer of time before she had to commence with planning her wedding. Kitty wanted to believe him. And yet, something about his answer didn't set right.

She trusted Collin. Of course she did. But she couldn't stop thinking of the man who'd approached them last night. That Mr Peters. And what had Garrick muttered when she asked Collin how long they'd be staying?

"I agreed to one night, Hastings."

Collin's reply to Garrick had been odd. "One night's all I need."

A knock sounded at her door, and her heart practically leaped from her chest. "Yes?"

"It's me, love."

Collin.

She opened the door and gestured for him to come inside.

He lingered in the corridor. "I thought I'd go for a stroll. Take in a few of the sights."

"Oh. I'm not quite ready to…"

"Don't trouble yourself m'dear. You need to rest. What say we meet up later for supper, and afterward I'll take you around, after I've scouted the area."

"Very well," she answered in no small relief. Collin had just afforded her the opportunity to wait for Zeke. "Is Garrick going with you?"

He frowned. "James? No, and I doubt my lack of invitation will wound him terribly."

"Collin," she began before she could stop herself, "that's the thing. He doesn't appear overly fond of either of us. Yet he presses for this marriage. It doesn't make sense. Perhaps we--"

Collin held out a palm to silence her. "Are you backing out of your promise?"

"Of course not, it's just—"

"Kitty, do we have to discuss this again? You know how much it destroys me to ask this of you. And I've already promised you'll be welcome to stay with me after your nuptials. That I'll continue to support you. What more do you want?

"Or should I simply accept my fate? Embrace my future as a penniless, landless, displaced aristocrat so you can avoid the responsibility embraced by many a well bred lady, to marry for the sake of her family?"

Kitty's heart sank. "Of course not."

He smiled grimly. "Thanks for that, anyway." He grasped the door handle. "Kitty, you really disappoint me. This again, after

I brought you here, after I went out of my way for you, sparing no small expense, to see to your happiness."

"I appreciate you doing so, Collin."

He nodded crisply. "Right. See you in a few hours, then, for supper. Maybe a nap will see you in better spirits."

He left, evidence of his lingering irritation reverberating in the slamming door.

***

Zeke was not in a good mood. He'd ridden all day. He was tired, sore, hungry, and damned if he wasn't as worried as a mother duck. Where was Kitty? Sure as hell not on her way to Maidstone County.

The possibility Maidstone and Hastings had somehow colluded to whisk her off for a quick ceremony had his blood running simultaneously hot and cold.

He saw the street lamps ahead and heaved an exhausted sigh. Reaching down, he smoothed a palm over his gelding's neck. "Almost done for the day, Sadie. You've worked hard for me today, girl."

Aylesford, the hanging banner read as he passed under the wrought iron arm. Fourth and last village today, damn his eyes. And he'd thought his plan so clever.

He first rode ahead of Kitty's brood to the town of Dunshire where he'd instructed Caden and the earl to send any pressing correspondence via telegraph. He received a cheery Good luck from his grandfather, and a cryptic message from Caden. It seemed he might have something of import to share, but he needed time to verify facts. Could Zeke please provide a telegraph station for Caden's message tomorrow?

Caden and his facts. Zeke would gladly settle for guesses, any damned thing he could use to untangle Kitty from her brother's web. Instead, he conferred with the telegraph operator to locate the next postal office equipped with telegraph service en route to Maidstone—where he thought Kitty's party headed.

Only after fruitless hours of waiting, Hastings' barouche never showed.

In mounting frustration, Zeke backtracked, and caught a lucky break when he traced Hastings' party to a rest stop from which they'd ventured west, decidedly not in the direction of Maidstone.

He'd searched two successive villages, turning up precisely nothing.

If he didn't find her here, he'd be forced to stop for the night. His horse could take no more today.

He paused on the narrow, cobbled street leading in to town. Night had fallen, and Aylesford spread before him like a London party. The streets teemed with life, as pedestrians strolled from one vendor to the next. Burning oil lamps lined the walks, and paper lanterns hung in trees. The smell of roasted meats and fresh baked bread wafted in the air, reminding him he had not eaten since his meager breakfast.

The summer festival, which had been the deciding factor in Zeke's choosing Aylesford over another village, was in full swing. Kitty's self-indulgent brother would be drawn to such an event. Now he had only to scour every inn in town to learn whether his theory proved correct.

***

Zeke turned the key in the lock of the room the innkeeper finally revealed was Kitty's. Persuasion had come in the form of a handful of notes, and the more subtle promise of a blistering beating should the half asleep man persist in withholding the information.

Zeke paused, hand on the door lever, praying the inn's proprietor hadn't steered him wrong, praying even harder that he'd find only Kitty in the chamber.

A moment later, he crossed the threshold into pitch darkness. He made out the bed centered on one wall. He didn't wish to frighten Kitty by rousing her from a sound sleep, but—

The rapid pitter-pat of bare feet on wood sounded moments before a lavender scented woman threw herself into his chest—half braining him with whatever cold, metal object she held.

"Ouch," he barked, one arm instinctively grabbing her around the waist to pull her close, the other hinging up to massage the base of his skull where she'd bashed him. "Woman, must you always try to concuss me?"

She pressed her face into his neck and shook with silent laughter.

"Glad one of us finds this funny," he grumbled, carrying her toward the bed.

"S-sorry. I grabbed it before I realized it was y-you."

His insides froze. She wasn't laughing. Silent sobs racked her body as her tears soaked the collar of his shirt.

"Shh. I'm not really hurt."

"I kn-know that."

He dropped onto the edge of the mattress, his arms tightening around her. "Why are you crying? What's happened?"

She sniffled. "I'm not crying."

Nothing too serious, then. He'd get to the bottom of this latest drama. In a minute.

With a bone weary sigh, he released her. She slid off his lap with an oomph, and he flopped flat on his back, his legs bent over the side. "At last. Now come here and kiss me."

To his great relief she didn't argue, but instead sprawled atop him, enveloping him with the scent of sleepy woman.

He thought briefly of his own malevolent odor having ridden all day. Sweat, horse flesh, and leather. Then she cupped his stubble covered, sunburned cheeks with her cool, silky palms, and he decided he didn't care. He just wanted her lips, pressed to his, now.

She took her time, first smoothing the hair off his brow, then angling her face just so. When she finally closed the distance between their mouths, he was half mad with the need to taste her.

His lips moved beneath hers, sucking, nibbling, urging her to give more. And she gave, parting her lips for him, torturing him with feather light touches of her tongue. When his arms came around her, hungry and possessive, she melted into him, turning his brain to pudding.

He twisted his head to the side, breaking the kiss.

"Zeke?" she murmured, sounding gratifyingly dazed.

"Give me a minute," he said hoarsely. "Can't think straight around you."

She pressed her face into his neck, and he felt the small, satisfied smile curving her lips.

Helpless to resist, he ran a hand down her back. She arched into him like a cat. He wanted to growl. Wanted to devour her. Instead he forced out the words,

"Kitty, tell me nothing of import happened today."

"Depends on what you mean."

"Damn it, Kitty, do not toy with me," he bit out, suddenly unreasonably angry. "I come in to find you crying and…You didn't…that is, you and James aren't—" He broke off with a curse.

"Are you asking if I got married today?"

"Yes, damn it."

Apparently Kitty thought the question concerning her marital status comical, because she snorted into his chest.

"Zeke. What on earth—don't you think he'd be in here with me now if we had gotten married today?"

Liquid rage burned though him at the mere thought of James—of any man—holding Kitty the way he was right now. He drew in a deep, calming breath. Tightened his arms around her. She was here, with him. No one else.

"Never mind. That's good. That's all right, then."

He sifted his fingers through her silky hair and the battle-ready tension gripping him since he'd lost track of her slowly eked out of him. Bone deep fatigue took its place, leaving him limp, save for one area of his body, which was getting harder by the second.

Unfortunately, Kitty's quicksilver mood seemed to undergo the reverse of his.

She rolled abruptly out of his arms and sprang from the bed. "What are we doing? What am I doing, Zeke?"

He craned his head to keep her in sight as she made her way to a chair by the window and dropped into it, pulling her knees up to her chest and wrapping her arms around them.

He sat up. "Kitty, I rode all day, searching for you. All. Day. My body aches and my mouth tastes like I swallowed sawdust. May I have a drink of water?"

She sniffed. "Of course." She got up, poured a glass of water and brought it to him. He grasped her wrist and held firm as he downed the night chilled liquid in several gulps. When he set the empty glass on the bedside table, she tugged to be free of him.

"Don't go, Kitty. Sit here beside me and tell me what's going through that pretty, stubborn head of yours."

After a brief hesitation, she perched on the edge of the bed, head bowed. "It's all a mess, Zeke. You and I both know we're biding our time. I have to do this thing. I have to, for Collin, much as I hate it. You would do no less for your family," she added with heat.

"Then there's you. You say you want to be sure I'm not pregnant. But you don't understand how it is with me..."

"What don't I understand?" He eased off one boot.

"I'm not like other women. At least I don't think I am."

He could have told her that much, but he wisely kept the thought to himself.

"I've never had the normal, you know, cycle women are supposed to have. I never know if it will be one month or six between my...um—" She broke off, wringing her hands in the darkness.

He dropped his second boot onto the floor with a thud, and leaned back to rest on one elbow. Helpless to stop himself, he reached over to caress the small of her back. She owned another nightdress, it seemed.

"I learned from other girls it should come every month. Only, for me, it never did. I always intended to ask mother about it, but never had an opportunity. I couldn't ask Collin or Grandfather." Her shoulders rose and fell in a shrug. "When it does come, it can be godawful. Cramps, mostly."

Zeke was fairly certain no woman had ever gone into this much detail with him about her menses. Still, he had the basic idea of how the whole process worked.

He imagined Kitty as a young woman. Needing someone to talk to. Someone to care for her. But she'd had no one, save her grandfather. He wished suddenly her mother hadn't died, so he could read her the riot act.

"I doubt I can conceive, Zeke. I would have told you if we became engaged, but we never were. Now you're waiting for proof I'm not carrying your baby. But what if proof never comes?"

"Sweetheart, there are other ways to know if you're pregnant."

Her head angled swiftly toward him. "Such as?"

He'd had as much of not touching her as he could take. He reached for her, encircling her waist, and slid her toward him. He lay his other hand on her flat belly.

"For one thing, you'll start to grow, here."

She flapped a hand at him. "I know that much."

He kissed her shoulder through her nightdress. "You might start feeling ill, especially in the mornings. I believe some women get a bit tender here." His palm slid up her rib cage to cup one plump breast.

Her breath hitched, but she didn't move except to raise her face to his. He kneaded her gently, his palm grazing over the bud of her ripening nipple.

A shuddering breath escaped her.

"Does that hurt? Or does it feel good?" He asked, not hiding the sensual edge in his voice.

He wanted her. Wanted her like he hadn't ridden all day, avoiding stops for meals or any form of sustenance save what was necessary for his horse.

"It feels...I feel..." She spoke in a breathy little whisper. "Like you're not taking me seriously," she finally croaked.

She twisted away, aiming her back at him.

"I'm sorry, love. I rather thought I'd addressed your concern. If you're pregnant, we'll soon know, one way or another."

She snorted softly, and he wrapped both arms around her, resting his chin on the curve of her shoulder. "As for the other thing you neglected to mention..."

"What other thing?" she asked.

"That engagement thing your brother's wrangled you into."

Her head moved to the side just a touch and he could practically see her rolling her eyes. "Oh, that."

"You're not marrying him, Kitty. You can't."

"Zeke—"

"You can't, and I can't let you. No, hear me out," he said when she opened her mouth to argue. "I understand about your brother. You want to make everything peachy for him. Sweetheart, give me some time to figure something out. Hell, I'm the future Earl of Claybourne. On my name alone I can make things happen."

She twisted around to face him. "Do you really think you can help him, Zeke?"

"I know I can."

"But, why? Why keep going through all the trouble, if you're only going to turn tail and-"

He silenced her with a slow, lingering kiss. When he felt the rigidity go out of her, he dragged his mouth from hers. "Don't move."

He rose from the bed and fumbled around 'til he had an oil lamp burning low.

He located a clean towel and her damned lavender soap and approached the basin. He pealed off his waistcoat and unbuttoned his shirtsleeves, all the while feeling her eyes on him, which in turn kept him in a constant state of semi-arousal.

"I assume it was as much a surprise for you as it was for me that you wound up here in this out-of-the-way town, hmm?" He laid his shirt over the wooden valet beside the dresser.

"Completely. I had no idea we'd changed course 'til the horses halted in front of the inn and I awoke."

He nodded. "You might want to cover your eyes."

His back to her, he stepped out of his trousers, then his drawers. "So you wound up here. Were you wondering if I'd find you?" Having asked, he couldn't not look at her.

She studied him, unblinking, lips parted.

He went rock hard, just like that.

Guileless as a newborn colt, and tempting as a siren, and he'd bet his last shilling she had no idea what she did to him.

She shook her head, as if to clear her mind, and shifted her gaze off him. "Yes."

He should leave it at that. His resolve lasted all of two seconds. "Wondering? Or hoping?" he asked softly.

She met his gaze for a heart beat. "Hoping."

He resisted the impulse to cross the room to scoop her into his arms. First things first. He needed to rid himself of the worst of the day's grime, for her sake.

He splashed tepid water over himself and soaped up. "Why did your travel plans change?"

The mattress squeaked.

He glanced over his shoulder to see her slipping her legs under the covers and leaning back against the headboard.

"I asked Collin as soon as Garrick was out of earshot, and he said he'd opted to take the long way home for my benefit. And yet..."

"And yet?"

"One would think Garrick would object to any delay."

"He didn't?"

"He seemed more smug. Like he knew something I didn't."

Zeke rinsed as best he could, then scrubbed the towel over his damp skin. "You think he and your brother colluded over something?"

"Of course not. Collin wouldn't hide anything from me. It's Garrick I don't trust."

He laid the towel beside the basin.

"There is one other thing. Trifling, really."

"Go on."

"This afternoon, after we checked in, Collin said he wanted a feel for the festival. He made it clear he didn't want my company." She paused. "We had words."

He strode for the oil lamp, extinguishing it. "Let me guess. He browbeat you some more about keeping your promise to him."

"You always think the worst of Collin. Just because he's had it rough these last years doesn't mean he doesn't love me. He's a wonderful brother."

"A regular paragon," he muttered. He crossed toward the bed, found the top edge of the covers and pulled them back.

"Oh. Are you"—she gulped—"getting into bed like that?"

"Like what?"

"You're naked."

"You'd rather I slept in those filthy garments?" He jerked a thumb in the general direction of his discarded clothing.

"I suppose not. Do you want to hear the rest of my story or not? I can't tell you're even listening."

He slid between the cool sheets, then propped a pillow against the headboard and leaned back, his arms behind his head.

"Let me see if I've followed you so far. Your arrival here was a surprise to you. Hastings says he made the last minute change for your sake. James's reaction tells you there's another side to the story. Later Hastings went out for an afternoon stroll. Right so far?"

"Hmm," she answered, noncommittal. "The thing is, Collin said he'd join me later for supper. But just before eight I received a note informing me he didn't feel well, and would see me in the morning."

Zeke felt not the least bit of sympathy. "Probably had too much festival food."

"I suppose. Only...it's nothing, really."

The hair on his nape prickled. "Humor me."

"I went out briefly, to stretch my legs, and thought I spotted that man again."

"What man?" His eyes had adjusted so he could make out Kitty's face.

"The man from the dining room last night. Mr Peters. To be honest, I don't care for the look of him."

"Are you saying Peters is in Aylesford? That you saw him?"

"I think so."

"You think so. That's an odd coincidence, him being here the same time as you."

Zeke didn't like coincidences. He crossed his arms over his chest. He had a strong sense he wouldn't like what she said next. "Go on."

"There I was, in the midst of the festival crowd, and I thought I recognized Collin's chum. So I tried to catch up with him, to be sure."

"The man you admittedly don't like the look of. Why would you do that?"

"I found it odd him appearing here, what with Collin making the last minute detour to Aylesford. If it was him."

"Very odd," he said, his voice raised several octaves.

"Quiet, Zeke. You'll wake the people in the room beside ours."

Ours. He liked the sound of that. It mollified him sufficiently so he lowered his voice. "You're right, of course. We don't want to draw attention. Move a bit closer so I can hear you better."

She hesitated a moment, as if sensing a trap. Still, she scooted to the center of the bed. "As I was saying, I tried to catch him. When he neared the tobacconist shop, I assumed he meant to go inside and make a purchase, but out of the clear blue, he turned into the alley."

He tapped his fingers on his biceps. "Tell me you did not follow him, Kitty."

"I didn't. But I wish I had. Thinking he'd merely taken the alley as a short cut to the other side, I hastened through the crowd, and 'round the corner. Unfortunately by the time I got there, I'd lost him."

Relief and fear for what might have happened co-mingled, stretching his already raw nerves to the breaking point.

"You said yourself you don't know for certain it was the same man. Maybe he simply resembled the man you met last night. For the love of God, promise you'll never do something like that again."

He hadn't realized he moved. Hadn't realized he'd reached for her, 'til one hand tangled in her hair, and the other encircled her low back.

"Zeke, it was still daylight, for goodness sake, in the heart of a religious festival. How dangerous could the man be?"

"When we're married, I won't be able to let you out of my sight, will I?"

"That's just it, isn't it?" she said, eyes shimmering. She half-heartedly pushed at his chest. "We aren't going to be married because you—"

"Enough talking," he growled. He pressed her back onto the pillows, lowered his head and kissed her.

Chapter Thirty-Two

Her arms snaked up and around his neck, and her lips clung to his.

He wanted more, needed more, desperately so, as if his life depended on it.

"You feel so good," he whispered against her lips. "I need to touch you. Need your skin against mine," he murmured as he fisted her nightdress into one hand and dragged it up over her hips. Fisted again and brought it to her waist.

When her fingers slid from his hair, and her arms came between them, he wondered briefly if she meant to push him away. Instead she arched up, grasped the fabric of her sheer gown, and pulled it over her head.

Now he wished he'd left the lamp burning.

"You'll make sure we won't get pregnant?" she whispered, raining kisses across his throat, the underside of his jaw. Her fingers kneaded the muscles of his chest, every so often stabbing him with the edges of her nails.

"Zeke?" she prodded.

He had to search his mind to recall her question. "If that's what you want, sweetheart."

Waves of heady desire rolled over him as she shimmied and shifted beneath him, her silken flesh gliding beneath his hardness till she had them hip-to-hip.

"Oh, God, Kitty, don't move like that," he ground out between clenched teeth.

She stopped moving—her body. Her fingers tickled the hair at his nape. He felt her touch all the way to the tip of his cock, which was presently cocooned between the twin pillows of her thighs and pointing straight at their apex.

"You don't like the way I'm doing it?" She sounded truly uncertain.

Before he could reply, she inched her legs apart and the head of his cock dove for heaven.

His breath hissed from his lungs. In the nick of time he rolled off her uttering a rapid-fire, "Oh-ho, God, Kitty." He jammed a hand into his hair and gulped air. "You feel too good. You make me lose control."

"Then I suppose you'll really despise this." He heard the sly lilt to her voice a moment before she rose onto her knees, twisting to plant her hands on either side of his face.

For a moment, he simply stared up at her, his gaze tracing the elegant arch of her neck. He reached up, twining his fingers in her ebony waves, falling in tangled curls all around him. He tugged, intending to pull her in for a kiss.

She lifted one knee, and straddled him.

Zeke hinged up at the waist, taking her face in his hands to kiss her like she held the key to his very existence. Sweat lined his brow, and trickled down the center of his back, as his body shivered with need.

Never breaking their kiss, Kitty wriggled her hips, sliding upward 'til her heat nudged the base of his erection. When it seemed she wasn't going to stop there, Zeke reached a hand between them, easing his fingers down the center of her belly to her curls. Gently he parted her, working his fingers into her damp heat.

With their lips locked, she gasped in pleasure, stealing the breath from his lungs.

She lifted her hips a fraction, granting him greater access, and whimpering with need. Soon she was shuddering against his hand, against his hips, the hot entrance to her core teasing his rigid erection with enough regularity he nearly lost it again.

All at once she reached between them, her cool fingers closing around his thrumming flesh, and he lost the ability to breathe. She nestled him into her heat and pressed her hips downward, impaling herself inch by precious inch.

She was so tight. So wet. So hot. Pulling him in. He lay back, unable to do anything other than drown in the cresting waves of pleasure.

She rode him, slowly, resisting his every effort to take control. He'd never been more desperate for a woman, or more captured.

He gasped in a breath when his head started to spin—lack of oxygen? He couldn't speak. Could only marvel at the intensity of wanting like he'd never known.

His turn. He grasped her hips in his hands, flipping her beneath him in one move. He had to show her. She was his and only his.

Using more restraint than he knew he had, he drove into her, again and again. Slow, deep thrusts, while she clung to him, wrapping arms and legs around him as if she couldn't get close enough.

"Zeke, Zeke, oh, please." She urged him faster, deeper.

Need twisted him inside out. But he held the reins tight, and drove her relentlessly toward her ultimate release.

Beneath him she arched and shuddered, crying out in nonsensical gibberish while she raked her nails into the sweat soaked skin of his back, until, crying his name, she came apart.

He drew out her pleasure, giving her all he had, pushing the limits of his own control 'til he had no choice but to rip himself out of her, erupting his own hot seed in the cold night air.

Afterward, he collapsed beside her and hauled her close, both of them breathing hard, their arms and legs entangled. Everything about them entangled. Jesus, didn't she see?

"I love you, Zeke," she whispered.

If he had the energy to speak, he'd tell her she owned him, body and soul. Eyes closed, his lips curved in a smile of total and complete contentment. With Kitty in his arms, he let himself sink blissfully into the sleep of the dead—and met the old baron once more.

Regal in his gray uniform, he stood, arms crossed, eyeing him askance.

"I did everything I could to protect her," Zeke argued. "I'm here, aren't I?"

The baron shook his head and dread filled him.

Looking around he saw he was no longer at the inn. He was in a shipyard. Cargo ships and sailing vessels jammed the slips. He glanced into the water at the quay and saw his own reflection. He'd grown old and haggard. A man utterly and completely alone.

He straightened. Spun in a circle looking for the baron. He was gone.

"Tell me what to do," Zeke shouted.

No answer came.

An emptiness he'd never known had his knees buckling, bringing him face to face with his reflection again. *Tell me what to do*, he repeated silently.

Like a whisper through his soul, he heard an answer.

"Open your eyes."

He was suddenly and completely awake, Kitty's supple, warm body in his arms contrasting sharply with the cold dread churning in his gut. Reflexively his arms tightened—and Kitty murmured sweet, unintelligible nonsense in response.

He released the breath he hadn't realized he'd been holding. Just a dream. Just an annoying, meaningless dream.

His manhood, it seemed, had awoken before him and now urged him to wake her, to prove to himself how not alone he was. But the church bells tolling in the distance told him to move.

He uncoiled his body from hers. The emptiness from his dream returned with a vengeance. *Get your head straight, man. Think about what needs doing.*

First, he'd see to his horse. Next he'd have a word with the innkeeper, assuring the man kept his mouth shut about Zeke's late night arrival. Then he had the long ride to the post where he'd stipulated Caden send his important telegram.

He still had to work out whether to return here or head on to Maidstone. He'd have to rely on instinct there, since he didn't know what Hastings was up to. If only he didn't have to leave.

He turned his head to gaze at Kitty, still sound asleep. He didn't want to go.

He traced his fingertips down the length of her hair, then slipped his hand beneath the covers to roam the curve of her hip, skim the softness of her belly. Her skin was like the smoothest silk, and warm like sunshine. He inched closer, helpless to resist cocooning her body with his once more.

She felt exactly right. It almost hurt.

She'd changed him. Somehow sneaked under his skin and taken up residence. If he lost her now, it would be like losing a part of himself. The truth slammed him like a punch to the gut. She'd made him need her.

Visions of his father swam before his eyes. Broken. Weak. All because of a woman. Zeke had sworn he'd never make such an idiot of himself. Except now that he had, he had an inkling of how his father might have felt. For the first time since his father's decline into depravity, Zeke felt a modicum of charity for the man.

Oh, he wasn't excusing the selfish, destructive tendencies of the man which had festered beneath the surface long before he lost Zeke's mother, and which eventually killed him. He simply understood for the first time in his life what it was to value someone as much as—no, more than himself.

He clenched his jaw, tamping down the unexpected well-spring of emotion that had the backs of his eyes stinging, for Christ's sake.

Get a hold of yourself, man. Focus.

He dragged himself to his feet. Minutes later, the sun barely reaching the horizon, he stooped beside the bed. "Kitty, I'm leaving."

She opened heavy-lidded eyes. "Oh, hello."

His gut flipped like someone had spun him around several times, blindfolded. He smoothed her hair from her face with trembling fingers. "I'll see you later tonight. Wherever you are, I'll find you."

"I know," she said, her green cat's eyes glowing—with love, for him. How had he earned such a rare and precious gift?

His throat tightened. "Try not to get into any trouble while I'm gone, hmm?"

***

Kitty awoke and sat bolt upright, a monumental epiphany clamoring to the forefront of her mind. Zeke cared for her.

He hadn't spoken the words. Yet, she saw it in his smoky blue eyes when he looked at her. She heard it in the way he spoke to her with that maddening combination of exasperation and teasing. When they were together, everything in him focused entirely on her—what she said, what she did, her life experiences. All of it mattered to him.

She touched her fingertips to her lips, and closed her eyes.

It was also there in his kisses, be they tender or devouring. In the reverent way he touched her, and the passionate, mind-emptying way he made love to her.

Last night, she had been desperate for him, completely unable to get close enough to him. She'd have crawled inside him, if she could. But then, Zeke seemed every bit as consumed with her.

Surely it all meant something.

Her body aching in places she hadn't known existed before experiencing Zeke's lovemaking, she eased off the bed and made for the basin.

She splashed herself, lathered, rinsed and dried, then picked up her brush to work out the worst of the tangles caused by

Zeke's fingers as they'd sifted through her hair. *I like it when you wear your hair down*, he said in that husky voice, laden with desire.

Maybe desire alone comprised his feelings for her. Maybe she saw what she wanted to see, grasped at straws, and all for naught. Her promise to her brother still bound her as surely as if she'd already married Garrick.

The truth was, regardless of what Zeke professed last night about his ability to see Collin's title restored, Collin was a bird-in-hand kind of fellow. Unless Zeke could pull off a miracle and accomplish what he promised immediately, Collin would never agree to void his agreement with Garrick.

But what if Zeke could convince Collin to trust him, and allow her to marry him instead? Would half of Zeke's heart be enough for her? She would have said no a week ago. But now…

Perhaps she should allow Zeke to speak with Collin on the matter.

A short while later, she stood outside Collin's door hoping he wouldn't take one look at her beard-scraped cheeks and know how she'd spent the evening.

She rapped her knuckles on the door and a young chamber-maid ducked her head out from an open chamber. "Excuse me, milady. Are you looking for the man who's letting the room?"

Kitty smiled and nodded. "He's my brother."

The maid stepped into the hall and cleared her throat.

Kitty glanced uncertainly from the still closed door to the somber looking maid. "He was ill last night, and now he doesn't answer. Would you kindly open the door for me?"

The chambermaid glanced toward the stairs. Kitty could practically read her thoughts. Go ask the owner of the establishment before opening the door and lose precious time from her many tasks, or trust the lady.

"Please," Kitty said in an urgent voice. That old feeling of dread was stirring the hair at her nape.

"The thing is, milady, his lordship isn't in."

"He's gone down to breakfast, you mean?" She asked, her pulse spiking.

"No, milady." The maid pulled a skeleton key from her apron. She unlocked and opened the door. "He's been out since yesterday afternoon, mum."

Kitty did a quick sweep of the room. Collin was, indeed, absent. His travel case lay open, but it looked as if little, if anything, had been removed. Someone had turned his bed down, but it did not appear slept in.

Collin hadn't spent the night here? But he had returned, had he not? The note she received from him eschewing dinner in favor of bed had been written in his hand.

Concerned and confounded, Kitty thanked the maid, and turned away. She headed straight for the dining hall. There she did a perfunctory check for her brother, knowing full well she wouldn't find him.

Minutes later, she set out at a vigorous clip. Something was very wrong here. Ever since Collin saw that man, Peters, he'd acted off.

If she was being honest, Collin had seemed different since his return. He had a coldness about him. She chalked it up to his traumatic experiences.

The day was gloriously sunny, a perfect day for festival revelry, and crowds swarmed the streets. The sounds of laughter caused a sick feeling to invade her stomach. Collin had brought her here as a respite from her upcoming trial, as she saw it. If something happened to him because of her...

But he had to be all right. She'd only just gotten him back. She redoubled her efforts, pressing through the clogged streets, her destination clear.

Resolve filled her as she spied the tobacco shop, behind which she'd lost Mr Peters. No one paid her any mind as she strode for the alley entrance.

Standing at the edge of the shadowed, narrow passageway, Zeke's warning against doing anything foolish flashed in her mind. He wouldn't be pleased with her right now. But what else she could do?

She took a bracing breath, and stepped into dark shadow. To her great relief no foul odor of urine greeted her. No broken glass crunched beneath her booted feet. No bats swooped.

She inched forward, letting her eyes adjust, sliding her fingers over the bricked wall to her left.

At what she guessed marked the half way point of the alley, a door crashed open. Raucous male laughter poured from the unknown establishment, and a pair of men clothed in gentleman's garb stumbled out. They appeared too intent on holding each other upright to notice her.

They started for the opposite end of the alley.

Before she could second guess herself, she called to them. "Excuse me, gentlemen?"

Two heads jerked around to gaze in her direction.

"Mr. Hawthorn, do you see a lady there? Or have my losses brought on hallucinations?"

"I do indeed, Mr. Stone. I do indeed." The man called Hawthorn raised his voice a little. "My dear lady, have you lost your way? There's no friar down this road, I can assure you."

The men's hardy snickers caused them to wobble all the more.

Kitty strode toward them with more bravado than she felt.

Up close, the pair reeked of spirits and stale tobacco smoke. She barely resisted the urge to wrinkle her nose.

"Actually, I have a brother who's lost."

The men exchanged glances, then guffawed uproariously.

"A brother, she says, Mr. Stone."

"So she did," Mr. Stone agreed. He stepped toward Kitty, tripping over his own slow feet, and fell into the brick fascia to his right. Evidently opting to rest there, he plopped his head in his hand, and gave her a smug grin. "Sure it's not a missing husband you're after?"

She blinked. "Positive."

Mr. Stone shrugged. "Why would you be looking here for your brother, miss?"

She decided to go with the truth as far as she knew it. "I saw Mr Peters come this way yesterday. He and my brother are friends."

"Peters? Peters ain't nobody's friend. Mr Hawthorne, let's be off."

They turned and resumed their plodding egress.

"No, wait, please. You know Mr Peters? Have you seen him? Perhaps you could point me in his direction."

One of the men gestured loosely behind him, toward the closed door.

Kitty approached the heavy looking wooden door, noting the chipped green paint and unpolished brass door handle. She considered for the briefest moment heading back to the inn. Then she thought of Collin, and the hard looking Mr Peters.

Before she could second-guess herself, she lifted her hand and rapped.

No one answered.

She pressed her ear to the door and thought she could hear the din of male voices coming from within. One way to find out. She squared her shoulders and grasped the knob. It stuck slightly, then turned in her hand.

The same awful smell of cigars and whiskey she detected on Hawthorne and Stone greeted her the moment the door opened. Was this a gentlemen's club?

She stepped into a narrow, dark passageway, allowing the creaking door to nearly close behind her. Tiptoeing on her boots, she headed toward the light spilling in from a room branching off a few feet down.

She could make out distinct male voices now, and paused while still safely in the shadows to listen for Collin's.

"I'll stay."

"Bloody bugger. He's bluffing again."

"Better hope you're right if you're going to call. He cleaned you out but good last time."

Poker, then. She'd wandered into a den. A gaming hell, she'd heard them called. She spun around and hastened toward the exit. Silly little fool. Collin didn't gamble.

She breathed a sigh of relief when she reached the door. She swung the door open and stepped one foot into the alley.

"Argh!" she choked, as a heavily muscled arm hooked around her neck and yanked her inside. She wanted to protest but couldn't speak. The brute had cut off her air supply.

She struggled with all her might, both of her hands tearing at the man's immovable arm.

He dragged her down the hall and into the light.

"Found this little package wandering in from the alley," her abductor announced in a gravelly voice.

A general rumble of male voices rippled through the room.

A tall man whose features she could not make out due to the brightly lit oil lamp hanging behind him approached. "I think she's trying to speak, Brawn. Loosen your hold a bit."

Brawn relaxed his grip enough she could stand on her own two feet and draw a full breath.

"I made a wrong turn, sir," she said when she could speak. "Now kindly release me so I may go on my way."

The tall man before her grabbed her chin, and jerked her face up to the light.

Up close, she recognized the man. "Mr Peters, you might recall we met two nights ago."

The room erupted with raucous laughter.

"Not exactly your type, sir," a man called.

Mr Peters rocked back out of her view. "Release the lady, Brawn."

Mr Peters obviously held sway here, as she was abruptly freed.

"Thank you. I seem to have taken a wrong turn and—m"

"When did we meet?" Peters demanded

She took a moment to glance at her immediate surroundings. Dark and high ceilinged, the room looked to be a converted warehouse of sorts. Four round baize-covered tables made up the furnishings. Four to five men sat at each. Oil lamps haphazardly attached to exposed rafters hung over the tables. Thick bands of cigar smoke coiled in the harsh lights.

The men all stared at her with varying degrees of pique or curiosity. None of them were her brother. Of course they weren't. She was the worst kind of fool.

"We both happened to be staying at the same inn, two days ago," she finally answered.

The man barked out a laugh of understanding. "You're Hastings' sister. The one he didn't want me to see."

Kitty sidled backwards towards the passageway. "I'm terribly sorry to have disturbed your games, gentlemen. As it turns out, Collin and I got separated. He'll surely be searching the streets for me, so if you'll excuse me—"

"Separated, eh? Do y'hear, men? Hastings and his darling sister got separated," Peters announced to the room.

"He's searching for her, all right. Nose deep in the corner yonder," someone volunteered.

Raucous laughter ensued.

Another man said, "Enough of this. I didn't come here to chat."

Several men apparently agreed, and voiced their assent.

Peters raised a hand, shushing the growing discontent. "Keep an eye on things, Brawn," he muttered to the man who'd grabbed her, and and gestured for Kitty to follow him.

She wanted very much to leave. But curiosity bade her trail the man to an unlit corner of the large room.

In horror she noted a man huddling on the floor. Dark haired, and lying on his side, his back to the wall, he emitted a small snore.

She peered down at the man. "Mr Peters why are you—" She gasped. "Collin! What have you done with him?" She crouched beside her brother and gave his shoulder a firm shake.

He did not open his eyes.

"He's passed out, thanks to his own overindulgence. I'd be most obliged if you'd get the pisser out of here," Peters replied.

"I'll be more than happy to," she said, attempting to wake Collin, to no avail.

What was she to do now?

"There's just a small matter of the debt owed me." Peters rocked back on his heels.

She straightened. "Debt?"

"He lost deep, as per usual, but I'm sure you're no stranger to that."

"Deep?" she echoed again.

"He's bet the farm, so to speak. You'd think he'd have learned after last time when he had to quit the country." Peters' face split in a broad grin. "You should have seen his face when he came to me two nights past, all apologetic and humble-like, telling me how he'd be coming into money soon, and how he'd pay off his debt.

"When I told him it'd been settled years ago by Lord Hastings, his grandfather, I thought his eyes would pop right out of his head." Peters cackled. "You fancies. You slay me."

"I have no notion of what you're talking about, sir. My brother was pronounced dead until recently. His ship was lost at sea."

"That's as may be, milady. I can't rightly say. I can only tell you, he fled like a scared girl when it came time to pay his debts last time because he didn't have the blunt. Meanwhile, his lordship cleared away his debts as always. Never bothered to tell his heir, though. I suppose he got tired of bleeding money." Peters stared down at Collin, hands splayed on his hips.

He sighed and disappeared, returning a moment later with a large tankard in hand.

"Never did trust a man what couldn't hold his liquor." He dashed the contents into Collin's face.

A sputtering Collin bolted upright, then brought a hand to his temple. His eyes were puffy slits of red. "What's that, eh? Kitty, love, is that you?"

"And here, Lady Hastings, is his marker," Peters thrust a small sheet of paper into her hands.

Kitty glared at her brother, then read the note. Her eyes went wide. "This can't be."

"Oh, but it can, Lady Hastings," Peters said. He pointed to a scribble on the bottom of the sheet. "Witness your brother's signature."

Chapter Thirty-Three

"There's no message here for you, my lord."

Zeke stared at the spectacled, bald little man who peeked at him from behind the telegraph machine.

Zeke shifted his gaze to the box of orange envelopes situated on the credenza behind the operator. How hard would it be to reach over that shiny head, grab the messages, and search them himself?

"Check again. My brother specifically told me he'd be in touch by today, and I'm sure I specified this office."

The man puffed out his cheeks and looked ready to argue, until he glanced up. Whatever he read in Zeke's eyes had him swiveling in his chair and all but diving for the box.

He searched the messages forwards and backwards, and with evident reluctance turned back to Zeke. "I'm sorry, my lord, truly. It is not here."

Zeke might have to kill Caden next time he saw him. He'd left Kitty's warm bed, ridden all this way, for the sole purpose of learning Caden's so-called important information.

Behind him the door to the post office jingled as another customer entered.

"I'll wait," Zeke growled at the machine operator, crossing his arms over his chest.

"Bullying a hapless public servant, Thurgood. Haven't you anything better to do?"

Zeke's brows shot up at Randall's voice. And, he'd be willing to bet the man had company. His mouth twitched and he made a slow about-face. "Caden, Randall," he said with a nod for each.

The pair of them stood side by side, their big frames taking up far too much space in the small office.

"Caden, how lucky for you to have arrived at precisely this moment." Zeke grasped his brother's shoulder and squeezed. Hard.

Caden shot Zeke a querulous look. "Why's that, brother?"

Zeke smiled coolly. "Because you just interrupted my very detailed plot of your impending demise."

Caden's mouth quirked in a grin. "Born lucky, I suppose."

Zeke gestured for the two men to precede him out of the office. They convened on the cobbled street, making a loose knit circle.

He wasted no time getting to the point. "Tell me the damned news I've been waiting to hear for over twenty-four hours, and after that, explain why you're here."

"As to why we're here..." Caden wrinkled his nose. "For one thing we brought you a change of clothes. We figured the ones you had with you must be ripe by now."

"We figured correctly," Randall added with a waft of his hand.

Zeke gazed heavenward. "You came all this way to see to my grooming needs?"

"That and we have news to deliver, of course. Thought it would be too wordy to express via telegraph."

"What is it?" Zeke bit out.

"Not until you've done a quick change—and we have some food in front of us," Caden said, without a trace of his usual lighthearted charm.

Zeke opened his mouth to argue.

Caden forestalled him, lifting one hand. "Before you waste your breath telling us there isn't time, think of your horse. She needs a break. While you're at it, think of yourself. You look half-starved. When's the last time you ate?"

Zeke's mouth snapped shut. He couldn't remember.

"There's an inn a block and a half down the street." Caden jerked a thumb over his shoulder. "We've already made arrangements to get you clean and fed." With that, Caden and Randall turned on their heels and marched off, leaving Zeke to grudgingly follow.

"How is the lady, by the by?" Randall asked over his shoulder. "You have been in communication with her since…er…she announced her plans?"

An image of Kitty as he'd last seen her sprang to mind. Zeke felt the blood rushing up his neck. "I have."

"Good. I for one have been worried sick about our Kitty," Caden said.

"She's quite well, despite her brother's best efforts."

"Poor darling. All ready to deliver herself up on a silver platter," Randall said, shaking his head.

Zeke grunted.

"Speaking of which—what's Hastings got to say for himself?" Caden demanded.

Zeke coughed into his palm. "I…er…haven't spoken to him."

Caden stopped short and Zeke nearly rammed into him. "How is it you can assure us of Kitty's well-being as if you spoke with her only this morning, yet you haven't made your presence known to her guardian?"

"Yes, rather neat trick, that," Randall added, also at a standstill.

"I'll be happy to explain my strategy as pertains to Kitty's safety as soon as you fill me in on this so-called news you felt the need to travel from London to continue withholding from me," Zeke barked.

"After food," Caden replied, and he and Randall resumed their brisk stride.

"Anyone ever tell you you're both stubborn as a mules?" Zeke groused.

"I learned from the best," Caden replied. "Here's the inn." He produced a turnkey from his waistcoat jacket and tossed it to Zeke. "Second floor, room two. We'll wait for you in the dining hall."

Within thirty minutes, Zeke was relatively clean, having availed himself of a quick shave with a sharp razor, thanks to Caden, and a quick scrub in the steaming bath he found waiting for him. He dried hastily and donned the clean travel clothes Caden brought, then made for the pub style eatery.

The rich scent of roasted meat and fresh baked bread assailed his senses when he entered the dining room. He was hungry. Ravenous. Taking time to eat over the last few days hadn't been a priority. Now his mouth watered to the point of a drool. Caden's instinct to clothe, feed, and water him was spot on.

But that didn't mean he wouldn't string Caden up by his boot straps if he didn't reveal his information immediately and let him get back to Kitty. Leaving her alone with James and Hastings left him uneasy. He couldn't help fearing they'd drag her to the altar while his back was turned.

She wouldn't go along with it in any case, he told himself. Not while there was a chance she carried his babe. A hot rush of tenderness and need roiled up in him. Oddly, it felt good. Right.

He spotted Caden and Randall and dropped onto the bench-style seat across from them.

Immediately Caden shoved a bowl of steaming beef stew and crusty bread under his nose.

"There's a frothy pint here for you, too, if you're a good boy and eat your meal," Caden drawled. "You almost look like yourself."

Zeke picked up his spoon and aimed it at Caden. "Tell me what you know."

Caden eyed the food meaningfully. "Eat."

Zeke glared. "Speak."

"Bloody hell. Caden will talk. You will eat." Randall shook his head.

Both brothers grunted their assent.

Zeke reached across the table to grab the pint Caden had thought to withhold and lifted it to his mouth.

Caden locked eyes with Zeke. "Garrick James never inherited Maidstone. Hastings is still the rightful heir by law."

Zeke managed to slog several gulps while frowning over the rim. He set the pint down with a thud and picked up his spoon. "That can't be."

"You yourself said you doubted James's ability to inherit, being the son of Lord Hastings's bastard brother," Randall put in. "You had it right all along."

Zeke spoke through a mouthful of stew. "That was before James produced the Royal Writ of Summons, calling him to appear at the House of Lords this spring."

Caden nodded. "That certainly had me convinced. Lucky for you, you asked the earl's man-of-affairs to look into James's background *before* the writ arrived to throw us off.

"When I arrived in London, I went to him for help digging into Hastings. Imagine my surprise when he handed me a set of documents showing Hastings, and not James, to be the, as yet, heir to the Maidstone barony."

Zeke broke off a piece of bread. "The mystery of the writ aside, I can see James being unable to qualify, but Hastings was pronounced dead."

Caden and Randal exchanged looks. "That's just it, Zeke. The crown only just began looking into his so-called death at James's insistence. Evidently, the powers that be never got any official certificate. Not one that got filed properly, at any rate. James did make a claim on the title, citing Hastings abandoned his estate, even if he wasn't deceased. His claim was summarily denied on the basis of bloodline."

Zeke sat back. "So James assumes he'll inherit. Finds out he's not only been beat out by a dead man, but prohibited from inheriting." He drummed his fingers on the scarred wooden table. "Theories?"

Caden shrugged. "Maybe James planned to act the part indefinitely. Hoped no one would notice?"

Zeke shook his head. "He's too crafty for that. He'd have to know he'd be found out sooner or later. No. He had an ace up his sleeve."

"Maybe James filed a petition with the queen? Maybe he's expecting his claim to come through any time?" Randall surmised.

"I could see that being relevant before Hastings showed up. But now James is bartering his supposed title with Hastings, the legitimate heir, in exchange for Kitty's hand. It makes no sense. We're missing something. Something vital."

Time to break down what he knew. Take each individual fact to its logical conclusion. He held up one thumb. "First off, Hastings clearly does not know he still holds right to the title, or he wouldn't be wasting time placating James by dangling Kitty under the cove's nose."

"Agreed," Caden murmured.

His pointer finger joined his thumb. "Second, clearly Kitty hasn't a clue, or she wouldn't have agreed to marry her cousin for her brother's sake."

"I still can't believe she has," Randall muttered.

"Zeke's not going to let that happen. Are you, brother?" Caden asked in a deadly soft voice.

Zeke slid a hard gaze to his brother in answer and lifted a third finger. "Which leaves James knowingly bartering a nonexistent title for Kitty. The bastard is bloody obsessed with her—so much so he produced a phony writ summoning him to parliament, then waved the damned forgery under our noses."

Caden knocked a fist against the table. "But why? Why would James want to make anyone believe he held the title? What would he gain?"

"Besides Kitty?" Zeke closed his eyes and blew air out his cheeks, trying to recall inheritance laws. He'd been forced to study the damned things in secondary school, but that was a long time ago.

Randall spoke up. "If we assume the Crown would eventually have concluded Hastings dead, what would have become of the barony?"

"'You mean, who would inherit?" Zeke asked.

"Precisely." Randall said.

All at once, the truth dawned. "Randall, you're a genius," Zeke said.

"Thank you," the viscount said with a jaunty grin. "Why, exactly?"

Zeke leaned across the table. "The title would have gone into abeyance 'til Kitty married."

A moment of silence passed as Zeke allowed his words to penetrate. It all finally made sense. Why James had been so intent on marrying Kitty—and Holy Christ—why he still was. He was after the title, and he wasn't letting anything like a prodigal son returned from the dead get in his way.

"My God," Caden whispered. "At her marriage, the title would pass to her husband."

"I am a bloody genius," Randall murmured, his hand to his heart. "Where are you going? Caden, where's your brother going?"

Zeke was halfway to the door, but he thought he heard his brother answer, "I think he's going to get his lady."

***

Zeke reached the mews, only to find his horse as yet un-saddled. He wanted to shake the groomsman. Instead he gritted his teeth and ordered the man to ready not only his mount, but Caden and Randall's horses, as well.

They arrived a few minutes behind him.

"Thanks for waiting." Caden slapped Zeke on the back a little harder than necessary.

"What took you so long?" Zeke asked, not taking his eyes from the barn door.

"We had to settle the bill. So tell us, where are we heading?"

"A little town called Aylesford."

"Kitty's there, I presume?"

Zeke met his brother's eyes. "One way or another, we're going to find her. But, yes, I suspect they're all still in Aylesford."

"Any reason in particular you think they haven't set out for Maidstone yet?" Caden asked.

Zeke stepped back to make room as the stable lad led his horse from the stalls. "Just a feeling. Something to do with why they stopped in the first place. It's a small village, not on the way to Maidstone. Kitty told me her brother claimed he'd made the detour for her, but..."

Randall came up on Zeke's other side and gripped his shoulder. "But you find it hard to believe her brother would put her interests before his own in any circumstance?"

Zeke smiled grimly. "Precisely."

The grooms led the horses out.

Zeke swung into his saddle, and waited while Caden and Randall followed suit. "Gentlemen, two words for you. Keep up."

***

Kitty was spitting mad. She'd gotten Collin down the alley somehow, and now they stood on the storefront walkway in full view of any and all passersby while she scanned the cobbled streets for a hansom cab.

Bother. Collin was heavy. Her discomfort only fueled her anger.

"How could you do it, Collin? You lost a fortune. I had to sign a waiver personally guaranteeing to cover your losses. Me! And if that Mr Peters fellow told the truth, this wasn't your first major loss. Not to mention, you lied to me. This was the real reason we stopped here in Aylesford, wasn't it?"

Collin winced. "Kindly stop your caterwauling. My head feels as though it's going to explode."

"It would serve you right. Aylesford?" she prodded, tapping her foot.

"Yes, yes." He put a hand to his temple. Their grandfather's ring, which he wore on his pinkie sparkled in the sunlight.

Suddenly her anger gave way to unspeakable hurt. Had her brother, the man she thought she knew, ever existed? "I'm surprised you didn't wager Grandfather's ring."

Collin held out his hand to study the gold band. "I would never part with it. It's a reminder of what's mine by birthright. Of what I nearly lost, thanks to the old man. But to answer your question, yes, Peters let me know of a game he had going when we happened into each other two nights ago. I didn't mention it because it wasn't your concern."

She laughed in disbelief. It was almost too much to take in. The fact she'd found Collin in a gaming den. The stunning sum of his loss. The fact she had to leverage their way out of the establishment by signing a promissory note.

How long had she been a fool? How long had her brother been a ne'er-do-well gambler? She frowned, replaying his last words.

"What did you mean you nearly lost your birthright thanks to the old man? You mean our Grandfather?"

"It was he who sent me away in the first place."

A flood of understanding assaulted her senses. Her stomach dropped and for a moment she thought she might be ill. "You bloody bastard."

"Excuse me?" he demanded, one brow arched over a red-rimmed eye.

She pointed at him, hand shaking, heedless of the stares she attracted. "You never went to America in search of our parents' belongings. You were running. Running from your moneylender. From Mr Peters."

"Now, Kitty, I can explain. It wasn't my doing. It was your beloved grandfather's."

People had stopped to stare. She sent them a warning glare before grasping Collin by the hand and dragging him back to the mouth of the alley. "You have the nerve to blame our grandfather for your disappearance? Your lies?"

"My losses were a mere drop in the estate's bucket. I would have recouped them in another game or two, at the most, like always. But the baron refused to see reason. So, as a matter of fact, yes, I do blame him. How do you think I got the money to go, anyway? The ticket to cross the sea? He told me to go and never come back."

Collin's words hit her like a punch to the gut. Her beloved Grandfather had sent Collin away, and then let her believe he was dead? He'd kept the truth from her every bit as much as Collin had.

A wave of nausea rolled through her. Her exertion coupled with the late morning heat wasn't helping matters. She closed her eyes and gulped air. "I've heard enough."

But Collin wasn't done venting his grievances. "He drove me from England, my home, Kitty. Told me he'd let that blackguard, Peters, kill me before he'd pay off another debt. I had no choice, don't you see?"

Drawing on all her will, Kitty tamped down on the pain squeezing her heart.

"Oh, I see, all right. I see you left me. You and grandfather both conspired to lie to me. And now that grandfather's gone, you've come back to reclaim your title by any means necessary."

Collin lifted his aristocratic chin a notch. "It is my title by right."

She locked eyes with him. "That it is, Collin. I wish you the best at recovering it from our cousin. But I promise you this. I won't be marrying him to aid your procurement."

Collin's previously ashen face suffused with color, and his eyes went hard. He drew himself up to his full height and closed the short distance between them with sudden agility. "You will if I say you will. I'm your guardian now, remember?"

Kitty had never seen this side of him. Hardened. Utterly without compassion. It broke her heart. But her spine had never been more stiff. "I don't care what you say, or what you threaten. I won't do it."

An arm shot around her from behind, a tight cord squeezing her waist so she couldn't draw in a full breath. Not Zeke's muscular, protective arm, nor Mr Peters' man, Brawn. But an arm with wiry strength. Garrick.

"Hastings, Hastings," Garrick said in a tut-tut manner. He turned his head to whisper in Kitty's ear, "I gather you've discovered your brother's dirty little secret, and now think to break our engagement yet again." As he spoke, he dragged her into the shadowy darkness of the alley.

"Let go of me," Kitty said through gritted teeth. She struggled to free herself but with her arms pinned to her sides, she could gain no purchase. "Collin, do something."

Collin did something, all right. He covered their movements like a walking shroud, glancing to and fro as if ascertaining no once witnessed the madness.

"Now, see you don't hurt her, James," he said.

As if that were the only issue. "Collin?"

He steadfastly avoided her gaze. He meant to let Garrick take her.

"No permanent marks," Garrick agreed. "She is my soon-to-be bride after all."

His calm arrogance galvanized her. She opened her mouth to scream, and found her face abruptly covered with a damp cloth reeking of chemicals. She turned her head violently, but Garrick's hand held firm.

"There now. Take a breath and go to sleep, my love," Garrick crooned.

She held her breath 'til her lungs burned from lack of oxygen and black dots danced before her eyes. Instinct drove her to suck in a breath, and everything went black.

Chapter Thirty-Four

Zeke, Caden, and Randall arrived at the Inn at Aylesford at half past noon. They hadn't met Kitty's party on the road.

His sense something was wrong had increased exponentially on the hard ride. He'd tried to deny the gnawing sense danger had found its way to Kitty, or she to it. He told himself he was letting his imagination run wild now he'd uncovered the truth. But the bone deep certainty had only grown more entrenched.

He slid from his mount and handed the reins over to the stable boy practically in one move.

"Wait for me," he called to Caden and Randall, already jogging up the steps to the entrance. He passed the front desk without responding to the clerk's cheery hello, and took the stairs two at a time.

He tried Kitty's door without knocking, and found it locked—a good sign. He rapped sharply, waited all of one second, then called out, "Kitty, open the door."

No reply came.

From the corner of his eye he saw a chambermaid pop her capped head out of a neighboring room.

He turned an urgent gaze on her.

The maid came out to the hall, wiping her hands on her apron. "The lady ain't about, m'lord."

"She's not on the premises?"

She shook her head.

"But she hasn't checked out?"

"Not that I'm aware, m'lord."

"Where is she?" he demanded.

She took a hasty step back.

He rolled his shoulders, stretched his neck, and tried again. "I'm looking for my fiancé. I thought I'd find her in her room. Have you any idea where she went?"

The maid relaxed visibly. "Aye, m'lord." She glanced around as if to ascertain no one was listening, then stepped closer to Zeke. "I was cleaning the rooms on another floor when I seen her standing in front of her brother's door who I knew very well wasn't in. When I informed her as such, she got upset. I got the idea she was going to look for him."

Zeke's skin went instantly clammy. "Thank you. That's very helpful. About how long ago was that, would you say, miss?"

His voice sounded strange. As if he were speaking from very far away.

"About two and a half hours, I'd say." She cocked her head. "The other gentleman asked the same thing."

Zeke's insides froze. "The other gentleman. That would be…?"

She shook her head. "Lord James." Her brows knitted in confusion. "He claimed he was the lady's fiancé, now I think on it."

"I'm sure you misunderstood. He's a distant cousin, nothing more."

She nodded, though uncertainty clouded her eyes.

Zeke thanked her and reached in his pocket to toss her a few coins. "If the lady returns, please tell her to wait for me here." He started to turn away, then added, "Lord Thurgood. Her fiancé."

✳✳✳

At the stables, Zeke quickly informed Caden and Randall of the situation.

"They haven't left town, but none of them are on premises. Additionally, the three left separately. According to the inn's staff, no one's seen Hastings come or go since he went out, day one.

"Kitty went off on a tear this morning, apparently on the hunt for him. James, it seems, left after that, looking for her."

Zeke felt downright grim. He'd known something was wrong.

"Any idea where to start?" Caden asked.

He had only one clue to go on—Kitty's possible sighting of Hastings' friend, Peters.

"We'll start at the tobacconist shop. Kitty mentioned it the other night. Said she thought she'd seen a friend of her brother's near the alley."

They set out on foot. The town wasn't large, and Zeke decided the horses might prove a hindrance in small, tight places, like alleyways behind tobacco shops.

The scent of baked goods, roasted meats, and sweets filled the air the closer they got to the ongoing fete. Sounds of laughter and conversation, of street vendors hawking their wares and buggies traveling the cobbled streets merged into a growing cacophony of noise—yet Zeke could still hear his own breathing. Could make out the distinct beat his heart. The clip of his boots on the street.

He needed to find Kitty. Needed to see her. Touch her with his hands. Nothing would be right until then.

"Is that the shop?" Caden pointed to the corner ahead.

Zeke's gaze followed the direction of Caden's finger, then shifted slightly to the alley behind the building. The hair on his nape stirred. "That's it. Let's go."

He crossed the street.

Caden and Randall followed, but remained a few feet behind as if they sensed his animalistic need to claim the territory. He would find something here. Something that would lead him to Kitty.

He stepped into the dark, narrow passage and started forward. Immediately, the sounds of the bustling town receded.

Halfway down the alley, he spotted a large, weathered door. Just past the door, someone had deposited what looked like a sack of refuse.

The low, weak groan of a person in distress reached his ears. He broke into a run. On the ground, the lump moved.

"What is it?" Caden demanded from behind him.

"I think the question is who," Randall put in.

Zeke crouched before the crumpled human—of the male persuasion, thank God. He touched the man's shoulder. Still warm.

A sneaking suspicion took root in his mind. Dark hair. Just about the right build. He rolled the man onto his back. Bullseye. "It's Hastings," he said over his shoulder.

Zeke lowered his head to Hastings's ashen face, checking for breath. When he felt the hair on his cheek stir, he patted him, chest to midsection. He pulled his hands back on reflex when he touched warm, slick liquid pooling at the man's low belly.

"Is he…" Caden swallowed hard.

"No. He's alive." Zeke glanced up at Caden. "Stabbed, is my best guess."

Hastings moaned and his eyes fluttered open. "Thurgood?" he whispered. "What're you doing here?"

Zeke resisted the urge to shake him. "Never mind why I'm here, just thank your stars I'm in time to save your sorry neck—if you tell me where Kitty is."

Hastings grimaced and closed his eyes.

"Hastings," Zeke barked. "Where is your sister? Tell me now, damn it, or I'll let you bleed out."

The door behind them creaked in protest as it opened wide enough for a dumb looking bit of muscle to peer out at them.

"What's this?" the man asked in thick cockney. His gaze hitched on Hastings. "Mr Peters," he yelled over his shoulder. "Someone's killed Lord Hastings."

Zeke noted the man didn't sound overly broken up.

Someone from within the building replied, but Zeke couldn't make out the words.

The man in the doorway leaned further out to glance up and down the alley. "No sir, the lady don't appear to be present."

Zeke was upright, door gripped in his hands and yanked open wide, before the man had time to draw another breath. "What lady? Peters!" Zeke snarled into the building.

"What's this?" the brawny man yelped again. He looked ready to pounce, but a tall figure materialized behind him, placing a staying hand on his shoulder.

"I'm Peters. Who might you be, my lord?" Peters stood eye level with Zeke.

"Thurgood of Claybourne," Zeke replied in a steely voice. "Is the lady of whom you speak this man's sister?" He jerked a thumb toward Hastings, who groaned as if on cue.

Peters stepped one foot into the alley and flicked a glance over Hastings. "So she claimed. She signed her brother's marker before they left, and was none too pleased about it. I didn't see her resorting to violence, however."

"She is not responsible for this." Zeke articulated each word through gritted teeth. "Who else was with them? Clearly a third party was involved."

"None that I saw." Peters glanced over his shoulder at the goings on within the building.

The look of the infamous Mr Peters, combined with the sounds and smells coming from within—the rumble of male voices, a haze of cigar smoke and spirit fumes—told Zeke all he needed to know about this place. A hell. Hastings had led his sister to a gaming hell. If Kitty's disaster-prone brother survived his wounds, Zeke would give him a thrashing he'd never forget.

Zeke flicked a last glance at Peters. Instinct told him the game master was a dead-end. He had no notion where Kitty had gone.

He turned to Caden. "Can you deal with this?"

Caden nodded once, crossed his arms over his chest, and eyed Peters. "Hastings isn't dead. We found him in this condition not five minutes ago. You say he and his sister were here earlier?"

Zeke crouched beside Randall who had taken over tending Collin's wounds. "Did you get anything out of him?"

Randall shook his head. "No, and we haven't much time. Whoever did this didn't stop at one thrust. He's lost a lot of blood."

Zeke smacked Hastings' graying face to bring him 'round.

"Hastings, you worthless piece of dog excrement. Do something right for once in your life. Tell me where Kitty is. She needs your help."

Hastings' eyes opened and focused on Zeke's face. "James took her." He gasped a shallow breath. "Plans to marry her...today. Had papers. Stabbed me. I don't understand."

Zeke cursed. "You were never part of his plan, you idiot, except the part where he got rid of you permanently. Where is this so-called marriage to take place? Hurry, man," Zeke demanded through bared teeth.

"Priory church. Hill top," Hastings wheezed.

Randall put a hand on Zeke's shoulder. "Go."

He met his friend's eyes briefly in thanks, then ran all out for the alley exit.

***

Her head ached and she wanted to sleep, but something kept dragging her awake.

"I said wake up." A sharp crack of a hand against her cheek punctuated the harshly spoken words.

Kitty's eyes squinted open. Her head swam at the intrusion of light, or maybe it was the pain reverberating in her jaw. She moaned.

"There you are. You were about to miss your wedding." Two Garricks smiled down at her.

She took a slow, cleansing breath and replayed his words. About to miss your wedding. Marry Garrick? She wouldn't. *Zeke*. If only he were here. He would swoop in, carry her out of here, love her...

Her eyes drifted closed.

"Oh, no you don't." Garrick gave her a rough shake. "The priest is waiting. A pretty penny he cost me, to boot."

"Priest?" Kitty peeled open her gritty eyes and glanced around. She was half laid out on a window bench in a small, wood paneled room. It seemed an office or waiting room of some sort. How had she gotten here?

She pushed herself onto her elbows. Images rushed her mind. "Collin," she said in a panic. "Where is he?"

"Finally you're asking the right question. Your brother's in a safe place. But he won't remain so if you don't accompany me down the aisle this instant," Garrick hissed.

Collin had badly mistreated her. He'd been more than willing to sacrifice her future for his own selfish gain. He was weak and undisciplined. But none of that altered the fact he was her brother, whom she loved fiercely.

How had they left him? She vaguely recalled Collin helping Garrick drag her to the alley, and then...nothing. "What have you done with him?"

"Nothing permanent. Yet. But defy me, and I promise you, he'll pay with his life."

She drew a shaky breath and sat up. Her mind was clearing, even as her head throbbed with a nauseating ache. "How do I know you have Collin? How do I know he's not simply visiting another gaming hell?"

Garrick barked out a harsh laugh. "You have learned a thing or two, haven't you? You'll have to take my word for it. Oh, and there is this." He held up his right hand. Flashed the gold ring he wore. Her grandfather's pinkie ring—the one Collin earlier swore never to relinquish.

She chirped in alarm, covering her mouth with her hand.

Garrick smiled in satisfaction. "I see you comprehend the seriousness of the matter. Now on your feet."

Chapter Thirty-Five

Zeke's lungs burned like he breathed fire. He hadn't run this hard, this far, since his days at university. Why hadn't he wanted to venture into town on horseback? Something about covering better ground by foot. Ha.

He pressed on, full tilt, keeping the gray stone church in his sights like a lodestar. If he was too late, even by a minute, James might decide to rid himself of both Hastings.

He couldn't be too late.

One final switchback, and at last he pounded up the church steps. He grasped the cold metal handle of the massive oak door and threw it open.

Cool, musty air greeted him. He moved inside the dark stained narthex and the heavy door swung closed behind him, engulfing him in deep quiet. Swallowing back the sick feeling in his gut, he rounded the partitioned wall.

Scores of empty wooden pews flanked either side of a narrow center aisle, leading toward a lighted nave—and Kitty. She stood beside James before the raised altar, facing a robed priest.

She was alive, thank God. The rest he could handle.

"Stop!" he yelled, his voice echoing off the vaulted ceilings of the church.

Three sets of eyes turned toward him as he charged down the aisle.

"Father, this woman is being coerced," Zeke told the officiator, moving down the aisle. He shifted his focus to James. "Move away from her, James." He held out his arm, beckoning Kitty. "Come away from him, love."

Ashen-faced, Kitty stared back at him with sorrow-filled eyes.

Seemingly at a loss for words, the priest glanced between Kitty, James, and Zeke.

Garrick suffered no such fate. "You have no business here, Thurgood. The lady's made her choice. She neither wants nor needs your interference. She's agreed to marry me of her own volition. Ask her."

Zeke skidded to halt, his gaze settling on Kitty.

He could see she'd been crying. More disturbing was the a silent plea for understanding that hung in the air between them as surely as if she'd spoken the words aloud. She intended to go through with it.

The hell she would. "Kitty, no—"

"If you please." The priest, looking gravely displeased, held up a hand. "Lady Hastings, are you being coerced into accepting Lord James as your husband?"

Kitty turned to the priest. "No."

Zeke barely heard her hushed response.

She looked at him. "I'm sorry, Zeke. I have to. Garrick's given me no choice."

Zeke edged closer to the small throng at the altar. "No, you don't. The title James dangled before your brother in exchange for your hand is nothing but a fabrication. Collin still holds sole claim to the barony."

"I'm losing patience, Kitty. Tell your lover to leave. Now." James shifted, placing himself between Kitty and Zeke. He reached for her arm.

Stumbling back, she evaded his grasp. "Why would he lie? To what end?"

Zeke stifled a frustrated curse. He needed Kitty safely away from James. But in typical Kitty fashion, she required the facts or she wasn't going anywhere. Stubborn, loyal, beautiful fool.

He took a fortifying breath. "His original plan was to keep everyone in the dark long enough to marry you. Once your brother returned from the dead, however, James adjusted said plan to include killing off your brother, then marrying you, or marrying you, then killing off your brother. Either way, marriage to you, the sole survivor of your line, was key from the start, because it's the only way he'd ever accede to the Maidstone title. Isn't that right, James?"

Kitty lifted her hand to her throat. "He told me he'd kill Collin if I didn't marry him."

Zeke didn't have the heart to tell her James may well have succeeded in carrying out that particular threat.

The priest lifted his hands, palms up. "Perhaps we should continue after the three of you have resolved matters."

"There's no resolution needed, Father. We're ready to proceed," James gritted out, the veins in his neck protruding. He grabbed her arm, anchoring her in place. "Kitty, remember what I told you."

She stared, unblinking, at James.

"Kitty," Zeke began, sounding desperate to his own ears—but he didn't care.

She held up her free hand, silencing him. "You'll kill Collin if I do marry you, Garrick." Twisting her arm from James's grasp, she fisted up her skirts and started toward Zeke.

"No!" James cried. In a flash, he rounded on Kitty, crooking one arm around her neck, the other around her waist.

Zeke's blood turned to ice in an instant.

James held a knife to kitty's throat. It glinted in the shafts of light pouring in through the tall stained glass windows. He shifted backwards, glancing between Zeke and the priest with wild eyes. "Stay back."

Kitty wrestled against his hold, trying to wedge her arms free as her slippered feet tried in vain to dig in to the polished floor boards.

"Kitty, don't fight him." Zeke's voice cracked. He held his breath, transfixed by the short blade. If she continued to struggle, she would get herself killed right before his eyes.

For once, she obeyed.

"Oh, dear," the priest murmured.

"Move," James commanded Zeke. "Far into the pew, or I'll slice her throat, I swear."

Zeke lifted his hands and backed into the first row he reached.

"I win, Thurgood," James bellowed and, with his quarry in tow, headed for the church doors.

Zeke wanted to roar as bloodlust practically blinded him. Instead he forced himself to speak in a calm, deliberate tone. "James, the game is up. You're a wanted man. Leave Kitty out of this. She'll only hold you back."

He laughed like a crazy man. "Wanted? For what? Manhandling my soon-to-be wife?"

No. I'll handle that infraction on my own. "Try attempted murder. We found Hastings. Or didn't you wonder how I knew where to look for you? Bad luck by the way. It looks like he'll survive." For Kitty's sake, Zeke hoped so.

Kitty's eyes bulged as she took in Zeke's words. She struggled anew—then winced as James' blade nicked her skin.

"Stupid wench, now see what you've made me do," James ground out.

Zeke gripped the backs of the benches on either side of him so hard he wondered that the wood didn't splinter in his bare hands. "I'll kill you," he said in a low voice.

"You won't find me, Thurgoood." James passed the last pew. A few more steps and he'd round the partition. Once he reached the church doors, he'd escape.

James paused, flicked a glance over his shoulder into the narthex, then shot a smug look of triumph at Zeke. With a furious looking Kitty in tow, he disappeared.

His throat so tight he couldn't have swallowed a drop of spit, Zeke leaped into the aisle, then charged, his boots slamming into the floor panels like guns exploding.

A very female, bloodcurdling scream drowned out the noise. Then came a loud crash and one agonized wail, in rapid succession.

"Kitty!" He heard his own anguished cry as he dove around the partition into the church entrance. He skidded to a screeching halt, nearly plowing into Kitty in the process.

She stood, chest heaving, staring down at her cousin.

James lay in a heap at her feet. Shards of potter's clay littered the area, with pieces clinging to his hair and clothing. He appeared...wet?

The door to the church swung open. Caden appeared in the doorway just as the priest joined the fray.

"Did I miss anything?" A broad grin split Caden's face. "Lady, you are a sight for sore eyes." He swung her into his arms, holding her so her feet dangled off the ground.

Kitty gave a little cry and wrapped her arms around Caden's neck. The next thing Zeke knew she was sobbing into the front of his brother's shirt. He didn't know what he wanted to do first. Kill James if he wasn't already dead, punch his brother, or kiss away every track of every tear Kitty cried.

Behind him the priest spoke. "Is that the holy water urn?"

Kitty's tears abruptly halted, and she shot the priest a look of innocence that would have done an angel proud.

Zeke grinned, despite the harrowing ordeal he had just suffered through.

Sniffling, Kitty wriggled out of Caden's arms. "Sorry, Father. I didn't know what else to do. He couldn't get the door open without loosening his grip on me, and the basin was the only means of defense I could conceive. I did say a prayer before I hit him with it."

After a moment of stunned silence, Zeke and Caden exploded with laughter.

"I say, what have I missed?" Randall asked, his head craning in from the open doorway. "My lady!"

Zeke curtailed his humor enough to grab Kitty's hand before yet another man engulfed her in his arms. He met Randall's eye. "Hastings?"

"Patched up and, according to the doctor, one lucky man. His vitals somehow escaped the knife, although he would have bled out if we hadn't stumbled upon him."

Kitty chirped in alarm and glared down at James.

Zeke wrapped one arm around her slender waist, anchoring her to him and offering what comfort he could. "Where is he?" he asked Randall.

"Resting in his room at the inn—under watch."

"Zeke, you must take me to him." Stark terror filled her eyes. She hadn't looked half as frightened when her own neck was on the line.

He'd expect no less.

"A hansom is waiting," Randall told him.

"Good man. Caden?"

His brother sighed. "By all means, I'll handle this mess, too."

***

Sitting beside Zeke in the street hackney as it made for the inn, Kitty gazed at Zeke's hard profile. A muscle ticked in his jaw. Considering the days' events, she could understand him being upset. She just wished she knew which things precisely bothered him.

One thing she did know. He was her hero, utterly and completely, and she loved and trusted him with every fiber of her being. She reached up to cup his cheek, urging him to meet her eyes. "I knew you'd come for me, Zeke," she said softly.

He jerked a nod. "Right. You knew I'd come, and what? Witness your ceremony? You were going to marry him, Kitty." Hurt and betrayal swirled in his eyes.

"Not by choice," she said, willing him to understand. "Can't you see I had no other option?"

He shook his head and his face flushed a dull red. "You could have trusted me to take care of you. Instead you nearly got yourself killed." He cursed and turned his face away from her.

Was she imagining things, or had there been a sheen of moisture in his eyes?

She laid her hand over his heart, gently caressing him through his clothing. "I didn't die, and I didn't marry Garrick."

"No, you didn't," he said in a gruff voice. Lifting her hand from his chest, he stripped her glove off and pressed his lips to her palm.

"Kitty," he choked out after a moment. "For a moment there I thought I might lose you. If anything happened to you, I couldn't survive it," he said, his voice so choked with emotion she could barely hear him.

"I'm so sorry I put you through it, my love." She drew a fortifying breath. "Zeke, I want you to know, even if I had gone through with marrying Garrick—for Collin's sake—I meant to slip away the instant his back was turned." She swallowed. "I told Collin I wasn't marrying Garrick. Then Garrick found us. He drugged me."

Zeke's head snapped in her direction.

She went on. "I woke in the church. I didn't know what he'd done with Collin, Zeke. I only knew Garrick swore to kill him if I didn't marry him. I had to try and protect him."

Zeke swore. "He should have been protecting you."

She cupped his hot cheek. "I know, Zeke. I never would have consummated that marriage, Zeke. You have to know that. And there are so many other things I wish to tell you. Things I learned about my grandfather and my brother which I can't go into now because there isn't time. The main thing I need to tell you is that I made up my mind to marry you. I love my brother. But not enough to spend the rest of my days without you."

Zeke sucked in a breath. He leaned forward, pressing his forehead to hers. "Kitty—"

"Let say one thing more." She gazed at him through misty eyes. "I accept you as you are. If you desire travel, to scour the globe for...for those ores you love so much, I will wait for you until you come home--if you still want me, that is, after all I put you through, and there is still the issue of me being unlikely to conceive." She pressed her lips together.

Zeke's brows furrowed and he shook his head. "Sweetheart," he began.

The hackney jerked to a halt.

"We've arrived. Perhaps you need time to consider." She leaped from the vehicle, leaving Zeke to pay the driver.

Her mind raced as she darted into the inn. She told Zeke he was free to not marry her, hoping beyond hope he'd reject the notion out of hand.

He hadn't. Had he finally given up on her? Had he finally had enough of the trouble that followed in her wake?

She forced the dreaded possibility from her mind. One disaster at a time.

She charged up the stairs and crossed to Collin's chamber as fast as her feet would carry her. She burst into the room half afraid she'd find her brother dead.

"Milady," the innkeeper's wife said, rising from his bedside.

Collin lay still, his eyes closed, his complexion practically bloodless.

Kitty stretched out her hand and moved forward. "Is he..."

"He's resting," the woman said with a kind smile. "I'll leave you to him, then." She stepped into the hallway, pulling the door closed behind her.

Kitty hovered over her brother, smoothing his greasy hair from his forehead.

He opened his eyes, wincing when he saw her. "Kitty, can you ever forgive me? I was wrong. Wrong to ask you, wrong to help him. I've been such a bastard."

"Shh," she whispered, and gave Collin a small smile. "Just rest now. We can talk about all that later."

"But did he...are you..."

"Married to Garrick James? No. And I don't believe we'll have to worry about him in future."

"Thank God. I'll make it right between us, Kitty, I will."

"I know. Sleep now."

He smiled and closed his eyes.

Kitty looked down on his battered form and couldn't have agreed more with his summation. He had been wrong. He had behaved terribly. But she loved him.

The door opened and closed softly behind her. Zeke stood there, glaring daggers at Collin.

"He's sleeping," she mouthed, moving toward Zeke, toward his heat, the innate strength of him.

He crooked a finger under her chin, lifted her gaze to meet his. "Perhaps we can finish that conversation now?"

She nodded, her heart in her throat.

He took her hand and led her from the room.

If she wasn't mistaken, his hand was shaking. Now if she only knew if that was a good sign or a bad one.

***

He didn't speak 'til he had her alone in her chamber, door locked behind them. Once there, he opened his mouth. "Now, then—"

Kitty erupted with rapid-fire speech. "I understand if you've changed your mind. I didn't mean to imply you had to make good on your previous—"

"—Kitty?"

"Yes?"

"Kindly shut up."

"Oh." She dropped onto the edge of the bed.

He knelt before her, taking both her hands in his. He removed her second glove, as he had her first, mostly to buy himself time. He feared he might stammer over his words, and he didn't want to make a mess of this. Not again.

"Kitty, I've done a lot of thinking over the last"—he huffed out a breath—"ever since you crashed into my life."

She winced.

He shook his head and traced his knuckles over her cheek. "I'm not good at this. Bear with me?" He gazed into her eyes.

She nodded.

"I thought I knew what I wanted. Thought I was so smart, setting up my life in such a way that no one could touch me, no one could hurt me, no one could make me or my family vulnerable, ever again. But the thing is, I had it all wrong.

"I thought my father was weak because he loved my mother so much her death wrecked him. But the truth was..." He stood. Scrubbed a hand over his face. "He was just weak. It had nothing to do with love."

"Weak like Collin is weak," Kitty offered in a soft voice. "But not you, Zeke. You're the strongest, bravest, best man I know."

He rolled his eyes, but her words filled his heart with warmth and yearning and so much more. "I don't know about that. I have been weak. Putting all my faith in things. In money and wealth. In my ability to stay detached. 'Til you came along."

He crouched before her again, taking her hands. "Somewhere inside me, I recognized the truth, but I kept rejecting it. Until today. Until this morning, when I woke beside you. I knew I didn't want to go anywhere without you.

"When I arrived back to Aylesford, and you'd gone missing, I realized...I realized—" He had to break off to force down the irritating lump in his throat. "Christ," he muttered. "This is damned embarrassing."

"Take your time, my darling." Kitty's eyes shone with unshed tears, and what looked like joy.

He'd put that light in her eyes. He'd never felt more proud or more like a man.

"I don't want to. I want to tell you how much I need you and…love you," he choked.

She emitted a high-pitched squeak, and covered her mouth with her hands.

"I want to tell you I won't rest until we are married. I won't ever leave you again, or England, for that matter, unless you're with me. I need you to know I want babies with you. Lots and lots of baby girls with your jet-black hair and tiger-green eyes, and maybe a boy or two.

"But if we don't ever have a baby, that's all right, too, as long as I have you." He broke off. Thought a moment. "I think that about covers it."

Kitty fell back on the bed, her body convulsing in silent sobs.

"Kitty?" He pounced on the mattress—only to find her choking on laughter.

That was the trouble with tigers. You just never knew what they'd do next.

"Oh, Zeke," she said when she had her laughter under control. "I do love you so."

"And you'll marry me?" He raked a hand through his hair. "This time I want a straight, yes answer."

"Yes. Oh, yes, my love." She reached for him.

He sprawled on his side, pulling her into his chest.

They lay locked together for a long time, Zeke running his hand down her back, assuring himself she was there, alive and well, and truly his.

"At last, you found your way, Thurgood. I can finally rest, knowing my granddaughter is happy despite our many mistakes. Just remember, I'll be watching."

Zeke's head jerked up from the pillow, and his gaze darted around the empty chamber. He heaved an exasperated sigh. "You again, Hastings? Don't you have something better to do besides harangue me?"

"Who's haranguing you? Darling, I think you're dreaming." She giggled and snuggled closer.

Zeke smoothed a hand over her hair. "Quite right, sweetheart. Did I ever tell you about the diamond I brought back from Africa? The one I named the Tiger's Eye diamond?"

It was going to look just right on her finger.

She sniffed and toyed with the buttons of his shirt. "I may have...overheard."

Zeke laughed softly, tracing his fingers over the curve of her cheek. "Never mind that. Come here, tiger." He pulled her in for a long kiss.

Epilogue

N ovember 1877

Chissington Hall,
Derbyshire, England

My Dear Collin,

Zeke and I are married. We said our vows in the Earl's beautiful chapel at Chissington Hall yesterday afternoon. Your absence was sorely missed—by me, at any rate. I'm sure you can understand Zeke's reticence after all that occurred. I truly believe after some time has passed and you have shown yourself reformed of your previous bad habits, he will warm to you.

We are soon to go on honeymoon—Zeke, myself, and, at my insistence, the earl. Zeke pressed for a tour of Europe, Paris in particular, thinking I would prefer not to travel so far from home. He listened, you see, when I told him of our parents' constant touring, and my desire to set down roots and have a warm, close-knit family.

The thing is, I now know home is not so much about where you are, but who you're with. As long as I'm with Zeke, Collin, I'm home. I am so very fortunate. He does love me so much, Collin, almost as much as I do him. He makes me very happy, happier than I ever knew I could be. When I know you are settled and at peace in your life, my happiness will be complete.

As to where we are headed. Zeke has long expressed a keen interest in the American Pacific Railway, and I, having read many accounts of the beautiful, untamed landscape of the American west, decided that we should go there. We leave in three days time. I shall expect your visit to Chissington Hall upon our return, at which time you can offer your felicitations in person. By then, you should be well recovered from your injury and able to travel.

I shall write you many letters detailing our journey, dear Collin, and will keep you in my prayers until we meet again.

Your loving sister,

Kitty

Sitting at her escritoire, Kitty re-read the letter before folding the parchment in preparation for posting it. Her heart still ached over the tumult her brother and grandfather's deceptions had put her through, but she had forgiven both of them. How could she not? She loved them both dearly, and, in the end, it was thanks to their shenanigans she wound up on the earl's doorstep, and married to the man of her dreams.

A scratch sounded a moment before the antechamber door opened.

She glanced over her shoulder to see Zeke hovering in the doorway. As always, the sight of him stole her breath.

"Good morning, my lord. I thought you had meetings scheduled."

The earl's man of affairs had arrived early this morning to help Zeke and the earl with their arrangements for the oversight of the Claybourne estates in light of their upcoming extended holiday—namely she and Zeke's honeymoon.

"Are you not pleased to see me, lady wife?" Zeke sauntered into the chamber, a cocksure grin on his face. He kicked the door shut with his booted foot.

Kitty twisted around on the wooden bench-seat. "Just surprised. I thought not to see you before we go out riding with Caden and Lord Randall later."

He grunted and wandered toward the crackling hearth, dropping onto the nearby chaise.

"Is everything all right?" she asked.

He eyed her. "I couldn't concentrate knowing you were up here, in the room adjoining mine, a room I can once and for all enter at will, with no one to censure me." He waggled his brows at her and she laughed.

Only yesterday, her things had been relocated into the room connecting with Zeke's suites. Last night, they had spent their first night of many to come together as man and wife.

His eyes lit on the letter she still held. "You wrote to your brother, informing him?"

She nodded.

"I'm sorry he couldn't be here for our wedding, Kitty. Much as"—He cleared his throat—"as he's not my favourite person, I know how much he means to you."

She sent him a brilliant smile. "You gave me a choice. Wait 'til Collin was well enough to travel or marry my knight and shining armor right away."

"Come here." He opened his arms and Kitty went to him without hesitation. He scooped her onto his lap.

"Sooner was certainly my preference. Sneaking to the conservatory or into your chamber late at night—"

"—And don't forget the secret garden," she murmured.

He barked out a laugh. "I could never forget that, darling." He kissed the tip of her nose. "Call me old fashioned. I like falling asleep and waking with you in my arms—and sharing a bed will make it so much easier to make a little tiger kitten to twist me around her pinky."

"Or a little lion cub," she said, tugging on a lock of his golden hair.

"And if all we ever do is practice making babies, I'll still die a happy, happy man, my love. One tiger is really all a man needs."

"Oh, Zeke, I do love you so."

He crooked a finger under her chin. "I love you more, Kitty." And in the brightly lit room, on a cool winter's day, sun pouring in through the windows, he proceeded to show her.

The End

Want more of the Claybourne clan? Don't miss **If the Slipper Fits** and **Beautiful Viscount, Beastly Bride**, books two and three of the Hidden Hearts Series.

About the Author

A word about the author...Kimberly Keyes knew before she was old enough to drive writing was her passion. She writes steamy historical and contemporary romance, laced with a bit of mystery and suspense. She loves crafting un-put-downable romances that take her readers away and leave them hungry for her next book!

Her favorite tropes are marriage-of-convenience, fake relationships, grumpy/sunshine and close/forced proximity. You can count on "steamy" yumminess intertwined with that delicious falling-in-love feeling romance readers crave.

The bulk of her time she spends writing and rewriting, plotting, and dreaming up ways to perplex the characters living inside her head. You can also find her toiling in her garden, walking her dogs and trying to keep up with her social media posts!

There's lots of ways to connect with Kimberly and she loves to hear from her readers. If you love one of her books, PLEASE let her know. It keeps her writing!

Want to learn more and stay in touch? Visit her website at kimberlykeyes.net where you can learn about her books, upcoming releases, watch book trailers and sign up for her newsletter. Every newsletter offers at least one awesome giveaway.

More ways to connect—my moniker is always "Kimberly Keyes Romance":

Facebook

Instagram

TikTok

Pinterest

Bookbub

Goodreads

Thank you for reading The Trouble with Tigers. If you enjoyed the story, Kimberly would appreciate you letting others know by leaving a review! Reviews are an author's life blood, and it really means the world to her to receive them!

Also by Kimberly Keyes

IF THE SLIPPER FITS a steamy, second-chance, Cinderella retelling, reformed rake meets widow, Just-one-bed, Victorian romance and book 2 in Kimberly's "Hidden Hearts" series.

A chance meeting at a summer house party re-unites CadenThurgood, charming grandson of an earl, with his childhood crush, Mrs. Anna Jones. His hopes of a renewed flirtation are dashed when she swears the two have never met.

"Loved the first book and loved this one too. The slow burn, the looks, the small touches, the gloves removed, the anticipation, it was all nail biting exciting. Just what I love from a historical romance book..." Amazon reviewer

BEAUTIFUL VISCOUNT, BEASTLY BRIDE, a steamy, enemies-to-lovers, grumpy/sunshine, forced proximity, marriage-of-convenience Victorian romance, and book 3 in Kimberly's "Hidden Hearts" series.

Lady Annabelle tracks Viscount Randall to the frigid north to demand a confession from him regarding her brother's death, and finds herself caught in a snow storm and forced to seek shelter in his remote castle instead.

THE LYON WHISPERER, book 1 in Kimberly's "First Comes Marriage" steamy Regency series set in Dragonblade's Lyon's Den Connected World. A Marriage-of-Convenience, Forced Proximity, Grumpy Sunshine, steamy Regency Romance. Available in Kindle, Kindle Unlimited, and Paperback.

When a fortune-wrecking wager at the notorious Lyon's Den tasks the "Iron Lion of Barrosa" with marrying an earl's reckless daughter, he'll tame her by any means—unless she shows him the true meaning of surrender first.

"...absolutely impossible to put down. It held the reader so very captivated that, once started, it was very hard to get any sleep. Two nights in a row this reader was up till 3:30am trying to find a good stopping point...A huge bravo to Kimberly Keyes." Dorothy C, Amazon reviewer

"This was my first foray into The Lyon's Den Connected World and now I can say I'm going to need a lot more reading time to explore all of the books! Kimberly Keyes has written a smoking hot romance novel that was so impossible to put down, that I had to stay up very late to finish it the same day I received it. I don't want to spoil it for anyone, but Amelia is a wonderfully strong protagonist and an animal advocate, so what's not to love? I'm going to lend the book to a friend, but not before I read it again." Sonya R., Amazon reviewer

THE LYON RETURNS, book 2 in Kimberly's "First Comes Marriage" steamy Regency series set in Dragonblade's Lyon's Den Connected World.

A fake marriage, forced proximity, bluestocking bride, widow/widower Regency romance.

Gwen, a wealthy widow with no desire to wed again must find herself a husband. After paying an exorbitant fee to the notorious Black Widow of Whitehall for a husband who, she's assured, is "almost certainly dead," her husband, the alluring Gideon Devereux returns from the grave.

"Fabulous historical romance. Great addition to Lyon's Den, and Keyes has a new fan. Rings every bell. Had a very hard time putting it down." Texas Librarian, Amazon reviewer

"...absolutely loved Gwen and Gideon's love story!! It was awesome!! The book was a lot of fun and very entertaining to read. It had just the right amount of romance and mystery within it that the story kept flowing and the pages turning....I highly recommend this book!!" GH, Amazon reviewer

A LYON'S TANGLED TALE, book 3 in Kimberly's "First Comes Marriage" steamy Regency series set in Dragonblade Publishing's Lyon's Den Connected World. A fake marriage, amnesia trope, rake and wallflower, Brother's Best Friend, forced proximity romance.

When unassuming wallflower Lady Georgina learns the dashing rake she's loved from afar, her brother's best friend, has returned home from the war an amnesiac, bound for a madhouse, a daring rescue mission ensues in which Georgina pretends to be Teddy's wife.

"Seriously one of the best in the Lyon's Den series. An emotional, exciting story from beginning to end. The Dove-Lyon dynamic is perfect. Georgina is a treasure. Teddy was...well...a serious hunk of treasure himself. Kept me reading almost straight through." Amazon reviewer

"Loved it!! Brother's best friend + successful novelist FMC + amnesia + rescue from the madhouse = histrom PERFECTION..." Hannah, Amazon reviewer

LOVER'S LEAP, a steamy, friends-to-lovers, mistaken identity, forced proximity contemporary romance.

Recovering from a break-up, Candace escapes to a friend's luxury vacation home and meets the lethally hot Logan Shaw, her temporary roommate who she wrongly assumes is gay, and her best friends lover.

"This book pulled me in from the first moment. I bought it for a plane ride and had finished it by the time the plane landed!" Amazon reviewer

"Take a smoking. hot photographer with striking blue eyes and a curvy blonde fireball on the run from a thunderstorm, put them together in a mutual friend's upscale Lake Tahoe retreat and you have the makings of a steamy, made-for-each-other romance." Kat Drennan, Award winning author

PLAYING HER SONG, a steamy, small-town, second-chance, contemporary romantic suspense.

Jackson doesn't do relationships, especially not with women like Julia, his one-time tutor, back after 13 years. But does that rule out a no-strings fling?

"Let me start by saying what we're all thinking, Jackson is seriously hot. And not just his looks. He's everything a rockstar hero should be and Julia is the perfect heroine for him..." Anij, Goodreads reviewer

"News flash: PLAYING HER SONG is SPEC-TACULAR! I'm OBSESSED with this book!" ~Betty Bookstagrammer @_Book__Cafe_

www.ingramcontent.com/pod-product-compliance
Lightning Source LLC
Chambersburg PA
CBHW061852310726
48972CB00004B/995